THE BIG GRAB

Karl Heisler used
having spent four
old. His wife just wants him to play it safe. But he's
still got one more job in him. Which is where Frank
Toschi, his former cellmate, comes in. Frank is a hard
young man with a fair amount of brains and good
old-fashioned guts. And he trusts Karl more than his
own father. All they've got to do is break into the cash
room at the Skyline House, a big gambling place, and
they'll both be set for life. The Skyline House is
owned by the mob, and what're they going to do
about it? Cry to the cops? Karl has the perfect plan—
his last big job. He may be getting old, but he will
make this one a work of art.

THE SAVAGE BREAST

D.B. Sadder is rich young girl who lives with the
husband her father provided her in an apartment in
San Francisco. D.B. is profoundly unhappy. Her
husband Gordon only disgusts her. Her father simply
frightens her. Then she meets composer Harry
Dazier and his two brothers at a party, and
everything changes. The connection she feels with
Harry is immediate. Sure, Harry drinks too much,
but then so does D.B. So do they all. All except
Harry's older step-brother Sandro, who doesn't like
women, and particularly the women who try to get
close to his brothers. But is he any crazier than
Gordon, who has his own revenge planned for being
kicked out of D.B.'s life?

JOHN TRINIAN BIBLIOGRAPHY
(1933-2008)

A Game of Flesh (1959)

The Big Grab (1960; reprinted as *Any Number Can Win*, 1963)

North Beach Girl (1960; reprinted as *Strange Lovers*, 1967)

The Savage Breast (1961)

Scratch a Thief (1961; also published as
    Once a Thief as by Zekial Marko, 1965)

House of Evil (1962)

Scandal on the Sand (1964)

The Big Grab
The Savage Breast
JOHN TRINIAN

Introductions by
Brian Greene and
Nicholas Litchfield

STARK
HOUSE

Stark House Press • Eureka California

THE BIG GRAB / THE SAVAGE BREAST

Published by Stark House Press
1315 H Street
Eureka, CA 95501
griffinskye3@sbcglobal.net
www.starkhousepress.com

THE BIG GRAB
Copyright © 1960 by John Trinian and published by Pyramid Books, New
York. Reprinted in a movie tie-in edition as Any Number Can Win, 1963.
Copyright renewed November 21, 1988.

THE SAVAGE BREAST
Copyright © 1961 by Fawcett Publications, Inc. and published by Gold
Medal Books, Greenwich. Copyright renewed November 13, 1989.

Reprinted by permission of the Estate of John Trinian. All rights reserved
under International and Pan-American Copyright Conventions.

"The Conflicted Character Known as John Trinian"
copyright © 2022 by Brian Greene

"Recidivism and the Price of Freedom"
copyright © 2022 by Nicholas Litchfield

ISBN: 978-1-951473-98-3

Cover design by Jeff Vorzimmer, ¡caliente!design, Austin, Texas
Book design by Mark Shepard, shepgraphics.com
Additional proofing by Bill Kelly

First Stark House Press Edition: August 2022

THE CONFLICTED CHARACTER KNOWN AS JOHN TRINIAN

By Brian Greene

It can be cliché to say a particular person is/was "a character." But, cliché be damned, the author known as John Trinian was A CHARACTER. For starters, the moniker John Trinian is twice removed from the man's original name. He was born Marvin Leroy Schmoker, in Northern California, in 1933. Somewhere along in his adult years, he became known to all as Zekial Marko. John Trinian is a nom de plume Marko utilized when authoring the seven novels he had published between 1959-1964. Confused yet? For the purpose of this introduction, I'll just call him John Trinian.

I wrote a career overview feature on Trinian that appears in the hard copy anthology *Girl Gangs, Biker Boys, and Real Cool Cats: Pulp Fiction and Youth Culture, 1950-80*, which was co-edited by Iain McIntryre and Andrew Nette, and published by PM Press in 2017. For that piece, I interviewed Trinian's daughter Belle Marko, a visual artist. During an enjoyable and highly animated phone conversation, she painted a picture of her late dad as a talented but troubled writer who was doomed to be a ne'er-do-well. She said he was never much of a father to her or her siblings, who were mostly raised by their mom. And when he *did* come into young Belle's world, things happened like the time he invited a bunch of his artistic friends out for breakfast and took her along. They all thought it was his treat and she felt proud that her dad was buying her and all these interesting people a meal. But when the check came, he suddenly told everyone present to bolt. It was a dine and ditch caper. She laughed about it during our phone chat, but also said the incident made her young self feel embarrassed.

One big mystery about Trinian is why he abruptly stopped writing novels in 1964, or at least having them published. His final work of fiction that made it into print, 1964's *Scandal on the Sand*, is a mini-masterpiece of a socially and ecologically conscious novel that describes how various people react when a whale washes ashore on a California beach. So why did he cease to write long-form fiction then, when his novel writing success seemed to be on the upswing? Or was he still writing novels and just not submitting them anywhere? When I asked his daughter about that, she pointed to his alcohol and drug abuse. She also said that the older he got, the more thin-skinned and embittered he became. Maybe he could no longer handle the experience of pouring himself into these books, then seeing what reactions they got from editors, critics, and readers? She also said he was always talking about "the big one," the grandaddy writing project that would dwarf all his earlier efforts . . . a project he seems to have never completed, or at least didn't show it to anyone if he did.

Trinian *did* write for TV cop shows like *The Rockford Files*, *Toma*, and *Kolchak: The Night Stalker* in the 1970s. So he didn't completely give up his work with the typewriter after *Scandal on the Sand*. But nothing more was heard from him as an author/scriptwriter after that. He died in 2008, and according to his daughter was homeless, or near to it, for most of his final years. Her last memory of his way of his life was him sleeping in a workhouse owned by a woman who made pottery and sold potted plants on the roadside in Santa Cruz; Trinian helped her tend to the plants and craft the bowls, and in exchange he got to crash on a cot in a little shed on her property.

The two Trinian novels in this edition showcase different facets of his writing abilities. *The Big Grab*, originally published in either 1959 or 1960, is pure noir. It's a downbeat, edgy crime novel that involves a heist. As a caper tale from that era, it compares favorably to Lionel White's *Clean Break* (1955), which was the basis of Stanley Kubrick's 1956 film noir classic *The Killing*. *The Big Grab* primarily revolves around Karl Heisler, a 54-year-old career con who's just completed a prison sentence for a botched armed robbery. Heisler's wife wants him to go straight now, get a job like tending bar, but he feels he's too old and unemployable to go that route at this stage of his life. With the aid of another newly-freed former jailbird, and the jailbird's brother-in-law, Heisler plans to rob the safe in an illegal gambling house. He just knows this job will go smoothly and will put himself, his wife and their 11-year-old son on easy street from then on.

Set in decidedly unglamorous sites such as the Heislers' modest home and San Francisco malt shops frequented by the working class, *The Big Grab* is a gem of a hard-edged, atmospheric crime novel. It was the basis of the excellent 1963 French film noir *Any Number Can Win* (*Melodie En Sous-Sol*), which starred cinema heavyweights Jean Gabin and Alain Delon. This American-noir-novel-made-into-French-film-noir pairing is on a par with David Goodis's *Down There* (1956) and Francois Truffaut's film version of it, *Shoot the Piano Player* (*Tirez Sure Le Pianiste*) (1960).

1961's *The Savage Breast* is less noir than *The Big Grab*, but more literary. It's a socially conscious novel about culture clashes, family dynamics, and the place where artistic aspirations collide with the cold realities of practical living. D.B. Sadder is a motherless 23-year-old San Franciscan who was born into a wealthy family and whose existence is micromanaged by her rich, domineering, status-conscious dad. He goes so far into controlling her as to force her into an arranged marriage with a judge's son whom she finds to be a bore. She divorces the dullard, unbeknownst to Daddy, and pays the guy a monthly allowance for his agreement not to tell her father that they've split up.

Before she's even met him, D.B. becomes infatuated with a struggling 37-year-old musical composer named Harry Dazier. Dazier has his own family drama. He's close to his two brothers, one a mentally unstable and violent misogynist and the other a reckless youth who's also a sponge. D.B. contrives a means by which to become acquainted with Dazier. They become live-in lovers, and then their respective families and other associates become involved in their affairs and everything gets a little nuts. The characters in the novel are almost always drinking, which of course contributes to the chaos.

The Savage Breast isn't a sweeping literary epic on the scale of a John Steinbeck novel (a childhood neighbor of Trinian's). But it *is* a well-written, highly engaging social novel peopled with believable characters ensnared in compelling predicaments. Like *The Big Grab*, *The Savage Breast* is also evocative in a way that puts the reader squarely in a particular place at a particular time. This novel is similar to Malcolm Braly's *Shake Him Till He Rattles* (1963), being an early 1960s novel set in Northern California that involves a high society woman becoming romantically entangled with a musician from the other side of the tracks, notwithstanding the stark differences between D.B. Sadder and Harry Dazier and their counterparts in the Braly book.

Based upon the biographical anecdotes so graciously supplied by Belle Marko, we can see that by whatever name, the author known as John Trinian was indeed a "character". We also know that he led an intriguing and ultimately sad personal life, which may have contributed to the cessation his published works in 1964, at the decidedly young age of 31. Or maybe there are other explanations that Belle wasn't aware of and that none of us can now know. Regardless, what the two stories in this Stark House edition tell us is that when Trinian was pumping out novels and seeing them published, he was a master of his craft, an author possessing a diverse range of literary abilities.

—May 2022

Brian Greene writes short stories, as well as journalism features on books, music, film, and visual arts. His writings on noir fiction and film have been published in print and online by PM Press, *Criminal Element, Paperback Parade, Film International*, Mulholland Books, *Crime Reads, Mystery Scene, The Strand, Crimeculture*, and *Crime Time*. Brian lives in Durham, North Carolina.

RECIDIVISM AND THE PRICE OF FREEDOM
by Nicholas Litchfield

In 1977, 44-year-old screenwriter Zekial Marko was at work on a Hollywood heist movie titled *Kingdom Come*. (Blank, 1977). The type of movie that promises tension, violence, fast-action, and multiple double-crosses.

In the bold, suspenseful opening, a hard-nosed gang of thieves rob a jewelry clearing house in the U.S. Steel Tower in downtown Pittsburgh. Their daring scheme concludes with them bagging two million dollars and fleeing in a Port Authority transit van, leaving behind a corpse in an elevator in the Steel Tower. When police discover the dead body, a precinct peopled by mostly Irish-American cops is soon in hot pursuit, installing roadblocks across bridges throughout the city, closing in on the gang early into their getaway. The main cop leading the hunt is perhaps the central character, although it is not entirely clear. That is about all we know of the script.

While the setup may not be far removed from other crime capers, you just know that in the right hands, the interesting makeup of the characters, their inevitable hostilities, and various unanticipated yet convincing betrayals would give the story a weighty punch.

Marko—apparently, he liked to be referred to simply by his last name—was a capable screenwriter by this point, with an impressive portfolio. He had started with teleplays in the mid-1950s, writing episodes for the long-running CBS police drama *The Lineup*. (Blank, 1977). Then came *Mélodie en sous-sol* (*Any Number Can Win*) in 1963, Marko's screen adaptation of his novel, *The Big Grab*, with a cast including handsome iconic French actor Alain Delon.

The movie was a sterling success—it hit the world box office jackpot and left plentiful film critics rubbing their hands with glee. "If you are looking for bright, warm, lively entertainment, you are guaranteed a win at 'Any Number Can Win'" (Bass, 1964). Slick direction by Henri Verneuil and strong performances by the cast, especially the two convincing leads, Jean Gabin and Delon, won over audiences, and the nerve-jangling execution of the robbery provided satiating thrills. "No suspense caper of this kind is any better than its problems, and this one's problems are realistic enough to give the viewer exactly the kind of heeby-jeebies which he has a right to expect and enjoy." (Kern, 1964).

Above all else, it is the droll ending—a snaked coil of "ironic bitter twists" (Crowther, 1963)—that elevate the film.

Serving as an instance of old-school cinema triumphing over the rapidly-emerging French art film movement, the movie outshone other domestic flicks and earned an Edgar Award for Best Foreign Film from the Mystery Writers of America. "In the country of the new-wave directors, 'Any Number Can Win' has far out-grossed the realistic shockers and experimental films of the so-called avante-garde." (Hale, 1963.)

By all accounts, it was a big success for Delon as well. According to a writer in the *San Antonio Express*, he "offered his percentage of 'The Big Grab' to Metro for $500,000 and they grabbed it." (Graham, 1963). In fact, Delon took the "film's distribution rights in certain countries instead of a straight salary," and "the gamble paid off well." (Thomas, 1965).

Marko's subsequent film, in 1965, *Once a Thief*—he wrote the screenplay from his novel, *Scratch a Thief*—did not garner the same warm praise nor the handsome box office return. Many argue that Ann-Margret was "out of her acting depth" (Elgin, 1965) and "no more alive or convincing than a stick" (Eichelbaum, 1965) and that her "limited two-speed performance" (*Star Tribune*, 1965) flawed what was otherwise a tense melodrama. Frankly, "Little Tammy Locke, the child, is a more natural actress than the decorative Ann-Margret." (M.L.A., 1965). Apparently, French film producer Jacques Bar had intended for Jane Fonda to play the female lead (Skolsky, 1965). Bar had worked with her on *Joy House* the year prior. For whatever reason, Ann-Margret was cast instead. Alain Delon, who worked with Bar on several films, including *Joy House*, was the central actor once more, and his "excellent" (*The Post Standard*, 1965) earnest portrayal was generally appreciated.

In contrast to *Any Number Can Win*, the movie lacked suspense, the main characters lacked complexity, and some complained about the "bitter" and overblown ending (*Star Tribune*, 1965). Ultimately, the shallow characters and their predictable situations turned this "sometimes gripping, but somehow unmoving film" (Howard, 1965) into a routine melodrama. However, the "hard, hip dialogue" and "the fascinating minor characters embroidered around the edge of the tale" (Bustin, 1965) added substance to the film, and when not confined to a jail cell, "charged with driving while under the influence of dangerous drugs" (*Oakland Tribune*, 1964), screenwriter Marko got a temporary out-of-jail card to play "an oily narcotics addict with conviction" (Elgin, 1965). He even managed to get his real-life sweetheart a part in the film (*Daily News*, 1964).

As for this collection's opener, *The Big Grab* (later reprinted as *Any Number Can Win*), the best-selling book that sold 250,000 copies (*Daily Independent Journal*, 1962) and brought Marko early fame, this first appeared in 1960 as a paperback original issued by Pyramid Books under the author's pseudonym, John Trinian. It was his second novel, after *A Game of Flesh*, published the year prior by Bedside Books. Unlike in the movie, *Any Number Can Win*, where "the posh elegance of the Riviera" adds visual appeal (Miller, 1964), *The Big Grab* is set in California, primarily San Francisco. Exactly why the title was changed is a mystery. Lee McInerney of the *Pittsburgh Post-Gazette* considered *The Big Grab* a superior title over *Any Number Can Win* (McInerney, 1964), and perhaps it is, but in my opinion, both titles seem fine.

The joy of the story is the robbery itself. Instead of a glitzy casino in Cannes, the target is a somewhat out-of-the-way illicit gambling house off the highway in a place called San Hacienda. You would be wrong to think it is a cramped, low-end joint. Bizarrely, it is a huge, opulent three-story greystone building resembling an old-fashioned theater and opera house. Sitting on a hill in a clearing bordered by giant redwoods, it has dark ivy up its walls and a marquee over the front entrance. An imposing, near-impregnable fortress with a concealed saferoom that's locked and alarmed and can only be accessed through an elevator. Security is so tight that a mosquito would activate the alarm.

Marko cranks up the excitement, inserting into the tense burglary some masterfully worked twists and surprises before drawing the story to a suitably wry finish. By the end, you feel rewarded for the slow build-up, for the author taking his time to flesh out these singular characters and exposing their foibles and fears, and failures. Men like gutsy old-timer Karl Heisler, stooped under the weight of longing and loneliness, haunted by the futility of the past, who clings to the memory of the good times—"the Weintzer job," the big payout—pulls at the heartstrings. Though respected by his peers, previous botched jobs have destroyed his pride, and the only way he can repair his self-respect is by pulling off one last impossible job. There is the insulting, abusive, cuckolded Leon, a high-level shill who is hurt and frightened and jealous of his associate to the point of lunacy. And there is the tough but cowed ex-con, Frank Toschi, whose attachment to his former cellmate, a fatherly figure to him, ultimately means he cannot escape a life of crime.

These and other finely drawn characters captivate the reader. Some you pity, some you revile, and some stir the reader with touching reflections, culminating in life-affirming messages. As crime capers go, few are as sharp, suspenseful, and stimulating as this tale of recidivism and the price of freedom, and truly, the payoff is worth the investment.

The second tale in this multi-volume, *The Savage Breast*, first emerged as a Fawcett Gold Medal book in May 1961 under the John Trinian pseudonym with this provocative description on the cover: "Born beautiful, spoiled rotten... Was she a goddess to be loved or a tigress to be tamed?" The rich, pampered central character, Debra Balmont Sadder—known throughout as D.B.—is conspicuously dissimilar to those who inhabit the previous story. She is fierce and feral and plainspoken and unapologetic in her actions. Near the start, there is a scene where she cuts her former spouse's face with sharp glass, not by accident. Pressured into marriage by her overbearing millionaire father, she has recently been granted a divorce but is now being blackmailed by her ex-husband to keep quiet about their split. Wealth aside, she is not unlike Karl Heisler—frustrated and wistful, despite her newfound freedom, she goes in search of a more rewarding life. Where Karl longs for the joy of the next "Weintzer job," experiencing rejuvenation while pursuing the biggest snatch of his career, D.B. has a different obsession: famed composer Harry Dazier, a man whose music soothes the savage breast. At a period in her life of doubt and misery, his music roused her aching heart.

In truth, *The Savage Breast* is a murky melodrama rather than a crime novel. A love story full of delusion and starry-eyed innocence, scheming ne'er-do-wells, mentally ill brutes, and savage passion. The guilt-ridden Harry is far from a catch. Creatively moribund and experiencing financial hardship, his preoccupation is not necessarily D.B. but a lust for money. D.B.'s family connections might provide the salvation he craves, but their affair is fraught with numerous challenges and unexpected peril.

Marko's writing veers beyond the confines of crime fiction, shifting into dark and unpleasant places at times and instilling disquiet and dread. Occasionally pulpy but often displaying a literary flair, his stories, whether sad and meditative, passionate and tender or heart-poundingly intense, hold one's attention.

"I started by writing 'pocket books' under three assumed names," he once told a veteran *Pittsburgh Press* reporter. The novels were of the sort that began: 'She was blonde, she was beautiful, and she was dead.'" (Blank, 1977).

Though dismissive of the fiction he produced in his twenties, these "edgy and meditative" (Greene, 2017) works helped establish him as a writer of note and paved the way for a career in TV and film, writing episodes for popular TV series like *Toma*, *The Rockford Files*, and *Kolchak: The Night Stalker*.

But what became of *Kingdom Come*, you might wonder?

Sadly, that is anyone's guess. All we know for sure is that Marko interviewed cops while in Pittsburgh, tried to get the cooperation of the U.S. Steel Tower tenants, and then retreated to his Northern Nevada cabin to hammer out the script. Presumably, the movie never got made. Or maybe the script is still out there, the rights sold to some company who subsequently shelved it, as was the case with "a musical version of "Casque D'Or" he'd written with composer Lalo Schifrin." (Blank, 1977).

Did he even finish it?

The sad truth is, a lot about Zekial Marko has yet to be discovered. I suspect that some of his writing credits on TV shows are undocumented, and one news report I came across detailing one of the author's run-ins with the law (this time, a fine for drunk driving) mentions that *House of Evil* is his eighth novel (*Daily Independent Journal*, 1962), making my question is there an additional novel of his that's been overlooked? In fact, the author even refers to having written under "three assumed names" (Blank, 1977) but doesn't elucidate. It is a pseudonym I could not uncover. A mystery yet to be solved.

In the meantime, relish these two exquisite gems that have fallen out of public consciousness, going undetected for way too long. Slim yet weighty novels that are well worth anyone's time.

—May 2022
Rochester, NY

....

Nicholas Litchfield is the founding editor of the literary magazine *Lowestoft Chronicle*, author of the suspense novel *Swampjack Virus*, and editor of nine literary anthologies. His stories, essays, and book reviews appear in many magazines and newspapers, including *BULL: Men's Fiction*, *Shotgun Honey*, *Daily Press*, and *The Virginian-Pilot*. He has also contributed introductions to numerous books, including thirteen Stark House Press reprints of long-forgotten noir and mystery novels. Formerly a book critic for the *Lancashire Post*, syndicated to twenty-five newspapers across the U.K., he now writes for *Publishers Weekly* and regularly contributes to Colorado State University's literary journal *Colorado Review*. You can find him online at nicholaslitchfield.com.

Works Cited:

Bass, M.R. (1964, January 30). 'Any Number Can Win'. *The Berkshire Eagle*, p. 5.

Blank, E. L. (1977, October 31). Pittsburgh Getting Starring Role In 'Kingdom Come'. *The Pittsburgh Press*, p. 10.

Bustin, J. (1965, October 29). Fringe Benefit. *Austin American-Statesman*, p. 35.

Crowther, B. (1963, October 9). The screen: Slick crime melodrama set in Cannes: 'Any number can win' at Sutton Theater Jean Gabin and Alain Delon are starred. *The New York Times*. Retrieved May 15, 2022, from https://www.nytimes.com/1963/10/09/archives/the-screen-slick-crime-melodrama-set-in-cannesany-number-can-win-at.html

Daily Independent Journal. (1962, May 10). Novelist Given Drunk Driving Fine. *Daily Independent Journal*, p.4.

Daily News, (1964, October 25). Life-Like Reel of Film. *Daily News*, p. 698.

Eichelbaum, S. (1965, September 16). Drama in North Beach. *The San Francisco Examiner*, p. 25.

Elgin, M. (1965, September 15.) Style outweighs suspense in film. *The Ottawa Citizen*, p. 39.

Graham, S. (1963, September 5). 'Prize' Won't Make Sweden Gasp; Rex Harrison Has Oscar Chance. *San Antonio Express*, p. 69.

Greene, B. (2016). 'Beat' in Fiction and Fact: The Books of John Trinian. I. McIntyre & A. Nette (Ed.) *Girl Gangs, Biker Boys, and Real Cool Cats: Pulp fiction and Youth Culture, 1950 to 1980*. Essay, PM Press.

Hale, W. (1963, October 9). Gabin, Delon Star in Suspense Movie. *Daily News*, p. 77.

Howard, E. (1965, September 2). 'Once A Thief' And Always a Detective. *The Memphis Press-Scimitar*, p. 25.

Kern, B. (1964, January 26). Penetrating Soviet War Movie Rates a Red Star. *Star Tribune*, p. 134.

M.L.A., (1965, September 23). Delon Handsome Thief In Paramount Drama. *The Boston Globe*, p. 26.

McInerney, L. (1964, July 22). Forum Has French Suspense Film—'Any Number Can Win'. *Pittsburgh Post-Gazette*, page 8.

Miller, J. (1964, January 30). 'Any Number' is a Larcenous Caper. *The San Francisco Examiner*, page 26.

Oakland Tribune, (1964, November 5). Nerve Pills Bring Jail To Writer. *Oakland Tribune*, p. 17.

Skolsky, S. (1965, March 2). Gossipel Truth for Hollywood. *Los Angeles Evening Citizen News*, p. 8.

Star Tribune (1965, October 10). Love's Teardrops. *Star Tribune*, p. 87.

The Post Standard, (1965, September 18). 'Thief' Is Hard-Hitting, Suspenseful Crime Saga. *The Post Standard*, p. 8.

Thomas, K. (1965, December 18). New Dream for Alain Delon. *Los Angeles Times*. p. a12

The Big Grab
JOHN TRINIAN

1

It was a cold day. The sun was hidden behind a dirty gray wall of clouds and there was the taste of late evening in the air. People either walked briskly into the wind or plodded into it with their heavy coats wrapped tightly about them. The ones who plodded were the losers.

Karl Heisler shivered in his thin suit, cold only on the legs because of the woolen sweater he wore under his shirt. Paper and loose trash swirled in the gutters; people hurried past him. Women passed, high heels clicking on the pavement, leaving a trace of perfume even in the wind.

Karl Heisler was a short, stocky man, with well-muscled shoulders and large, heavy hands. His legs were thin and he walked with a slight stoop. He was getting old. He was fifty-four and he had been in prison fourteen years of his life; three hitches served, and the last one, the one that had ended at eleven-thirty that day, had been for five years. And maybe that was why he was old. Another man his age wouldn't be considered old, but Karl looked old enough to retire. His face was hard and weathered, tough, wrinkled. His white hair was thick and cut short to his scalp. His gray eyes were deeply set under white eyebrows, the creases of his neck like scars, his lips stiff and cracked with puckering lines.

When he first realized he was fifty, he had felt suddenly tired and he had caught himself secretly testing his stamina and reflexes. Then it had passed. He forgot about it, but he continued to take his time without bothering to ask himself why.

He stopped at a corner. He knew San Francisco well but there were quite a few new buildings and he had to look twice to see where he was. The intersection cop blew his whistle and Karl crossed the street with the rest of the people, his eyes hard and brooding as he walked. He stood with his back to a building, as if he were confused or unsure of himself.

There were those sounds and smells. Cocktail lounges, a traffic signal, hurrying people, newsboys with jailhard eyes, a laughing couple, pigeons sidestepping the crush; and there were no whistles to regulate the movement, no schedules to follow.

He wanted to see Frank Toschi, but right now there were other things that he had to do. His business with Toschi could wait—it was important, but it could wait. His son, little Karl, was the more important thing right now. Five years made a lot of difference to a growing boy. Maybe he wouldn't remember his old man—and, Karl thought reluctantly, maybe he wouldn't remember the kid either....

Karl and Toschi had been cellmates for the past two years. Frank had been released three weeks ago. He was a young man, almost young enough to be Karl's son, but, as young as he was, Karl trusted him, liked him. The trust was important.

Karl walked the streets of the city and sniffed the air. It was good to be out again. He stopped to look at the flashy new cars that were parked at the curb. He wasn't impressed by them, he merely stopped and looked. He had seen them in the movies and on the television, and they meant almost nothing to him. Perhaps he looked at them because he had once measured his absences by the changes in their design, and he did so now out of habit. At any rate, he was no longer impressed by the changes on the outside. He expected them. He looked at the cars only to satisfy an old man's curiosity.

He caught the Mission Street bus going southwest, sat next to the window and watched the people along the street, pushing baby buggies, standing, walking. Once he had been fascinated by people who were free, but now they held no meaning for him. If you were poor, as they all were, what good was freedom? What could they do with freedom on eighty bucks a week? Freedom wasn't something you could buy with eighty bucks—it took much more than that.

The bus passed a bank and he looked at it indifferently. It would take the brains of an expert to get a return a supermarket bandit could get on a payroll night.

That was the trouble: the return had never been worth the risk. The story of Karl's life. But he wasn't worried about that now. He had put all the old wishes and the old regrets behind him. The only true profit from the past was experience. To cry over it was a waste of time.

No more little pickings. It wasn't worth it. If you were after, say, a quarter of a million, (he smiled knowingly to himself) it took a quarter-million in thought to get it. You had to invest the amount in experience and expect only an even money return. You give what you've learned, and you take what you've earned. It was as simple as that. But it took people a lifetime to learn that. And, even then, most of them never learned. Karl, however, had learned it many years ago. And he had parlayed his thought and experience into fairly large rewards in his time. But, of course, there was none of it left now. And that, too, had been a mistake for him to learn from. Once you've got it, keep it.

He left the bus at his stop, walked a block, and, when he turned the corner off Mission Street, he saw the familiar south hills in the distance. Like the heavy thighs and breasts of a woman, dark green brown, rolling in solid earthen waves and connecting with the dark ragged sky. A few blocks and the neighborhood became poor, rows of shabby flats and apartment houses, empty lots and dark corner groceries. The neighborhood hadn't changed. He felt the tender excitement of homecoming, smelled the familiar odors, saw the familiar sights.

A few kids were in the street, kicking a ball and making the echoing lonesome sounds that only kids could make on a cold dark afternoon. He stopped before his apartment building. The yellow paint was peeling from it and many of the tobacco-colored shades were drawn in the gray windows. There was a low bench on the sidewalk with soft-drink signs nailed to the backrest. A young kid with high-heeled boots was lounging on the bench, looking decoratively medieval with his black silk club jacket and pegged trousers. Karl entered the building, feeling the hostile eyes of the kid on him. Who did he think Karl was? A solicitor? A bill collector?

The stairs were steep, with a loose railing along one side. Paint blistered from the walls. The landing was dimly lighted. There were the familiar odors of damp wood and sour paper. A bare bulb burned at the end of the first passage. From somewhere upstairs, perhaps from a nearby flat, someone was practicing "The Daring Young Man on the Flying Trapeze" on the clarinet. The stairway railing shook under his hand. The wooden apartment doors were lacquered a sickly kidney-bean color. He stopped before his door and knocked lightly, waited a minute, then tried the knob. It was open.

Edna stood uncertainly in the front room, a tall woman with a strong face and body. She had never been beautiful, not even in the good days when he had struck it rich on two of the best jobs of his life. She was almost forty now, her face was red and smooth, almost flat, the lips wide and without makeup.

Karl shut the door and removed his hat, feeling terribly moved, almost saddened as he looked at her. He nodded. "Hello."

Edna returned the nod, a small embarrassed movement of her head, as if they were strangers. She moved a bit toward him. "How do you feel, Karl?"

"Fine. I'm all right."

She looked at her large hands. "What time ... I mean, how long you been in town?"

"This morning, eleven-thirty or so."

"Well ... you look good, Karl."

"Thanks. I feel all right.

There was an embarrassing silence, and when he looked at her he saw the suffering in her face and he felt a stab of guilt, even a little pity. He knew that he loved her and he wished that he could show it the way kids and newlyweds did. But he didn't say anything. He wondered if she thought he loved her. She said nothing, and he had been away from her too long to be able to read her expressions.

He held his hat self-consciously at chest level, like a first-time kid or a clever solicitor. He moved the brim nervously around in his fingers, pinching at the felt.

"Well," Edna said, "it's sure kind of funny seeing you without a screen between us."

"I think they took the screens down. They don't use them anymore."

The tiny smile died on her lips. "Are you mad at me because I never came to see you this time?"

"No. I told you that."

"I wanted to."

"Sure, I know that. But it was better this time."

She looked uncertainly toward the kitchen. "I was just going to have some coffee. Would you like a cup?"

He nodded, silently grateful for something to do. He wanted to move directly into the atmosphere of home. There was so much already lost…. "Sure, coffee's just the thing." He tossed his hat onto the sagging sofa and followed her into the kitchen. He removed his coat, rolled his shirt sleeves up high on his thick arms. "Coffee's the best on a cold day. It warms your hands more than it does any good for the stomach."

She poured the coffee and deliberately reached out and patted his hand, almost maternally, and broke the spell between them—or, at least, made an effort to break it. "I see you wore the sweater I sent you. I'm glad you did. I had an idea, one of my old-fashioned hunches, that it was going to be cold at this time of year…."

"I'm glad you sent it," Karl said.

They sat for a long while, smiling self-consciously when their eyes happened to meet. The window behind Karl, the one that had always been loose, shook when the wind grew stronger. They had more coffee and Edna put out half a loaf of black bread and a dish of cucumbers. Karl ate slowly.

He remembered, for no particular reason, how Edna had looked the first night he had seen her. It had been in Detroit, at Max Hunt's house, many years ago. Karl had just turned thirty and he had brought a new 1936 Packard touring car. He had gone to Max Hunt's to drive his sister and her girl friend to Terre Haute. The girl friend had turned out to be Edna. She wore a dark blue dress with velvet trimming and her face was red from the cold, and in the back seat, while Max drove, she had allowed Karl to kiss her and put his hand on her knee under the heavy coat. Outside it had been snowing and the quiet Indiana landscape looked bewitched, surrealistic, with the thin naked trees, white fences, snowcapped mailboxes, barns.

Karl had whispered to her. "Gee, I sure get a kick out of Indiana. Is this where you're from, kid? Indiana?" Edna had whispered a reply. Then Karl: "Me? I'm a salesman. I had a good week so I bought this car. Kind of a celebration...."

Karl sighed, forked a cucumber and ate on the left side of his mouth. The partial plate bit into his gums. He chewed carefully. He wondered why that midnight ride in Indiana was so clear to him now. He remembered that a few months later, after he and Edna were married, he had been arrested for the warehouse robbery in Illinois. He sighed again.

Edna said, "You didn't worry about me ... running around?"

"No," Karl answered. "I don't think of those things anymore."

She said nothing.

He watched her from under his heavy white eyebrows. She was still the same silent woman, he thought, almost like a deaf person, rarely showing her feelings; and when she did she always managed to do it in a clumsy, embarrassing way. But Karl didn't mind that at all. It had been good between them. Of course, there had been a few rough moments, like in all marriages, but all in all it had never been bad. He thought of her still as a good, simple woman—actually she was probably a complex woman, but since she said so little and revealed even less, it was easier to think of her as being simple and uncomplicated.

"I'm glad you didn't think I was running around."

He shook his head. "I used to. I remember when I used to accuse you, and I'm sorry about it. But it's all done now. Let me tell you, Ed, these last five years ... well, it didn't hurt me too much. That's because I love you, I really do, and hell, maybe I didn't when I was accusing you. But I mean it now." He thought a moment, frowning. "I feel kind of like a kid. I don't mean young and horsy, but kind of mixed up inside and not really knowing how to say what I feel."

She studied him with her sad Russian eyes and flat handsome face. "You only say that because I'm old now and kind of beat up. It's easier to trust me this way."

"Don't say that, kid. Don't you believe me?"

She touched his hand again, squeezed it. "I believe you." She smiled. "You know, you haven't even asked me about little Karl."

"Sure, I was just about to. Where is he?"

"In school."

"I forgot. I saw some kids outside but I guess they were playing hooky. Is the kid's report card good?"

She smiled and seemed to come to life. "He's a perfect gentleman, Karl. I don't know where he gets it...." Karl gave her an uneasy look. She said, "I didn't mean it like that. I mean, he's a fine kid. The best. But, like I wrote you, he's still not very strong...."

"Doesn't he take the vitamins you wrote about?"

"He takes two kinds."

"Doesn't it help?"

"Probably, but it don't show too much."

He thought of the steep stairway out in the hall. What if the kid happened to fall down there in the dark? What would happen then? Little Karl was weak, probably much weaker than Edna wanted him to know. A fall on that stairway would probably kill him.

Little Karl had been weak since birth. In the beginning, when the child had just turned two, they had believed him to be retarded because his growth had been slow. His understanding of danger had been that of a one-year-old. His vocabulary had been only grunts at his second birthday. When Karl took him to a specialist they found out that the boy had a chemical deficiency. And, even with the pills, his physical growth had been slow. Mentally, after the treatments, he had improved almost miraculously, but physically he had remained retarded. Now, at eleven years of age, he looked more like six or seven.

Karl had a fierce love for his son, and at times he became frightened when he thought of his love, felt uncomfortable with the tenderness he had for his family.

But all this sadness would pass; they would leave it. This place, this shabby old house, the relief checks and the powdered milk would all be gone and dead. This was the promise that he had made to himself while in prison, and, he recalled with a guilty wince, it was the very same promise he had made to Edna the day before his last job.

He had known it was a sucker play before he had tried it and still he had let himself be lured by the hope of reward. But it had been too much for one man. Karl had always been a loner. He had never been able to trust anyone else. But there was someone now. If Frank Toschi had been with him on the last one he would be in Alaska, or Canada, or even Australia—one of the new lands where freedom was more than just a word, and he would be in a paying business for himself, helping little Karl grow strong, living the fat rich life that others only dreamed about.

"Have you thought about getting a job?" Edna asked.

"That's just what I've been thinking about."

"Maybe you can get another bartender job. It was good times when you were working at that bar."

"I might. I've been thinking about getting a job."

Later, after three o'clock when the schools were out, he took a walk around the neighborhood with little Karl. He found that he had very little to say to the eleven-year-old with the slightly protruding eyes and limp blond hair. His son had even shaken hands with him. What was Karl supposed to say to him? What do you say to kids?

They walked past the green lace of a pepper tree, crossed the weed-grown lot with the water tower in the center. The wind shimmied the beads of the tree. Karl lit a cigarette and chanced a side glance at his son. Little Karl had been watching him, so he looked away. "Do you play much in this lot?"

"Sometimes. I cut my knee right over there, playing War."

"That's good," Karl said absently.

"But I cut my knee."

"What did you put on it?"

"Iodine."

"Did it burn?"

"Yes, kind of, but Mama said it was the good germs fighting the bad ones."

"Everybody gets hurt in a fight," Karl said. "Before you were born I used to work over that hill. There was a big shed there. We used to build fires on cold mornings to keep us warm. Smoke used to go up in the sky and then we'd go to work."

"You know what's there now? There's a great building with a chute on it, like a slide, and there's a guy there that's a watchman and he chases all the kids off."

"That's the same place I used to work at. It was there before you were born."

They walked in silence and Karl thought of what the boy had said. He wondered if the same watchman worked there. They crossed the lot. The gloom of the day brought out the bits of color; the bleeding rust on the tank, yellow cabs, red firebox, blue neon signs in grocery windows. There was an alley with a steel-blue shadow and the death odor of wood and paper rot. Further down there were the smells of cooking food and gasoline.

Karl stopped at a corner. "How do you get along in school?"

The boy stood, imitating his father with his hands thrust deep in his pockets. "The other kids pick on me, I guess."

Karl felt suddenly helpless. "Did you tell your Ma that?"

"No."

"That's good."

"Why?"

"I don't know. It's just not good to let a woman know that other people can pick on you." Then he felt ashamed for having said that. "Can you fight?"

"No, not very well."

"Why?"

"I'm not strong enough."

"You will be."

"When I get big like you?"

"That's right." They walked again. "What do you call me?"

"Dad."

"Good. Pretty soon I'll teach you how to get even with the kids that pick on you."

Little Karl nodded uncertainly. "I don't like fighting."

"It's just like the iodine though. When there's a wound there's bound to be a fight. Like when you got wounded, the good germs fought the bad ones. It's like that. Someone wounds you somehow and then you've got to fight him because he's a bad germ. It's like that."

"I still don't like to fight very much."

They returned to the house when he saw that the boy was beginning to shiver from the cold. The wind became stronger and he put his arm around him and they hurried. The wind continued to grow and it didn't die until after dinner when Edna was helping little Karl to bed. Karl lifted his head, listened to the sudden dying of the wind, then went to the loose window and looked out at the rear garden. It was silent, eerie. He picked up his coffee cup and went to say good-night to the boy.

"Dad, can I get a brother?"

"I don't know. Why?"

"I could play with him."

"Yes, well, we'll see."

"I remember what you said about the germs, Dad."

They left the night light on and Edna kissed little Karl. Karl wanted to kiss him, but he didn't know if it was still the right thing to do. It had been right, had even been expected, five years ago, but he wasn't too sure now.

When Edna closed the door he handed her his coffee cup and returned to the room. He said, "I want to kiss you good-night." He kissed the boy and they held each other tightly for a moment. Then Karl said good-night and softly closed the door after him. He felt warm inside. He returned to the kitchen.

"How was the walk this afternoon?"

"Fine," Karl answered. "We talked about this and that."

"He worships you, Karl. Did you know that?"

"No, I didn't."

"He thinks you're an oil man."

"He didn't ask me anything about oil."

She looked sad again. "I didn't think that he would."

"You know, Ed, I worked in a gas station once before we met. It was in 1933. Jobs were hard to find then."

He put his arms around her, standing behind her, and he moved his hands on her, touching her stomach and remembering when little Karl had been there. She kissed the side of his face.

Late at night he thought that he had heard the sounds of the streetcars. He left his bed, moving carefully so as not to waken Edna, and went into the kitchen and out onto the porch.

At one time he had worked for a year in the neighborhood, tending bar during the day where there was now a gas station. After work he had made it his custom to sit on the rear porch in a wicker chair and watch the sun set behind the water tower and the streetcar barn further on. He had been able to listen to the gritty iron jingling and creaking sounds of the big cars being turned on the wheel by the night crews. But the streetcars had been converted to electric busses long ago and he no longer listened to them.

He thought that he had heard the sounds of the streetcars, but it must have been a dream. He sat heavily in the old wicker chair and looked out at the secrets of the night. The backyard, the washline poles, the moonlit flowerbeds.

He thought of Frank Toschi. Lately it seemed that he thought of him even more than he had when they had been in prison together. Riding the bus into town from the prison gates he had thought of him. Karl needed a man like Toschi to get the money from the big one. He trusted him completely, because, for some curious reason, he reminded Karl of himself when he had been a younger man—there was the same shrewdness, the toughness, the pride.

In 1936 Karl Heisler had been successful, nearing the top, with six good jobs behind him and a score of small ones. And, most important of all, there had been no criminal record. He fell for the first time in early 1937. After that he grew more cautious in his ways. He became more of a loner than before. He had no close friends, even Max Hunt stopped writing to him. Karl had drifted in those early days, first in Illinois, then in Indiana and Michigan, then, finally, California. The years just after the war—1946 and 1947—were his best ones, the good years of his life. That was when he had pulled off the Weintzer hit. Of course, he had been caught on that one, but prison wasn't as bad as before. He had been something of a celebrity. A magazine that specialized in factual crime stories had written an article about him, saying that he was the last of a vanishing breed—a master at his trade, a professional. Edna hadn't liked that article, and for that matter neither had Karl. But still, he had felt a certain secret pride in it. Every man wishes to be the best at his chosen art. It was only natural to feel pride in true accomplishment.

Sometimes Karl still daydreamed about the Weintzer job. It had been his best job. He had always hoped to do another one like it, just as fat, just as big. But this time he knew that he would have to execute it with even greater care. He was getting old. He would have to put behind it everything that he knew. He would have to make this one a work of art.

He sighed, sitting in the lonesome darkness in the sagging, battered wicker chair. He could feel the cheap shabbiness of his surroundings pressing him. He wanted to get out of here. He wanted to get back on top, wanted his family to have something better than they had been getting for the past ten years.

Karl had always been in business for himself, but the business that he was in was marginal and the penalty for failure wasn't bankruptcy but jail. Toschi seemed to be the answer to that. A hard young man with a fair amount of brains and good old-fashioned guts. The good kind of guts. Not the crazy, reefer-puffing guts of the new switchblade breed, but strong, old-fashioned guts like Karl's father, and like Karl himself....

His son wasn't that way. He was weak and sick. But he was a bright little kid. When he had first started school, the teacher had told Edna that little Karl was the brightest in the class. So, if he didn't have the strength to fight the bad germs of the world, then he would out-think them. That's what really paid off now anyway. The brains were coming in. The old-time guts were going out. The thinkers were the ones who were making the big money. Guts only got you one of two things these days: eighty lousy bucks a week or a stretch in prison. No, in a way it was better that little Karl was going to be a thinker, a bright one, even if the price for this gift was his strength. Because guts come in different packages. It didn't take guts alone to get into prison. Anybody could go. People were fighting their way into jails every day. Honor students were cutting up little girls and quiet, baby-sitting neurotics were becoming snipers. That wasn't guts. There was a decision to be made to accept a life that contained combat for reward. To make the decision, to stake the camp peg outside the big wall, that was the hardest to do, and sometimes this was accomplished with old-time guts and sometimes you did it with brains. It was the way that things were. And no matter how you looked at it, the man on top, the man who could sneer at the big wall, was the man with the money and the courage to get it.

The getting of it was a business, and Karl Heisler, after all, was merely a small businessman hoping to eliminate the risk and increase his profit by taking in a decent partner.

He heard a small sound and when he looked up he saw that Edna was standing next to his chair, wearing a denim robe, holding it closed at her waist with one hand. Again, he remembered that night crossing the Indiana line in the new Packard with Max Hunt driving and Edna in the rear seat with the blue velvet-trimmed dress.

"I couldn't sleep," Karl said.

"I heard you get up. I was still awake." She touched the top of his head and let her fingers rest in his white hair. "It's been a long time since you've sat out here. I never threw away the wicker chair. See? It's the same one you used to sit in. I didn't get rid of it because I was hoping you'd sit here like you used to. Those were good times."

Karl said nothing. He felt at peace with himself for a moment.

"Have you been thinking about working?"

"I've thought about it," he whispered. "I'm too old, Ed. No one's going to hire me as a bartender. It's my record, too. The only guy I knew in the saloon business died and they built a gas station over his grave."

"You were a good bartender."

"I don't really want to be a bartender again, Ed."

"Maybe Mr. New can help you get a job. You remember him."

Karl remembered. Mr. New had been Karl's parole officer years before. He would be more than seventy now—if he was still alive.

Edna said, "Has prison changed much since the last time?"

"Not too much. A few new guards, new faces. The food's better now. In fact, the food was pretty good this time. I didn't mind it too much."

She looked at him with an expression of curious understanding. Her voice was low. "Is that why you're trying your damnedest to get back in? Is it because you miss the food so much?"

He looked up at her, then lowered his eyes. So, she knew about it. He said, "It's a good job this time. Better even than the Weintzer job. This is the best...."

"This time?"

"I know it sounds corny, like all the other times, but it's not like that at all. I'm going to take you and little Karl to Alaska, or Australia. It'll be real good, Ed. You wait and see."

She sighed, shook her head in deep disappointment. Her fingers were heavy on the top of his white head. "Why did they let you out? Don't they know that you'll do it again? Don't they honestly know that it's all you know how to do? You're a thief, Karl. They ought to know that by now—they've had you enough times."

"Just bad luck, Ed. I tried to pull off things that one guy couldn't swing."

"I hope you don't get put into jail again. I hope they bury you in the ground." She shook her head again, this time more for herself than for her husband. "Maybe it would be better if they buried you." She blinked and her eyes were wet with a great sadness and self-pity.

"Don't talk crazy like that," Karl soothed. "Hell, you don't want to see me dead."

She put her arms around him, holding him tightly, the robe opening and her warm belly pressing against his ear. "They catch you again and you'll never get out. They'll put my big tiger away and throw the key into the ocean. Is that what you want?"

He stroked her arm. "They're not going to get me...."

"You always say that, too."

"They won't."

"Are you going to carry a gun to use?"

"I didn't mean that."

"But if they get you ..."

He said nothing for a long while. His eyes clouded and his throat went dry, hurting. "No, if they come for me I won't let them wrap me up. I guess I'll make them kill me."

"Thank you."

"For what?"

"I don't want to see you in again. I'd rather see you dead."

"Well, just don't go thinking that. Because this one's plenty different. I've got me a guy I can trust, and for the first time in my life I'm not going it alone."

"Will it make that much difference?" She sounded vague, uncaring.

Karl nodded, enthusiasm for his thoughts blinding him to her indifference. "This guy is right for me, Ed. I got the place and a pretty good plan for it, and now I've got me a guy I can trust. It makes a big difference in my business. You know that. And believe me, it's going to work, click-click, just like that. It's going to take an act of God to—"

She put her hand on his mouth. "Don't talk like that."

"I'm sorry. But it's going to work this time."

She kissed him, still on the side of his face, and left the porch. He sat and watched her bare feet moving in the kitchen darkness. He thought of the warm bed two rooms away from his wicker chair on the porch, but he didn't stir. His thoughts were still feverish with the dream of Toschi and a quarter of one million dollars.

2

The room that Frank Toschi sat in was painted a foggy blue; the linoleum on the floor was the same blue, but it was broken by occasional squares of dirty cream. The group photograph on the showpiece mantel was of a large family: father, mother, uncles, brother, sister, and, somewhere in the background, almost lost in the shadows and hardly seeming to be a part of the family was Frank Toschi. The wallpaper in the hallway was gray with tiny flowers. The boat-shaped clock said that it was four o'clock. There was a kitchen off to one side and swinging doors held back the rich cooking odors from the living room.

There was a chalk statue of Popeye the Sailor on top of the radio. Frank sat on the sofa, listening to the radio music, his foot patting time to it on the blue linoleum. A cigarette hung from his thin, unmoving lips. He wore no necktie and his cheeks were dark with a single day's growth. The smoke curled slowly around his eyes and he narrowed them.

Frank Toschi was thirty years old but he looked older, tired. He had light brown hair, hard brown eyes that were almost gray, a strong nose that was probably a little too long for his face, cheeks caved in below the high cheek bones. He had never been a heavy eater, unlike most of his family, and he was lean. His eyes seemed sad, his thin mouth hard. He was just shy of being handsome and women had always been attracted to him.

Women didn't interest him very much. He figured that he could have any of them if he desired them enough, and the knowledge of this seemed to satisfy him. He was a fierce personality, quick, curious, but lazy and wrapped in himself a great deal of the time. He had no close friends and it was usually pretty difficult to approach him. He rarely drank and he was highly suspicious of jovial people. He often wondered where he was going, and what he would do once he arrived.

He liked money. He liked the potential of power that money could offer, liked the idea of the women that it could attract. But more than that, he liked the power of decision that money afforded, the decision to reject the very things that the power could attract. He wanted only to be a completely free agent. And yet, all of his life, he had never had to answer to anyone. He felt that he needed the money because what he wanted seemed to require money. The trouble was that Frank didn't honestly know what he wanted. It was a strange thing that gnawed inside him. He figured that once he had the money then he would automatically know what it was that he wanted. He put a high value on possession simply because everyone else did. In reality his needs were very simple, his wants very vague.

He felt bitter.

The kitchen door swung open, flashing sudden light into the dark living room. His mother looked at him from the doorway, one hand on her hip, eyes glittering. Her hair was white and, with the bright kitchen light behind it, it looked almost glowing, like a halo. Her eyes were dark and her powerful little body was shapeless in the severe dark dress. She held her free hand under her apron, as she always did, almost as if she were concealing something.

"Why don't you put on the light? You can't see anything."

"Because I'm not looking at anything," Frank answered tiredly.

His mother nodded with the misled wisdom of those who believe that since they were humble they were also wise. "You should get married, Francis. You should get yourself a good wife. Settle down."

The door swung after her.

Frank shrugged. His mother was like that: she would brood in silence for a few minutes and then come forth with a statement that would solve, or could solve, all existing problems. If it wasn't a spiritual solution it was a practical one, true and correct, because she believed that the answers to all questions needed only to be studied in the proper light. The proper light, of course, was herself. She was a failure as a domineering person, but her personality remained as though she had made a success of it. She simply ignored any who opposed her.

Frank smiled softly to himself, ignoring his mother's solution. Marriage wasn't the answer to anything. Marriage was a bad thing for a person like Frank. He could picture himself with a pregnant wife. He knew he wouldn't be the type to run away from it if it happened, and paradoxically, he knew also that he wouldn't be the type to stay. So, he shied away from marriage completely. It was out of the question for him.

He had visited the neighborhood house twice since he had been released from prison and that had been more than sufficient for his needs. Frank had his own solutions. Give it to two-bit Molly and get it out of the system. It was a fuel, like food, only in reverse. A pleasurable form of vomiting.

The kitchen door swung open.

"You should get a job. What're you now? Thirty? Think of that! Thirty years old. Thirty years on the face of this earth and no job. Thirty years is just less than one third of a hundred. You know what a hundred is? That's right, Mister Smartypants—a century."

"Leave me alone," Frank said woodenly.

"Sure, I should leave you alone."

"Yeah, leave me alone."

"You should have joined the YMCA when I asked you to...."

Frank thought back to when he had been a small boy. He said, "That was a long time ago."

"So what? You should have joined like your brother."

"I should have done lots of things," Frank said.

She nodded, again the wisdom of the humble. "Well, I'm glad that you can see your wrongs, Francis."

"Don't call me Francis."

"It was the saint! Remember that it was the saint! It was never your uncle. Your uncle was a Red, a Communist. Remember that it was Saint Francis, the lovely man who kissed the birds and the dogs."

"I'll remember it the next time I see a dog."

"Comedy. Go on television and make yourself a million dollars. Go get money from laughter."

"What're you trying to say, Ma? You think I'm going to steal?" He spoke calmly, his voice icy, low, controlled. His narrowed eyes never moved from the Popeye statue.

His mother's eyes grew large when he mentioned stealing, and she began to solemnly nod her head. "So, it's out in the open now. No more kidding in the bushes, Francis. That's true. I think you'll steal again. Your Uncle Francis stole the Party funds in Palermo and they shot him. You look like him. I fear for you."

"Don't fear for me. I'm not going to steal."

"That's good. You're a good boy, Francis. You won a silver medal in the basketball game."

"That doesn't make me a good boy."

"Your father never won a medal. And he's a good man."

"Well," Frank said, "he never played basketball."

The door swung shut again.

Frank crossed his legs and listened to the radio. His thoughts wandered. He automatically lit another cigarette.

Ex-convict Toschi, the black sheep, the kid that should have joined the YMCA fifteen years ago, the tough guy that had shoved a pistol into a man's face and demanded money. He smiled bitterly and tapped his foot on the linoleum, listening to the music. He thought of his old cellmate, Heisler. He was a funny old guy, quiet, always brooding and pulling on his leathery old lip. He had a good reputation, was considered one of the top men in the business. Frank remembered how old Heisler used to put his lower partial plate in the toe of his shoe at night so he would never forget it in the morning.

Frank had to admire old Heisler. Who would ever think that a quiet old guy like that would go for a big payroll all by himself and nearly pull it off. It was an admirable thing. Not necessarily a good thing, but yet it was admirable. Heisler looked like a tough old Prussian soldier, the kind that would have told Hitler to go pee up a rope and get shot for it.

The door swung open.

"Hey, lazy man, you going to be here for dinner?"

"Yeah."

"Your father says he wants to see some rent money from you."

"He didn't say anything to me about it."

"He asked me to tell you."

"How much does he want?"

"Just so you get yourself a job and be a good boy, that's rent enough for the both of us."

The door swung shut.

It was like taking orders from a waitress. *Two cheeseburgers to go.*

He sighed, sunk lower in the lumpy sofa. If Frank had had old Heisler with him he wouldn't have failed at that loan office. He felt positive of that. When that guard had shot him in the hip the old man could have covered him to the car. They would have made it and they would have split better than ten thousand dollars. He sighed again, deeper, heavier. You can't have everything.

He felt the house around him, his father's house, and he felt lonely and hungry for something unknown. It was the familiar gnawing. He wanted to move ahead. But which direction was that? He didn't know.

Frank's father was a good, strong Italian who had worked in a San Bruno machine shop all his life and was now the shop steward for his union. He was a courageous man, in his own way, but Frank felt that he had wasted his life making machine parts and striking with the union and functioning as the secretary for the local Italian-American club. The structure of his father's life was no more than that, and the substance reflected it. He owned his own home and had two cars, one a small family Ford and the other an old pickup that he used for work and for his annual vacations. His was an uncomplicated existence, asking for no more than his worth and receiving his rewards without complaint; the rewards were always fair enough in his father's eyes. The Toschi family seemed a contented lot. But, as in most families, there was the disturbing presence of the shadow offspring, standing in the rear of the family group, almost as if he had wandered accidentally into the well-knit serenity of the family. Frank was the shadow. And, in spite of his mother's near-morbid concern for him when he had been a child, he had retreated into a secret shell and produced a code entirely of his own making. He had found it nearly impossible to exist in his family's image. He felt a desperate need to answer to his own code and not have to dance to unfamiliar tunes. He was a loner. Frank was a man who didn't think of toughness, but was tough because his fibers were unyielding to the demands of the world outside his code. And so, Frank Toschi had been sent to prison, five years for armed robbery.

In his parents' bedroom, over the baroque brass post bed, was an engraved sword and crossed Italian and American flags. A wood-and-silver crucifix was on the other side of the room on the bureau top, along with red-glass votive candles and a colored portrait of the Virgin Mother. His father was a devout Catholic and he wouldn't have a bedroom without religious representation, but over the bed were the two flags and the decorative sword.

Frank drew on his cigarette, smiling to himself.

His thoughts moved again to old Heisler, as if they had never left him, had glanced away for only a moment. Frank remembered how he had felt that Heisler was so much a part of his own code. The old guy was a thinker, had always been on his own, and had been busted three times. But, the way Frank figured it, Heisler wouldn't have gone for the strikes if he hadn't been by himself. And still, he thought of the guts, the sterling reputation with the old-timers who truly knew. The iron craw of Heisler. One old man, not being silly or trying to get caught the way the prison psychiatrists said most criminals were, but alone, a professional, trying to take an impossible payroll all by himself. And, the most amazing thing about it, he had missed by only a few seconds. Rotten breaks all the way down the line. Nobody was perfect, of course, but rotten breaks can sometimes make you believe that you're rotten yourself.

Heisler had said very little to Frank during their two years together, but Frank had expected that. The old ones, the good ones, weren't too eager to fraternize with a younger man. They weren't snobs, but they weren't friendly either. There was an air about them, some of the old ones, something like a cloak of dignity, of class. They had something that the rapists and juvenile terrorists lacked. And whatever that elusive, indefinable air was, it demanded respect. Frank had given that respect and he had never pushed himself on the old man. Of course, since they were cellmates, they had exchanged the usual words and had once shared a bottle of contraband bourbon together.

There had only been that one time when Heisler had acted close to Frank.

It was the time when Lover had cornered Frank in the laundry, behind the big hot rollers with the steamy-dry smell and the acrid tang of yellow soap, and Lover had had a tape-handled knife pointed at him. Others stood in a rough circle, vague figures in the steam clouds. The boilers clanked and the wet laundry carts rolled with the casters hissing on the concrete. All that activity and noise, and yet it was so terribly silent in the corner behind the rollers. Frank had been scared. He could have slammed the big blond Lover through a wall if it hadn't been for the knife.

But there was the knife, and Lover was going to cut him because he had made cracks at Lover's five-to-life sweetheart.

There were several of Lover's girls working the rollers and they stood in the circle, flitting excitedly, waiting for their top queen to prove his local authority.

Then Heisler had come behind Lover and smashed a blocky fist into the back of his neck. Lover's eyes popped. The knife fell to the floor and his jaw snapped and he dropped to the concrete. Heisler stopped him from trying for the knife by planting the heel of his boot hard at the Lover's Adam's apple. Frank kicked the knife under the rollers. Heisler said, "No more now, Lover. Or I'll make you lose your voice and your talent."

The circle backed away, not taking their eyes from the weathered face of the old man who had felled their queen. Lover thrashed around, trying to look tough again, but the old man merely pushed his heel harder. He looked at the circle of men in the steam. "You guys talk of this and I'll break you all up. We don't want no bad marks on us." Then to Lover, "I don't like you, sweetlips. I want you to leave us alone. No funny business now." He released his foot and slammed his toe into the soft flesh of Lover's side between the hip bone and the lower rib.

The guard came to their end of the laundry.

"What's going on here? Patterson, who knocked you down?"

"Our friend tripped," Heisler said. "Didn't he trip, Toschi?"

"Yeah, he tripped," Frank answered. "I think he fell over a piece of metal or something."

The guard looked to the rest of them.

"He tripped, Mr. Langdon," a bald-headed lifer said.

The guard looked to Heisler, pursing his lips. "You're a model boy, Heisler. You've never been in any trouble...."

"No sir, Mr. Langdon. I'm never in any trouble."

"Sure you didn't strike this man?"

"I'm sure, sir."

"Well, he's a jocker. Sure he didn't make a pass at you?"

"At an old bird like me?"

The cons laughed. The guard smiled.

"All right," Langdon said pleasantly. "You're supposed to be on the other side of the rollers. You're feeding. You're not even supposed to be on this side."

When Langdon left and the crowd broke up Frank sided up to Heisler. "Thanks. Looks like I was in a bit of trouble."

"Forget it, kid. We're cellmates. You're a good man."

That had been the end of it.

And now, Frank figured, Heisler was probably out of prison. He had most likely gone back to his family. Maybe he had even retired.

The door swung open again and his mother blocked it from swinging shut with her shoulder. "Dinner's almost ready, Francis."

"Good. I'm hungry."

"How can you be hungry? You sit in the house all day. You should go see your sister. She wants you to babysit for her because poor Louis has to work nights for two nights now."

Poor Louis! Frank liked his brother-in-law, Louis Goodwin, and he always thought it strange that his mother always referred to him as "Poor Louis." Louis was poor all right, but not because he was underpaid, but because he preferred working for himself, running his dingy auto-repair shop with hardly any capital and being forced to situate his business in a cheap low-overhead district in Daly City. Poor Louis! Louis was a hustler—he probably wouldn't remain poor for very long.

"You should babysit for your sister and poor Louis."

"What the hell's wrong with my sister?"

"She wants to see a movie."

"I'm too old to babysit. I'm one-third of a century."

"Comic!"

"Forget it. When's Pa coming home?"

"In a little while."

He wanted to say something to please her, anything; he felt that she had borne a heavy cross all her life and that somehow he could ease the weight by saying the correct thing to her. He felt guilty, felt a sudden surge of remorse. He thought desperately, digging around in his parcels of pity for a word that would encourage her. He grinned reassuringly, having found something that he felt sure would appease her, ease the weight of the imagined cross. He said, "I'm going to go to work, Ma. Get a job."

"Where?"

He looked at her, surprised. Why did she have to look his gift horse in the mouth? Why did she have to spoil his good intentions by taking what he had offered so seriously? He said, "Well ... pretty soon now I'll go to work. Maybe I'll get work in some kind of a garage. After all, I like cars

…" Then he realized that it had been the wrong thing to say. He saw the bitterness pass across his mother's face and he knew in advance what she was going to say. He almost groaned aloud.

"I know you like cars, Francis. You stole one when you were but a little baby."

"I was sixteen," he corrected bitterly.

"So don't sound so proud."

He sat in the darkness, almost pouting, feeling like a small boy, anger burning inside him. He had to remind himself that this was only his mother's way. He had tried—honestly tried—to say the magic words that would ease the weight of her cross, and she had rejected his offer with sarcasm. The hell with her then. If she didn't appreciate what he had tried to do, then the hell with her. He wasn't going to get down on his hands and knees for her. He no longer cared that much. The entire affair was too depressing. He felt more lonely now, more isolated from the family. He almost felt that the shadowy photograph of himself in the group was bleeding, becoming fainter, dissolving. Hell, pretty soon he wouldn't even be there. He would only be a memory. He would only be a sarcastic remark—like his late Uncle Francis who stole the Party funds in Palermo. Frank Toschi, ex-convict, a disgrace, a grown man who had stolen a car when he had been a baby; a kid who should have joined the YMCA and who now should get married; a grown man isolated from his family because he couldn't accept their code.

The hell with them.

"Go wash up, Francis. Your hands are dirty from thinking up dirty schemes to get rich quick."

"Shut up."

"You don't talk to me like that, Francis!"

"Just shut your goddam trap. I try to say good things to you, try to be the way you want me to be, and you slap me down. I feel like kicking your head in."

She began to cry then and he grabbed his sweater and hat from the hallway coat rack that was shaped like antlers. The door slammed behind him.

For the next two days he drifted aimlessly, was rarely home, rarely saw his family. He needed money, but he didn't try to look for a job. He went downtown to Market Street and went to the three-feature movie houses for four bits. He saw twelve pictures and he wasn't able to recall any of them. He went to a hotel that a freelance Tenderloin cabbie had steered him to, but had walked out when he saw the woman standing by the sink with a chip of soap in her hand and a Woolworth smile on her face. The two days passed slowly, lost in a maze of Hollywood deserts and penthouses with Scotch drinks fizzing, huge half-bared breasts and roaring western pistols. He felt cheated, and the more he drifted; the more somber and melancholy he became. He stood for several hours in front of the Powell-Market bank and he watched the people go inside and freely draw out money. He went to Antonio's Ice Cream Parlor, where he had often gone as a high-school kid. He ate ice cream. He took a long walk around the city and he bought a quart of beer to drink on the Embarcadero piers. He watched the free white gulls and the olive drab oily swells of the bay. He watched the tankers and pleasure liners head out to open sea. He stopped once in front of the Howard Street California Employment Office, but the long dreary lines only discouraged him and he felt more melancholy than before.

On the morning of the third day, Karl Heisler telephoned him.

"I'd like to speak to Mr. Frank Toschi please."

"Speaking. Who's this?"

"Heisler." The voice was muffled.

Frank frowned for a moment, then a certain warmth spread through him. His thoughts picked up speed and the shell of lassitude that imprisoned him cracked open. He felt a breath of fresh air. "You sound good, Heisler. I mean, it's good to hear from you. I've been going slightly nuts the last few days."

"What have you been doing with yourself, Toschi?"

"Just knocking around, going to movies, drinking beer. I can't get settled, I guess."

"Sure, it's like that, kid. That's sort of what I've been doing. Right now I'm walking my kid around town. I'm in your neighborhood as a matter of fact. I'm buying the kid an ice cream soda."

"Which place you at?"

"Some little joint with white tile like a subway."

"Antonio's. I know the place."

"Come down and see me, Toschi. Let's talk over inside times."

Frank hung up and put on his hat. He felt vaguely excited. His mother was coming slowly up the sagging front steps as he was leaving.

"Where are you going now, Francis?"

"I'm going to get me an ice-cream soda."

"If you're going to Antonio's, then bring back a pint."

"Sure, I'll bring back a pint."

Antonio's was a small, white-tiled shop two blocks from Frank's house. The tables in the booths were gray-streaked marble with white iron legs. Frank saw Heisler in the booth next to the window. He was drinking a chocolate malt. Grayish light came through the window and a fat tiger-colored cat was stretched out on the tile sill. Heisler was watching the kids that were at the long counter, his hard gray eyes resting on a slope-shouldered boy with pale cheeks and limp blond hair. The boy was watching another kid, heavier and taller than he, who was hitting a red rubber ball attached to a wooden paddle with an elastic band. It wasn't hard to see which boy was Heisler's.

Frank slipped into the booth, sitting opposite Heisler. They shook hands warmly.

"How are you, Heisler."

"Good. I feel fine." The older man smiled. "And you?"

"I can't complain."

Heisler continued to smile, the gray eyes under the shaggy white brows surrounded by hard weathered lines. He looked older in the grayish light.

"How long you been out?"

"Almost a week."

"How did it go?"

"Not too bad," Heisler said softly. "Only this time I think it was my family and my age. An old white head is the best gimmick there is to get sprung. People get wiser when their heads become white and their hands start to shake. It's sort of like the old snake in Kipling that had lost its fangs and its juice." He chuckled softly. "And how about yourself? You say you aren't settled yet?"

"I'm staying with my old lady until I can get enough walking money together. Meanwhile, I rot."

"Sounds like a tough thing, paisan."

Frank frowned. He knew why Heisler looked older now. It was the civilian clothes. The suspenders and hat, the cheap chambray shirt and the woolen sweater under it. Heisler dressed with the calculated functionalism of an older person. The way the chess players in Golden Gate Park dressed. Frank felt slightly disappointed. He had half expected Heisler to be dressed more in keeping with his reputation.

"You don't like being called a wop, do you?"

"Who me? I'm only half wop."

Heisler shrugged. "The wops put out some good men," he said absently.

"Like Mussolini?"

"I was thinking of Caesar."

"He was a white dago. At least all the statues are white."

Heisler spoke slowly, sipping his malt. "You like statues?"

"They're all right. I used to go to the museums when I was a kid, out to the park or up by the golf course—looking at statues, things like that. Used to pick up girls in the museums."

"You know, kid, the best read people in the world, I think, are merchant seamen and convicts. First time in, that was in Illinois in '37, I thought I'd go nuts. See, I'd just gotten married and I was still a peppery young guy. Then this old forger turned me onto the library. Prisons were tough in those old days, not like it is today. They didn't have any movies, television, radio, no psychological recreation forum, no nothing. The screws used to carry wooden pickaxe handles with a carved spike on the end. The food was the lousiest ever put out. If a guy didn't have friends on the outside to send him grub he'd damn near starve to death. The beds were so thick with lice in those days that every morning you'd wake up needing a transfusion." Heisler smiled wryly. "So, believe me, everybody buried themselves in the books. Some of the brightest guys I've ever met were in prisons."

Frank was amazed, not so much by what Heisler had said—he had heard stories of the old prison systems before—but by the length of it. It was the most he had ever heard the old man say in one sitting. He nodded when Heisler finished. He lit a cigarette and didn't say anything. Of course, he was curious as to why Heisler had wanted to see him, but he said nothing. The old man would come around to it in his own good time. Frank could wait.

"I was just taking a walk," Heisler said, "walking around with my kid. I thought I'd drop over to your neighborhood."

"I'm glad that you did," Frank said.

In the background the boys were slapping the red ball with the paddle; the milkshake machine was spinning, the point hitting the metal with a sharp whine when the cup was removed from the rod. Heisler bent over to suck at his malt. Frank ordered one for himself.

"You tried a loan office and got plugged, didn't you." He didn't voice it as a question. "That was a rotten break. I asked about you up there, before you became my cell buddy. Some big spade, name of Akar, said you were from around here, some kind of armed fall. I was curious."

"Why?"

"Just shopping around. You know, during the spawning season, hot spell weather when most of the new fish take the fall ... everyone gets curious about everyone else."

Frank nodded.

"I liked the way you kept to yourself. Not just because you were some kind of screw loose, or because you thought you were above prison. It wasn't like that. I saw that you were just a stick-to-yourself kind of guy. That's a rare thing these days. Especially with an Italian."

Heisler didn't explain his remarks and Frank didn't press him. It was always best to keep quiet, say nothing, let the other person feel you out. That way, in case anything goes wrong and the other person pulls out of whatever he was trying for, you've given him nothing about yourself. The advantage was that you learned about the other man, but he knew nothing about you. Frank kept it that way, he said nothing.

Heisler said, "I see where there's plenty of gang-looking guys in this neighborhood. I looked in a bar, the dingy one with the purple stripes on the canvas over the door. It looks like you could have had the cream of the tough guys, or at least as creamy as this generation can get. How come you never cliqued with the purple-striped bar people, or some of the others around here?"

"My old man came from Genoa," Frank said.

Heisler chuckled. "You're a cagey guy, Toschi. That's a helluva funny answer. That's no reason at all. Now take me for instance, my old man was a butcher, came from Hamburg, but that isn't the reason why I was a loner." He paused, sucked again at his malt, the straw darker with the liquid in it. "I just don't trust people, or at least I didn't. I got in plenty bad squeezes because I was alone, the same as others have gotten into bad squeezes because they weren't alone."

"You're telling me the story of my life," Frank said. He studied Heisler's face for a minute. "You're thinking about me for something."

"That's right."

"What about me?"

"Have you anything going?"

"I haven't thought about anything."

"That's good. A young guy with only one strike should keep his nose clean."

"What's on your mind."

"I have an idea."

"I'm willing."

Heisler looked at him, not smiling. "Why?"

"I trust you."

Heisler nodded, apparently satisfied. He pointed to the thin boy with the limp blond hair. "That's my kid over there. The little one. Isn't he something?"

"He's a fine looking kid," Frank said.

"Not really. Look at me, I'm a big guy. I mean heavy, and his mama's a big woman, kind of flat and Russian. You know the big wrists the Russians have sometimes? Well, I can't understand it. My kid's so damn skinny it makes my teeth hurt just to look at him."

Frank nodded.

"He's eleven years old. Look at him. Eleven years old. Edna buys clothes for him with colored rocket ships on the undershirts because his size is for smaller boys."

"He's just growing slow."

"No, he's not growing slow. He's never had anything, that's what's the matter with him. His papa's always in the Joint."

"You're not inside now."

"That's right, I'm not inside now."

The bigger kid finally missed the ball and he slapped the paddle angrily onto the marble countertop. He made a gesture to a fat kid, his turn to try it.

"I've got one that's going to go for plenty," Heisler said with a low voice. "I figure it—this of course is all pretty rough in my mind—I figure it for the best cut for the two of us. There has to be one other person in on it. I hate to do it that way but I can't see it any other way. The third party gets a flat salary for the job. He has to be a good driver and a good man. We'll pay him the flat fee and you and I will cut the rest Charlie McCarthy, right down the middle."

Frank thought a minute. Then, "How much do you figure on?"

"I'm afraid to tell you, Toschi. You won't believe it. It's a cash pile, no checks, no serial numbers, and no piece of cake to grab."

"I'll trust you. How much?"

"Upwards of two-fifty. Maybe more than a quarter million."

Three teenage girls entered the shop, giggling hysterically, wearing yellow slickers, six tough-looking, pimply-faced boys following them. They settled noisily into the far rear booth and lit cigarettes. They played the jukebox, arguing over the selections. The boys stood around the table, looking self-conscious and self-important, thumbs hooked in the pockets of their faded jeans, ducktailed haircuts greasy and messy looking. A cloud of cigarette smoke hovered over the jukebox.

"I got a driver," Frank said.

"I can't have one that's hot pants. I don't want a hot rodder or a pool hall John Dillinger."

"I've got a good man in mind," Frank said. "He doesn't even have a traffic ticket."

Heisler pulled on his lip, a familiar gesture to Frank. "Well," he said quietly, "I'll take your word for it. But I don't want him to know anything. You're sure he has no record?"

"No. Nothing at all. He's my sister's husband. Name of Louis Goodwin."

"Don't get your family into this."

"He's not my family. He's just the guy that happened to marry my youngest sister. He's a top mechanic and he can drive sweet. He's all right, otherwise I wouldn't have recommended him."

"He's not a wop?"

"No."

"Good. Wops like a crowd."

Frank nodded uneasily.

A teenage girl from the rear booth stopped at the counter for a package of cigarettes. She had removed her bulky yellow slicker and Frank sat and watched her. When she returned to her booth she noticed him and smiled.

"What're we going to hit?"

"It isn't a *what,* it's a *who.* We're going to hit Leon Bertuzzi."

Frank swallowed dryly and then managed a smile. He had heard of Leon Bertuzzi and he knew who he represented. He said, speaking quite simply, "You're nuts."

"No, I'm not nuts. You and me, and a driver, we'll take Leon's entire monthly grab from the Skyline House. It's not impossible. It won't be easy, but it's not impossible. Nothing is impossible if you work at it long enough."

Frank shook his head.

"It isn't Leon's place anyway. He's just the mink-lined shill, kind of a well-paid fall guy in case the state gets nosy about the house. The whole works belongs to—"

"I know who it belongs to. I've had my ears open in my time."

"Pietro DeVinci, Roger Dolan."

"That's what I hear."

"They're in New York, or Vegas. We just have to face Bertuzzi."

"He's big enough." Frank picked up his malt and didn't bother with the straws. He took three big gulps. "Well, we sure as hell won't be messing around with any peanuts. What hole do we crawl into after we finish the job?"

"We just hike out of the country. At least that's what I'm going to do."

"Can you tell me anything more about it? It's a pretty big idea and I—"

"I can't say anything more than what I've already told you."

"We'll need finances."

"Don't worry about that end of it."

"I don't have any money at all. Maybe sixty bucks in the bank."

"We'll use that sixty, and more."

"But you don't tell me anything more than what I already know. Right? We're going to visit Leon Bertuzzi and walk off with a quarter-million of his dough. That's all I know."

"That's all you need to know for right now. The rest of it can come later … once we're up in San Hacienda, where Skyline House is, then I'll fill in the rest. You'll have to trust me."

"I trust you," Frank said. He felt it inside, a warm something growing, blotting out the old gnawing sensation. Something big brewed in its place. He knew that he had allowed himself to become stale since prison. He had been losing his juice, but now he felt in command of himself again. The apathy was gone and he felt the excitement of scheming inside him, feeling the old heat of purpose give him the full pleasure of his abilities. He said, "Getting out of the country is the best idea. At least for you and me. We've got records and the cops may tie us in. Louis won't have to leave at all—"

Heisler smiled again. "There won't be any cops, Frank. That's one thing we won't have to worry about, not once we're across the San Hacienda County line. You see, Bertuzzi won't blow the whistle if the house gets hit. Skyline House is illegal. Gambling isn't allowed. So, if he blew a statewide alarm he'd be in plenty of hot water. And not only from the cops but from guys like Dolan and DeVinci. They won't want to lose a paying situation like Skyline just because of one robbery. So, the way I figure it, they'll try to catch us within the county lines, or else, if we get through, they'll concentrate their own facilities on us. The beauty is, they don't have the means that the cops do. They'll have to play it by ear. And, if we don't open our mouths, then they won't hear a word."

Frank nodded again. He liked the idea of no police action involved, and, he knew, Heisler had probably figured that much of it correctly. It was obvious, now that he thought of it, that Bertuzzi wouldn't send out the alarm. But, there was the one thing, there were the local police, which Bertuzzi obviously owned. He had to own them, or else Skyline wouldn't be allowed to operate as successfully as it did.

"What about the local cops?"

Heisler pursed his lips and looked thoughtful. "You've probably already figured it, Frank. Bertuzzi owns them from the D.A. on down. They're all on the payroll. But once we clear the county line we won't have to worry about the law."

"We only have to worry about the organization."

"Right."

"That's enough to worry about."

"You still with me?"

"I'm with you," Frank said. He thought of the dreary lines at the Howard Street Employment Office.

Heisler's skinny kid was watching the fat boy slap the ball. Little Karl was standing in a circle of larger boys.

"I bunked with Larry Con before they put you in with me. Remember Larry Con? He's the guy that died just before you were transferred."

"I remember Larry. I never met him but I'd seen him around." Frank remembered only that Con was a balding man with purple splotches on his neck. He couldn't remember anything else that had impressed him. Only the old-timers had talked to him, and when he had died two years ago, only the old-timers had mourned him.

Heisler continued, "He was a pistol for Bertuzzi at Skyline House, one of the guards. He worked there for—I think he said about three years. I'm not too sure, but, anyway, he and I knew a few of the old-timers in Detroit in the late twenties. We buddied pretty good in those days. We were even in the Illinois Joint together in 1937. He was getting out just about the same time I was going in. After that we didn't see too much of each other. He got mixed up with some organization action in Pennsylvania, something to do with unions, while I drifted out to here." He sighed heavily. "Well, anyway, I think old Larry knew he was going to die. The doc up in the last place showed him X-rays of his lungs. Larry didn't talk very much about it. But, just before they shipped him off to the hospital, he told me a skeleton layout of Skyline. After all, I was an old friend, used to be a good one, and I didn't have any money to speak of. Since he was going to die anyway I guess he figured he didn't have too much to lose by telling me what he knew. It wasn't too much, but it was enough to get me thinking. After all, Frank, a quarter-million is a helluva lot of money ... and I'm not too young anymore." The old man's eyes glittered and his face looked hard. "I haven't had a good thing since the forties. I've been in this business long enough that I think I can even smell a good one."

"And this smells good?"

"The best."

"Then I'll take your word for it—and Larry Con's word. I'll go along with you all the way."

The fat boy finally missed the red ball with the paddle and the kids laughed. They had been tickling him to force him to miss. Little Karl asked if he could give it a try. The other boys turned their backs to him and didn't bother to answer.

"Come here, Karl," Heisler called out from the booth. "I want you to meet a friend of mine."

Little Karl shook Frank's hand.

"This is Mr. Toschi. He worked with your Dad in the oil fields and we're going into business again."

"Hello, Mr. Toschi."

Frank made room for the boy on his bench. "Well, I guess I got enough to spring for a round of malted all around. How about it, little Karl?"

"Thank you."

Frank called the counterman and made the order for the booth. A thick cloud of unmoving blue smoke still hung over the back booth where the teenagers were. The fat tiger-colored cat finally moved from the window and the grayish light.

"I wish I had a cat," Little Karl said.

3

The Sutro Heights District was at the west end of the Richmond District, bordered by Golden Gate Park to the south and Lincoln Park to the north; it was the farthest point of the city, with only the blue expanse of the Pacific Ocean beyond it. The district was a quiet one, a retired district, sheltered by the north hills and the windbreaking eucalyptus of Sutro Heights Park. The houses were generally tree-shaded and much older than the monotonous crackerboxes of the neighboring Sunset-Parkside homes. The district had a quiet and dignified personality. There wasn't much traffic. Old men puttered in their gardens and there were no children playing in the streets.

Karl Heisler stepped from the Clement bus and walked three blocks with his hands deep in his pockets. The sun was warm on his shoulders and the woolen sweater under his shirt was hard against his skin. Tuttle's Nursery was at the end of the next block.

Karl had wanted to take his son with him; he could have studied the nursery plants while Karl spoke with Walter Tuttle. But the boy was in school until three each day.

It wasn't going to be easy with Walter. It never had been. Sometimes they had lost, but it had never cost Walter as much as it had Karl. And Walter had, over the many years, made quite a bit of money with Karl.

They had known each other from a long time back. In the Terre Haute days Walter had been a good man in the business, but he had finally been caught with a bad one and he had had enough independence to voluntarily end his active days. When he was out three years after his fall he had turned to contact work. If you had a bullet in you and wanted it out Walter Tuttle was the man to contact for a doctor who would remove it without the usual inconvenience of a police report. Walter took a third of the cost. He worked with abortionists for a third as well, and he could get you a gun or a car for cost plus one third. He worked only with the old-timers, men that he knew of and had known, men he could trust. He was a cautious man.

Karl entered the nursery. The small bushes and trees were set in planters and the long cool green racks of clover and dichondra were on both sides of the shaded, graveled pathway. Fuchsia hung from the overhead latticework and long striped shadows swept the nursery grounds. The smells of manure and rich damp earth were strong in the warm air.

A white-haired old man was putting young plants into tins, cutting them from a seedling flat with a putty knife and transplanting them into the larger cans. He heard Karl's crunching footsteps on the pathway and he looked up, straining his tiny eyes through his thick tinted glasses.

"Karl Heisler!"

"Hey, Walter, you're pretty sharp. You can't hardly see me, but you know who it is right off."

"I always know the ones from a long time back," Walter croaked. "You walk kind of flatfooted so's nobody can knock you down." He grinned and set the putty knife on the lid of the seedling flat. He pulled off his glove and rubbed his earth-colored hand on his trousers.

Karl came forward and warmly took the old man's hand.

"You're looking good, Walter."

The old man looked bad. He had lost most of his teeth and hadn't replaced them with plates or a bridge. His breath was strong and smelled almost of death. His thin chest rumbled when he breathed. But still, his face and neck were burnt from the constant outdoor exposure and his body movements were steady and quick. The good air and relaxing work and atmosphere of the nursery seemed to be the only thing that held the life inside him. Tuttle seemed to be the type who was sickly but yet lived to be a better-than-old age. As a matter of fact, Karl had never known Walter to be in good health, even in the old days when they were both much younger.

Walter was at least seventy now. Maybe a little more. He had quit the business when Karl had been twenty-three. That was in the later part of 1929. He had been a good man until they had caught him. Then, after his time in prison, he hadn't had the appetite for the work and he had entered the percentage business.

"What brings you around here, Karl?" Walter returned to his work. He cut into the flat with his knife. "I thought you were still living off the state. I didn't hear about you getting out."

"I got out about a week ago."

"So I see. You get them books I sent?"

Karl smiled. He was sitting on the heavy-legged table, smoking a cigarette. He had taken his jacket off and the perspiration was damp along his forehead under the band of his hat. "Yeah, I got the books all right. I figured that they were from you. I didn't write to say thanks because I didn't want the front office to know you were still around and talking to guys like me."

Tuttle nodded, not looking at him. "You're a good boy, Karl. It's good you're out." He looked up at the clear sky through the latticework overhead. "Because the weather's getting good now. And the pen ain't no place for a man to be when the weather's good and clean."

Karl looked around at the nursery. There had been a few changes. "Looks like you're doing all right here, Walter. The place looks fine."

"Not too bad, I guess. The old folks around here like me and I like them. I talk grassy talk with them and we get along just fine."

There was a new sound to the rear of the nursery. Karl looked through an uneven wall of young fir and saw a small green shed and office. There was a seedling house with a slanted roof of opaque glass, a clearing with a rack of redwood planter boxes stacked to one side. A young woman, about twenty-five, was pulling light paper sacks of leaf mold and setting them by the glass house wall. She looked once at Karl with large brown eyes, then returned, expressionless, to her work. She was dark-skinned, Indian or Negro, and wore a soiled pair of denim coveralls and a patched polkadot shirt. Her figure was almost boyish.

Karl pulled uneasily on his cigarette. "Who's that back there? Is it okay for us to talk?"

"It's okay," Walter answered. "I guess I forgot to tell you. I couldn't write to you while you were inside...." He grinned, showing empty gums. "I got married two years ago."

"To her?"

"Surprised? Hell, I was surprised myself. She can hardly speak English, but she's a darn good worker and she's learning this business fast. She'll get this whole place, even all the mad money I got stashed, the minute I die." He looked down to his hands, then, almost as if he were ashamed, to Karl. "That probably won't be very long from now, Karl."

"You'll outlive me."

"Maybe so. But I doubt it, and so do my doctors. That's why I married her legit."

"Is she a spade?"

"No. She looks it though, doesn't she. She's Guatemalan. Her name's Rosaria. Sounds cute, kind of—Rosaria Tuttle. Did you ever know my first wife? Her name was Myrtle. They don't name girls Myrtle any more. I guess it kind of went out of style. Like most things. They just go out of style."

"I never knew you were married before," Karl said.

"Sure. Five years of it. She divorced me when I took my one and only fall." Walter shook his head, then looked back toward the glass house. "Rosaria came to me from a whoremaster in Bakersfield. It was her first time up from the borders and she was pregnant when she came. But she didn't show until about a month after she got here. I got her fixed up through old Doc Bertoli. Yeah, he's still around, still sawing bones." He lit a cigarette, coughed wretchedly for a minute. "Anyways, Rosaria didn't want to whore and she had no place to go. She was only up here on a work permit for this Bakersfield guy. So I married her legit and she's a citizen now. We get along real fine."

Karl nodded. He felt the peace of the nursery getting to him. He said, "I'm happy for you, Walter. I really am."

"Thanks." He smiled and winked. "But you're too old for your wish of happiness to do me any good. It only counts when a young bucko wishes you real happiness."

Rosaria finished with the leaf mold sacks and she disappeared behind the shed. Karl heard her at work on something else.

"Well, you didn't come all the way out here just to discuss my life—or my death. What's up with you, Karl?"

"I thought we'd be social for a little while."

"No need to be that way. Time's an important thing. You're old enough to know about that."

"I came to see if you could help me out."

"Always. That's why people come to see me. They need something I got, or I can get. Sometimes it's flowers and other times it's hardware. I'd rather see you come for flowers."

"I'm needing hardware."

"I figured as much."

"I need guns and a good car."

"You just got out of the Joint, Karl. You want to go back for the whole book?"

"No fall this time, Walter. This one's going to be better than the Weintzer job."

"Weintzer was a good one," Walter admitted. "But those kind of jobs don't grow on trees. Companies pay off with checks and everybody carries credit cards. Cash isn't floating around anymore these days. The only cash in large enough amounts to attract a good professional is registered by serial numbers." He shook his head sadly. "You have to face it, Karl. The big company payrolls like the Weintzer job are gone. Cash money has gone out of style. Like the name Myrtle. Lots of things go out of style, Karl. And, I've been thinking, that maybe the old ones like you and me, maybe we've kind of gone out of style too."

"There's still cash in plenty of places. And besides, there's still furs and jewelry, negotiable bonds, narcotics. There's still plenty of ways."

"You're talking like a kid," Walter said. "The business is rotten and you know it. Only juvenile delinquents left. They stick up a grocery store for six bucks and pump eight bullets into a half-blind old man. That's what the business is these days. These punks ain't got no respect."

Karl nodded. "I've still got an idea."

"Want to tell me?"

"I can't."

"Then I won't invest in it. It's that simple."

Karl bit his lip, lit another cigarette, debated with himself. He knew that of all the people he knew, Walter was one of the few he could trust implicitly. "All right. It's Skyline House. Bertuzzi's place in San Hacienda."

Walter merely nodded. "Okay. It's your neck. How can you pay me for the stuff?"

"When I get finished with the job."

Walter laughed softly as he eased wet earth around a tiny plant.

Karl said, "You don't have any reason not to trust me."

"I trust you. I was just laughing at myself because I knew that I trusted you. If you did the trick and got clear you'd take the chance of coming back here to pay me. That's just like you, Karl Heisler. You pay your debts and nobody's ever said a word against you. You've got one of the best reps I know of. You've always been real straight."

Karl felt better. For a second there he had feared that Walter would turn him down. But it was all right now. He had always tried to play fair and he knew that his word was good. He had confidence in the Skyline job because it was the best that he had ever heard, and he knew that he would be able to repay Walter for the financing. Otherwise he never would have asked for credit. Credit was a bad way to run any business, but it was a good thing to have a clear rating in case you had to take a safe plunger now and then. But only if it was safe, one that had a better than seventy-five per cent chance for success.

He said, "I'll need something heavy, something with plenty of bogeyman value. A sawed-off shotgun, one automatic, two pistols. I don't care about the model or year, just so's they're thirty-eights. No little stuff and no forty-fives. And I've got to have a car, one that I can ditch and that can't be traced back to you or anybody else."

Tuttle squinted behind his thick glasses and rubbed his stubbled jaw. "What're you going to do? Start an army?"

"No."

"How many going in with you?"

"Two."

Walter nodded, looked down at the work at his hands. "I like working with young things, little plants. I put them into the dirt and they grow and bloom. It's a good feeling to watch things grow. I like to watch these plants grow and get stronger each day. I don't like it when they get brown and droop." He paused. "I get sick to my craw when I think about death. It's like a dirty old man who hides behind things. Just like the way I do. That's me: Death. Anyways, we all have to go some time, but I don't see why we have to hurry it along." He shook his head. "It's funny, Karl, I don't like to talk like this, all full of butterflies and frogs, but I do."

Karl was silent a minute. A bee hovered near a box of fuchsia. The fuchsia looked like a flowery Portuguese man-of-war, trailing in the still air, colored bright with purple and red. He said, "Will you take my tab for the stuff and two thousand capital?"

"Sure, I'll take your tab. But if you make it don't come back here. Mail it to me."

"Okay."

"I'll have the stuff ready for you in two days. But, I'll tell you, I don't like doing it. I'd rather preach to you like a social worker. This way I'm only putting nails into your coffin. I could be digging your grave … and I don't want to do that for an old friend."

Karl pushed himself from the tabletop and removed his hat. He ran a handkerchief that Edna had ironed for him across his brow. "You don't think I'll make it?"

"No."

"Why?"

"Guts."

"I've got them, Walter."

"You always have. But you were younger then, too."

"You think I'm old?"

"Age is a funny thing…."

"I'm only fifty."

"You're older than that, Karl." He stood by the table, a small bent figure of a man with his snow white hair and thick eyeglasses. He didn't look very tough, not tough the way he had years ago. "I suppose you heard about Larry Con dying…."

Karl smiled. "You're a sharp guy, Walter."

"I can figure things out pretty well," Walter said. "Well, I wish you all the luck in the world, old friend. Take that for whatever it's worth. I wish you all my luck."

"Thanks. I'll see you in two days."

"Sure. Two days."

Karl walked to the nursery entrance and looked back at Walter. The old man seemed to caress each plant as he moved them from the flat to the tins. He had only a little life let in him now and he was holding onto it as gently as he could. He was older than Karl, much older, and there wasn't much left for him but his hands to midwife young plants; and a wife, probably a good thing, maybe even one of the better things. But she could hardly speak English. Karl wondered if Walter had learned to speak Spanish. Then he wondered if it really mattered.

He walked into the sudden bright sunlight, leaving the nursery, moving like an old man. But Karl wasn't old. He was twenty years younger than Walter, and he wasn't holding onto life with death cold hands. He looked at his hands, thick, with lumpy fingers. He knew that he could easily kill a man with those hands if he wished. If there were no other way, he could kill cleanly and simply with his hands.

He stopped at a public phone on a corner by a gas station. He dialed Toschi's number and waited for the voice to answer.

"This is Heisler."

"What happened?"

"In two days. We can have the stuff in two days."

There was a pause. Then, "That's fine, Mr. Weidman. I'd like to think about it."

Karl smiled at the dial face of the phone. Frank's mother had probably entered the room. He said, "I want to meet your brother-in-law tonight or tomorrow, whatever the best time would be for all of us. I want to be plenty sure about him."

"Yes, sir," Frank answered pleasantly. "I'll let you know as soon as I see you."

"Meet me in front of Antonio's in about an hour."

"Yes sir," Frank said, "I'll be happy to do that."

Karl hung up and walked out to the bus stop.

4

At Antonio's, Karl sipped from a cup of coffee. The shop was empty. The kids weren't out of school yet. The bright sunshine glared from the white tile. Karl watched the window for Toschi.

He had come early. He hadn't known that it only took the bus forty-five minutes, including the Mission transfer, from the Richmond-Sutro Heights District. He had guessed an hour. He ordered a French pastry and waited and watched.

He thought about the driver. He didn't have to worry about Toschi. He could trust him and he had confidence in his judgment. But the brother-in-law, Louis Goodwin, as far as Karl was concerned, was a pig in a poke. He knew nothing about him. But if Toschi said he was a good man for the job then he probably was. And still, he had to think of it this way, Goodwin was Toschi's brother-in-law, practically a relative. He wondered about that. Perhaps Goodwin couldn't support Frank's sister on what money he made. Perhaps that was why Frank was bringing him in on the job—so he could keep his sister off public welfare.

He thought of what Walter had said. It had been something about getting old and losing your nerve, or becoming too cautious. But that was senseless. Karl had never feared anything. He knew that he would never come across anything that he would fear. He had known violence and danger in every form and he had never buckled before it. He had always seen his enemy, seen the dangers, and he had been able to face them. No, there was no chance of his ever losing his nerve. No chance at all.

Karl prided himself in one thing, his strength, his ability to face danger without breaking. He had always had that. And he felt that he would still have it—no matter how old he became.

He ate his pastry and drank his coffee. He waited, ordered more coffee, decided to call his wife. The phone was on the wall near the jukebox in the rear.

"Hello, Edna?"

"Did you see Walter?"

"Yes."

"How is he?"

"He got married. A nice little Guatemalan girl. I didn't get to talk to her, but she seemed to be a nice woman."

"Are you going to be home for dinner?"

"Yeah, sure."

"Stop at the market for me then. Do you have enough money?"

"Sure."

"Get a pound of hamburger, the reddest you can, and a pound of cucumbers and some spaghetti."

"I'll remember. Do you need anything else?"

"I suppose some beer for yourself if you want it."

"All right."

"Are you going out again tonight?"

"I think maybe I'll have to."

"I wanted you to take us to the movies. There's a Marlon Brando picture playing, and you said that you'd never seen him."

"Maybe we'll go tomorrow night. Is the picture a western?"

"Yes."

"Good girl. I only like the westerns and the comedies." Back at his booth by the window he sipped his coffee and waited.

Ten minutes later he saw Toschi coming down the street, wearing his sweater and looking more like a hungry college joe than a man of thirty who had already completed a sizable piece of time. When Frank came in he ordered coffee and joined Karl at the booth. He didn't say anything. He stirred his coffee, adding cream until it was the color of autumn.

"Okay," Karl said. "What about your brother-in-law? Did you tell him about the trick?"

"I only told him that I'd heard of something that might come up and might be needing a driver. But I didn't say anything about it."

"Good."

"Don't worry about him, Karl, he's a pretty sharp guy and he'll keep his head. He's a clean liver. He doesn't drink, he isn't a junk man, and he wants to make a good dollar for himself. My sister's pregnant and he'll be needing the money. That's my youngest sister. I have two of them. So now I'm going to be an uncle. Uncle Frankie. I can see it now."

"When can I see him?"

"Tonight. My sisters are both going off to the movies, some kind of a western they want to see. Louis will be home by himself all evening. The feature doesn't let out until ten-forty-five." He smiled boyishly over his coffee cup. "I called the movie house and asked about the schedules."

"Then it'd be safe for us to drop by say about eight o'clock. Where does he live?"

"Only five blocks from my place. About three from here."

"I'll meet you here at seven-thirty or so."

Frank nodded agreement. "You got the stuff okay? No hang-up?"

"Don't worry about it."

"He took your tab?"

"Like I told you, he's an old friend of mine from Terre Haute. And I guess there's another reason, but that doesn't matter very much."

He thought of Walter Tuttle and the other reason he was taking his tab. It was because Karl had asked for them—and because Walter believed that this was to be the last time for Karl Heisler. He wouldn't deny a man the opportunity to dig his own grave if he wanted to badly enough.

But Walter had been thinking of the way things had been in the old days. He suspected the set-up because he knew of Larry Con's background and knew his connection with the organization's man, Leon Bertuzzi, and the Skyline House operation. But he didn't know, couldn't know, of the many nights that Karl had thought of it. How could old Tuttle know of Karl's sleepless nights, thinking of a hundred and one general plans? Larry hadn't given many details so Karl had been forced to improvise. He had established fifteen basic layouts. He knew for certain that Skyline would have to be set up along one of his lines. He had exercised all of his ability in planning. And, he knew, that the moment he saw Skyline, the plan itself would fall like a leaf, crackling, gold-colored from the sky.

Out of the years Karl had built up an amazing talent for guessing the total picture of an operation. Quite often he had never seen the layout until he had actually stepped into it. But, even then, he knew almost by instinct where the money was, where the entrance was, and, most important of all, how to get in and out. The writer of that article in the factual crime magazine had known of this, and it had been that talent that he had focused on; Karl Heisler was indeed a professional, a master, and he felt certain that the Skyline job would be the greatest stroke of his career. He was betting all on it. He could smell its success. How was an old, fate-shaking, doom-rattling, dying man like Walter Tuttle to know that?

Walter was no more than a faded photo of the past, whiskey-colored, staring, one-dimensional, a figure that had long died and only his ghostly shadow remained in a sunny garden that reeked of death. He was one of his own plants, once bloomed, now brown and drooping, shaking the air with foreboding. The hell with Tuttle. What did he mean by his cracks? Karl Heisler wasn't old. He was still on top and he intended to remain there.

What about Skyline? Some plush organization house with white dinner jackets and gleaming foreign cars in a graveled driveway with polished finishing school hoodlums with sunglasses and television-emcee dialogue. Karl knew them. He had seen a hundred and one fancy mob clip-joints. They were all alike. So, what about the Skyline House? Were they impregnable? No. No one would ever suspect it because Skyline had never been hit before. No one ever dared hit the big houses with the big eastern backing. It was like holding a lily in your hand at your breast and signing the death registry.

Karl Heisler smiled, almost chuckled. That was all too true. But, only if you intended to live. And, since he was going to disappear completely, retire for good, it would be the same as dying. There would be no way for Bertuzzi to touch his finger to Karl Heisler. Karl would be gone, buried in a free land. All he had to do was get in and get out, cross an imaginary line out of San Hacienda. He sipped from his coffee, lost in his thoughts, excited with them, unconscious of his shabby clothes and the cheap jailhouse tile of the ice-cream parlor. Toschi stood up, carrying his coffee cup. "Do you want more coffee, Karl?" There was a note of respect, admiration in the younger man's voice. Karl smiled and nodded, slip his cup across the grayish, sticky marble top. "Sure thing, Frank."

A good kid, reminded Karl of himself when he had been young. He liked Toschi, felt surprisingly good with not being alone on this one. The coffee came and he lit a cigarette. They talked for twenty minutes more, then shook hands and Karl stepped out into the street.

What was it that Edna had asked him to get at the market?

5

Karl sat in the darkness of the living room of the old apartment, the sour dusty odors of the faded flowered carpet and broken, bleeding furniture staining the air. Smoking a cigarette, still dwelling in the tinseled plain of the Skyline job, feeling older now with a full stomach, he was keenly aware of the close dinner hour atmosphere that lingered; the tiny comforting clack of dishes being stacked in the chipped sink, the liquid whispering of tap water, knives and forks jingling in the enamel pan, the radio playing softly. His watch said that it was six o'clock. It was becoming dark outside. He could hear Edna picking up each plate and turning it under the tap. Then the water gurgling in the drain, the cupboard door opening and closing, the heavy black pan being moved on the stove.

The boy sat at the kitchen table, swinging his small feet, chewing thoughtfully on a yellow pencil. Now and then he glanced toward the front room, squinting quickly at the darkness where he could see the glow of his father's cigarette from the sofa; then he would squirm in his chair, smile secretly and contentedly to himself, cup his thin face in his hands, and look back to his mother.

Five minutes past six. Karl felt himself relax and grow confident under the influence of the dinner hour. It was good to be home. He was at last becoming accustomed to his freedom, to the intimacy of his family. He felt accepted, a part of it all.

He sat and looked at nothing in particular. He felt time slip past him with no feelings of anxiety. By now the neon signs were probably lighted in the streets and the automobiles were probably driving with their headlights on.

The boy came into the living room and sat in a chair. The pencil was behind his ear now.

Little Karl had finished his dinner, had only picked at his food, moved it desultorily around on his plate. He had finished his cucumbers and his milk, but the hamburger and rice had hardly been touched. Karl felt concerned, as if he could see his son wasting before his eyes. A growing boy should eat to keep himself growing. It wasn't right to pick at your meal. But Karl said nothing. He had only exchanged knowing glances with Edna during the meal. He felt somehow that it would be out of place for him to criticize the boy.

"Do you like cucumbers?"

"I sure do," the boy said.

"It's one of my favorite foods. Probably my favorite. I like them when they're ice cold with a little lemon juice on them. Sometimes they're good with chili powder."

Little Karl nodded. His hair was hanging to one side of his face. It was amazing how much the boy resembled Karl's own father. Karl remembered having seen a photograph years ago, during the Depression, when he had returned to Detroit to visit his great uncle. The picture had shown his father standing by a white horse and a flatbed cart in Hamburg. There had been the same large gray eyes and sad mouth, and, especially, the limp blond hair.

"Can we go to the movies tomorrow night?"

Karl looked up. "Sure. Do you like westerns?"

"Yes."

Karl fell silent again. He sat, looking at his son, thinking of how much he resembled the photograph of his father. But the resemblance was only in the features, the bodies weren't alike. Karl's father had been a giant of a man, not particularly tall, but sturdy and thick like Karl himself. His father had been a butcher. He could remember helping out in the shop at night after school, going over the hardwood floor with the fan-shaped bamboo rake, pushing and laying the sweet-smelling yellow sawdust, leveling it around the fat legs of the bloodstained chopping block. Then wiping the block with clean waste rags and putting the meats into the big coolers for the morning. He also sharpened the knives and tools on the stone wheel and helped deliver the sandwich meats for the free-lunch counters in the neighborhood saloons.

"I sure wish you didn't have to go out tonight," the boy said.

What would his son remember of him years from now? Would he know that his father had been in prison? A useless thought. Of course he would know. If he ever applied for a civil or government job they would question him about it. And then what? Would he reinterpret the past to serve the angry moods of his present? Would any favorable memories become bitter?

"I have to go out tonight, son. It's business."

"Will you be gone for very long?"

"No. I'm only going out to see a few men about a job. We may be able to make some money. And, if all goes well, then maybe we can start our own business somewhere, just you and me and your mama. Then you can help me with it, just like I used to help my father when I was your age. I'm getting old and I'll be needing a good boy like you to help me carry the load."

"Like the butcher shop you told me about?"

"Yes."

"Tell me about your father."

"There's not too much to tell. He was a very honest man."

"Is he still a butcher?"

Karl shook his head. "No, he's dead now."

"I'll bet he was a real old man when he died."

"No, not too old."

"Did he have lots of money?"

"No, we were poor."

Edna came to the doorway, wiping her reddened hands on the apron about her waist. "Don't bother your father now."

"That's all right, Ed, he wasn't bothering me."

The boy returned to the kitchen and Karl lit another cigarette. He sank back into the moldy sofa. He still had a little time before he was to meet Toschi. It was early yet.

He wondered what the ones still in prison would be doing at this moment. He couldn't bring himself to remember. It all seemed far away. Still a close reality to him, but yet, far away, indistinct. like watching details from the reverse end of a telescope. All he remembered now was the grim monotony. The yellow ceiling lights in the long corridors, the clean smell in the air, the blankets neatly rolled at the foot of the bunks. He remembered the trays that you carried your food in. He remembered the sign on the wall of the cafeteria. And there was the long curved road that bordered the gray water, going east to the parking circle and the last gate. There were the naked brown hills that rolled on the north side of the walls. Isolated towers dotted the hills, and at night the main tower light moved and an occasional airplane would drone overhead, winking red, green, humming and throbbing under the stars. There were many other things, but they had merged into a single hazy picture. And he felt too content at the moment to unravel and decipher it all and force himself to remember....

How different everything could be if there was money.

But there hadn't ever been enough money and he had to accept that. He knew that there were other things in life besides money, and, if he were alone in this life, without Edna and little Karl, he felt certain that he would ask for nothing more than what he believed would be his worth. But he wasn't alone in this, and he didn't feel cheated or bitter because of it. He was glad that he had the family. It gave him something to look forward to. He had a great responsibility to them, greater than the responsibility to himself. He had missed so often lately that he felt a great deal lost between himself and his family—a great deal to make up for. There was no other way. There had never been any other way for him.

He didn't wear a necktie. Edna helped him with his coat.

"Are you going now?"

"Yes."

"It's still early."

"I'll stop for a drink and kill a few minutes."

"There's still some beer in the icebox."

"Beer is for laborers." He smiled. "I'll have it when I get back."

She kissed him then. It was the first time since he had returned that she kissed him on the mouth.

"You look worried, Ed."

"I guess I am. I want you to make it, Karl. I'd rather you don't even try, but since you're going to anyway, I hope you make it."

"It'll be like the days after the Weintzer job. Remember? We had a time, a good time, in Mexico, Tucson, that new car they took away from me. The whole works." He patted her and left the house.

It was warmer outside than he had expected. San Francisco weather was like that, cold one day, then beautiful and warm the next. And often it was warm in the evening, especially in the Mission District where the offshore breezes didn't reach. Always in October it was the best weather.

He stopped at a nice bar, small and well-lit with a large chandelier, and had brandy with cloves. Then he went to Mission Street and caught a jitney. When he reached his stop he had to remove his coat. It was warmer now, and he walked slowly, deliberately pacing himself so he could arrive at Antonio's right on time. He stopped in front of a theater, the colored neon blinking overhead, and studied the glossy stills in the glass cases. There were many people on the street; couples walking in their shirt sleeves and holding hands, young girls with tight shorts and close-fitting blouses, young men with oil in their hair and a glossy shine on their heavy boots. He saw a pair of women entering the theater, one tall and thin faced, the other short and pregnant. He wondered if they were Toschi's sisters. He continued walking, almost in a dreamy state, aware of the warmth of the night, the lurid honkytonk blinking glow of the neon, the strolling couples, the tiny mysterious sounds from the saloons and cafes.

Antonio's was crowded and Toschi was waiting in front of the store with his back to the window. He removed his hat when Karl came up to him.

"Did you call your brother-in-law?"

"Yes. They left for the show already. He's all alone."

"Good."

"I don't know how it got so damned hot all of a sudden. I thought it was going to cool down there for a while."

"It feels good," Karl said.

"I'm not complaining. I like the heat."

They walked slowly. They turned a corner off Mission and the street became dark and lonely, leaving behind the traffic sounds, the crowded sounds. Mexican families were sitting on the porch steps. Someone was singing *Tu Recuerdo Yo,* a guitar thumping in the background.

"I wish it was all over with," Frank said.

"It will be in a few days."

"How long do we stay in San Hacienda?"

"Long enough. I'm going to rent a cabin by money order under the name of Lars Anderson."

"Will it be close to Skyline?"

"Close enough. Are you nervous?"

"Not just yet. But I know I will be."

"Good. It's not right not to be spooked."

They stepped into a bar, a long one with pictures on the wall of faded prize-fighters, baseball stars, and Mexican theater people. They sat at the bar and a thin-faced Latin took their order.

"Two brandies."

Toschi smiled. "You got fancy tastes."

"Brandy? There's nothing fancy about brandy." He chuckled lightly. "But, maybe you're right. I like good things. It's because I'm getting old. When I was younger I never had the patience to look at a painting, smell a flower, or even finish a good book. But now … I guess I have the patience. Brandy is one of the good things. A brandy warms you, brings out little fires in your wrists, makes your eyes become a separate part of your body."

"You make it sound good."

They finished their drinks and left the bar. When they paused at a corner for Toschi to light a cigarette, Karl saw for the first time that he looked older than thirty years, harder, that he didn't even stand like a young man. He also noticed that there was something appealing, something uncommonly sensitive in Toschi's eyes, something that most of them didn't have. It was a curious thing to see in a man that you had lived with for two years. Karl was surprised. And, because of this, he felt warmer and closer to him. The teasing identification between Karl and

Toschi fused, came closer, and Karl felt almost giddy. It was good to be with a man you could trust, a man that could be your own son.

"Did you ever feel like a crook?" Frank whispered in the darkness.

"I never ask myself. Do you?"

"Yeah, sometimes I feel like a crook. I think about it."

"Have you ever killed a man, Frank?"

Louis' apartment was in a two-story flat, the lower story occupied by a rundown grocery and a shoe-repair shop. A sagging wooden staircase separated the two stores and led up to the outer door of the second story. Frank led the way and rapped lightly on the door. No light showed.

A young man, perhaps twenty-five, opened the door and nodded at Frank. He wore natty gray slacks and a white sports shirt. His hair was long and dark, his sleepy eyes a deep moist brown, the Adam's apple pronounced in his thin throat. He was as slim as Toschi but not quite as tall. They shook hands all around and Louis nodded to the rear of a long narrow hallway that smelled faintly of floor wax and camphor.

"We've got the whole place to ourselves. I was just going to have some coffee, but maybe it's too hot for it."

"Coffee's fine," Frank said.

There was a single light fixed in the ceiling of the all-white kitchen. An avocado seed had split in a water glass and a new green shoot was emerging. Karl thought of Walter Tuttle and his plants. He studied Louis Goodwin's gestures, watching him out of the corner of his eye, pretending to look at the plant. You never could tell very much by looking at a man, or by talking with him for that matter. It was something else that made Karl decide on a person. He had to know about a man from inside himself. And if he tried to judge someone without that elusive something, he knew he would be acting arrogant. If Toschi liked Goodwin, then Karl could find no honest reason to doubt and object. After all, Toschi knew the young man and Karl didn't. But still, in spite of this, he felt that he had to make the final judgment himself. He was new to working with a group, but he felt that this was the proper procedure. He could trust no one. It had to be done exactly as if he were working alone. But this time, with the others. The combination of them, must work as a single unit. Karl realized, deep inside, in spite of his self-denials, that he was indeed growing old. He couldn't do everything by himself. He had to have someone who had the instincts and the guts that he himself had once had. Toschi supplied that need. Toschi was merely an extension of himself. And, since Karl was extending himself with the challenge of the Skyline job, he needed him the same as he needed his right arm. But Goodwin was something else. He needed a lookout, a dummy, someone who moved quickly and asked no questions, who was faithful.

Often a small group would form to complete a single job, but they would be formed on the individual ability of each person, completely overlooking the personality incompatibilities. Karl wasn't going to make that mistake. So, he watched Goodwin, studying him, feeling him out with the judge that was within.

"Glad you guys came by," Goodwin said. "I probably would have gone to the movies with the girls if Frank hadn't called."

"You don't like the movies?" It was the first thing Karl had said.

Louis Goodwin's smile was genuine, easy to appreciate. "It's not that. I like movies. I like musicals, dancing, singing, that kind of stuff. But it's just that those two girls yak all the time once they get into a movie. Especially my wife, that's Frank's kid sister. Yak-yak-yak, all the time while the picture is on."

Karl nodded, feeling good already. There was something oddly theatrical about Louis' looks, like an old-fashioned actor, dark, heavy-lidded eyes, dashing smile.

They sat at the table and Louis poured three cups of coffee in thick cafe mugs.

"Would you like red wine instead?"

"No."

"I've got some beer on ice."

"Do you drink much?" Karl asked.

"No. A glass of vino now and then. Usually when I visit with Frank's folks they push wine on me. And I usually don't refuse."

Karl nodded, smiled, feeling relaxed with the coffee in front of him, the clean white kitchen. "That's the idea, Louis. I'm a married man myself and the first thing I learned was walk soft with in-laws. You never know when you may need to borrow a couple of bucks."

Louis laughed.

"Have you ever been in any kind of trouble?"

"No," Louis said.

"You were in the service?"

"That's right. The Navy."

"See any action?"

"No."

Karl appeared thoughtful. "Have you ever been in on anything? Anything, I mean, like I may offer you."

"No," Louis answered seriously.

Karl looked to Frank and Frank nodded. Karl looked away. He knew that Louis was lying, but that was to the good. It proved, if nothing else, that Goodwin could keep quiet about whatever past he had. "Frank tells me you're a pretty good driver."

"I know cars okay."

"You're a mechanic?"

"That's right. I've got a shop over in Daly City. It's not very much though. It's kind of small."

"How're you doing with it?"

"I get by." Louis shrugged, his dark eyes looked directly at Karl. "Every now and then I make deals with a used-car lot, but I didn't like that too much. It's almost like working for someone else."

"I guess it is," Karl said. "Would you like to make a few extra dollars?"

"That depends."

"On what?"

"On what I'd have to do, how much I have to put out, the risk, the people I work with."

"Did Frank tell you anything?"

"No, only that some guy may want a driver and would I be interested if the proposition was sound." He nodded to Karl. "I guess that you're the guy he meant."

"That's right. I'll tell you what I'd want from you. Can you get away from your business for a couple of days without anyone knowing about it?"

Louis looked mildly surprised. "A couple of days? Sure, I suppose so."

"How would you work it?"

"If I get a used-car deal, making a few heaps sound like new and run for a short time without trouble, then I work late. Sometimes I shack out at my shop. It's not too uncommon for me and if I tell my wife that that's what I'm going to do then she'll never try to get in touch with me. And, even if she does, I can always say that I've been at the used-car lot, working over there. That's not uncommon either."

"I see. What I've got in mind may take two or three days. Maybe four."

"All three of us?"

"Frank's been in on it from the start."

Louis looked to Toschi.

Karl continued, "We want you to drive us up, and back after the strike. It's about ninety miles from here. Can you do that?"

"Yes. Isn't there anything else?"

"We want you to be lookout for us. It may be tricky."

"I can do it."

"Okay. Do you want to be in?"

"I don't know the details."

"You're not supposed to."

"How much do you pay me?"

Karl pursed his lips, touched the saucer and coffee cup with his thumb. "Twenty thousand," he said softly.

Louis swallowed and his lower lip moved, hung a bit. "You mean just for driving?"

"Yes, that and being lookout and keeping your mouth shut."

Louis stood, hands concealed in his slacks pockets. He leaned against the stove and looked seriously at both Frank and Karl. "Twenty grand! I was thinking in terms of a few thousand at the most."

"You've got to be worth that kind of money, Louis."

"Sit down, Lou," Toschi said softly, "you're slobbering on your shirt."

That was true. Every time Louis moved his lips a tiny fleck of gathered spittle would drop on his shirt front. It seemed to be a habit of his, and now that Karl looked he noticed that Goodwin's full theatrical mouth was set loosely rather than being sensual and expressive. Still, even with his full mouth, he was a good-looking fellow.

Louis looked at the stains on his shirt and smiled nervously. He wiped at the spots, holding his lips closed with conscious effort. He returned to his chair.

"When you get paid off I don't want to hear of any big spending. Just a few bucks here and there. Take it real easy and it'll last longer. We'll all last longer if you do it that way."

"Don't worry about me, Mr. Heisler."

"Call me Karl."

"Okay—Karl."

"I want this to be kept completely quiet. If anything, and I mean *anything,* goes wrong then we'll all be dead. We won't be sent to prison for this one. We'll be killed. It's as simple as that. Do you understand that?"

Louis looked calm. "Yes, I understand."

"Good. Now, I don't want to die, at least not just yet, and I'm pretty sure you don't either. I'm not threatening you. I'm telling you the truth. If anything goes wrong we'll be in the ground."

"I understand," Louis said again.

"Have you ever heard of Skyline House?"

"I've heard of it. It's a big gambling joint in San Hacienda. Supposed to be some kind of a mob joint. Is that ...?"

Karl nodded. "That's the place, kid."

Louis moved his lips again. It was an embarrassing thing to watch.

Karl pushed his coffee away from him. "Now you can get that cold beer you were talking about."

The beer cans were opened and set on the table. Karl swallowed. He would have preferred a good brandy, but the beer tasted good. He drained half of it with three swallows.

"Is Louis okay?" Toschi asked quietly.

"He's perfect."

Louis showed his pearly teeth and his face flushed.

"Here's to a good job, lots of luck."

They raised their cans, the frost sparkling like wet little jewels on the sides of the cans.

"Now remember," Toschi said wearily, "don't say a goddam thing about this to my sister...."

6

Leon Bertuzzi awoke, after a long and troubled night, and saw himself on the ceiling, reflected there in the six-foot mirror that had been fixed over his bed. He saw himself lying on the rumpled sky blue sheets and blue electric blanket. He moaned and narrowed his sleep-filled eyes. He hated to wake in the mornings and see himself reflected on the ceiling. It was the first thing he saw every morning, and he always felt a bit startled at first, then uneasy, as if the suspended Bertuzzi might suddenly peel away from the silver and glass and fall on the reclining Bertuzzi. He always closed his eyes and experienced a slight wave of nausea and vertigo. Then, by turning to one side, he managed to ignore his reflection and crawl quickly out of bed.

It was the same way every morning. It was no different now.

He shut himself in his private washroom and removed his silk pajamas. The sun poured through the bubble glass dome that bloomed in the ceiling over the leafy green tropical plants that surrounded the tiled sunken tub. He noticed, without caring, that it was a clear, bright day. His own room, which faced the west, was heavily curtained and he never knew what kind of day it was until he stepped into his washroom.

He turned the gold-plated water tap and splashed cold water on his face, shivering and making small animal sounds. He saw, looking into the amber mirror, a short heavy man with narrow shoulders and wide hips. What had once been tight and solid was now flabby and soft. His stomach was broader than his chest and there were sagging hairy breasts where there once had been solid mounds of muscle. He was fifty-seven years old. His once-black curly hair, which had long ago been his secret pride, was streaked with silver and there was a bald patch with the hair worn long and brushed toward the spot in an attempt to conceal it. His face was sagging, the thickness drooping, the lines under his eyes and around his mouth becoming deeper. His heavy-lidded black eyes were no longer exotic and menacing, they merely looked wicked and cruel. His lips were bloodless and his large nose a trifle lumpy from heavy drinking. Whenever he was naked he always felt ashamed and a little sad. He was an ugly little man.

"Good morning, Mr. Bertuzzi," he said to the face in the amber mirror. "How do you feel, tiger?" Then he scowled at the sound of his own gravelly voice.

He fished out his partial plate from the glass of overnight solution and slipped it into his mouth. The metal hooks caught and bit and he gritted his teeth to accustom them to the plate. Each night, or so it seemed to Leon, his gums shrunk a little, leveled out, and each morning the plate wouldn't fit into the natural ridges and grooves of his gums. He always considered having a false plate a nasty business, and when he did the fitting he didn't look at himself in the mirror.

He bathed in the tub, wallowing in the water and spitting mouthwash at the tropical plants, then he dried himself with a fresh towel. He began to hum a tune from his young manhood. He left the water in the tub for Jane, the housewoman, to empty out. He dressed, smoothed the white silk necktie into his gray silk vest and patted his stomach. Then he carefully lit a cigar and watched his little act in the mirror.

"Go get 'em, tiger."

He stopped at his wife's bedroom door in the hallway and knocked. He realized, wistfully, then angrily, that he hadn't been in her room since her twenty-third birthday. And that had been five months ago. Each morning, since that time, he had tried to see her.

"Janet?"

Her voice was indistinct, muffled, most likely coming from under her covers.

"Go away, Leon."

"I want to come in."

"I'll bet you do."

"I'd like to talk to you."

"No. Go away, Leon."

He tried talking to her again, but she didn't answer him. He stood outside her door, almost suspiciously, and set his ear to the wood. He listened for the sounds of her breathing, of her body whispering against the silk of her sheets. Then, when he heard the housewoman's steps downstairs, he moved quickly away, as if he had been caught in the nasty act of spying on his own wife.

The morning sky was cloudless, almost white. The sun streaked through the wall of trees and reflected on the surface of the huge, freeflowing swimming pool. The house, called Leon-Jan, was in a natural clearing in the redwood, like a bowl, situated three miles north from San Hacienda and six miles from Skyline House, the base of Leon's operations. It was always deathly quiet in the bowl. The air was always clear. The giant redwoods surrounded the expensive two-story house. Dry needles and cones littered the narrow, twisting private road. And leaves floated on the surface of the pool and clogged in the run-off gutters.

"Will you have breakfast by the pool, sir?"

He nodded absently to Jane and went out to the pool. He sat in a pink beach chair a few feet from the water. A bluejay racketed overhead. He puffed thoughtfully on his cigar and fished in his vest pocket for his usual handful of pennies. He did this every morning when the weather allowed him his breakfast at the poolside.

Jane stood by, waiting for his permission to start his meal. She was young for a housewoman, but was too careless with her appearance to seem unusual for the role. Leon ignored her. It was a breakfast ritual of theirs. She didn't speak until spoken to. She stood and watched him. He waited, as he usually did, building the seconds into minutes, every gesture calculated because he knew that he was being watched and waited on.

Ever since Janet had frozen him out he found that he spent more time with Jane. Of course, it wasn't the same, because with the housewoman he was usually acting out a role, a part that he always enjoyed. So, he said nothing and he ignored her. He liked to keep her waiting. He tossed a penny into the pool and watched it sink slowly to the bottom with a coppery wink. Then, deliberately, he flipped another penny after it.

Jane watched. Leon had often wondered if she had ever thought for herself, had ever made a decision that she could rightfully call her own. He doubted it. And, since this seemed to be the case, he feared her, doubting even his own decision, suspecting that all the time he talked to her, abused her, she harbored secret thoughts of hatred and violence. He was afraid of Jane. He was afraid because she was too passive, too noncommittal.

He saw Artie, the silent man, standing near the edge of the woods, watching him.

Artie was his night bodyguard, who watched the house and road. Leon knew nothing more about the man. He had been sent to Leon as a bodyguard in 1948 and Leon had never questioned it. He knew who had sent him. There was no need for questions.

He tossed in another penny. That was three cents so far today. He had eight cents left.

Jane shuffled her feet. He looked at her with a critical eye. He was always amused with her plain, almost homely features, her short mousy hair. He knew nothing of her teeth because whenever she smiled, which was rare, she never showed them. He wondered if she had ever truly laughed gayly, showing her teeth and throwing back her head. He rather doubted it. She wore no makeup and despite her acceptable figure she was a dumpy person. She was young, probably about Janet's age, and occasionally when he watched her from the corner of his eye he was surprised to discover a certain feeling of lust in himself.

"What time is it?"

"Ten o'clock, sir."

He thought of his wife, wondering why he had ever bothered to marry her. Had it been loneliness? Or had he thought that somehow the freshness of her youth would infect him? He wasn't sure. He was sure, however, that Janet had been the most beautiful showgirl in Las Vegas. And, at that time, two years ago, he believed that she could learn to admire him. And, if that failed, to at least fear him. But it hadn't worked out that way. It had all been a terrible mistake. Like so many other things.

He narrowed his eyes at Jane. He said, "You're not very bright, are you, Jane? You say you've worked here a year?"

She hadn't said, but she nodded anyway. Her rain-gray eyes were empty, her sad mouth drooping slightly at the corners.

"Ah, a year, unh? Well, it seems like forever. You know that? Looking at your dumb face, it seems like forever. How could a broad like you live with the dumb face you got? How can you brush your teeth in the morning?" Then, under his breath, whispering, he asked himself again if she had teeth. This, somehow, made him angry. He felt like stamping his foot, shrieking at her, demanding that she laugh, act alive. The house and the woods were always so still.

"I don't know, sir," Jane answered.

"You don't, unh? Well, you should. You got yourself one of the dumbest faces I've ever seen." He flipped a penny into the pool, watching Jane's rain eyes follow it until it settled on the tiled bottom. There were many pennies on the bottom, like freckles on the tile, winking in the wet cobwebs of moving light. "Okay, go get me my breakfast, stupid. I'm getting hungry."

Artie, the silent man, moved in the bushes a hundred yards away, watching.

Jane left and Leon watched her until the kitchen door closed after her. He knew that he wasn't angry with the housewoman, because whenever he talked to her as he did he spoke casually, even if he did growl his words, and his manner was almost always relaxed. He was angry at

Janet, his wife. It had been like this for four months now. And, before that, he had only ridiculed Jane on special occasions. But now he talked to her every morning, abusing her, calling her foul names, and generally trying to get a rise out of her. Nothing worked. She was like a wooden pole. The more passive she became the more vicious Leon became. He threw every malicious remark he could think of at her, and he delivered it all with his controlled snarl. He was a past master at snarling at underlings and servants.

When he saw Jane again he motioned to her, a wave of his hand, like calling to a dog. She came, sullenly, flatfooted, with her square hands concealed under her starched apron.

"Get me my phone."

When the ivory and gold telephone was plugged into the crane-necked poolside socket he waved her away and sat in silence, staring glumly at the water, feeling a bit better with the phone at his side. He always felt safer when he was near a phone, as if he was plugged into immediate contact with the rest of the world.

It was quiet again; the bluejay had long ago flown away. He sat on edge. Didn't she ever make any noise? Why did she creep around the house, like a ghost, a spy, a cat? Didn't anything ever impress her? He wondered what she would say or do if he made a pass at her. The idea had lately begun to intrigue him, caught in the outer webbing of his thoughts, snarling, gathering yarn there, a monotonous little tune whistling over and over again. He would like to make love to her, awaken her, have her naked, but only because he considered her an unattractive girl.

Did she know why he abused her? He didn't dare ask. If she admitted that she was certainly aware of his reasons then he would have to quit because he didn't want to be thought of as childish. And, on the other hand, if she didn't know his reasons then he would have to quit also, because he didn't want to abuse her without the sense of combat; there wasn't anything to be gained by kicking a dumb animal. No, it was best not to think about it. The mystery of the ugly girl was what made his cruel little game with her enjoyable these days. And there weren't many things that Leon Bertuzzi enjoyed these days. Life had gone sour on him. He felt cheated, power-stripped, rolling rapidly downhill, driven to his petty acts of cruelty. He was bitter, and often he had moments of genuine despair and self-pity.

Jane brought his breakfast. She rolled it out to him on a special cart. She locked the sparkling chromium wheels at the side of the pink beach chair. Leon began to eat, without tasting: weak tea, stewed prunes, and one bowl of bran flakes. The sun glittered from the silver.

"Do you like working in this joint?"

"Yes, sir."

He waved her to a beach chair near his own. She sat down. He returned to his food, ignoring her again. He often asked her to sit with him. She sat carefully, primly, using only the edge of the chair. Her hands were folded in her lap, her mouth drooping.

"Are you scared of me, sister?"

"No, sir."

He didn't know why he called her "sister." It was a hangover from the old days. It sounded cheap and he knew it. Perhaps he wanted to cheapen her. He watched her, over his prunes, looking at her legs out of the corner of his eye. He had never made a direct pass at her because he feared she would report it to his wife. And, if that happened, he would only have another miserable situation on his hands. He wouldn't be able to cope with the superior look that his wife would torture him with if she knew he desired the ugly servant girl.

"I like the desert better," Leon said between mouthfuls of prunes. "The desert is cleaner, and at night all the smooth clubs open up, wide open, the wheels spinning, the ball going click-click. The desert. It's a great life. Palm Springs. Vegas. The little ball going click-click." He sighed, looked up to the trees that surrounded the house, the sun splintering white, yellow, spewing through the lace of leaves. The bluejay had returned. "Do you like these mountains, sister?"

"Yes, sir."

He spit out the last prune seed and it clicked in the dish, like the Vegas ball. He burped, felt for his heart that thumped somewhat under his gray silk suit, white silk tie.

The morning before, he had asked Jane about her home life; before that it had been her opinions on dumb animals; before that, finances. This had been going on for four months, and he felt confident that he would never exhaust his supply of topics. At any rate, they always ended in the same fashion. And that, after all, was why he bothered talking to her. He liked to have the final bitter word.

"Why do you like these mountains, sister?"

"They're pleasant," Jane answered.

"How about them trees?"

"Yes."

"Why do you look guilty when I talk with you? I ain't no cop. You look like a wet dog all the time. You scared of me?"

"No, sir."

"Yeah, I'll bet you are. I'll bet you quake every time I look at you."

"No."

"How much does the Missus pay you?"

"Seventy dollars a week."

"Seventy bucks, unh? I'll bet you knock down half of that every week. Cheat on the meat bill? That kind of jazz? No? What do you do with all your dough, your seventy bucks a week? Do you bury it in a coffee can?"

"I put it in the bank."

"Sure, that's the safe thing. In the old days it wasn't none too safe. Them goddam bankers was always running off with the kitty. But you're too young to remember them days. What're you? About twenty-five I'd say. I'll bet you were born in the Depression. Am I right?"

"Yes, sir."

"I thought so." He leered. "You know why I knew that? No? I'll tell you. It's because you're the most depressing looking broad I've ever seen." He roared with laughter until the tears began to form. Then, just as quickly, he stopped. "Don't you think that's funny?"

Jane shook her head.

"Well, it *is* funny, sister. Laugh."

She stared at him, puzzled.

"I said laugh, sister."

She managed a weak smile and a few forced chuckles.

Leon looked satisfied. "That's better, Jane. I'm glad to see you got yourself a sense of humor. Yeah, an ugly broad's got to have herself a sense of humor, or else she ain't got nothing at all. Am I right? Of course I'm right."

He picked up his coffee cup, scowling at the weak tea.

"Would you care for cream, sir?"

"No. Cream's fattening. Things like that put little things in your blood. Very bad." He shook his head sadly. "So, you like the mountains, unh? Well, let me tell you, sister, the desert's better. It's legalized gambling in the desert, but up here it's strictly against the law. Even then, sister, you got to keep your fingers crossed. I mean, no matter how much local law you buy up. Am I right? Sure, I'm right. Do you gamble?"

"No, sir."

"Well, you should. A dumb broad like should learn to gamble." He made a fist and shook imaginary dice close to his ear, simulating a lucky-wish expression. "You'd get some kicks out of living if you gambled. When that old fever hits you I understand it's just like going to bed with someone. And since you're so stupid looking I guess you don't know about things like that. So, you should gamble to get your thrills. You sure as hell won't get them any other way." He paused, narrowing his eyes. "Now laugh, sister, I just said something funny."

She smiled again, weakly.

"That's better. You'd better earn your seventy crummy bucks around here." He dismissed her with a wave of his hand and watched her shuffle dejectedly back to the house. Leon's dark, aging face became sour, hating Jane, hating himself, hating his wife....

The telephone rang.

It was Max West, the accountant who came to Skyline House once a month; he was calling from his apartment in San Francisco, apologizing in advance. He might be late in arriving this Friday. He had to bring his wife, who was pregnant, to the hospital. She was having complications with the baby. Max wasn't sure he could get away on time.

"You get here Friday, Max. I don't care about your baby." Leon wondered what an ugly runt like Max wanted a baby for. He had never had children, he didn't understand them, and he had only recently felt a faint regret for this. The children that belonged to others made him feel envious and angry. "What're you trying to do? You want to give me baseball-sized ulcers? I got the Vegas runners coming into San Hacienda Friday night. So what'm I supposed to tell Roger Dolan if the payload is late Saturday? What'm I going to say? I'm sorry, boss, my accountant is worried about his wife? My accountant thinks if he's in the city he could do what doctors can't do? I tell you, Max, you got to be here. No one here is authorized to okay the deliveries. That's your job. If you don't show up here Friday, then I'll phone Mr. Vince in New York and tell him you're going to be on the first plane for New York. I'll let you do the explaining to them. I'll wash my hands of it."

"But I thought—"

"Yeah. Well, your job ain't thinking. I've never missed a cut delivery in twenty-five years and I'll be goddamned if I'm going to start now just because your baby's coming out sideways. Your job is here on Friday and you'd better be here to see that it gets done."

He hung up angrily, then sipped his tea, telling himself to calm down, take it easy. But it was hard to do. It was things like that that got his blood pressure up. Max was a good accountant, and since the Vegas circle had appointed him, which was out of Leon's jurisdiction, then he couldn't very well fire him. It was the same with Stanley Nagel. Nagel had been sent to Skyline by Mr. Vince, Pietro DeVinci, the same as Max. So, Leon couldn't fire any of them. Whom could he fire? Practically nobody. He could fire the croupiers and the waiters, but that was about all. He couldn't even fire Artie, the silent one, even if he had hired him in the first place. Artie knew too much by now.

He curled his thin bloodless lips over the rim of his tea and stared at the swimming pool.

Everything was wrong. It was a mess. Even the swimming pool affair had gone wrong. Janet had bitched about wanting a pool, so Leon had spent better than sixty thousand dollars having one installed. And now no one used it. Leon hated swimming because he was ashamed to be seen in a bathing suit. And Janet wouldn't even look at it. She called the pool "that damned thing." So, the pool was used exclusively as Leon's private wishing well. The bottom was freckled with his pennies.

Later, when the sun rose over the redwood trees, he left the poolside and took the car from the garage. Artie moved from the woods and stood, waiting, at the foot of the road. Leon drove to the side of the house, just under his wife's bedroom window, and honked the horn twice, short blasts. He waited, and when her window swung open, he honked again. She drew back the gauzy curtain and glared down at him. She looked beautiful up there, like an angel, her ginger-blonde hair pulled back and clipped with a pearl ring, her large blue eyes watching him. She wore a watermelon-colored blouse and white Bermuda shorts. She didn't move. He honked again, irritated that she didn't answer him.

"Shut up that damned horn, buster," Janet said tightly. "You think you're calling a moose?"

"I'm going to the club."

"Is that supposed to be something new?"

He hated her for her trick of ignoring him, to dislike him so passively. He had always thought that disliking brought anger. He felt like punching her lovely face, then making violent love to her. He said, "Don't wisemouth me...."

"Shut up, Leon, it's too early in the morning to spar with you. Now what is it you want?"

"I thought maybe you'd like a ride into town."

"Well, you thought wrong. Now leave me alone and quit playing with your horn."

"Will you be here if I come back for a late lunch?"

"No. I'm going riding."

"Your car's in the garage."

"I'm going riding on a horse, Leon. A horse."

"With Stanley Nagel?"

"That's right."

"I think you see too much of that punk."

"No. I don't see enough of him...."

He cursed her, jerked the automatic shift and drove angrily away from the house. Artie stepped out on the road and waved his hand. Leon picked him up. Artie sat woodenly beside him, his coal-chip eyes staring straight ahead. The big car bumped over his narrow private road, winding through the cathedral forest, climbing up to the highway. The redwood and wrought brass sign at the gate said, Leon-Jan. That was a laugh. Leon and Janet, like two little lovebirds tucked away in their isolated nest. One a vulture, the other an eagle. Leon smiled. He fancied himself as the eagle.

"Do you feel tired, Artie?"

"No."

"It's a nice day...."

"Yes."

Leon frowned. He was vaguely frightened by Artie. He couldn't understand a man with so few pleasures in life. He knew nothing of Artie, despite the years together. He knew that Artie stayed awake all night, watching the house from the woods. And, every morning, when Leon drove to Skyline, Artie went along. He slept in a small room at the club. Then, late at night when Leon was ready to return home, Artie awoke and accompanied him, only to stand, watching and waiting for trouble, in the woods. Leon couldn't understand it. He wasn't even sure how much the Vegas circle paid Artie. He knew nothing, so he feared.

He parked the big car in the graveled parking lot, the tires crunching, raising dust. Benny looked out from the clearance shed and waved a greeting. Artie, now that Benny was there, left the car and disappeared somewhere into the building. Benny opened Leon's door and nodded.

"Morning, boss."

Benny Coca was a tall, rangy man with a shiny black chauffeur's suit and the red turkey neck of a cowboy. He was someone that Leon could trust. Someone that Leon had no fear of; he had been with Leon in Nevada, and, before that, in the early thirties, in Dade County. He had replaced old Larry Con as clearance guard when Larry fell on a six-year-old charge.

"Is Stanley Nagel here yet?"

"Sure, boss. He's in the office with the doc."

Leon stopped. "Doc? What doc?"

"That doctor you called that time you had the heart attack."

Leon's mouth quivered with sudden fear and anger. He grabbed Benny Coca's arm and squeezed until Benny winced with pain. "I never had no heart attack, Benny. Who told you that? It's a dirty lie."

"Mr. Nagel said—"

"Mr. Nagel's a goddam liar. You hear me? It was just gas in the stomach."

"Sure, boss."

Leon left him and slammed the front door when he entered the building. That kid, Stanley Nagel, had him worried. If word of his attack, or even a rumor of it, leaked to Dolan and the Vegas circle, or to

Mr. Vince in New York, then he would surely be eased out of the picture. And that, of course, was exactly what Stanley Nagel wanted. He wanted everything. Leon's job ... even his wife. Leon clenched his fists. Well, Stanley already had Leon's wife, but, by God, he wasn't going to get his job! No ivy league college joker was going to muscle out Leon Bertuzzi.

He had taken steps to rid himself of Stanley. But he had to be extremely cautious. If, after Leon's plan was completed, the Vegas circle suspected anything, then again Leon would be in danger. He intended to be careful. He had planned it too well for anything to go wrong.

In the old days it would have been different. Leon would simply have a punk like Stanley killed, and he wouldn't have to fear corporation disapproval. Because in the 'twenties, there had been no corporation. The entire structure had been composed of independent companies all operating within their own declared territories. But it was all different now. It had to be. Because the old way hadn't worked out to the satisfaction of everyone concerned.

They had been drawing too much unnecessary publicity to themselves. And, at that time, Leon Bertuzzi had been one of the first to recognize the inadequacy of the old set-up during the early stages of the conferences between the more powerful of the independent groups. He knew that a central corporation leader was the only choice for the survival of the minor companies. So, he was respected because he was one of the originals to acknowledge corporation, had been one of the first to swear loyalty to the rules and follow them through the years without once stepping out of line. His reputation was excellent. He knew that Mr. Vince and the others thought highly of his pioneer work in Nevada after leaving Dade County without argument. Yes, Leon had stuck to the rules and had never once overstepped his appointed authority. His position, at least for the past five years, with the west coast subsidiary had been secure.

But recently doubt crept in. He began to notice a slight change. Why had he been assigned such a dangerous and touchy position in California? His set-up in Nevada had been going smoothly, in fact, better than anyone had ever hoped. Why the sudden change? Why Stanley Nagel? Nagel was, after all, just a kid from left field who had suddenly become a power. Why was Nagel assigned as Leon's small-end partner in the Skyline operation? It was puzzling, and, even with all that looming before him, he steadfastly refused to read the signs. He still clung stubbornly to his job.

He stopped by a covered roulette table and looked at a dropchute cart in the aisle. He wheeled it to the janitor who was sweeping a green felt dice table with a soft white brush.

"What's this doing here, Herman?"

"I don't know, Mr. Bertuzzi."

"Put it in the back room, will you?"

Leon was pleased with the comforting sight of the neat green tables and gleaming chipracks. He had always liked the atmosphere of a gaming room.

He found Dr. Sheldon in Stanley's office, the first office in the private corridor behind the huge game room.

Stanley smiled his bland superior smile when Leon stepped into the office. He was a young man, tall, with crewcut hair and English-cut suit. His boyish face was suntanned and the wide blue eyes glowed like neon. Every day or so Leon felt, Stanley was becoming younger.

"Good morning, Leon," Stanley said.

Leon deliberately ignored him. He looked at old Dr. Sheldon. "Did you tell Stanley some kind of nonsense about me having a heart attack?"

"No, sir, I didn't. I told him that it had been gas."

Leon looked suspiciously to Stanley. "Then why did you tell Benny Coca that I'd had a heart attack?"

"Gee, did I say that? I think maybe he heard me wrong."

"It was gas."

"Why, of course, Leon. That's precisely what I'd told him."

"You're lying."

"Don't be so touchy, Leon."

He ignored him again. He asked Sheldon to step into his office, then, as they were leaving, he looked back at the smiling Stanley Nagel and narrowed his eyes. "You bastard. I'll see you in my office when I'm through with Sheldon."

In his own office he carefully lit a cigar and sat behind the wide executive desk and looked calmly at Sheldon. The older man stood in the center of the large room with his Stetson hat held nervously in his wrinkled freckled hands.

"Well?"

"I said nothing to him, Mr. Bertuzzi."

"What're you doing here then? Did Nagel call you?"

"Yes."

"Why?"

"He said that he had a stiff leg, and since he intended to go horseback riding this afternoon, he wanted me to take a look at it."

"And did he have a stiff leg?"

"I doubt it."

"What did he want then?"

"He didn't say anything direct. But indirectly he asked me about your health."

"He asked you about me?"

"That's right, Mr. Bertuzzi."

"And you told him nothing?"

"That's right. He asked about the incident of five months ago. I told him it was just a little gas."

"Sure, I believe you, Sheldon. Stanley wants my job."

"I'm sorry if you believe I'd told him anything about your heart attack."

Leon slammed his heavy fist on the desk top with such force that the telephone jumped. "Don't you use that word around here again, Sheldon!"

"I think you'd better relax, Mr. Bertuzzi."

"I *am* relaxed!"

"Have you been taking the pills?"

"Sure. You think I'm stupid? I want to live, just like you want to live." He paused. "You understand?"

"Is that a threat of some sort?"

"Take it any way you want. But if I have another one of them attacks I'll make damn sure you feel the hurt just as bad as I do."

Sheldon drew his thin frame erect. "See here, Mr. Bertuzzi. You're not in Chicago any more—"

"I never was in Chicago," Leon snapped.

"Well, then wherever you're from. You're not a tough guy to me."

"Whether I'm a tough guy or not, I'll cut your guts out if I have another attack. What do you think you're getting my money for? I'm paying you good dough to prevent them things. You think I'm paying you to sit around on your hick behind and watch me kick off?"

"You're being awfully childish about this...."

"Get out of here, Sheldon. I'm through with you now. The more you run your mouth off the more you bore me. And one thing more, don't say a goddam word about this to anyone. Get me?"

Sheldon didn't answer. He closed the door softly after him.

Leon drummed his stubby fingers on the desk top. He hated doctors. But he knew that they were now necessary for him. Their services were a burden that he had to live with ... or die with. There was nothing he could do about it. If he was sick, he needed a doctor. It was that simple. But still, he hated them because they were a constant reminder of his fallibility. Doctors meant sickness, and sickness meant weakness; weakness meant deterioration and eventual death. Old Sheldon, with his hick mannerisms and John B. Stetson hat, was still a doctor, a threat, a cold reminder that death was inside every man.

Leon fumbled in his desk drawer, reached far to the rear past a few blank scratchpads, then touched a hidden button. A section of wood, molding strip, flipped open. He took his keys from his vest and inserted one of them into a lock behind the exposed wood. He opened a side drawer. He replaced his key and locked the wood strip. Then he removed the bottle from behind a small metal index box. He held it up to the light, swished it, watched the rich mahogany liquid bubble briefly. Brandy. Expensive, French brandy. The best. He fingered the plastic strip that locked the neck foil. A beautiful job, perfectly done. The label was a cobweb of French writing, flutes, whorls, dandelions and unicorns. A beautiful bottle. One sip of it, half a teaspoon, and you're dead. Leon chuckled, replaced the bottle.

Not now, he thought. There would be time for it later, perhaps next week. How would he do it? Have a party? No, he rarely gave parties and it might look suspicious. There was still time, time enough for many things; he would wait until next week.

He touched the floor buzzer with his foot. It was a device that Stanley Nagel had had installed four months ago. Leon had tried to explain that there was no need for a buzzer, explaining that the office door was always open to Stanley, but Stanley had insisted, saying that it was there in case Leon had another attack of "gas."

Stanley entered the office, having heard the buzzer in his office. He glided to the center of the room and stood casually in his tailored suit and smiling suntanned face. He wore his clothes and his face like a uniform. He said, "What's happening, Leon?"

"You. You're happening, Stanley. You're a troublemaker."

"Aw … really, Pops, you're too sharp."

Sarcasm. Leon winced. "You're nothing but a cheap hoodlum with a lousy college education. That's all you are. I'll bet you sit in your office every night and wait for that buzzer to sound, like a vulture." He liked the sound to that word, he repeated it. "Like a vulture. Waiting for me to be in trouble. You'd love it to come rushing in to my rescue, wouldn't you. Then you could crow it up to Mr. Vince. You cheap hoodlum."

Stanley arched one eyebrow and managed to look bored. "Oh, come now, Leon. Are we going to lock horns again? Can't you accept the inevitable?"

"Shut up!"

"Sure thing, Pop."

"And don't call me that!"

"Sure, Leon. But you'd better watch the old blood pressure."

"It was gas," Leon muttered sullenly.

"Then you'd better watch your gas gauge."

"How long have you worked for me, Stanley?"

"You must be mistaken, Dads. I don't work for you. I'm your little partner. I was asked to come here. You didn't hire me. I was appointed."

"How long?"

"Six months."

"And how long have you been sleeping with my wife?"

"About four. I'm a slow worker."

"You're a sonofabitch, that's what you are."

"Come off it. Let's be sophisticated about this thing, Leon old boy. Janet digs me. I dig her. It's chemistry, pure and simple. You're an old dog and you're on your way out. I'm a young dog and I'm on my way in. You've already had one heart attack and you might have another, a bigger one. For a while there you were walking around as if you had weights on your shoulders. You were weak as a kitten and you sweated. They had you in oxygen for seven hours and you were in a San Hacienda rest home for six days under the name of Browning. Now you're taking little pills with TNT in them. Wise up, old boy. Don't insult my intelligence and try to tell me that you only had a touch of gas in your tummy."

"It was gas," Leon insisted weakly.

"Okay, so go ahead and insult my intelligence. But remember this, old boy, you're becoming rather useless to the whole set-up here, and you know it. But I'm not. I'm smarter and tougher—"

"You're not tough," Leon said tightly.

"Yes I am," Stanley corrected pleasantly. "Of course, I don't carry a violin case with a machine gun in it. And I don't have a corny old rep that stretches back to the turn of the century...."

"I'm not that old."

"The 'twenties then. Have it your way. Anyway, Mr. Vince told me quite a bit about you before I was assigned, and my father, rest his soul, even mentioned you once or twice."

Leon tried hard not to show it, but he had twisted nervously when Mr. Vince had been mentioned. He said, "What'd Mr. Vince say?"

"You honestly want to know? Real McCoy?"

"Why not?"

Stanley Nagel sat on the corner edge of Leon's desk and casually lit one of Leon's cigars. He used Leon's lighter. "Okay, I'll tell you, Pops. Mr. Vince said that once upon a time you were some kind of a tough guy, a real killer. You killed old Charlie Eagan with your bare hands and dumped him down the garbage chute. You bossed the games in Detroit and had workings with Capone, O'Bannion, and the rest of those old-fashioned maniacs that gave everyone a bad name. Am I right?"

"You might be."

"He also said that I had a damn good chance of being the new wheel here at Skyline. And, if I worked it good for a few years, then who knows? Maybe even Havana for a while, if it opens up again by that time."

"So, you're sitting on top of the world, unh, Stanley?"

Stanley looked smug. "I guess so, Pops."

Leon couldn't sit still for any more of it. He lunged and slammed Stanley with sudden violence, catching him unaware and easily throwing him from the edge of the desk. Stanley almost toppled to the carpeted floor, but he managed to catch himself and he regained his balance. He stood with the long cigar hanging stupidly in his mouth, the boyish eyes wide, he look of smug self-assurance gone from his face.

"You may be sitting on top of the world, kid, but my desk ain't the top of the world. Go sit somewhere else. This is my office, it's *still* my office, and when you're in it you act like it. You understand?"

Stanley smiled nervously, gaining poise. "Don't get so hot, Leon. I dig you."

"And don't talk bop to me!"

"That's not bop. That's the new lingo. Everything's new these days. We don't carry violin cases anymore."

"I know, kid. You carry a book of poetry and sunglasses. But when you're around me you're nothing more than a punk kid. Just because you're Threefinger Nagel's kid don't mean you're any aces in my book. Maybe with Pietro De Vinci you're somebody big. But not to me. You got that?"

"I dig you, Leon."

"You're only here because Mr. Vince wants it that way. If I had my way I'd dump *you* down a garbage chute."

"I realize that, but you don't have your way. Not anymore. Your time has gone. Your sand has shifted, Bertuzzi." He opened the office door and smiled. He didn't look very boyish now, and his usually oily purr was now a harsh stab. "And besides that, Bertuzzi, they don't have garbage chutes any more. They're out of date. Old hat. Everything's done automatic now."

"Get out of here!"

"Sure, old boy."

The door closed softly.

Leon cursed and lit another cigar, watching his hands holding the heavy gold lighter. They were shaking.

He opened the desk drawer and looked at the bottle of deadly brandy. He remembered that Stanley liked to pose with a huge bubble glass, liked to sniff it and slowly shake his head as if the fumes were some invisible narcotic, nostrils quivering, electric blue eyes dazed. Stanley was a phony, arrogant, punk kid with a limey suit and a fat puffy butt that cantered in the saddle; an eager face drawn to the soft watermelon-covered breasts and dove-white Bermuda shorts. He walked on Leon's property, depositing his little tracks, dirtying up the belly and the breasts.... Leon thought back to that hot Vegas night with the pineapple-shaped flames, passion-orange, yellow, rose, surrounding the still night pool, shimmering gold on the liquid tar-looking water, hissing, swaying in the desert warm breeze. It had been that night, at Dolan's Hawaiian party, that he had first met Janet; in the background there had been quivering electric guitars and leis of fragile orchid and cream-white, scented gardenia.... And now, only one day distant in memory from that night, Stanley Nagel altered it all with his fake tweedy youthfulness and brash bop-talking remarks. So, Leon's time was supposedly gone, his sand shifted, outdated like the mythical violin case and the very real garbage chute. Leon glowered. There was still the brandy bottle, very real, in his hands, winking mysterious redwood winks, glugging when he tipped the bottle. It was such a simple thing. One sip ... no more Stanley Nagel. Leon chuckled, feeling better. And, after Stanley was dead, he would have the terrified old man, Sheldon, sign the death certificate. Natural causes. Brain tumor. Something like that. It would be perfect.

He was only one small sip of brandy away from his wife....

7

The radio was set on the rough ledge frame of the open cabin window, the plastic handle hooked over a rusted nail, the dance music turned low. Frank Toschi leaned against the porch railing and yawned, stretching his shoulders, his back muscles feeling stiff from sitting in the car during the long ride that morning. The trip hadn't taken them as long as he had thought it would. But it had been cramped in the rear seat with the many bundles and boxes they had brought with them.

Louis was working on the first car, bent into the open hood, his coveralls streaked with grease. He seemed absorbed, his tool kit opened on the covered fender. Frank listened partly to the radio music and partly to the unfamiliar sounds of the dense forest around him. The sun was high and warm and the leaves had a thin film of yellow dust on them.

The cabin that Heisler had rented under the name of Lars Anderson was one of twelve, more isolated and farther up on the wooded slope than the others. Through the wall of trees Frank could barely make out the doll-house roofs of the other cabins and the gas station-general store that housed the proprietor and his wife. He couldn't see the highway at all. Occasionally, he could hear a truck pass, but he couldn't hear the cars. The great forest acted like insulation, muting most of the road sounds. The stillness was new to Frank. The enchantment almost disturbing. He had never been in the woods before.

Louis stepped back from the car and wiped his hands on his coveralls. He lit a cigarette, mechanic's style, by plucking it carefully from the package with his fingertips and holding it by the filtered tip.

"Don't start a forest fire now," Frank said lazily.

Louis grinned, shook his head.

The car was an old Pontiac Louis was under the hood again. A bluejay sounded overhead, like a Halloween noisemaker, screeching, racketing. A cone plopped to the forest floor. There was a clean, woodsmoke odor, probably someone cooking in one of the other cabins, and a thin cloud of blue smoke drifted through the trees. Frank rolled his shirtsleeves high on his arms and looked up at the ragged patch of cool blue sky that showed between the leafy towers of the redwoods. It was good to be free of the city, even if it was for only a few days. He decided that he liked the woods, liked the atmosphere of quiet strength.

"Wonder where the old man went," Louis said from under the hood.

"He went to the store." Frank handed Louis a waste rag. "Anything wrong with the car?"

"No. I'm just checking it out." He wiped his face with the rag and pulled hard on his cigarette. "You know, Frank, you never told me how you met Heisler."

"Didn't I?" He shrugged. "He was my cellmate."

"I suppose he knows his business."

"He's the best."

Louis hesitated, looking puzzled. "I can't figure it."

"What?"

"Well ... about you and me, Frank."

"What about us?"

Louis seemed reluctant to say. He made vague gestures with his cigarette, still wiping his face with the piece of waste. "Well, we were never real buddies. At least, that's the way I always felt. Even your sisters and your older brother, Al, they never talked much about you. What I mean is, how come ... how come you wanted me on this job?"

Frank didn't answer right away. He thought about it.

Was it for his sister? Surely it wasn't because he honestly wanted Louis to make good with some money. He said, "I don't know, Louis. You're the first guy I thought of. I knew you'd go for it. I knew you'd be good for it."

"Yeah, but how'd you know, Frank? How'd you know I'd go for it? I mean, I've never even so much as had a traffic ticket, and that one job you know about was years ago. I mean, I'm not the criminal type...." He winced, then tried to smile. "I'm sorry, Frank. I didn't mean it quite like that. Hell, you know what I mean. You've been inside and all that. Now, I don't mean to say that you and Heisler are a bunch of crooks. I don't mean that at all."

"I know what you mean, Louis. I guess I wanted you in because I knew that you've got what it takes."

Louis nodded.

Frank hadn't meant that. He had no idea if Louis had what it takes. After all, it doesn't take too much to drive fast when you're running from something. So, it wasn't that. Louis was a good driver, and Frank had known that when he had recommended him. Then what was it? His sister? He wasn't sure. He had never been very close to any member of his family. He remembered that one of the first things that had come to mind when Heisler had mentioned a driver was that his mother always called his brother-in-law "Poor Louis."

He looked up now at the mystery of the trees; he felt older, more tired, yet still not beaten by it; he felt the tiredness that comes before the second wind. The bluejay racketed overhead, then flew away. He realized, for the first time, that all his life he had been a lonely man. He stepped out his cigarette and walked slowly back to the cabin.

Karl entered the general store section of the proprietor's cabin, the patched screen door slamming after him, the sudden cool dampness and darkness of the store surprising him. He stood by a book rack and picked up a magazine without looking at it. There was no one else in the store.

Both sides of the large room were shelved and filled with canned goods. There were cluttered pyramid islands in the center, wire snack racks on the main aisle, large enamel coolers with frosted glass doors behind the rough wooden counter. A tobacco display case was beside a fishing equipment stand. He went to the stand, still carrying the magazine, and pretended an interest in the poles. He fished with his free hand into the raised glass lid of the tobacco display. He ran his fingers along the pipe sacks and wire cleaners until he found an open carton. He took two packages of cigarettes, not caring about the brand, and hurriedly slipped them into his mackinaw pocket. Then he smiled softly to himself, feeling almost childish....

He looked out at the road.

The drive from San Francisco had been easy. They had left early that

morning after stopping to buy food at the cut rate store and had arrived
in San Hacienda County three hours ago. The cabin had been waiting
for them and they had moved in without a hitch. Karl felt good. The
operation had gone smoothly so far. Karl had driven the Studebaker, the
second car, and Louis Goodwin had driven the first, the Pontiac. Toschi
had sat in the rear of the Studebaker with the coveralls and weapons
and equipment. Toschi had remarked, Karl remembered now, that he
had never been in the mountains before, that he was looking forward
to it. He had said little else, even when Karl had pointed out Skyline
House and the parking lot road, and then, a few minutes later, when he
had pointed to the rough wood sign with the Lion's Club shield nailed
to it. Toschi had smoked in silence, using his trouser cuff for an ashtray.
A curious guy, that Toschi. He seemed quite different now that he was
out of prison, more quiet, more reserved. There was a hard dignity about
the man. And again, he reminded Karl of himself when he had been a
young man.

The road outside the store was empty. The sun was flat and hot on it
and a dragonfly hissed silver lights.

"Hello, Mr. Anderson."

It was the proprietor's wife, Mrs. Kovall. He had seen her three hours
earlier when he had informed her husband that he had moved into his
cabin. She must have just now entered the store through the gathered
green cloth over the doorway. She stood behind the counter, smiling and
watching him. He wondered if she suspected him of having stolen
anything. He cursed himself for the two packages of cigarettes. It had
been a stupid thing to do, an amateurish stunt.

Karl tipped his dark gray hat and returned the smile. "Hello there,
Mrs. Kovall."

"Do you like your cabin all right? Is it comfy?"

"It's real fine." The two packages of cigarettes made a large lump in
his mackinaw pocket.

She smiled, looking chatty. "You say you're from San Francisco?"

"Yes, Ma'am. I'm just on a little vacation right now. First one in five
years. Five long years. My friends and I, we thought we'd take to the
mountains and see what they're all about. We hear quite a bit about the
mountains."

"You say you're in the hardware business?"

"That's right."

"Well, mountain air, they say, is supposed to be real good for you. But
I wouldn't know about all that. Originally, I'm from Cincinnati. I met
Nat, that's my husband, there during the war. I've been up here ever
since. Anyways, I don't feel any healthier now than when I was in

Cincinnati."

Karl opened a package of his cigarettes and offered her one. She shook her head. He lit a cigarette, noticed that he still held the magazine. When he replaced it he noticed that it had been a crime magazine, with a handsome young burglar on the cover, holding a huge .45 to the neck of a trussed up girl wearing only a black lace slip. Karl shook his head.

Mrs. Kovall watched the highway, her body resting against the counter. She was wearing a faded red sunsuit. She had small pointed breasts and long white legs with a faint roadmap of veins. She had enormous lips and hair under her arms. When she smiled she showed crooked teeth and pink gums. Her long brown hair was worn in the dated style of the years during the war, and Karl wondered if those years had been the best for her and if she were still clinging to them.

"I suppose you've got enough fishing equipment, Mr. Anderson?"

"Yes," Karl answered. Had she spied on him when he had unloaded the car? He touched one of the fishing poles on display. The feel of it was foreign to him. "How much is this one? Is this a good pole?"

"Sure is. They're all good. But I can see that you know your poles, Mr. Anderson, because that's an especially nice one. I don't know too much about them, but my husband pointed it out to me. He said it was a good buy."

"How much?"

"Twelve-fifty. And that's a pretty cheap price for a pole like that."

Karl had no idea if it was, so he made a noncommittal gesture and pretended to handle the pole. He held it as if it were a pool stick.

He bought it, even though his funds were low. He wondered if he had bought it to atone for the cigarettes.

"You'll like that pole, Mr. Anderson."

"I'll try the creeks around here tomorrow."

"For the fish? Oh, here you have to go farther out, way up in the hills where the little lakes are. Nat says they're best up there."

He left and walked back through the trees to his cabin. He saw Goodwin working on the Pontiac.

"Anything wrong?"

Louis was practically black with grease. "No, not a thing. I'm just tightening up here and there, cleaning and checking."

"Where's Frank?"

"I don't know. He was here a minute ago." He looked curiously at the fishing pole. "What'd you buy that thing for?"

Heisler glared at him, then to the pole, then back to Louis; he wasn't sure of the answer himself. He said, "We're fishermen, aren't we? Well, this is a fishing pole. I don't want anyone snooping on us, so I'm going to leave the pole right outside in case anyone looks our way."

Louis merely shrugged and returned to his work. Karl entered the cabin and set the pole on top of the table.

8

The creek was practically hidden at first, but he had heard it and found it easily enough, walking cautiously down the steep slope through the fairyland sprays of wild fern and Tokay-colored skeletons of manzanita and past a solemn dark stand of redwood. He paused at the flat bank and watched the water flow smoothly past him, cold and clear. The water seemed to be motionless in spots, except where the natural walking stones channeled it, and there it rushed in gurgling sluice fingers, babbling, planing the gray rocks smooth. The rocks on the bottom were smeared with olive-green moss and quick, skinny water spiders pinched the surface of the deep pools.

Karl sat on the spongy mattress of needles and leaves and opened his bundle. He held the heavy revolver in his hand, looking at it for only the second time. Then he began to clean it, carefully, running the wire rod through the long barrel and shell chambers. When he was finished, he loaded it and snapped it shut. He sat, bewitched with forest sounds, and watched the smooth flow of the creek.

A mood of longing for the unknown stole over him and he remembered something that his father had asked him many years ago. He had been just a kid. They had been standing ... where? He couldn't remember that part of it. But he could hear his father's voice, asking, "What do you want to become when you grow up, Karl?

He removed his hat and looked around him, his wrinkled flesh squinting, crowsfeeting around his quiet gray eyes. His hands folded themselves on his lap and his heavy shoulders sagged. The sun glowed in his snow-white hair. He felt drowsy and suddenly tired. He was fifty-four years old, and he found, at times, that he had to remind himself.

His jaw ached where the partial plate bit. His vision clouded and his head nodded down to his chest. He crossed his legs, looked down at his shoes, old, high-topped, out of style. He forced himself to stay awake. He wanted to hear his father's voice once more. Then it came to him, softly, gently, riding a warm mountain breeze.

What do you want to become when you grow up, Karl?

He wondered why, of all the memories in which to choose from, his mind had brought back such a seemingly innocent remark as that. Certainly he hadn't been that impressed with it at that time. And yet

... Now the picture returned to him. His father had been standing in
the snow, with a heavy fur cap over his head, his mustache drooping,
his rubber boots hitched over his trouser legs. Karl had been riding the
big wooden cart with the brown heavy-hipped horse. They had been
delivering meat. His father had turned to him, quietly, in the breath-
steaming darkness moonlit, snowy, and had asked him, *"What do you
want to become when you grow up, Karl?"*

Why should he remember it now?

He sat, spellbound, and watched the cold flowing water, listened to the
soft music-box sounds of the birds. He thought of his mother, a beautiful
woman with thin cheeks, and long pale hair spun into a golden bun. He
remembered the midnight ride in Indiana, his wife at his side, snuggled
against the cold, riding in the new Packard. 1936....

While in prison he had thought quite a bit, trying to piece together the
complex paper mosaic of his past, trying to feel it, smell it, know of it
more than a memory. But none of the memories were quite as clear, as
strangely frightening, as the voice of his father.

He returned to the cabin on the hill, carrying the heavy revolver free
from the soiled cleaning rags and box of shells.

What was the good of all these memories? They were the prints of his
past. And he trod slowly ahead, looking back, seeing the prints, and
wondering if he were, after all, alive.

Weren't the prints of his memories proof enough? What was he
seeking? What was he trying to prove? Wasn't it enough for him to
simply breathe and realize that he must be alive? Wasn't that, by
itself, an answer? Why then did he painfully search into his past?
What was it that he hoped to discover there? So far, during the
melancholy iron nights of the many imprisoned years, he had discovered
only bitterness, pain, sadness. Why did he still look back? What good did
it do him to see his prints stretched far behind in the gloom? He had no
idea. And it brought him only more pain and confusion.

But still, in spite of this, he wandered vaguely on, an old man, looking
wistfully back, feeling certain that he had lost something somewhere—
that behind him lay the answer to a question unasked. In his heart, he
had neither the question nor the answer. He had only a deep emotion,
a painful weight of longing and loneliness. What was it? He was still
strong, and yet he felt feebly for the damp red tissue-paper of his pulse,
wondering what he feared. What demon did he pursue, and what
demon pursued him?

He feared a complete death. He feared failure. And, most important,
he feared a realization that what he presently sought was pointless.

Still, he continued, planning, scheming, waiting for the excitement of the past to catch up with him. This job, Skyline House, was his final challenge. Why didn't he feel it then? Why did he still hear the haunting voice of his father, see the image of his weak son, remember so clearly his wife on that magic Indiana night; why was he, Karl Heisler, so cursed with a search for meaning when he had long ago convinced himself that it was all meaningless? He knew that it was unwise to curse his life. He was alive. He shouldn't curse it. He knew of no other way to live. It made no difference to the outcome how he stepped ahead, so long as the memory existed, whispered in the darkness of his soul and reminded him that he had indeed lived that lost moment—for see, there in the soft trail, the prints. Listen to them. Ignore whatever is ahead. Listen to the prints. They speak of the pain of the past, of the futility of other years. The excitement will come later....

In the late afternoon the sun began to set, gently at first, with soft coral and blue, then the sky glowed as if it had been smeared with hot red oil. Far above the horizon line the tissuey-paper clouds burned with deepening color.

Karl dressed slowly. He put on a brightly-flowered silk shirt and fresh lemon slacks. He tied the laces to his white canvas sneakers and stood up from the cane chair. The cabin window was open. The air was warm and still. The cabin walls glowed like wine and the black silhouettes of the trees were outlined with fiery tinsel. Chipmunks danced airily along the tree trunks, sniffing, waving delicate plumed tails. The cabin road was a peculiar yellow, cracker-colored, twisting through the woods past the peaked roofs of the other cabins.

Karl sighed, the memories lingering, the sadness evaporating slowly. He wished now that the job was over. He wanted to be home, away from it all. He admitted to himself that he was tired. He wanted to retire from the business.

He inserted two creek stones into an empty camera case. He hadn't been able to afford the camera. He allowed the case to hang free from his neck by the leatherette strap. He picked up his cheap felt hat and left the room. The scuffed bulky briefcase was by the door where Toschi had packed it. Karl nodded hesitantly to Louis and Frank.

"Well, how do I look?"

"Ah, just like a tourist. A work of art, Karl."

"Fine," Louis nodded. He lit a cigarette. There was no light in the room and the tiny golden flare illuminated Goodwin's dark, handsome features. It all seemed so mysterious.

Karl picked up the heavy briefcase. "I'll be back later."

"Take the Studebaker."

"I will, don't worry about that."

Frank followed him out to the rose darkness of the porch. They stood side by side, watching the cabin path. The crickets were beginning to sound.

"It makes you kind of sad being up here," Frank said softly.

The half question came as a surprise. Karl studied him for a moment. Then, "How come, kid? What makes you ask?"

"You're more quiet."

Karl nodded.

"I think Louis is anxious."

"Jumpy?"

"No, I don't think so. He's going to be all right. I'm becoming anxious myself. After all, we still don't know the details yet. To me it's just a job. It hasn't become a fact yet." He shrugged. "I'm not knocking you, Karl. It's not that. I'm proud to be working with you. In fact, I consider myself kind of lucky."

Karl said nothing. He held his briefcase and stared down the road. Finally, he said that it was becoming late. He had better be going.

"This is Wednesday," Toschi said. "We'll make the plans tomorrow night?"

"Yes," Karl answered. "I'll give you everything I know tomorrow. We'll make the go for Friday night. It has to be this Friday for sure."

Toschi touched his shoulder, a gesture of luck, then retreated into the cabin. Karl remained on the porch for a long moment, then, finally, he followed the path past the Pontiac. The Studebaker was parked off the shoulder of the main highway, about a quarter-mile from the Kovall general store.

"Why, hello there, Mr. Anderson."

It was Mrs. Kovall, still wearing the cheap red sunsuit, sitting on a flaking white bench in front of the gas pumps. A black puppy was squirming on her lap. "All dressed up, unh? Going into town?"

"No, just an after-dinner walk."

The air was becoming dark blue. An occasional cab light peeped yellow through the trees. She sighed, moved her bare shoulders. "Gee, isn't it a warm night?"

He agreed. He realized that he had paused to talk with the woman because he still felt foolish over the theft of the two packages of cigarettes.

"Nat's in the City on business. Would you like to come in for a cold beer?" She grinned, showing her gums under the sickly pump light. There were moths flickering against the bulb. "You wouldn't have to pay for it, you know."

"No, thank you, Mrs. Kovall. Some other time."

"Well, whatever you say, Mr. Anderson."

He found the Studebaker where Louis had left it. He drove into San Hacienda and found a parking area in an alleyway next to the red brick Fabelhaft Hotel.

The town's main street was gently sloped at each end, becoming level in the center. The expensive shops had peaked roofs. The street was lined with pine and redwood. There were no neon signs. In the town square there was a fountain with greenish bronze figures of lumbermen and mules. An obelisk was printed with fading names of the long-ago war dead. A single patrol car cruised the street. Tourists walked along the brick sidewalks in their shirtsleeves. Most of the shops were arts-and-crafts affairs. There were a few verandas with curving archways. Near the Fabelhaft Hotel there was an old blacksmith shop, faintly smelling of leather and alfalfa.

The town had been restored from a once-booming lumber settlement. In San Hacienda it was considered a local sacrilege to employ neon, advertising of any sort, or to restore a building along lines other than its original. Skyline House, which was three and a half miles south of the town limit, was housed in what had once been the county theater building.

There was still time, so he stopped in a bar and had a pony of brandy. The interior was cool and dark and there were the waxy odors of polish and leather soap. The walls were illuminated by flickering gaslight and the lofty ceiling was a jungle of lanterns, team halters, chains, axes, and two-handed saws. The bartender behind the Victorian bartop wore zircon studded arm garters and long fuzzy sideburns.

"You stopping here?"

"Yes," Karl answered. "At the Fabelhaft. I've read quite a bit about this town in the magazines back home. Thought I'd take a look around."

"It's a good town. Nice. Quiet. No commercialism."

Karl sipped his brandy. The bartender drifted away. A thin, pink-faced man wearing a white cashmere vest emerged from somewhere in the gaslit gloom. He settled hesitantly on the nearby barstool. There was the scent of gardenia. His eyes were large and wet looking. He licked his rosebud lips and nodded an uncertain hello. Karl returned the nod.

"Not too much to do around here, is there. I mean, after Frisco it's a bloody drag. And I mean, a bloody drag."

"That's right," Karl answered.

"You live around here?"

Karl didn't answer. He wondered what the man was pimping for.

Skyline House? A woman? Himself? He sipped his brandy and lit a cigarette, taking his time.

"Looky here, my name is Archer. Archer Cameron."

Karl paused, narrowed his lips into a tight line. He nodded shortly. "Anderson. Lars."

"Really? Whenever I hear the name Lars I always think of this friend of mine. We went to this costume party, a big drag affair. In New York. And he dressed up as the God of War. A Roman outfit with one of those red shoe-brush things on top of his helmet. The Martian God. I'm digressing now. But, to get to why I think of Lars, his name was Larry." Archer Cameron shrugged, looked dreamily up to the ceiling. "Anyway, whenever I hear the name Lars, I always think of that."

Karl was aware that Cameron was drunk, and was holding onto the bar for support. Karl wanted to leave, but he didn't. He was sorry now that he had wanted a brandy, sorrier still that he had chosen this particular bar. But what could he do about it now? If he left now he would only draw unnecessary attention to himself. He cursed under his breath and ordered another drink. Archer Cameron insisted that he buy the round, supporting his request by shouting a brandy for the two of them.

They had a brandy. Through the open doors Karl saw that it was much darker now. There were less tourists on the street. It was the dinner hour. The Fabelhaft restaurant across the street was brightly lit and a man was studying the outsize menu card on the brass grill stand on the sidewalk. Beside him, Archer Cameron had settled more permanently on his stool and was now pointing out the wonders of the old equipment on display behind the bar.

"What I mean is, I adore old cap and ball guns. Think of the lumbermen, so goddam strong, cutting an empire and all that lusty jazz. Think of it. God."

"Are you in lumber, Mr. Cameron?"

"Me? God, no. I'm a photographer. Fashion. When you think of Cameron, think of cameraman. That's sort of my motto back in New York. Fashion is the thing now. Only way to make a good living. Exotic backgrounds. Green trees, yellow and gold autumn jackets. Ancient buildings crumbling, cracking, and flaring, white-and-cantaloupe gowns. Big-eyed models like newborn colts. Fashion, Mr. Lars. New York. Old San Hacienda. Exotica and the Great American Female. God."

Twenty minutes later, after more drunken rambling from Archer Cameron, Karl left. It was warmer outside. There were hazy magic rings of gold around the ornate street lamps. He returned to the Studebaker. He hunched down on the seat and stared blankly at the wrinkled folds about his lumpy knuckles and thick wrists.

He had to be positive that Skyline House would be busy. He waited, thinking back again, occasionally glancing at his old-fashioned pocket watch.

For the first three years during his last sentence old Larry Con had occupied the lower bunk in Karl's cell. And, as the final months approached, his cough became worse and he grew noticeably weaker. Finally, when the prison doctor thought it advisable to move the old man to the hospital ward, Frank Toschi was moved into his place.

But, before that, during the last months, the old man and Karl talked long into the nights.

"See, Karl, he told me to make it into Frisco and get myself picked up. I could of stayed up in San Hacienda, but no, the bastard says get caught. What else could I do?" The voice whispered like a frantic moth caught in a steel coil. His yellowish toad eyes watered in the sagging skin, the sunken mouth flapping and foaming. The only sounds were the night coughs and the occasional tread of guard steps. "Karl? Are you awake? Hey? Listen to me, Karl. I wasn't kidding you about the deal. It's the up and up, the goods. You know that."

"Sure, I know that, Larry. I know that."

"Good, good. You see, the way it was, Bertuzzi gave me the word. The way it started was this old bird wanted a parole pretty bad so he gave them information on a six-year-old job in L.A. He named me for it. Sure, yes, oh yes, I was in on it. But hell, I got a right to live just like everyone else. So, here I am, in the Joint, and I'm going to die. I know that. The doc knows it, too. You can smell it sitting inside me if you get close enough. Death smells, Karl. Did you know that? Death smells like a cold rabbit hole, with no more rabbits living in it. That's what death smells like."

Karl nodded uneasily and the tight springs whispered underneath him.

"It's just like I said. About the deal. And why do I tell you? Why? It's because I'm getting out of this joint. God is granting me a parole. So, I'm telling you. You'll be out of here in two more years, and I figure you'll be about fifty-five. Right? I always liked you, kid. Even back in the old days. You need the breaks."

The breaks ...

Larry Con continued, whispering, the ebbtide voice holding back the rattling cough that lurked deep in his stringy throat. "The breaks, Karl. Like the old days when you were on top. Like that last big one. What was it? Weintzer? That was a good one, kid. We all admired you for that one. You used to be the best. And with Skyline you can be right back there. This one is good."

This one is good.... Karl wondered with a stirring of excitement, his thoughts boiling in the darkness of the cage, his pulse keeping time with his thoughts.

"Bertuzzi can stand it. You just remember the layout I gave you. You'll work it. I know you can pull it off, kid. When I was there I used to give it lots of thought. It was kind of automatic with me. I guess I'm really a crook at heart. That much dough down in that hole! I suppose I had to kind of keep my fingers in just for practice. So, I thought about it during each count day. I can't get to it now, I'm too old, too washed out. So, I give it to you. You're one of the old ones. I'll be goddamned if I'd give it to one of these punks around here. See, I'm going to hell when I die, Karl. But you—"

"Take it easy, Larry. Relax."

"Sure, Karl. You're right. I don't want to start coughing again."

"Now, you say the only way into the hole is by the elevator."

"Yeah."

"And only Bertuzzi can get into the elevator?"

"The only one. The big safe down in the hole is opened only by Max West. That's the accountant I told you about. Bertuzzi don't even know the combination. Only Max West. And the safe is hot, the whole joint down there is wired. Like I told you, the only way is the elevator. But remember—you're an elevator, too."

"And once it's in the hole?"

"It stays there. Only Bertuzzi can bring it back up. Once it's down there it stays until the count is finished. The last Friday of each month is the count day. I can tell you the whole routine, step by step. The count starts at ten each time."

"You said there's only four in the hole. Bertuzzi, Max West, and the two counters. And none of them are armed."

"That's it. Bertuzzi never carries a gun. He's too afraid of the law. It's an old habit of his from the Florida and Nevada days. I've never known him to carry a gun. And as for Max, he's a little bug who wouldn't know a gun if he saw one."

"How about the guards? Tell it to me again."

"Upstairs in the corridor. I used to be one of them. They wait right at the elevator door and don't move. The only way into the corridor is through the front, which is the rear of the game room where the dropchute carts come in from, and the side door. The side door is locked on the outside, bolted from the inside, and is guarded from the elevator post."

"Okay, Larry. We're going to go over everything every night until they haul you off to the hospital."

"That's okay, kid. I don't mind. Go ahead and pump me dry. I know that's how you work."

It always impressed Karl as strange to be called "kid." He remembered that old Walter Tuttle, the heist financier, had always called him that.

"Who're the guards?" he asked. "Tell me about them."

"A guy named Artie, a zombie, new breed from Vegas. The kind that lives only to pack a gun and comb his hair at night. The other's a nice guy, Benny Coca. He's got my old job."

"How about the tree, Larry?"

"Jesus, it's a monster, big around like a house, couple hundred feet tall. Redwood, I guess. I never was too good at naming trees. They all look alike to me. But this one, it's the biggest I ever seen. That's probably why no one ever thought of it as a way up there."

"Okay."

"You can do it, Karl." Larry's whisper became intense with emotion. "Bertuzzi tossed me to the wolves. He said it was to protect himself from a possible investigation. He was afraid that if I was picked up for the L.A. job in his stamping grounds there might be an investigation. And, if that'd happened, his deal would've blown sky high. So, the bastard tossed me to the wolves. What could I do, Karl? Once them guys tell you to do something, you do it. There ain't no place to hide if you screw the organization."

"What about me, then?"

"Bury yourself somewhere, retire from the business. You'll be too old to keep pushing yourself. And, believe me, you won't find cash money, unmarked like this, anywhere else. Only casinos and race tracks have money like that. But this's even better than banks, or Federal raps like that. They're not going to blow the whistle on you. They won't be able to. The Federals would be too interested in the income angle if they reported it with an out-of-county or state-wide alarm. The most they can do is say you hit the restaurant for a few bucks. And, believe me, the state fuzz aren't going to break their asses over a cafe robber who made off with a few crummy grand."

"Thanks, Larry."

"Think nothing of it. When I get paroled, I'll put in a good word for you with the top man. I don't want to see you in hell like I'm going to be, Karl. I want *you* to go to heaven."

"Okay, Larry."

"Skyline's a tough nut, but you'll make out all right."

"Nothing's tough," Karl said.

He drove slowly out of town, picking up speed when he passed the Lion's Club shield nailed to the post. The headlights reflected from the dusty roadside leaves and picked out the red mailbox reflectors. He passed the Skyline cutoff road. He could smell the forest droppings and the scent of woodsmoke rushing through the car. He slowed a quarter-mile past the cutoff and stopped where there was a creek bridge and a wide, hard-packed car park.

He left the camera case behind and carried only the heavy briefcase. He crossed the bridge, holding onto the guide-rail with his free hand. On the opposite side there was a plank patio before a darkened two-story cabin. He crossed the deck and followed a narrow path that seemed to lead north through the woods. The ground was soft and damp underfoot.

He stopped once. From the case he drew out a pair of felt window dresser's overshoes and a black duster. The black slippers covered his feet and the duster buttoned clear to his throat.

He continued softly through the woods.

A quarter-mile later he crouched behind a lightning-blackened trunk behind Skyline House. He was at the southwest side of the building itself, at the top of a gradual slope, fifty feet from the car park area.

A young attendant with a white smock and straw cap raced up the dimly-lit gravel aisle, coins jingling in his smock pocket. He stopped before a dark gray Bentley. He checked the stub number on the half that was fixed to the wiper. He drove the car carefully to the front entrance of the building.

Then it was quiet.

Karl left the briefcase at the base of the tree and crept quickly and silently down the slope to the lot. The gravel whispered. The first car was a cream-colored Cadillac. He checked the pencilled time under the purple stub number—one o'clock—then made a dash back up the slope and hid behind the blackened trunk.

He felt excited now, but there was the familiar lid of control that clamped it and held it inside him. His movements were quick and sure. His senses were alerted. He watched and listened, breathing heavily after his brief run to and from the car park. It was hot under the black duster. He felt the armpits of the silk shirt clinging to his skin.

There was a high moon, the color of wax, and the outlines of the trees above him were daubed with moonlight, the leaves glowing like silent silver moths. From where he was stationed, he could hear the watery hiss of the creek two hundred yards away. There were still the crickets. The mulchy ground was soft and damp to his touch and the odors were sweet and earthy.

His briefcase had two separate sides. On one, the long thick leather strap, waist belt, climbing irons, clamp rings. The other contained a dark cloth bag with a bar of soft soap, hand drill, pliers, Phillips screwdriver, flashlight.

He moved through the underbrush to the building at his left.

Skyline House was a huge three-story affair set in the center of the flat clearing three hundred yards up a gentle slope from the highway. The long graystone sides were covered with dark leafy ivy. In spite of its present employment the club still resembled an old-fashioned theater and opera house. There were no windows or fire escapes. Over the front entrance, there was a marquee with a glowing underbelly of tiny yellow lights.

The cutoff road passed over the creek a hundred yards from the highway. The bridge was covered. When the cars passed through, there was a deep irregular roaring sound as the tires whumped along the planks and echoed through the wooden cave.

The nearest tree to the building, which was quite near, was the giant redwood that Larry Con had mentioned. The first of its branches were considerably higher than the roof of the building. The crown disappeared far into the night.

"The tree's the only way, Karl," Larry had whispered in the darkness of the cell. "Sure, Bertuzzi goes down into the hole, but that isn't the only thing. Something else goes down there, too—the elevator. And remember that grill—no one knows about it—it's lined up with the chimney, maybe a little east of it...."

At the rear of the building he stood at the base of the tree and looked up. It looked impossible to climb. The dark red shaft was grooved with the bark hide and towered straight into the sky. Even the roof of the building appeared higher than he had imagined.

He ran the long strap around the body of the tree and clamped the ends to the thick waist belt. He fixed the irons to his legs, tested the bite of the spike by stabbing it into the bark. He left the briefcase hidden in a clump of spiky fern, looped the cloth bag around his neck, then, inch by inch, began to ascend the shaft of the tree like a lumberjack.

He was quivering with exhaustion by the time he reached the top. He rested, leaning back against the belt, his feet clamped to the coat of bark. The lip of the roof was only two feet from him. There was a slight breeze at this new height, warm and mountain scented, and he sighed, breathing heavily.

Far below, he saw the west end of the car park and a row of shiny automobiles. He felt free and safe from harm. Could it be possible that he had only been released from prison such a short time ago? It all seemed far away to him. Larry Con, the cramped cell, the hours, seemed to belong to another age. High in the tree he felt a mixed sensation of freedom and panic. He almost giggled. A fifty-four year old man climbing a redwood tree like a lumberjack monkey. It all seemed unreal. He heard the muffled roaring of the cars, the shiny dragons passing through the covered wooden cave. He heard the creek, smelt the forest, was aware of the frightening nearness of the sky.

What would happen if he were to fall? Would Bertuzzi shoot him? Would he be able to crawl painfully away into the forest? Would he break his fool neck?

He swung the cloth bag onto the roof and carefully lowered himself down the tree. It was quite a bit easier for him on the way down.

"It can be done, Karl. It's that grill that fixes it. Just remember, wherever the elevator goes, you go. But you won't be able to do this one by yourself. Not the way you used to. With this one you'll need one, maybe two guys. But you'll have to figure it out, about getting away and all that...."

The dry run was completed. Some of the necessary equipment was on the roof, and he had checked out the building to his satisfaction. It was exactly as he had pictured it. And the two points that he had been able to check out were done. First, the automobiles parked to the far rear of the lot were pencilled for approximately one o'clock. And, by far the more important of the two, he had been able to climb the tree. He had proved it to himself.

It was with a more youthful step that he re-entered the woods and made his way to the south path. Somewhere a night bird whistled. Karl removed the duster and felt slippers and stuffed them back into the case. The bird whistled a second time, as though trying to win attention, and Karl smiled softly.

9

Darkness closed in early the next night and a thick fog rolled silently through the forest. It devoured in misty jaws the dark roofs, the trees, the ferns, rolling softly, wet and purring. The radio played quietly in one corner of the cabin, almost unheard by Karl and Frank Toschi.

It was nine o'clock when Louis returned from the store with the second load of beer. He set the bag next to Karl's cream-colored drawing sheets.

"It's a big fog tonight," Louis whispered fearfully. "It's like walking through a cold Turkish bath out there." He was wearing his hat at an angle, the brim pulled down on one side, and it gave him the ridiculous air of an old-fashioned actor. Again, he looked vaguely handsome to Karl, and what with the angle of his hat, more theatrical than before. He was under the greenish-yellow light, his dark eyes turned toward the closed windows.

Karl watched him. Even Frank looked a bit pale and nervous. "What's up, Louis? You look as if you'd seen a ghost."

"No, no ghosts, Karl." He smiled sheepishly. "It the woods out there; they spook me. When I went to the store just now I was walking on my toes all the way." He swallowed nervously, still speaking in a low voice. "It's nothing I can point out, it's not like that at all. It was like I was a kid again, whistling in the dark, passing a cemetery. That sort of thing. It's kind of funny, isn't it."

"I know what you mean, Louis," Frank said thoughtfully.

Karl looked to Frank, and suddenly, as if a film had begun in his mind, he remembered a bleak afternoon when there had been a thick fog and the dampness had clung to the prison metal. Frank had looked worriedly up to the sky beyond the hazy walls and towers and hills of mist. They had been on medium security detail near the cyclone fence and the bay.

He frowned, remembering so clearly; he wondered why he did. Prison tended to draw men very close to one another, binding their lives together until a deep understanding, almost a dependence, was formed. Then, just as mysteriously, freedom unwound that net and alienated men. Toschi was different, however. If anything, he was closer. The bond between Karl and Frank was stronger because of the memory, the print of the recent past, and Karl felt an unusual tenderness toward the younger man stir in him.

Then, possibly because of this, he felt his age. It stole into him as did the fog creep through the trees outside. He had to remind himself that he had indeed climbed the huge tree the night before. This he did to convince himself that he couldn't possibly be as tired or as old as he actually felt.

Louis nodded to Frank, obviously encouraged now that he found support over his ill feelings toward the fog. "Coming back up the path was even worse. The fog gets on them trees and it falls the same way raindrops fall. You ever hear them drops click when they hit the ground? It sounds like someone's walking around on the leaves, creeping kind of. I kept thinking that someone was going to reach out and touch me on the shoulder. It's kind of funny, because I'm carrying my gun, and I figured I'd just start shooting if someone touched me. Of course, I probably wouldn't do a silly thing like that, but still, even with the gun and all, I was scared. I forced myself to walk real slow on the way back, just to kind of prove that I wasn't really scared." He looked hopefully to Frank. "You know what I mean?"

"I know just what you mean. I don't like the trees myself. Me? I'm a city man. The daytimes is okay, but this fog and this night is strictly for the hicks."

Karl puzzled as he listened to them. He wasn't capable of feeling the uneasiness they confessed to. He had found that he liked the woods, and, for some queer reason, liked them even more at night. There was a security about them, as if nothing could go wrong if you kept yourself on their side. And, besides, the great quiet served to remind him of other times, of picnics in Indiana with Edna, of Michigan trips with his father, of quiet times, secure times.

He was aware, however, that Frank and Louis weren't necessarily uneasy because of the fog. It was the job set for tomorrow night that had set them on edge. He knew that. He felt no immediate fear for himself. He had been through it too often in the past. But he felt something new, something deeper than an immediate fear. It had begun the moment he had been released from prison, when he had first talked with Edna, walked near the shimmering green pepper tree with his son, and, even later, in the sun-striped nursery with old Walter Tuttle. He recognized it now. He had tried to tell himself that it had been a sadness that he had felt. It wasn't a sadness, however, it was a foreboding....

The atmosphere of the cabin was strange. The weak light, sufficient for the table, wasn't enough to illuminate the entire room, and the shadowy corners seemed more ominous since Goodwin's tale of fear. Even Karl was beginning to feel the infection of uneasiness.

The fog grew heavier. The branches over the cabin became heavy with the collected moisture and the tapping of the swollen drops on the shingles was a pleasant sound. Louis kept looking nervously to the ceiling.

Karl forced himself to be at peace. There was nothing for him to fear, he told himself. There was no reason for him to carry this sense of foreboding. He felt now as if the three of them were the last humans left in the world, cut off from everything, wrapped in the fog and isolated in the gray depths of the mountains. The air became stale and blue with tobacco smoke. The beer cans glinted under the light.

"This is the general idea," Karl finally said. He ran a heavy black marking pencil on the first of the cream-colored drawing papers. He outlined the basic floor plan of Skyline House. Where the first X was placed on the southwest side he indicated the metal-covered door that had resembled a stage door. "There's a heavy bolt inside and a brass lock on the outside. This door opens onto the parking lot, which is right here, along the south side of the building. Behind that is a slope, a bit steep, with trees beyond that. It's fairly well covered with underbrush. The main floor plan is simple: the entrance foyer with the hatcheck stand on the right, public telephones and reservation desk on the left. The dining room is just past the foyer."

"Where's the gambling room?"

"In the rear, behind the dining room. There's a kitchen on the right at the rear of the dining room. Now back here—see where I've oblonged the floor plan?—is the corridor. It runs north and south in the far west rear. The tree another X "—is here. It's about halfway from the rear of the parking lot to the north side. This corridor here, is beyond the game room and is always locked on the count days. North in the corridor are a few offices, south is the metal stage door. In the middle is the elevator." He pulled out a second sheet. "The second floor plan is easier than the first. High-stake poker rooms back here, and a private dining room in the front. From this floor to the third, there's a narrow stairway. This is closed with a barred gate, a lock, and an alarm. The front section is used to store extra chips, dropchute carts, chipracks, felt tops, dishes, utensils, cooking supplies, uniforms, and so on. The rear part is always kept empty. There's another barred and locked and alarmed gate between these two sections."

"And the money?"

"It's down in the hole. That's a solid concrete block set in the basement directly under the corridor and the offices. In Bertuzzi's working office there's a slot an inch wide set in the floor under his desk. He counts the nightly take with two counters present. Then, when he's sealed the packets into money piles about half an inch thick, he drops them down the slot. The money goes down a steel corkscrew shaft through three feet of concrete and lands in a catch cart in the belly of the big safe down in the hole."

"Jesus," Louis said under his breath.

"The only entrance to the hole is through the elevator. And the only entrance to the elevator, for all purposes, is in the corridor between the stage door and the offices. The elevator is unlocked with a key by Bertuzzi. The key is used again to operate the panel to open the button to get down into the hole. When the elevator gets down, it opens directly into the count room. The outer doors lock into an open position. At all times, night and day, that room and the safe are wired up so bad that a mosquito would touch off an immediate alarm. Bertuzzi has the system turned off two or three minutes before they go down. He has to make a phone call to the protective association and give them the word. It's all very routine. Been going on like this for almost six years."

Frank nodded thoughtfully, leaned on the table with his elbows. He watched the carefully drawn sheets. Only Karl spoke. The others were silent and intent.

"The routine at Skyline never varies. On the count days, which is the last Friday of each month, Max West, an accountant from the City, arrives at Bertuzzi's house. That's a big place north of here, called Leon-Jan. At eight o'clock, or thereabouts, they arrive at the club with Leon's personal bodyguard. His name is Artie. Artie goes into the corridor and waits there with the house guard, a guy named Benny Coca. Max and Bertuzzi eat in the dining room, almost always toward the rear near the game room door. At ten o'clock they both go through the game room and enter the corridor. They lock the door behind them. They wait until the two guards search the two regular counters. They also search Max West. Then Bertuzzi makes the call to the protective association and opens the elevator door with his key. The key, by the way, is always in Bertuzzi's home safe at Leon-Jan and is only taken out on the count days. Artie and Benny Coca stand double guard at the elevator entrance and the group enters the cage. Then they go down into the hole.

"There are two desks, one to the left facing the cage, and one to the right facing the safe and the count bench. The bench is about waist high and has two stools. The counters face the concrete wall until Max West opens the safe, then they start to count the money, making the take official and packing it."

"How do they get it out of there?"

"In six yellow cases. Bertuzzi has runners that come up to San Hacienda late Friday night. They stay at the Fabelhaft Hotel in town and drift into the club separately. They each take a small portion in a sealed yellow case and run it into Vegas, or wherever the organization cut goes to. Whatever they carry is a minimum and Bertuzzi figures that if they're going to be hit it wouldn't be worth it. If they were all hit it would take seven or eight guys, and that, as you can probably figure, would be damn near impossible. The bags are sealed and signatured by Max West. The entire operation is slick and tight as a drum. They've never been hit before and they probably never expect to be. That's in our favor. Now, this's the good part. There's always at least a hundred thousand in cash in the safe that belongs to Bertuzzi. It's his private fund box. The rest of the take is made up of Bertuzzi's monthly split, the organization's split, and the monthly gross from the restaurant. Totaling it all up, it's usually upward from a quarter of a million in cash. Unmarked, tax free."

Frank sat quite still. Louis gaped and made a dry swallowing sound deep in his throat.

Karl's hand continued to sketch smooth clean lines, the job seeming to take place before him. He drew a side view of the three-story building, sketched in the bulk of the big tree, shaded the walls to indicate the thick ivy growth. He crossed a small *x* to show the narrow grill imbedded in the ivy on the north side of the building. He lined the *x* up with a chimney stack. He ruled a line from the grill mark to the lip of the roof. Six feet. In the far rear of the third floor he shaped an enclosed shaft, like a long thin box, that extended as far down as the hole.

"This's the elevator shaft. Remember now, there are two locked and barred gates leading to the rear of the third floor. It's impossible to get back there, cut through those locks without selling off the alarms, and then what? Steal chips? That's not the reason for their being there. They're there to discourage anyone fooling around near the elevator shaft. However, to the right as you're facing west to the shaft, there's a small grill. It's an old air vent used by the stage hands. The building used to be a theater and opera house and the third floor rear was the top of the curtain and property loft. The grill is barely enough to squeeze through. It's entirely covered with ivy and can't be seen from the outside. It's doubtful if it can be seen from the inside since it shows no light. The only way to get to that grill is by lowering yourself from the roof. There isn't supposed to be a way up to the roof. But look at this tree…."

"Is it really that big around?"

"I think it's actually bigger than I drew it here. That's the one I climbed last night."

"And you and I climb it tomorrow night?"

"Yes. We make the roof, fix the short rope ladder to the chimney and lower ourselves six feet down to the grill. We'll have to push ivy apart and look for it, but once we find it there won't be any problems. We just crawl inside and that's that."

"It doesn't sound very easy."

"It isn't. Everything like this is complicated. It always is. But then, I didn't expect it to be easy. The toughest part is climbing that damned tree."

"Okay." Frank nodded and bit thoughtfully on his underlip.

"Now I'll tell you the part that we'll have to go over until we get it right." He opened another round of cold beer. He talked slowly, sipping his beer. "At exactly nine o'clock Louis drives the Pontiac to Skyline House. He's well dressed, all jazzed up for a night out, and he tells the parking lot attendant that he'll be four hours. Remember that. Say four hours and don't be vague about it. That'll put you at one o'clock when the attendant will expect you to leave. Frank and I will be in the trunk with the equipment. The attendant will park us as far to the rear as he possibly can because the late outgoing cars are put back there. The one and two hour cars are put up in front where they can be quickly reached. Louis enters Skyline and has a leisurely dinner. Bertuzzi and Max West will probably be there, eating at a rear table near the game room. Louis orders a big meal and takes his time in eating it. Meanwhile, Frank and I crawl out of the Pontiac and make for the rear of the building. We bring with us the two rope ladders, the short and the long one, two waist straps, climbing spikes, straps, the shotgun, a handgun, a roll of friction tape, a spool of wire, and the two denim bags for carrying the money.

"We'll wear the dusters and the slippers when we get into the trunk. Now, shortly after nine o'clock, we climb the tree, lower ourselves by the short ladder into the third floor through the grill. Then we cut the lock on the shaft door with the hand drill. This opens onto the top of the shaft where the cable wheel and motor is. We lower the long ladder down into the shaft. Once we climb down the ladder we'll be sitting right on top of the elevator. Like all elevators, there's a small safety door on the roof. We pry it loose and just sit tight and wait. We may have to sit on top of the cage for half an hour. At ten o'clock Bertuzzi calls the association and has the alarm turned off in the hole. When Benny Coca and Artie wait outside to guard the elevator the group enters the cage. We go down into the hole with them.

"We wait about fifteen minutes to make sure that Max West has opened the big safe and everybody feels secure and is in the middle of the count. Then I open the trap and drop through, carrying the shotgun. I cover everyone until Frank drops the equipment and follows through the trap. Then we pick up the money, tie them with the tape and wire, and return the same way, taking the ladders with us. We return back down the tree and crawl into the trunk with the equipment and the two sacks of money.

"At exactly fifteen minutes to eleven, Louis leaves the dining room and asks the attendant for the car. Then we all drive away, snug as a bug in a rug, rich, tax free, with the mob's money."

"Are any of the guys in the hole armed?"

"No. Bertuzzi never carries a gun, the two counters aren't allowed to; after all, that's why the guards search them both. If there is shooting, which there won't be, but *if* there is, then it wouldn't be heard anyway. You wouldn't be able to hear a bomb go off in that hole. It's pretty far down there. And, like I said, it's three feet of solid concrete."

Louis seemed relieved to be assured that there would be no shooting.

He frowned and scratched his jaw. "What about the car switch, Karl? Where do we make that?"

Karl moved his hands through his jacket pocket until he came out with a state map. He ran his heavy, wrinkled hand along the green marbled areas used to indicate mountains, the tiny blue veins of rivers and waterways, the red veins of roads, the arteries of highways and freeways, the dots and stars and bullseyes of the cities and towns. He tapped his finger at a single dot deep in the dark marble. "This is where we are right now. This little purple box line is the county. That's as far as Bertuzzi's crooked police force operates. Beyond that line we're relatively safe. We drive the Pontiac across the line and abandon the car facing north, then take the Studebaker and return back across the line, coming south."

"You mean come back where we just came from?"

"Only as far as here." A dotted winding line that left the red line of highway and wound through the forest toward the ocean. "This's a jeep road, little used, kind of rough as you can see by the broken line. But it takes us right to the ocean. From there we follow the coast highway right into the city."

"We leave the Pontiac—how far from this road?"

"About five miles north from it. That seems to be the safest. Frank and I crouch in the back seat of the second car until we get to the jeep road. By then we should be out of it. Look, I figure we'll have more than enough time. Bertuzzi won't be able to free himself for at least two hours, and by that time we'll be almost to the coast highway. By the time he's able to blow his whistle we'll be almost into town."

"Where do we go once we're back?"

"We'll split the money at Louis' Daly City place. Louis takes the Studebaker apart and completely dismantles it, putting the parts in his stock pile. The hull of the car can be put out in the rear yard and burned. It won't look suspicious. It's done all the time. And then he sighed and smiled softly, "we bury ourselves and split up."

It was quiet. Frank looked at the old man and nodded. "I guess you'll be leaving the country."

"Yes," Karl answered. "I guess we won't be seeing each other after this."

Frank looked thoughtful for a minute. "I suppose not," he finally said. "Are you going to retire after this one?"

"For good, Frank."

"I guess I will, too. If I get out of this—I mean, when I get out of it, I'm going to quit. I was becoming kind of fed up with it all anyway. Now seems to be as good a time as any to pull in my horns. After all, it's a perfect deal for me. There won't be any cop's or citizens out looking for me. It's not as if we're hitting a bank or anything legitimate like that…."

"No," Karl agreed, "it's not like that at all."

They opened more beer and began to go over the plans and the timing. Karl didn't speak. It was difficult for him to concentrate now. The mist tapped on the shingled roof, began to look like gray prison walls, blotted out the dark sentries of trees. The radio played softly in one corner.

Karl felt again the crawling memory steal over him. He had a vision of Edna and Walter Tuttle watching him, smiling secretly at his antics under the greenish light. Their voices hissed in the fog. Sadness crouched in the dark corners of the room; little Karl limped somewhere, asking his father to tell him again about his own father, about the good and kindly butcher in the snowy midwestern twilights.

He saw Larry Con at the wheel of the Packard, and his son next to him in the rear seat. *"You need the breaks, Karl…."*

He forced himself to concentrate on the plans at his fingertips. Frank was reciting the movement again, ticking off the nine o'clock trunk ride, the dash to the rear of the house, the climb up the tree, the long wait on top of the elevator….

10

The trees which surrounded Skyline House sighed in the warm mountain breeze. The restless night birds flew overhead like bits of windswept rags, phantoms under the murky bowl of sky, black and silent. The narrow path of gravel and dry needles crunched and whispered underfoot.

The doorman saluted with his white-gloved hand and opened the brass door for Leon, Artie, and Max West. They walked quickly up the wide stone steps under the yellow glow of the theater marquee. Everywhere there was the clean sweet odor of forest.

Max West, thin, balding, queerly mushroom-colored, followed Leon into the dimly lighted foyer. Artie nervously hitched his shoulders and glanced suspiciously around. The headwaiter looked bored. Leon led Max into the high-ceilinged dining room and they sat at their usual table in the rear behind a boxed hedge of ferns. The uniformed waiter removed the reserved sign, took their order, then moved silently away. Artie had disappeared behind the game room door. Overhead, the chandelier glittered like a suspended clump of glass shrubbery.

Leon looked haggard. There were ugly dark splotches under his eyes and his thin lips were pale and turned sullenly down at the corners. He sat hunched over his soup dish, not looking at the food, smoking his tenth cigar of the day.

He was terribly upset. His ritual bout with his housewoman had gone very badly that morning. And, as if that had augured the remainder of the day, the weather had turned toward evening. It had remained warm, of course, but a wind had come up quite suddenly and the birds became restless in the sky.

He began to wonder if Jane, his housewoman, had decided to rebel against their morning sessions. He hoped not. What would he do with his otherwise empty mornings if he had no Jane to execrate? Who could he turn to during the day? It was foolish to consider talking with his wife. Ever since her affair with Stanley Nagel, Janet had become impossible to reach. Her indifference toward him was becoming greater. And, Leon realized, it was all Stanley's fault. Nagel—Nagel—Nagel— the name tolled in his mind. He hated the very sound of it. He had never hated anyone as much as he did Stanley Nagel.

This recent attitude of his was bordering on all consuming insanity. Lately he had been sleeping very poorly. He could barely eat. He was obsessed with his hate. He believed that Nagel was the root of all his problems.

It was going to be a relief once Stanley was dead.

Then why, after all, was he still alive? Leon asked himself why he had waited this long. Was it because he was afraid? Was that it? Or did he naively believe that the situation would somehow solve itself? Was Leon that great a fool?

He could wait no longer. It was senseless to continue putting it off. It would have to be done now—tonight. He could no longer allow a punk like Stanley to torture him. He wanted his wife to become his property again. He wanted his position at Skyline to become secure again. That wasn't asking for too much. He deserved that much, at least.

The cold soup was removed and a salad was placed before him. He didn't even glance at it. He heard Max West's prissy voice chattering aimlessly about his wife and the recent arrival of the baby. Leon remembered something about it being a girl. He wasn't too sure, however.

At the other tables people talked in quiet tones under the glittering chandelier. A waiter led a single party to a small table near the rear, two tables from Leon. A darkly handsome young man, with theatrically full lips that trembled now and then, carefully studied the outsize menu card. He didn't look to the right or left. He glanced only once at Leon's direction.

Leon took no notice of this. He was still staring blankly at the dishes before him. His thoughts, which had been none too clear all day, now turned inward. He began to brood, and he had a sudden, eerie, vision of himself in the old days....

He crept silently along the stuffy, poorly lit hallway. Dirty Victorian wallpaper of purple-and-yellow flowers were on the walls. Outside, in the hot summer street, the children were yelling; old couples sat in the darkness on the porches; a gramophone played; somewhere an automobile horn sounded. It was 1927. He stood before a partly opened door and peered in at Big Charlie Eagan who slept on the bed. Eagan woke quite suddenly when Leon's hands grabbed tightly around his bull's throat, the thumbs punching in the windpipe. He tried to scream, to reach the revolver on the nightstand. Then, after many struggling minutes, he was dead. And Leon wept silent tears of relief and pride, rising above himself on magic new murderous wings. He dragged the bulky figure along the purple-and-yellow hallway to the rear porch near the smoldering stone incinerator. He lifted the body into the garbage chute opening and watched as the patent-leather shoes and fawn-colored spats disappeared noisily down the trash-gummed tube....

Max West was still talking to him, describing nervous little arcs in the air with his thin, blue-veined hands. He chuckled now and then and owlishly blinked behind the rimless glasses. Leon hadn't been listening. The vision of horror and triumph still lingered. The Victorian wallpaper and strangled body swam spectrally in the gelatine-coated memories behind his heavy-lidded eyes.

It was true that he had fought hard all his life to get where he was. Why should he stop now? Why surrender without a battle. After all, Leon Bertuzzi had once enjoyed a certain reputation for tenacity and toughness. Why quit? There was no reason to simply throw up his hands and cower like some old man on a park bench because some college boy with smart ideas wants to squeeze him out.

No, Stanley would have to be taken care of. He was a symbol of this new breed. He would have to be taken care of now, tonight after the count, over a friendly glass of rare brandy....

"Shut up, Max," Leon said.

"I was just telling you about

"Yeah, well I don't want to hear about it."

Max looked momentarily hurt, then he shrugged it away and forked at his food. "You seem kind of edgy tonight, Leon. Anything the matter?"

"No, not really, Max. I've been feeling kind of punk lately. Just a case of the blues, is all. Nothing important."

"Well, maybe what you need is a vacation. Get down to the beach, do

a little swimming and take in some sun. It really works wonders. I know.
Last year I took the wife up to Lake Tahoe for five days. We really had
ourselves a jimdandy time. Boating, swimming, gambling at Stateline,
just lazing around in the evening, or maybe taking short hikes. It
makes a guy feel like a million dollars. It really does."

Leon nodded indifferently. "Maybe you're right at that, Max. Maybe I
do need a vacation."

They finished their meal in silence. Leon didn't wait for tea or coffee.
It was ten o'clock and they were a bit late already. He lit another cigar,
signed the check, and led Max through the game room door.

The dark young man with trembling theatrical lips two tables away
put down his fork and nervously gulped at his water.

Leon led Max through the game room and locked the corridor door
after them. Charlie and Nels, the two regular counters, were already
waiting by the steel elevator door with Artie and Benny Coca.

In the rear office Leon saw Stanley Nagel, talking on the telephone.
He hung up a bit too quickly when Leon entered the room. His powder-
blue eyes glittered and his narrow necktie was biting into his suntanned
neck. Leon felt the boil of hatred and revulsion that he lately felt
whenever he saw Stanley. He made a sarcastic face and gestured with
his cigar.

"What's up, kid? Were you just talking lovey-talk with my wife?
Making a date? A midnight horseback ride through the woods?"

Stanley flushed. "Knock it off, old boy. You're becoming a bit boring.
Don't be so childish. You're old enough to take all this with a little more
flair, more sophistication. Remember, you're not talking to a roaring
twenties mobster with a sailor straw hat. This is me, Stanley, your loving
partner. So don't try to act so flip. It's unbecoming in a grown man."

Leon snorted. He wasn't too concerned with Stanley's smart talk
now that he had come to an agreement with himself, now that he knew
that Stanley would no longer be around to torture him with his
presence, his smart-talking ways.

He shut the door behind him and glanced at his watch. Five after ten.
He waited until Artie finished searching Charlie and Nels, then he
checked the stage door bolt and the corridor door that led to the game
room. Everything was locked tight.

His footsteps clicked hollowly in the corridor. The counting group
looked, as they always did, unreal and discolored, like wax figures, under
the naked fluorescent lighting. Benny Coca searched Max West and
nodded an okay. Leon returned to the office, ignoring Stanley again, and
called the protective association. After speaking a few brief code words
he hung up. Stanley was standing on the opposite side of the room with

a black-papered cigarette between his white teeth.

Leon opened the desk drawer and picked out his leather cigar case. He saw, as he usually did, the revolver resting on top of an unused linen handkerchief. The gun had always been there, and Leon had always ignored it. Now, for some reason, he picked it up, hefted it, then slipped it casually into his coat pocket. Stanley hadn't noticed this movement.

It might come in handy, Leon was thinking, in case something went wrong, in case Stanley suspected something with the brandy. Leon made it a rule to never carry firearms, but now it made him feel easier. After all, he was going to kill a man, and the carrying of the gun somehow made it seem all the more official.

He opened the locked drawer and drew out the bottle of brandy.

"What've you got there, old boy? A bit of the grog?"

"What's it look like, kid? It's brandy. Felix gave it to me from the bar. It's supposed to be something rare, something special." He smiled appreciatively at his own morbid joke.

Stanley looked indifferent, as if he had other, more important, things occupying his mind. "I want to have a talk with you first chance you have. I feel it's about time we cleaned out the attic, dusted away some of the cobwebs up there, get a few important things settled between us. You understand?"

"Like my future?" Leon asked pleasantly.

"You seem terribly jolly, Leon. That's not like you."

There was a too-bright glint in Leon's eyes. He smiled stiffly. "Is it a crime to feel jolly? I had a big load taken off my back tonight and I feel better now than I have in months."

Stanley looked at Leon closely for a moment, then shrugged. He slapped Leon on the shoulder and bit the exotic black cigarette between his teeth. "You know, Leon, you're not such a bad sport. I think I'm going to have a ball with our little chat tonight."

Leon was enjoying himself immensely. He flashed his pasted-on smile. "Well, Stanley, you sound like you might have an ace up your sleeve. Sounds like you've been second-carding me."

"Perhaps I have, old boy. You see, I've been chatting with Roger Dolan down in Vegas. No, not just now when you came in—but earlier." He paused dramatically. "I've got a few things to tell you. You might call it a message from the top...."

Leon let that pass. It was after ten and he had to leave. Stanley said that he would drop down into the hole later on, about half an hour. Leon nodded. Nagel was going to die. He grinned, tucked the brandy bottle under his arm, and started down the corridor toward the elevator.

Stanley didn't need a key for the elevator. He already had one, the same as he had everything else.

Artie scowled under the fluorescent light and hitched his shoulders. Doesn't he ever say anything? Leon wondered. He inserted the key and swung open the door. The others filed into the cage. Leon paused, frowned, pointed to the roof of the elevator cage. "Look at that up there, Benny."

"What's that, Mr. Bertuzzi?"

"What do you mean, what's that? Take a look."

"Looks like the light flickered," Benny said.

Leon scowled. "That's right. I want things to run smooth around here. You'd better replace that bulb first chance you get. Tell the janitor about it."

"Yes, sir."

The machinery hummed and the elevator descended into the hole. The automatic door slid open and locked into place. Leon flicked on the light. He set the brandy on top of his desk in the count room and sat tiredly in the padded swivel chair.

The hole was always quiet, always a bit cool. He had generally been able to relax for a moment in the restful hush of the concrete tomb.

He waited until Max opened the safe. The thick steel circle swung noiselessly on the polished hinges. There was a whirring sound, then a click, as Max opened the slot chute box and the wide panel that enclosed the spare currency cabinets. Charlie and Nels wheeled out the heavy catch cart and went to work. Max sat at the executive desk opposite Leon and removed the black dustcloth from the green-and-chrome adding machinery. He opened the ledger book and removed his coat. Leon noticed that Max wore old-fashioned arm garters.

The only sounds now were the click-hiss of the machine and the soft ruffling of banknotes at the count bench.

Leon wearily closed his eyes. He watched the brassy colored blobs and spangles behind his lids. He wondered what it was that Stanley had to tell him.

Was it all over? Had Roger Dolan told Nagel to let him know he was through? No, not that. He was too old and too faithful an employee to be given the word that he was being sent out to pasture by a small-time punk like Nagel. No, when his time came, he would be told by the top man himself, by Mr. Vince, or maybe by Roger Dolan. Not a Nagel.

So, if that wasn't the answer, what? Maybe it was to simply tell him that Stanley was, from now on, going to receive a greater cut of the profits. Bitterly, he accepted that idea.

If Stanley was to get a bigger piece of Leon's end, what did he do to deserve it? What the hell did Stanley Nagel do around Skyline? Ride a goddam horse with his wife, go to bed with her, drink free Scotch at the bar—that's all he ever did. Was it fair that he should get a raise in the percentage for doing that?

It was all so tiring and confusing. Lately Leon was always tired and confused. Quite often he felt the edges of his mind slipping into something like a black, red-tinged cloud. And, at those times, he almost welcomed it. He became more irritated now, more confused than before. He tried desperately to erase the image of Stanley rising in his place but it was a difficult thing to do.

Nagel—Nagel—Nagel—the name tolled in his mind. That punk would get his tonight. And if the brandy failed then Leon would shoot him the way he would shoot a diseased dog.

Meanwhile there was work to be done. There was the money to be counted and distributed, the gambling profits that would see their way to the organization in Vegas, then to New York, and from there perhaps to Italy or to other points to enlarge the power of the organization.

Thinking of it in exactly that light always made Leon feel warm inside. He felt that he was a definite part of the organization. In spite of his relatively small California role, he felt that he was indeed a necessary and important wheel in the vast apparatus that strangled and milked and collected and grew fat on the money of others and spent money to grow even more powerful. That was the dream that he had nurtured in the old days when the small, squabbling gangs were first combining to create the organization—and now it was a reality. He felt proud knowing that he had been instrumental in its birth and its growth.... A man had to belong to something, something that he could look to with pride. He had to have a child, a machine, a business, something that performed in his image. He had to leave his mark.

He became aware of the comforting sounds. There were the occasional slaps of currency packets being transferred to the adding desk, the ruffling of money, the low murmurings from the count bench.

It was peaceful and quiet. And still, deep with Leon, he could feel the great beast that was his madness coiled and poised, waiting for Nagel. Without opening his eyes he took out a tranquilizing pill and swallowed it. He crossed his arms and bowed his head, listening, feeling, waiting.

There was a sound, an unnatural thump.

He lazily opened his eyes, half-expecting to see a few dropped money packets in the center of the floor. He was half-expecting to chew out Charlie or Nels for their clumsiness.

But there were no packets on the floor. All in a second, he saw Max and the two counters as if they had suddenly become a monstrous photograph. There was a look of absolute horror on their faces. Leon turned toward the elevator cage. His face became suddenly gray as the blood drained from it.

When he was a child, his mother had told him old stories of night things, crawling black things that lurked up in the hills, higher among the rocks than the bandits, evil, devilish things that visited only once; he remembered the tales of the black angels, the ones who had fought at Lucifer's side, wielding the black swords against the greater angels— the figures of death. He was faced now with one of these phantoms— an angel of death....

Then he shook his head and the childish vision evaporated, draining into the recesses of memory.

The figure that stood at the mouth of the elevator cage was wearing a long black cloak, a dark hat, a black mask with grotesque eyeholes, shapeless black slippers, black leather gloves. The figure was also holding a sawed-off shotgun at waist level, covering the count room. He looked like a cloaked demon, a wizard who had appeared magically from thin air. Then Leon saw the equipment bundles drop into the elevator from the overhead trap-door. Then another figure, dressed the same as the first but taller and thinner, followed the bundles.

The first clear thought that flashed in Leon's mind was the fact that he was, for the first time in years, carrying a gun.

The tall figure carried only a revolver. He picked up the two bundles and moved into the room. No one spoke. Leon could detect the sharp odor of sweat about him.

The entire scene—the two black figures, the frosty white faces of Charlie, Nels, and Max—seemed too quiet and carefully-acted, too theatrical to be real. Charlie and Nels stood with their backs jammed against the count bench. Max, if it were possible, was paler than usual, looking as if he had been whitewashed; the usually owlish eyes were glazed and slightly crossed with intense fear.

Leon raised his hands; the others followed his example. Max raised his so high that he seemed to be standing on tiptoe. So far no one had spoken a word. Then the short figure—slightly stooped, older-seeming, slower-moving—spoke to Leon in a deep grating voice. There was no fear in it, and none of the cheap dramatics of the nervous amateur.

"You, Bertuzzi. Get away from the desk."

"Where do I stand?"

"Over there." He waved at Max's desk with the shotgun. Leon stepped to Max's side, hands still raised. The situation was taking shape his mind. He carefully studied the movements of the two black figures. He noticed nothing familiar about them. All that he could tell was that they were professionals. He had seen enough like them during his life to know. And these two were very good indeed. He watched them, detached and almost admiring them, and he didn't move a muscle. He wasn't particularly afraid now. His strained heart had lost its irregular beat and a bit of color had returned to his face.

They had come through the trap door in the elevator cage. But how, he wondered, had they come to be in the elevator shaft? Had Artie or Benny Coca planned this? Had they allowed the two gunmen to pass through the steel door? No, that was ridiculous because only Leon had access to the key ... but no, there was Stanley. He had a key. But how could Stanley have managed to get his accomplices past Benny and Artie? It was becoming more puzzling as he thought of it. He began to imagine all sorts of enormous plots. Were Artie and Benny on Nagel's side? Did the entire group plan this to insure his downfall?

Was this simply some monstrous plot intended to break him? Were they *all* against him? His heart began to thump wildly again. His thoughts whipped into the whirlpool of suspicion and blind hatred. All that he suspected seemed as impossible as the presence of the two black figures.

The short figure picked up a denim bag and opened the drawers in Leon's desk, looking, presumably, for weapons. Then he picked up the bottle of brandy. Leon held his breath. The short one looked at the label and grunted. Perhaps he was even smiling behind his mask. He dropped the bottle into the bottom of the bag and slid it across the floor to the tall one with the revolver. The short one searched Max's desk, then, apparently satisfied, stood once again in the center of the room and covered them with the shotgun.

Leon swallowed. They seemed to be deliberately fouling his plan to murder. They had stolen the brandy. The fools. The simple fools. Leon's professional fellow-feeling for the gunmen almost moved him to warn them about the brandy. No, let them have it. One swallow of that and ...

The tall one was quickly scooping the currency from the bench. It had taken less than two minutes so far. Their motions were quick and smooth. They seemed to know exactly where everything was. The tall piles of green were disappearing from the top of the bench. The one yellow case already sealed was broken open, the contents dumped into the bag. The other yellow cases were looked into.

Leon was feeling feverish now. His black eyes burned with near madness. *What about Nagel?* How was he supposed to rid himself of his tormentor? Could he shoot him? Why not? Why should he wallow at the cowardly level of a simple poisoning? He was made of sterner stuff than that. He had no real fear of punishment. He would simply gun down his opponent. It was more direct that way, more real, as the strangling of Big Charlie Eagan in 1927 had been direct and real.

Let them have the brandy, let them knock themselves off, Leon still had the gun. He could get rid of Nagel's body far out in the ocean … *watching the shoes slip into the glossy black water, the rising bubbles, salty cobwebs the grave marker….*

The tall one finished taking the money from the catch cart. Leon's straying attention returned to the more immediate problem that confronted him. He frowned. *Why hadn't he been watching?* He was being robbed. He had to realize this. What were the organization, Mr. Vince, Dolan, going to say? This had never happened in all his years of operating clubs. It seemed incredible that anyone could have the audacity to consider, much less execute, a plot against the organization. Did they actually believe they could get away with it? Were there still fools like that left in the world?

It seemed that there were fools like that, for the two gunmen were now busy scooping money into the two denim bags. Leon watched the green packets. He wondered how much he would lose. A quarter-million? Three hundred thousand? He recalled that this month had been a particularly good one. It must be better than a quarter-million. Of course, he realized bitterly, this figure represented his own savings and the restaurant take, as well as the gambling gross.

"Look—" Max West croaked.

"Keep quiet," the short one said.

"I don't want to … die. Look … I've got a little girl—"

"We're hardly murderers," the short one answered. "We only came for the money."

Max nodded, continued to shake.

Leon relaxed. No, these two weren't murderers. How many professional thieves were? There was no reason for them to start blasting away. He saw the rolls on the floor—wire and tape. They would simply be bound and gagged.

The tall figure finished cleaning out the safe. Both bags were filled and drawn shut. The short one looked at his old-fashioned pocket watch. Then he ordered Charlie and Nels to kneel. The tall one bound them with the wire and taped their mouth and eyes with the friction tape. They repeated the binding with Max West. Then, just as they were about to turn to Leon, they both whirled and faced the elevator.

There was a humming sound, like a muffled harmonica. The door of the elevator slid shut. The interior light rose beyond the wirenet glass of the viewing window in the outer door.

Leon felt the hard stab of the revolver muzzle in his ribs. There was fear in the voice of the tall one. The short one had gone almost rigid, the shotgun poised. The elevator leaving obviously hadn't been a part of their plans. They hadn't known about Stanley having a key.

"Who's that, Bertuzzi? Who's coming!"

"My partner—"

"Your *what?*"

"His name is Stanley Nagel." He narrowed his eyes, controlling himself with difficulty. A sudden, wild thought had come to him. The unsteady pendulum of sanity had swung the other way, hesitantly at first. He said, "You'd better let me get back to that desk. When the door opens and I'm not there he'll get suspicious. And if he shuts that steel door and goes back up you'll be through."

The short one looked curiously at him. Through the clumsy holes in the mask Leon saw a pair of hard gray eyes, scarred at the edges with deep age lines. The eyes nodded.

Leon sat at his desk. He realized, without caring, that once he saw Stanley he would no longer be responsible for his actions. He would do what he had to do, and Nagel would die. He knew what would happen then, but it didn't matter....

The elevator whirred to a stop at the main floor level.

It snapped inside him. The tension whirled around. He felt like a god, executioner, judge, prosecutor. All the wrongs of his past became pure and white. The snap inside drove him quietly mad. The black, red-tinged cloud descended. All the bitterness and fury of his life raced in his veins. His forehead glittered with perspiration. The pistol was heavy in his jacket pocket. His hands twitched uncontrollably.

So, he was going to be pushed out was he? He was going to be squeezed by a punk kid with a crew haircut, a smart college boy with bright blue eyes who had stolen Leon's wife, his job, his possessions, and now, most likely, was thirsting for his life.

The two black figures were pressed against the opposite wall. The elevator hadn't started down yet.

Leon's hatred for Stanley burned, consuming him. He saw his fears creeping down from the hills, higher than the bandits, the black swords poised with black robes flowing, pushing him into a corner, stripping him, robbing him.... *Nagel ... Nagel ... Nagel ...* He saw a never-ending legion of bright young punks with grinning masks, pushing Leon out, shoving their way into the organization. *They had no right to be there!* They had not brought it to birth or trained its growth. These punks knew nothing of the filth and hardships of the old days. *They had no respect.* (The elevator began to hum again.) They knew only bright shiny new law offices and ivy league colleges. They hadn't risen through pain and sadness. They hadn't fought face to face to gain possession. No, they just made love to Leon's wife! Buttered the Vegas crowd! Demanded a bigger share of Leon's profits!

The steel elevator door slid open.

Now.

Perhaps Leon had indeed consumed himself, eaten the insulation from his sanity; he stood now naked and primitive with a pistol in his hand.

"You punk! You faceless bastard!"

Stanley saw the pistol before the two gunmen could do anything about it. He ducked, clutching for his own small automatic just as Leon squeezed the trigger and began to laugh, unreal, high-pitched. The gun continued to fire and Stanley spun in the cage, red flowers blossoming on his shirt front. Stanley's only return shot caught Leon directly in the stomach. He dropped the revolver, fell back, stumbled, slid heavily to his knees. The pain bit sharply into him. He smiled knowingly to the concrete floor. The acrid cloud of gunsmoke boiled like mist in the sudden silence. There were no sounds from above. The concrete hole had absorbed the noise of the shots. Stanley's body twitched only once. Leon sagged. The dark patches under his eyes were like soot patches. His skin was like snow.

He had killed again. Again. He had ridden himself of his tormentor. He was back on top. He was borne again through the air on the magic murderous wings through the purple-and-yellow Victorian hallway to the smoldering incinerator. He wasn't dead. He was still alive. The pain wrenched at his breath, trying to rob him. And, just as he was drifting into warm unconsciousness, he muttered softly to himself. *Big Charlie Eagan....*

The black figures came to life. They scrambled for the elevator, carrying the swollen denim bags around their necks. Using Stanley's body for a platform they hoisted themselves up into the gloomy quiet of the oil-smelling shaft. The long rope ladder dangled against the wall.

11

It was this way every time. His hands shook and his knees felt cold.

He hunched in the grubby darkness of the Pontiac's trunk, conscious of the stale odors of rubber and oil and dirt, of the sweaty bulk of Frank Toschi next to him. The face mask itched. With each jolt of the car his cramped position became more torturing. His skin felt feverish and damp, his heart thudded hard against the wall of his chest, the hatband acted like a leather vise against his temples. Suspense and tension were gnawing at him. And still, as he always had after the other times, he felt both weakened and relieved.

He listened for familiar sounds, felt the vibrating trunk deck for familiar movements: the hollow echo as the car rumbled through the covered bridge, the pause at the highway crossing, and, finally, the slow left swing as they headed north.

He pressed his shoulder against the cardboard separation. He waited until he was positive they had passed through town, then, when he felt the car resume speed, he grunted loudly and nudged Frank Toschi.

Karl had been badly shaken by the shooting in the hole. When he had climbed the rope ladder past the corridor door he had experienced an overpowering sense of fear and weakness which held him frozen momentarily to the rope rungs. The only sounds had been their heavy breathing amplified in the gloomy concrete shaft. Then, after a long minute, he had been able to place hand above hand on the shaking rungs and gain the cable-wheel shack at the third floor. He had been dazed still—so, he had seen, was Frank. The shooting had happened too quickly, too unexpectedly ... like a dream.

In the trunk, they were both still sweating freely from their scramble across the Skyline roof and their quick but careful descent down the big tree. The jumble of equipment pressed against them, bunched against their faces, practically suffocating them. The swollen denim bags whispered soothing papery sighs under the weight of their bodies. The Pontiac took a curve with a faint whine. Karl's buttocks slid into the spare-tire scoop and the protruding frame bolt jabbed painfully into the small of his back. The black duster was like a hot damp sheet. He was sweating inside his gloves.

The air became closer. He thought how wonderful it would be to have a cold beer, something biting, something that would rake his dry, grimy mouth with icy bubbly fingers. An ice-cold beer. It was strange that he should think of beer at a time like this. He should be thinking of escape. He should be fearing for his life. But all he could think of was cold beer.

He pushed hard against the rear seat until it gave way. The fresh air that rushed through the widening crack tasted incredibly clean and sweet. He stretched his body until head and shoulders were through the crack. He lifted his buttocks from the scoop and massaged the sore spot in his back. He breathed the air. The thought of beer left him. He thought of the piles of money that rustled under him.

Frank Toschi chuckled softly, as if he were enjoying a private joke. Karl began to laugh as well. The joke, after all, was one to be shared. They had beaten the organization, and, for once, the law wasn't going to be after them for having committed a crime.

"Are you back there?" Louis asked.

"Yes."

"Did it go right?"

"It went right," Karl answered.

"Hell," Frank said quietly, "it went better than that. It went righter than right."

They crawled through the rear seat under the back rest and pulled the equipment and denim bags after them. Karl checked the trunk to make sure that nothing remained. Then, quickly and without words, they removed their slippers, dusters, waist belts, and masks. They didn't take off their gloves.

They built a single large bundle with the loose equipment and bound it together with the longer ladder. They pushed the seat back into position and remained crouched on the floor, their knees pulled up close to their chests. It was still cramped, with the heavy bundle between them, but the air was better. Toschi lit a mentholated cigarette, took one long drag, then passed it to Karl.

It had the air of a toast. The smoke tasted cool. Karl's hands were still shaking. He noticed that Frank's thin face had a pasty, worried look to it. But they were both quiet, the excitement and panic wearing off. Louis coughed once to clear his throat but said nothing. Karl wondered what the others were thinking. For that matter, what was he thinking? It seemed to him that he hadn't had a single clear thought other than cold beer. How strange. Why didn't he think of the money, of his victory, of his having won after the many years of thinking and scheming?

"How do you feel?" he asked Toschi.

"Tired. Kind of shook up. We both froze on that ladder. I thought sure as hell they must have heard the shooting—" He shrugged and made a noncommittal face.

"What shooting?" Louis asked. There was an edge to his voice.

Karl explained what had happened, speaking as briefly as he could. When he finished, Louis asked him with a whisper if he was kidding him. No, Karl answered, he wasn't kidding him. It had happened exactly as he had told it. Louis simply said, "Jesus," then became quiet.

Karl didn't understand it himself. He knew *what* had happened, but he hadn't the slightest idea *why* it had happened. He hadn't expected anything like that. It had happened too violently, too quickly, for him to grasp what had gone on.

Bertuzzi had, after all, been carrying a gun all the time they had been in the hole. Karl should have searched them. And the young fellow, Bertuzzi's so-called partner, had come down in the elevator. There had been a brief, insane exchange of gunfire. The kid in the elevator had gone down and so had Bertuzzi. Karl could still hear Bertuzzi laughing as he pulled the trigger. Then, after the last shot had finished echoing, Karl and Frank had made a run for it. Something close to panic had infected them. What else could they do?

"Where are we now?" Karl asked.

"Just passing Kovall's place."

Karl knelt on the floor and peered out the window. The car gathered more speed. The leaves flickered under the sweeping yellow lights, the road markers winked red on the small white posts. A truck rumbled noisily past, going south, and drove a gush of warm air into the car. The rig lights burned amber and red and the black Diesel stack spit out brilliant little sparks of flying gold. The Pontiac slowed for another bend in the road.

"You know," Louis said, "that waiter back there in Skyline put me at a table practically right on top of Bertuzzi and that accountant. Bertuzzi looked kind of beat, like a real old man. It was all I could to eat my meal without staring at the guy."

"What'd you order?" Frank asked.

"A steak. Just a steak. I should of asked for a pheasant under glass, or something like that. But I couldn't think. I've never been in a place like that before. So what do I do? I order a plain old steak. But it was like butter, like hot butter that tasted like a steak."

"I don't know why I should be," Frank said quietly, "but I'm hungry. I could eat a horse."

Five miles north of the San Hacienda County line they pulled to the shoulder of the road and carried the money bags to the Studebaker across the highway, pointed south. There was no traffic. The crickets seemed noisier now that they were away from the town and the cabin areas. The forest seemed blacker. Karl felt a need for haste, but didn't have to say anything to the others; the car switch was done quickly and without words. Again, Louis drove, and Frank crouched in the rear with Karl.

When they crossed the line Louis said, "We're over," then was silent. The Studebaker slowed a few miles later and made the right turn onto the jeep road going west. The darkness closed around them. The rough, winding road forced Louis to gear down on the steep, rutted drops.

In spite of everything, Karl found himself relaxing. He thought about the shooting back in the hole, but it made so little sense that he soon abandoned it. By now he was fairly convinced that Bertuzzi had cracked under the strain and had started shooting wildly without thinking of who he had been aiming at. The young fellow's returning fire had been automatic. Either way, there was nothing Karl could do about it now, so he settled back, lit another cigarette and watched the black leafy wall pass his window.

Toschi sat huddled in the opposite corner, rubbing his hands thoughtfully. Louis drove slowly and surely, taking the unknown winding road as easily as if it were a paved highway. The spray from the headlights wobbled crazily to the trees and down to the road again as the Studebaker jounced over the deep ruts and pits. The engine whined in the low gear.

The knotted tension seeped from Karl. The warmth stole back into his knees. He was surprised to find that his hands no longer shook.

"This would be a fine place to have a flat," Frank said.

"Don't think about things like that," Karl answered.

It was all over. They were going to be safe now. Karl had planned it very well. He had milked Larry Con for every eagerly-given drop of information. He had pieced it together, had thought of several possibilities, weighed them, and had pulled it off as best as he had been able. Of course, he couldn't know of everything that could possibly happen. There were always a few unexpected twists with each job. But, in spite of those, he had succeeded. And now he felt that it was the right time for him to retire. His age flooded through him. And, like an actor who had been performing a role intended for a much younger man, he was relieved now that the curtain had fallen on the last act. There was still the escape, of course, but he felt that the greater part of it was over and that he was going to be safe.

His emotions were elusive, unclear. They were a hundred and one small colors that entered and left a tiny mark, building a pattern that was more like a taste than a thought.

He felt no guilt about what he had done. He had hurt no one. If you took what belonged to someone else, that was a crime, yes. But there were other questions involved. To whom did the Skyline money actually belong? What crime had he committed? The law wouldn't be hunting him for anything; so he had committed no crime against society. He hadn't *stolen* the money from society—he had simply transferred it from a set of crooks to ... another set of crooks....

He had committed a crime; and then again, he hadn't. It depended entirely on how you looked at it—.

Louis braked the Studebaker. Karl came to life and picked up the shotgun from the seat beside him. Frank Toschi pulled the revolver from his jacket pocket.

"We're not out of it yet," Louis said fearfully.

"Take it easy," Karl whispered.

"But—"

"Just stop and act natural. It's not a road block."

At the base of the short slope they were descending there was a tiny point of light swinging back and forth. The light grew brighter when they approached and they saw a square cabin light through the trees on the right. A figure stood in the center of the road, swinging a warning red lantern. The Studebaker stopped several yards from the temporary shack half-hidden in the pines. The signalman was tall and sunburned and wore a checked yellow shirt and a silver helmet. He stood in the glare of the headlights. His heavy boots crunched on the dirt. Frank and Karl put the guns out of sight. Louis rolled down his side window.

"What's up?" Louis asked.

"Howdy, there," the signalman said cheerfully. His face was wrinkled with age cobwebs and he wore shell-rimmed glasses. When he grinned, he showed long yellow teeth. "We're pulling out a damaged piece of equipment 'bout half a mile down the road, so's if you'll wait a few minutes until we get it up here, then I'll flag you right on through." He peered into the car, bending to see. "Not many folks come along this way."

"What kind of equipment you pulling out?" Karl asked.

"Cat. Slid off during the rain, green driver, skinned right off the hill a piece down there. You'll see it, left a big track bite where it slipped. It's a pretty tricky turn and in the rain it was kinda rough goin'. It just slipped." He chuckled softly to himself, then squinted into the car again. "You fellas come far?"

"We're heading back to work," Karl said. "The gravel works down on the coast."

"Carter's?"

"Yep. I'm foreman down there."

"Well, I'll try not to hold you boys up. Soon as they get that machine up I'll give you the word."

"Okay, thanks."

The signalman waved a gnarled brown hand and walked back to the tiny yellow shack. He set the lantern in the center of the road.

"How long do you think it'll be?" Louis asked.

"Not very long," Karl answered absently. He could already hear the straining whine of a truck motor far down on the road.

"I'd like to be in San Francisco right now," Frank said.

"So would I," Karl said.

"You think those two counters and that accountant are still tied up?"

"Probably. And even if they aren't, we're still all right. We won't be here another five minutes. And it'll probably take the truck and the cat a half hour or better to get up onto the man highway. And when they're past us and going up the mountain no other car coming down will be able to pass it."

"Then it kind of seals us off from San Hacienda."

"That's it," Karl said.

"But what if the cops radio ahead to the next county? Cops can be waiting for us at the bottom of the mountain, maybe even all along the coast highway."

"No they won't," Karl said. "If they put out an alarm for us they'll have to give a damn good reason. If the cops from another county, or even the state police, pick us up the whole San Hacienda Force falls into hot water. The D.A. up there would probably even get tossed into the clink. How could they explain our having a quarter-million dollars? They couldn't say we'd robbed the bank, then the FBI would be called in. They can't say we heisted Skyline restaurant, because of all this dough." He chuckled quietly. "Hell, they can't even say we're driving too fast or without tail-lights. We'd be searched and the money found."

Some of the color returned to Frank's thin face and he smiled. "You sure figured it, Karl. I got to hand it to you."

"Larry Con gets some of the credit, too."

"Sure, but you did the figuring."

They were silent. After a minute they could see the approaching lights of the truck that was hauling up the cat. Frank began to whistle happily.

"I'm not so hungry anymore," he said. "But I wish I had a drink."

It was then that Karl remembered. There had been an unusual bottle of brandy, probably quite rare, on Bertuzzi's desk, and he had dropped it into the bag as an afterthought. He opened one of the bags, buried his hand in the money, and groped about for the bottle. The packets rustled, felt fat under his thick fingers.

The noise of the truck was coming closer, the lights larger and more glaring. The yellow-shirted signalman stepped from the temporary cabin and stood by the lantern with his back to the car.

Karl gave up on the first bag, muttered that it must be in the second one, and closed the end with the laundry cord. Frank opened the second bag; it was closer to him. He felt the outside of the bag and rapped his knuckle against the bottle.

"It's in this one, all right," he said, and started to dip into the money.

The signalman swung the lantern and walked toward the car.

"Put away the bag, Frank," Karl whispered.

The signalman chuckled again. "Here she is. Didn't take as long's I figured. Sorry to've held you boys up."

"That's all right," Louis said.

The truck rumbled slowly by, dragging the huge yellow cat with a thick chain. The track bite plowed up the road. A Negro worker with a silver helmet and a Van Dyke beard came out of the shed and jumped on the running board of the truck. The two machines passed and the signalman waved the lantern again. Louis started the motor and drove out onto the road. They passed the spot where the cat had missed the bend and had skidded off the slick wet shoulder and tipped into the deep ditch.

They drove slowly, taking the turns with extra care. Once Karl saw a bright pair of raccoon eyes watching them from the side of the road, caught in the glare of the lights. Farther down, they saw a doe leap the road. There were no road markers or signs, but Karl figured that they must be halfway to the ocean highway.

He settled back a second time and closed his eyes. No one spoke, but there was the feeling of tired victory in the air. He removed his hat and pressed his face against the cool of the side window.

He felt, for the first time in many years, completely free. He was dead tired and he was becoming thoughtful, but still, he felt completely free. He had nothing to fear from the law, from society—and not much to fear from the underworld either.

"This's a rough road," Louis said.

Karl and Frank didn't answer him. Karl barely heard him. The dash glow illuminated Louis' features with a sickly greenish glow and Karl was vaguely reminded of the Louis who had stood under the cabin light, frightened, like a child, of the fog and the forest. It all seemed long ago, even Skyline seemed far away to him now.

He remembered the creek behind the Kovall cabin on the hill. Other questions came to mind. Why had he been torturing himself with his past that afternoon?

He had a frighteningly clear vision of himself by the creek. He saw his high-topped shoes, snow-white hair, old-fashioned pocket watch, the sun sparkling on the clear water, his aged hands folded over his stomach, his head rolling sleepily on his chest. Like an old man on a park bench. A tired old man.

What had he tried to find in his past? Why had he been so frightened upon hearing the voice of his father?

"What do you want to become when you grow up, Karl?"

He realized now that it hadn't been the hearing of the words themselves that had frightened him. It had been something else. He had feared what they meant to him now, what they implied. He knew what they meant:

"What have you become now that you have grown up, Karl?"
"When are you going to grow up, Karl?"
Either way, he had puzzled in fear and shame over those simple words. He had been deeply ashamed to discover that he had failed his father, his wife and his son, that he had indeed spent fourteen long years of his life in prison, and that he had accomplished all too little during his life.

He had been afraid, unknown or denied to himself, to commit yet another crime. He hadn't honestly wanted to start it again, but, he had told himself, this particular job was the big one, and would take a real master to pull it off. No young kid could do it. Only old Karl Heisler.

And he had convinced himself with the same fancies and excuses that had served him so easily as a young man, the same foolish lies that had hurt him in his confused past. The Indiana night ride in the new Packard had been a shameful night for him, not a romantic memory as he liked to believe. *"Me? I'm a salesman."* And later, his arrest in Illinois—all these had haunted him, warned him.

But the fancies of youth had won him over, had overshadowed the shames and the fears. He had known all along that he was no longer a young man, not even a good fifty-four—prison and failure had taken too much from him. And still he had denied himself the memories of his father, the responsibilities toward his family. In spite of his sadness, his forebodings, he had executed the robbery. He had listened to his memories, to his conscience. He had ignored everything and everybody.

But now, what was right? What was wrong? Why didn't he feel guilty?

It was over, that much he knew. And now he was deeply relieved and grateful to find that, with honesty as he felt it, inside himself, he hadn't committed a crime in the true sense after all. Society was no longer a body for him to hide from. He was a free man. He had only the forces of the organization to hide from. And to that he merely smiled. He didn't care about the organization, about the underworld. He was through with it. The roles had been reversed. There would be no more demons now....

Karl was at last a quiet old man with thick white hair, grizzled weathered flesh, and high-topped shoes. He tasted the warm forest air that came through the window. There was a break in the trees now and he saw that the wax moon was still in the sky, dimpled with gray craters and seeming close enough to touch with an outstretched hand. The entire scene, vast and moonlit, looked like a steel engraving, so clear and sharp. Far away the jet-blue silk of ocean shimmered and glittered under the white moon-bath. Karl contented his thoughts with Edna and little Karl.

He was going home. It was over. He had climbed the big tree high into the sky and had taken the golden goose that the man-eating giant had stolen. And now he had cut the tree and had trapped the giant in the sky....

"You want me to dig up that bottle now?" Frank whispered.

"Not right now," Karl answered absently. "We're almost there."

Benny Coca bent noiselessly on one knee and looked over his shoulder to the others that stood by the couch in the darkened room. Dr. Sheldon gave a brief nod and Benny touched Leon's shoulder gently. Artie stood silently against one wall, hitching his shoulders and looking suspiciously at Loren Snyder, Leon's hand-picked district attorney. Benny nudged Leon again, whispering. "How do you feel, Mr. Bertuzzi? Can you talk now? Mr. Snyder and Artie say they have to talk to you...."

Leon coughed and half opened his eyes. What were they all talking about? Wasn't the pain in him great enough? He said, "Lousy." Then he glared up to the ceiling at the acoustical squares.

Always before he had been convinced that there was no pattern to the punctured dots in the squares, that they had been punched at random and without a pattern in mind. But now, at last, he knew better. He saw that they had a pattern after all, but had been set on the ceiling in such a way to confuse. Each square had a series of three dots in one corner, then a blank, followed by one dot, a blank, and two more dots. It was the same on each acoustical square.

"Everything's a fake," he whispered drowsily, painfully. "Even the goddam ceiling's a fake. You can't count on anything. There's a lousy pattern to it." He turned his head and looked at old Sheldon, who still wore his John B. Stetson hat and string tie. Leon said, "How am I? No, don't answer that, you lousy fake...."

He sighed and the sound bubbled deep in his throat. He coughed again. He ignored everyone in the room. He thought wistfully of Janet, of the pennies on the bottom of his sixty-thousand-dollar wishing well, of Big Charlie Eagan, of his set-up in Nevada, the set-up in Dade County, of his dark-eyed mother telling him of the crawly night things that lived in the hills higher than the bandits.... He looked to Benny Coca. "Did I get him?"

"Stanley? Yeah, sure, Mr. Bertuzzi, riddled him like cheese."

"Good. Guy tried to out-squeeze me, take everything. Yeah, well ... I showed him."

Why was it so dark?

He tried to sit up but he couldn't move, was too weak, too weak. What had happened to his strength? Where was Jane? Why didn't she bring him his breakfast? *Where was his hoop?* He had left it right there in the street. The neighborhood kids probably stole it. The Greeks, or Irish, or maybe the Jewboys got it. They stole his hoop. And his mother told him what would happen to them....

He forced his eyes open and the other men in the room noticed that the whites looked blurred, as if something had tried to erase them. His face was doughy and his carefully concealed bald spot was exposed. He looked small and pitiful. His stomach was bound but there was a great deal of lost blood on his silk suit.

"I got that bastard Stanley."

Snyder knelt at his side. His eyes were colorless behind the steel-rim glasses. "You said something about brandy, Mr. Bertuzzi. You poisoned a bottle of brandy for Stanley to drink. You said it had been on the desk and that the gunmen had taken it by accident."

"That's it," Leon said, his voice far away. "Here, Stanley, take a drink with your old pal."

"The organization has to know, Mr. Bertuzzi. They took the brandy with them?"

"Lemme alone, Snyder. Get out ..."

"I have to know about that brandy, Bertuzzi."

So, they had dropped the "Mister" already. He brought his mind back to the brandy. He said that if the gunmen took one sip, to congratulate themselves, one sip, then they would be dead in just a few minutes. He asked Benny to tell Roger Dolan to watch for the buzzards in the sky, and that Leon Bertuzzi hadn't missed a payment in twenty-five years. Then he looked vague and uneasy and he asked what difference it really made. He was dying. And somehow it didn't matter about the payment.

Snyder looked worried, perspiration shined on his brow, and he worked his lips nervously over his slightly protruding teeth. He clutched at Leon's shoulders, shaking him, bringing him to consciousness again. "But what if they *don't* take the drink! No one says they have to, Bertuzzi! What if they don't drink *any* of it? What'm I supposed to tell Roger Dolan?"

Leon started to laugh to himself, then, when it became too painful, he smiled shyly. He remembered a small boy. His voice was barely a whisper. "Then it looks like they'd get away with it, don't it?"

He sagged slowly back onto the soft leather of the couch and his eyes drooped shut as he felt the dark night people, higher than the bandits in the hills, come for him and wrap their cloaks about him. Then it was quiet.

THE END

The Savage Breast
JOHN TRINIAN

Book I — Fitzroy

1

It rained twice during the night, and she had listened with closed eyes. The rain whispered against the window panes, and, again, she felt the dark presence of madness threatening her; lurking on the rain-splattered balcony, crouched in the cool shadows of the room.

She finished the rest of the first bottle of Scotch, hardly noticing it. The madness told her that she must come to a decision; that she could put it off no longer. Already she was beginning to feel that she no longer belonged to herself.

When the night passed the sky turned a soft April blue, the light pressed gently into the stone-colored shadows of the city, and the madness that was indecision burned away with the coming of the dawn. She knew what had to be done.

She stood now on the long balcony, watching the sky, holding onto her highball glass as if she were afraid she might drop it. The dark tiles were damp against her naked feet. Her skin was feverish, diamond beads of perspiration glittered on her temples, her eyes were bright and glassy, her lips slightly parted.

She was young, not quite twenty-four, but she was cursed with a suspicion that the greater part of life was behind her, that she had no true identity, that she belonged to no particular time or place. As she paced the balcony she watched the sky as if she expected it to do something other than grow lighter, and when she tried a swallow from her drink she could barely taste the Scotch. She was drunk. Drunk at dawn—but it meant nothing to her. She stood before the dark windowpanes seeing her reflection, seeming unreal to herself, as if she were wearing some sort of disguise.

Her hair was dyed champagne gray, worn long and coil-piled in a casual acorn shape—loose swirls of ice-white and steel and mist. Her large doe-shaped eyes were pale green, framed with dark natural brows and long sooty lashes. She knew that she was a beautiful girl, but her beauty meant nothing. What did it matter if one was beautiful and one had to live in a cave without light?

She returned to the room.

Before her, in the quiet darkness, Gordon Fitzroy sat stiffly in the black Gothic chair near the brass parrot cage. His cornflower eyes were moist and angry, his cupid mouth tight and colorless, his fingers touching in a tent near the blunt point of his chin. He was thirty years old, handsome, but smudged with a weakness that had always repelled her, even from the beginning. The dawn light brought his figure into a milky blue focus, and she was able to pick out the white of his shirt front, the blond crown of his crewcut, the ice sparkling in his glass.

She knew that he was still afraid to speak to her. He hadn't said a word to her all night. The two of them, Gordon and herself, had remained in the one small room in her apartment since midnight, drinking steadily, not speaking, not sharing the night but simply enduring it.

"Have you ever heard of a man called Harry Dazier?" she asked.

Her voice—her question—seemed to startle him. He blinked at her and rattled the ice in his glass. "No—no I can't say that I have—"

She shrugged. "That's because you're a cluck, Gordon."

He glared. "Well, then, who *is* Harry Dazier?"

"He's a composer."

"Oh—I see."

"No, you don't. You don't see anything."

She returned to the balcony, to the cool air. She had ignored her problem for the past two weeks but she knew what had to be done now—Gordon was finished. He was going to have to leave. She had been afraid of what her father would say—would do—when he found out that her marriage with Gordon had failed, but she realized that her father didn't have to find out. She knew what Gordon was going to suggest. He was going to ask for money to keep it from her father.

She paced the balcony. Airy sprays of fern and bamboo were lined against the elaborate iron railing, and at the far end, near the lacquered wicker furniture, there were the two stone gargoyles, hunchbacked, grotesque, blindly staring out at the city.

The apartment stood twelve stories above the peak of Nob Hill, and below her San Francisco seemed a huge toy city of gray stone, miniature streets, fake little trees. The balcony faced north toward the bay, the green and brown hills of Marin County, the graceful red bridge, the small wooded islands. Other apartment buildings surrounded hers, some old and rich, others new and rich. Hers was one of the newer ones, a white concrete-and-glass shaft of what appeared to be staggered levels, with wide balconies, high windows, eight rooms to the apartment and one apartment to the level.

She removed the ice cubes from her drink and dropped them over the balcony. Bombs away. But it was too shadowy at the street level for her to see them burst on the concrete. She finished her drink, wandered back to the room.

"I don't think I'll be able to make it to work this morning," Gordon said.

"So? I don't think my father will miss you. He can make another goddam million without your help, anyway."

"What I meant to say, D.B., was that if Malcolm calls will you answer the phone for me? You can tell him that I'm ill."

"If Malcolm calls," D.B. said, "I'll simply tell him that you're too drunk to go to work. Malcolm loves honesty."

"He doesn't like drinking," Gordon said.

"My father doesn't like anything that's pleasurable."

"Well, if he calls will you tell him that I'm sick?"

"Of course. Because then I'll be telling the truth. You *are* sick." She refilled her glass and moved to the automatic couch.

"I resent your attitude, D.B."

"I thought that you would."

"Can't you *try* to be civil about this—"

"No. It's not worth it," she said. She removed her robe, piled it carelessly on the floor, and sat on the couch. She was naked but it no longer mattered if Gordon watched her; whatever went through his mind was no longer her concern. She touched a switch and the black leather began to crumple and wheeze as the unseen machinery slowly hoisted and lowered the movable mid-section. She settled back, set her glass on her stomach, and traced moist lazy circles on her skin.

"D.B.?"

"What now?"

"I wanted to ask you if you've come to a decision yet. I mean, do you know what you're going to do?"

"Yes."

"And?"

"Shut up, Gordon. I'm trying to think. I can't think if you're whining."

The couch continued to purr, like some monstrous leather beast, with D.B. Sadder riding its back, going nowhere, just up and down—up and down. Fatigue buzzed against her eyelids, her thoughts were washing slowly back and forth, like wet smoke in a swinging bucket, mixing everything up, confusing her. She felt trapped; needing fresh air, a new life. She was bored. She wanted identity, something—someone—larger, more secure, more real than herself.

What Gordon wanted was easier to understand. He wanted the money. A weird form of alimony. Blackmail. Whatever they called it, Gordon wanted it.

She didn't want to think about it. She allowed the imaginary bucket to slip from her grasp and the confusion of her thoughts splashed free. The couch wheezed, lifting, falling. The sun moved slowly into the sky, slanting lemon rays into the room through the tall French windows.

The trouble had started more than seven months ago when her father, Malcolm Sadder, had said: "It's for your own good, D.B. You've got to get married and settled down once and for all. As I've told you, your Aunt Eva has given me a full account of your behavior in Dublin—No, don't bother to give me an argument, young lady. We've been through all that before. I've thought it over and I've decided that what you need is a husband—"

"I don't think it's that simple, Malcolm," she had said.

D.B. had always wanted to become someone different. As a child she had buried herself in Oz, disguised herself with shoe polish and poster paint for games, worn her father's old clothes. And still she could never become the person, the daughter, that Malcolm wanted. Marjorie, D.B.'s older sister, had been that daughter—but Marjorie had died of leukemia five years ago, on the day before Christmas when D.B. had just turned eighteen.

When she was eight she had had a huge doll house, big enough to crawl into, and she had invited Prentice Wilder, a neighbor boy, to play Charlie McCarthy with her. When her father had caught her with Prentice, both naked, wearing monocles and cardboard silk hats, he had whipped her and said: "You're your mother's daughter!"

Two weeks after her return from Dublin Malcolm had said: "I *order* you to be at the house for dinner, D.B. Don't get the idea that just because I've allowed you to take an apartment away from home gives you any right to stop coming to the house. Do you understand?"

"Yes, of course—"

"Good. Now, this Gordon Fitzroy that I've mentioned is going to be there with his father, Judge Fitzroy. You remember the Judge, don't you? Tall fellow, reddish face, attended your debut. I believe he mentioned having a son in the Navy—Gordon is now a coming young man with one of my firms—Are you listening, D.B.?"

"What? Yes, Malcolm. You were saying about someone named Gordon Fitzroy—"

"Yes. I feel certain—and I hope you understand exactly what I mean by that—I feel certain that you'll find Gordon to your liking—Need I say more?"

"Is this a marriage arrangement, Malcolm?"

"Call it whatever you like. I believe I've made myself clear. The rest—as they say—is up to you."

"Yes, Malcolm."

It was no secret to herself that she hated her father, but still, she always sought his approval. Once, when she was six years old, she had made him a birthday card of leather sheets with glued silver sequins. Instead of being pleased with the gift Malcolm had jumped at her, demanding to know where she had found the leather. She had told him that it had been a discarded briefcase she had found in the basement. Malcolm had raged then, telling her that the basement was a forbidden place, then he had grabbed the gift and had thrown it into the fire. D.B. stood crying, shaking with rejection, and had watched as the flames kicked and curled at the bright sequins and leather.

It was always that way: she hated Malcolm and yet feared to do anything that might displease him. She sought his approval but feared his attention.

In high school she was a lonely girl, making few friends. She never learned how to dance and never dated. She was always under Malcolm's suspicion. And, after spending four years at four different colleges, she eagerly jumped at the chance to tour Ireland and England with Aunt Eva.

Once in Ireland, away from Malcolm, from the disapproval, the constant comparison of herself with her late sister, D.B. discovered something new and exhilarating—complete freedom. She had managed to escape from Aunt Eva and had gone on a tour of the museum. There, she met a wild man with a loud screaming voice and a sheepskin jacket, and she believed she had fallen in love with him. She lived with him for three hectic weeks. He had been a sculptor and he had claimed to be in contact with Jesus Christ once every week. Three times she went to the countryside with him to kneel at a certain spot and recite certain prayers. Aunt Eva had finally tracked her down with the aid of a private detective. D.B. had returned to the States and the local authorities had put the sculptor into a hospital for observation. D.B.'s taste of freedom had come to a sudden halt.

She had asked Malcolm: "Do you want me to marry a perfect stranger? Just to make sure that I don't do anything—like I did in Dublin?"

"Of course not, D.B. Gordon won't be a perfect stranger to you. When you come to the house for dinner tonight I'll introduce him to you."

"But why? Is it just because of Dublin? Do you think I'm a—a tramp?"

"No, I don't think you're a tramp. No daughter of mine is a tramp. But I do think that you're a starry-eyed little fool. Don't question what I say. This is all for your own good."

She didn't argue. Reluctantly she attended the dinner and met her future husband, Gordon M. Fitzroy, a polished bore, a Young Republican, a skin-diving enthusiast and an ex-Navy man. Exactly two weeks after their meeting they were married in a simple ceremony by Judge Fitzroy.

The marriage was an empty lie, not even graced with the strange adhesive of mutual dislike. They were indifferent toward one another, moving through the marital motions like bored children playing a game under adult supervision. The whole thing was a terrible mistake. It became worse when she found out that Gordon's family had more background than substance and that he had married her for her money. So for six and a half months she lived with the ache of the lie, all the while trapped in her mink-lined web, batting her head against diamond panes. Finally, two weeks ago, she had divorced Gordon, but hadn't worked up enough courage to tell her father.

Of course, there was a solution now. Gordon would leave the apartment, would give her her freedom, if she agreed to pay him to keep it from her father. It was blackmail. She could think of no other way. She had to be free in order to try to recapture the wild exhilaration of the break that she had had for three weeks in Dublin.

She realized that she was relatively inexperienced as a woman, but she was willing to make up for lost time. She wanted to meet new people, taste new experiences, live without the need of her father's approval—

"Have you come to a decision?" Gordon asked again.

"Yes."

"Have you decided to wash it up? Do you really want to make this divorce the final word?"

"Yes. I want it to be the final word."

He began pacing the room, running a hand over his blond crewcut, jingling the coins in his pocket. He stopped at the foot of the couch and gazed at her naked body, at the hips and thighs moving up and down with the purr of the massage couch.

"What do you think Malcolm's going to say about all this?"

"I've been thinking about it," D. B. answered.

"He'll cut you off without a dime. You'll have to go out and—and get a job. You'll have to work at—at Woolworth's, or some place like that."

"Shut up, Gordon. You make me sick."

"Listen, D. B. We don't have to go through with this, you know. We could run down to Mexico and get married all over again. That way Malcolm wouldn't have to know a—"

"I don't want to remarry you, Gordon. You're a bore, a phony; you are the Great American Myth—The Husband. Now shut up and leave me to my thoughts. I'm drunk. I'm sick. I'm tired."

"Well—if Malcolm ever finds out—"

"For God's sake, can't you come right out and blackmail me? Name your price and get it over with, Gordon. I don't need the build-up. How much? What's your price to get you out of my life and keep you quiet at the same time?"

He coughed behind his hand. "How—how about a hundred?"

"A hundred what?"

"Dollars a week—"

"Fine. What makes you think I can afford to give you a hundred a week?"

He coughed again. "Well, if you want to know, I've been doing a little snooping. I happen to know that you're getting eight hundred a month from Malcolm for your allowance. You have seven thousand six hundred in the bank. Your store expenses are charged to the Sadder account. And, you don't pay rent on this apartment because your father happens to own the building. Do you want to hear more?"

"No. I see you've been peeking into my desk. All right, since you've figured it all out, I'll pay you the hundred a week." She closed her eyes wearily, and when she reopened them she saw that he had moved closer, that he was staring at her body, his boyish face feverish, his cupid mouth puckered tightly. She said, "Get away from me, Gordon. You're standing in the way of my sun."

"*Your* sun?"

"Yes, *my* sun. And if you've got any ideas about touching me you'd better get rid of them. I haven't been in the mood for one of your childish assaults for months."

"What would you do if I touched you?"

"I'd smash my glass into your stinking, blackmailing face."

He gave her an unbelieving look and when he reached for her she tensed and drew back her glass. His hand brushed on her breast, the thumb passing over the pink nipple. She swung and clipped him viciously just over the right eyebrow. Glass cracked, ice flipped out into the pale sunlight, Scotch splashed into his face. Pink blood blossomed on his forehead and he screamed, staggering back and throwing his hands to his face.

"You should have taken my word, stupid."

While he slumped against the wall she calmly went to the bar and prepared another drink, using a heavier glass this time. Gordon touched his forehead, gaped at the blood on his fingertips. It wasn't a bad cut but he stared at the blood with an expression of complete horror and self-pity.

The parrot had been awakened by the noise, had jerked its head from under its feathered armpit, and was now skrawking, filling the silence with loud green sounds. D. B. returned to the couch and soothed the bird with puckered kissing noises. Gordon dabbed at his forehead with his handkerchief, sat in the black Gothic chair and glared at D.B.

"I—I hate you," he hissed.

"You're sick, Gordon. You don't know what you feel."

She touched another switch and a record began to move noiselessly on a turntable hidden behind the ferns. A mechanical arm settled on the disc and Scarlatti burst from four hidden speakers.

D. B. drank more Scotch, and as the music played she envisioned wild scenes of silk pennants fluttering atop stone battlements, of creaking moat bridges, of mad medieval harlequins laughing and cavorting in parti-colored abandon. The fight had upset her. The music soothed her. Who was it that had said that music soothes the savage breast? She couldn't remember. And, thinking of that, her thoughts again turned to Harry Dazier, the composer—

More Scotch. She began to grow sleepy. She didn't like the idea of her marriage ending badly, but there hadn't been much of a choice. Gordon wanted one of two things—either the money and D. B.—or just the money. And since she could no longer stomach Gordon and the marriage lie, it would have to be just the money. It was sordid, but at least it was over and done with—or so she felt.

She turned to the parrot. The bird screeched and blinked at her from behind the brass spokes, his ugly little claws rustling on the perch. "And where are you, little parrot?" she asked. "Where are you?"

"I'm in hell!" the parrot croaked.

They were the only words she had bothered teaching the bird. She made kissing sounds. The music poured from the hidden speakers. Gordon sat in the Gothic chair, glaring at D. B. The couch continued to purr and the sun rose slowly in the sky.

"I'm in hell!" the parrot said.

"So are we all," D. B. answered softly.

2

The tiny sea-coast village of Darker's Bay was north of San Francisco, beyond Bodega Bay and Duncan's Mills on old Highway One. The village consisted of a run-down gas station, a general store, a few ugly houses, and a once white Victorian hotel that stood along the shell road which separated the small bay from the sharp hills that rose on either side. A rickety pier led from the shore; a few fishing boats were tied near the old pier shed.

The mountains formed two craggy breasts and were thickly wooded with eucalyptus, pine, and redwood. Halfway up the slope of the south hill, called Canaan, and buried deep in the forest, was the Dazier house, a huge two-story frame affair that for some reason resembled a Mississippi riverboat.

Harry Dazier came awake by the sounds of the birds at nine o'clock in the morning. He turned on his mattress and bleakly stared up at the purplish ceiling, tracing a thin line which led to a large irregular crack that, for him, always looked like a huge moth sitting on top of Abraham Lincoln's head. Harry closed his eyes, moaned, and worked his tongue in an effort to start the saliva past the brackish gum of last night's wine and vodka.

He remained on the floor mattress for many minutes, waiting for his eyes to adjust to another morning, then he pulled himself from the floor and staggered to the window. Another foggy day, the mist blotting the trees, smudging the branches and leaves like an out-of-focus watercolor.

Harry Dazier was naked but he didn't bother to hunt for his clothes. He had no idea where they were, anyway. He filled the yellow bowl with cold water and plunged his head into it, made bubbling animal noises, rinsing his mouth and forcing himself awake. He dried himself with a dirty T shirt.

The walls of the room were decorated with old RCA and Columbia posters of conductors. A bulletin board near the door was tacked with yellowed clippings reviewing Harry's works. He wandered about the room, poking under books, under sheets of music, until he found a crumpled package of Alpine cigarettes. He sat on the floor, smoking, scratching his feet.

"I wonder what happened to my clothes."

Harry was a tall man, rather thin, thirty-seven years old, with thick black hair prematurely streaked with gray. His eyebrows were unusually thick, his nose slightly hooked, his mouth wide and expressive. His eyes, set deep under the thick brows, were the color of a mild bourbon whiskey. His hands were long and bony, the wrists matted with black hair.

He sighed, spoke to the walls. "Yes, the duck is represented by the oboe. The cat by the clarinet. The wolf by the horns. And I?—I'm represented by the tuba and the banjo—Oompah. Plinky plink. Another day, another hangover."

He squashed his cigarette out on the floor and wandered out into the hallway and stood at the head of the stairs. Along the wall behind him there were several elaborate horoscope charts with feathered darts stuck into them.

"Where's everybody," he said. He went to his brother's door and knocked. "Birsha? You up yet?" There was no answer and he started down the stairs. "Birsha? Sandro? Sophie? Anyone up yet?"

Sophie's answering voice echoed through the lower rooms: "I'm in the kitchen, Harry."

He shuffled down the hall to the kitchen and stood in the doorway, glumly staring at the solid row of empty wine and vodka bottles under the sink, the heaped dirty dishes, the pots and pans. He tried to recall the night before but as always only certain parts returned to him. There had been the usual argument, with his older brother Sandro, about Sophie. There had been a raccoon out on the front porch. Not much else came to him. Up until the second bottle of vodka everything was clear, but after that it was sketchy, the blanks becoming wider, darker.

Sophie was at the table, hunched over one of her horoscope books. She was a young girl, about twenty—Harry wasn't too sure—and had wide gray eyes and soft greenish hair. When she had first come to live with Harry's younger brother Birsha she had promised to keep him amused—and she had. She had dyed her skin with a special washable dye. Last month she had been blue, which Harry hadn't objected to, but right now she was green. The color didn't help Harry's hangover.

He slumped into a chair and held his head in his hands. Again, he wondered what had happened to his clothes.

Sophie looked up from her book with her usual childlike expression. She smiled, not paying any attention to his nakedness.

"You're a Libra," she said brightly.

Harry nodded. "Yeah. I'm a Cuba Libra."

"No, I mean, you're late October, aren't you."

"Very late October. Around October the forty-second to be exact."

"You're Libra," she insisted. "Wouldn't you like to hear something about yourself today?"

"No. I already know about myself. I'm under the symbol of the tuba and the banjo, the whips and the jingles."

"Oh? Really?" She looked in her book, ruffling the pages. "It's not here. It's not in my book, Harry."

"Then you were gypped, because that's what I am."

"Gee, Harry, you're so smart," she said, quite innocently. Then, without asking, she turned the gas ring on under the pot and set out a cup for him.

"Where's Birsha?" Harry asked.

"He's still asleep, I guess."

"And Sandro?"

"Gee, I don't know. I guess he's still in bed, too."

Later, still unable to find his clothes, Harry went into the large front room and sat at the piano. He picked up his pencil, marked the date on the margin of his sheets, stuck the pencil behind his ear. He drank some coffee, hit middle C on the keyboard, stared blankly at the walls. Sophie brought the coffee pot to him, refilled his cup, and sat in a carved chair near the window. Sandro and Birsha hadn't wakened yet and it was quiet. Outside, the fog was growing thicker, burying the old house in the wet gray forest.

"Aren't you going to put on your clothes, Harry?"

"I can't find them."

"They're probably still out in the front yard."

"Oh."

He didn't bother asking how they happened to be out in the front yard. He hit middle C again and the sound held in the musty air, washing slowly from wall to wall. Middle C held no meaning for him.

"Play something for me, Harry."

"Like what?"

"Do you know Cocktails for Two?"

"No, I don't."

"How about *Stardust?*"

"I don't know that either."

She smiled and remarked, very innocently, "Gee, Harry, it must be wonderful to play the piano."

He chuckled softly. "Yes, it is."

"Do you like jazz?"

"Sure. Do you?"

"I love the music from *Peter Gunn,*" she said.

Sophie reminded Harry of a little girl hidden under the flesh of a grown woman, pretending a secret little game against the adult world. She attracted him, but he had never made an advance toward her. She was his brother's girl, Birsha's property, and Harry respected that. Sophie was an absently gay child, always a little removed from reality, like a color photo out of focus, a lovely green girl with silver lipstick and wide gray eyes.

"If I took off my clothes, Harry, would it be better?"

"No, I don't think so."

"You look lovely naked. Did you know that?"

"I'm thin."

"Gee, but not where it counts. I mean—" she smiled—"you've got wide shoulders."

Harry laughed, drank more coffee, then he began playing the opening of his Two Saints: *Vitus, Walpurgis,* but his fingers were full of wine. His soul was full of fog, his eyes were full of blood, his veins were full of hot spiders. He could use a shot of vodka but knew that if he started drinking again he wouldn't be in any shape for tomorrow night's party and recital.

Sophie seemed to remember something and she smiled. "Harry, why don't you get a girl? Wouldn't that be great? If you had a girl we could all sit around and sing."

"Sing?"

"Don't you like singing?"

He shrugged. He was becoming used to Sophie's scatterbrained notions. She had been living in Harry's Darker's Bay house for the past two months. At first Harry had thought it a fine idea, imagining that a girl around the house might improve the general conditions, that his clothes wouldn't be scattered about all the time, that the kitchen would at least be cleaned once a week. But it hadn't worked out that way— Sophie was just as irresponsible as the rest of them and the house continued on its merry way. However, Harry hadn't been disappointed. Sophie was a happy person, never interfering, and she, at least, seemed to keep Birsha contented.

Birsha was the youngest of the Dazier brothers, Sandro the eldest. Of course, Sandro was only a half-brother to Harry and Birsha, but a brother nevertheless. Sandro lived in San Francisco, in a warehouse, but came often to Darker's Bay for several days at a time.

Perhaps Harry should return to the city. He missed the noise, the sense of direct contact. It wasn't that he disliked Darker's Bay, but he felt the change might do him good. Lately he felt himself growing stale. He was drinking too much. The music was coming too slowly and often it had to fight its way past a vodka haze. He hadn't completed a major work in two years. Last week's television showing of *Walpurgis* had brought in just enough money to pay his back property taxes and his liquor bill. He was trying to finish the score now, trying to convince himself that the *Vitus* was equal to the *Walpurgis*. If only he could find a way to be free of financial worries long enough to finish the new *Kadesh*, and the old *St. Vitus*. Both pieces were commissioned but he wouldn't receive the balance of the money until he completed them.

Perhaps—

No, he couldn't ask for an advance.

He hit middle C, yawned, stretched, scratched his stomach, stared at the floor, the walls, the windows. He forced himself to look at his manuscript. He was working on *Kadesh* and for the speaker's part he had written: *But God came to Abimelech in a dream by night, and said to him, Behold, thou art a dead man, for the woman which thou hast taken; for she is a man's wife …*

"Why don't you, Harry?"

"Why don't I what?"

"Get yourself a girl."

He nodded absently. That was all he needed—another goddam mouth to feed. Sophie drifted off, humming *The Rat Race*, and Harry finally started thinking seriously of how he was going to get God to tell Abimelech that he was a dead man.

3

D. B. Sadder slept soundly and when she awoke she saw no sign of Gordon Fitzroy. She had slept for five hours and she felt better now, the sleeping having washed away the jerky, gassy mood of the morning. She stood under shower, hot, lazy, slipping soft piles of perfumed suds along her body. She toweled herself and walked naked about the apartment.

She dressed carefully, having no plans for the day, but knowing that in the evening she would go again to Pendragon's Bar, a gloomy North Beach tavern that she had happened on quite by accident three nights ago. She had been drawn to it, had been drawn by the haunting sounds she had heard. And she had sworn to herself that this time she wasn't going to deny her curiosity. She was going to go all the way. As in Dublin. After all, what was freedom for?

She brought her breakfast tea to the balcony and stood near the gargoyles, watching a freighter move sluggishly out to sea. A few clouds, small, mushroom-shaped, had gathered. She hummed softly to herself, trying to recall the mood at Pendragon's, two nights ago.

When she had first entered the bar and had seen the TV set she had almost turned and left, but when she heard the weird music she became curious.

"What's that?"

"What's what?" the bartender had asked her.

"That music on the television?"

The bartender frowned. "Don't go turning me on, baby."

She moved to the set, joined a small ragged group at the end of the bar. A fat woman and a pale man with a straggly beard moved to allow her room.

She had always been a compulsive listener and since she had studied music in high school she felt she understood whatever she heard, but yet these sounds were different, eerie in fact, and she remained there in the gloomy bar, drinking draught beer and listening.

"Pardon me, could you tell me what this is?"

The fat woman mumbled in reply: "Dazier's *Walpurgis*."

"Dazier?"

"Yeah, honey, but don't ask me. Ask that guy." She pointed to the pale man with the straggly beard. "He studied music, not me. He knows Dazier, I don't—"

When the performance ended the smooth announcer talked briefly about the composer, referring to him as "A very great local talent—" Dazier.

The name, now that she thought of it, wasn't unfamiliar to D. B. She recalled that she had heard his works discussed one afternoon on the FM radio. In fact, she remembered having a magazine with an article written about him. The television performance was, however, the first time she had heard his music.

When she returned to the apartment she hunted up the article and read it twice. It was called: *"Rebel with Cause—Demonism in Music"* It was an essay on Dazier's unsuccessful ballet, *The Owl and the Pussycat.*

The next day she went to a music store and bought the only LP recording of works by Harry Dazier. Three quarters of the record and the entire jacket had been given to the major artist. The rest, twelve minutes, was Dazier's. A sketch called, *The Legend of Peter Klaus.*

That evening she returned to Pendragon's Bar, as she had known she would, having been jolted from her post-divorce lethargy and wanting to live, wanting to fight the suspicion that the greater part of life had passed her. And when she entered the bar she heard again the Dazier score, but this time from a battered corner piano. The straggly-bearded man—who supposedly knew Harry Dazier—was sitting at the piano, bent over the yellowed keyboard.

She bought him wine, glass after glass, listening to his playing.

"Can you tell me about the music?" she asked.

"Sure. It's good."

"Do you really know Harry Dazier?"

"Yeah." Then he stopped and turned on his stool, staring at her for a long minute. She could feel his eyes undressing her, then looking at the labels of her clothes to see how much she was worth. He said, "Are you a fan of Dazier's?"

"Yes. Does he live around here? I'd like to meet him—"

"He lives pretty close by."

"Does he come in here very often?"

"Not too often."

She remembered that evening now with a disagreeable ache in the pit of her stomach. She hoped that Harry Dazier wasn't anything like that piano player.

She finished her tea and went into the parrot's room. She set the

Dazier on the record turntable, returned to the balcony. The freighter was gone now. The sun was behind her and the city was jigsawed with yellow light and blue shadows. The music swirled into the warm air. Magic, wine, mountains, strings, kettledrums, flutes.

She stared at the city.

She had been born in San Francisco, in the St. Francis Woods district, in a large Spanish type house. The attic had been a place of eerie sounds, the basement of winds and mice and travel trunks. School had been mixed odors of flower-wax and chalk and camphor.

She had been plain as a child, thin-legged, green-eyed, with straight hair the color of wet sand. She had breasts early, experience late, a curious mind, a silent house. Marjorie had never been a sister to her. D. B. could barely remember her. Her childhood had been a wretched hazy film of staring relatives with denture breath, of running the faucets loudly whenever she went to the toilet because she was ashamed of even that. She had decided that to be seen was to be disapproved of, so she preferred to be hidden in the shadows, in a room that others could not enter, a colorless world. She lived under the constant suspicion of her father.

She had never known her mother and whenever she asked Malcolm about her he became pale and silent. Marjorie had told D. B. that their mother had died but she had never believed her. Somehow she had the impression that her mother was still alive, denied her by her father. She still held that suspicion but it was deeply buried, locked inside her, never allowed to rise in her thoughts.

From the very first magical moments she had felt that Dazier's music had the sadness, the hope, the happiness that was hers. She needed it. With the Irish sculptor she hadn't had this feeling. With him it had simply been the savage animal thrill of the forbidden. But with Dazier's music, coming to her as it did during her period of doubt and rebirth, she felt the first stirrings of true identity—

When Gordon came to the apartment with a man from a moving company, D. B. let them in and withdrew quietly to the bar in the front room. Gordon gave the moving man instructions on what to pack and how to pack it, then he joined her in the front room. He picked up two bottles of Dewar's Scotch.

"I bought *these* with my own money," he said lightly. "I'm taking them with me."

She shrugged. Gordon made himself quite at home, sitting in the large couch before the picture window, a freshly made drink in his hand. He had changed his clothes since that morning and looked rather handsome with his black silk suit and white cashmere vest. He arched an eyebrow, smiling. "Aren't you going to say anything to me, D. B.?"

"We have nothing to say."

"I think we do."

She didn't like the tone of his voice, the suave performance. She studied him through narrowed eyes. "Such as?" she asked.

"Such as when are you going to send me my hundred and twenty-five a week? After all, we hadn't made any definite arrangements this morning."

The blood drained from her face and she started to hurl a bottle at him, then checked herself, simply stood there, her knuckles white on the neck of the bottle.

"Your *what?*" she demanded.

"My hundred and twenty-five," Gordon said blandly.

"You're out of your mind."

He held up a warning finger. "If you're going to persist in name-calling then I'll up the ante to a hundred *thirty*"

Barely controlling herself she paced the room, nervously touching the silver-white pile of her hair, clicking her nails together.

"Well, where do you want to send it?" Gordon asked.

She was trapped and she knew it. It was outrageous but he had her in too tight a spot. She tried to think of a way out but nothing came. She would have to give him the extra cash.

It wasn't the money. She could easily afford twice that amount. It was the principle. The humiliation was much more damaging than the cost. She couldn't stomach the idea that a hungry little weakling like Gordon could force her to give in.

She finally asked, "Where are you staying."

"Now that's being smart, D. B. For a second there I thought you were going to explode or do something equally stupid. But I can see that you understand the situation—I'm staying at the Mark for about a week, under an assumed name of course—we wouldn't want the press to find out about our marital difficulties, would we?—So in the meanwhile, just mail the check every Friday to Gordon M. Fitzroy, General Delivery, City. Are you agreeable?"

She nodded and Gordon rose smoothly from the couch, offering her his hand. She stared at him without expression. She would pay him his money but she was damned if she would shake his hand in the bargain. Without a word, she turned and left the room.

The mover had carried the packed crates out to the service elevator and Gordon quietly left the apartment. Alone, D. B. cursed aloud, damning Gordon's soul, damning her father for having forced her into this mess. She poured a stiff drink and threw herself onto the couch. She drank hungrily, waiting for the alcohol to hit her, to set her thoughts going.

After reaching the desired alcohol plane she thought of Harry Dazier, and tried to comfort the ache of need and fear and confusion.

4

The uniformed doorman swung open the door and saluted with a quick white-gloved hand. "Good afternoon, Mrs. Fitzroy."

"Hello, Norman."

"I see Mr. Fitzroy's been moving a few things."

"Yes, some books—and things."

Her German sports convertible was parked in her private slot in the adjoining brick court. The sun was dipping but it was still warm, and the clouds that had threatened earlier had drifted away. There was a pale sliver of moon in the sky. She drove to Chinatown, then, to avoid the snarl of one-way traffic, crossed toward Jackson Square and parked at the first spot she found on the south slope of Telegraph Hill. While she was putting the top up and locking her car a group of hoodlums roared past and whistled at her.

When she walked to Grant Avenue she didn't stop but went past Stockton and stood at the corner, feeling pensive, looking at the grass of the square, the statue, the baroque spires of the old church. She hadn't eaten, so she wandered along Columbus Street until she came to a restaurant. She ordered a light dinner and a Scotch-and-soda.

It was over, she was no longer Mrs. Fitzroy. But now with her new freedom she began to feel a little lost. Nothing had really changed. Gordon was still around her neck. She couldn't think which was worse: being blackmailed by him or being married to him. Either way she was still trapped. She ordered another drink—a double—and when her dinner came she found that she had lost her appetite.

There was still the threat of Malcom Sadder. If he discovered what she had done he would cancel her apartment arrangement and force her to return to the St. Francis Woods house, and if that happened she knew she would never have another chance for a new life again. It would be over, completely finished.

When she finished her drink she crossed the street to the square. The street lights were lit now. When she walked up Filbert to Grant she stopped at the corner where an old woman stood, wearing a dirty tweed coat. The woman had two crates of live chickens at her feet.

Feathers dappled the sidewalk.

"Hullo," the woman mumbled to D. B.

D. B. looked at the crated birds, feeling a queasy turn in her stomach. The chickens were cackling, blinking, lifting their yellow legs nervously.

"A body's gotta eat," the woman explained mysteriously.

"I beg your pard—"

"These chickens. I hate them. But you gotta eat. Am I right?"

"I suppose—"

"Let me tell you," the old woman hissed, "once out in the country I saw a bunch of chickens pecking at a man's vomit. Can you imagine that, young lady? These filthy creatures would do anything. They'd pluck your eyes out if they had half a chance. I hate them. I like to wring their bloody necks. Do you know where I do that?"

D. B. stared at the woman, suddenly identifying with the birds.

"In my bathroom," the old woman said. "In the bathtub. I wring their necks in the bathtub. Did you see that picture—*Psycho?*"

"No—"

"Well, that's where I got the idea. Put 'em in the bathtub and wring their necks."

The woman picked up her cackling crates and trudged off. D.B. wondered if she was drunk already. Then she slowly started down Grant. When she came to Pendragon's Bar she pushed aside the heavy doors and entered. It was dark. Dirty sawdust was strewn on the floor, piled in little dunes around the fat tablelegs. A grimy light glowed overhead, nude photos hung on the walls. The bartender wasn't the same as the night before. This one was tall and thin with a black Vandyke beard, sunglasses, and yellowish teeth clamped on an empty Medico cigarette holder.

"A white wine, please."

She sipped, not liking the taste, lit a cigarette and looked around her. She didn't see the straggly-bearded pianist. There were few people in the bar. The bartender remained stationed before her, watching her with obvious appreciation.

"Has the piano player been in tonight?" she asked.

"He was. Why? You a friend of his?"

"Not especially. I'd just like to talk to him."

"You don't look the type."

"The type for what?"

"For Auckland."

"Is that his name?"

"Sure. Auckland. He's a dirty little stud." He removed his sunglasses and studied her a moment. "You don't look the type."

She didn't know what to say to that so she pretended to sip her wine.

"Would you like to know where he is?" the bartender asked.

"Yes."

"He's at Hajek's, eating. That's a little joint exactly three doors down from here."

"Thank you."

"Wait a second. Before you go let me give you a bit of advice. Don't let Auckland con you into paying for his dinner. I've already paid for it."

She thanked him again and left. Three doors down she stopped before a small cigar-store with race-result sheets tacked to a sidewalk board and a row of girly magazines. A giant man with a bald freckled head stood behind the candy and tobacco counter. When she entered he eyed the front of her blouse, then said: "The restaurant's in back."

She stepped through a heavy curtain and found herself in a long airless room without windows. Electric lights burned dimly along the bare walls, there were no carpets, no linen on the wooden tables. The atmosphere was choked with the greasy odors of lamb fat and olive oil. She found Auckland in the rear, hunched over a book.

He was a thin little man with a white monkey face, pale beard, gummy eyes behind thick plastic-rimmed glasses. When she stopped at his table, sat without his invitation, he looked at her and smiled. His smile said that he remembered her from the night before. D.B. lit a cigarette and noticed the title of his book: *The Care and Handling of Dogs*.

"Well well," Auckland whispered, "here you are again. Still asking questions about Harry Dazier?"

"Yes—"

"Making some kind of mystery?"

"How do you mean?"

"I mean, intrigue. You didn't have to buy me wine the other night. Anyone could have told you that Harry Dazier lives nearby."

She sat without speaking, feeling his eyes on her, feeling suddenly cheap and terribly out of place. The odor of lamb fat was overpowering now. She felt her blouse clinging to her back.

"I suppose you know my name?" he said.

"Yes—it's Auckland."

"Ah. That's not my real name. No, don't look bugged—I'm not Harry Dazier in disguise. My name's Harrison. I called myself Auckland when I deserted the goddamned Army in 1943." He chuckled. "I don't tell many people about that."

She didn't know what he expected her to say to that, so she was silent.

Auckland said, "I know what you want."

"What's that?"

"Harry Dazier."

She wasn't too surprised. She sensed a plot brewing behind the gummy eyes. She asked, "How do you know that?"

"Because I can spot your type a mile away. You know what type that is? No? You're a dilettante."

She said nothing, feeling an uncomfortable twinge. She remembered now that with her Irish sculptor she had made some pretty wild plans for furthering his career. She had felt that in order to repay him for the borrowing of his identity she should help him in his work.

Auckland grinned, watching her expression. "You see—I'm right, aren't I?"

"Perhaps."

"I'm glad you understand. It makes it easier for us to talk."

"You mean—like conspirators?"

He pushed his plate aside and lit a stubby cigar. "If you wish. This, by the way, I find very interesting. Go ahead. Ask me any questions you want."

"I want to meet Harry Dazier, that's all."

"And you think I can help you?"

"Yes."

"Why?"

"You said that you knew him and I—"

"No. I mean, why do you want to meet him?"

"I like his music."

"Is that all?"

"Should there be more?" she asked.

"But of course. I like Dimitri Shostakovich but I don't write him letters. I'm wild about Ann Sheridan but you don't see me going to Hollywood to meet her, do you?"

D.B. said nothing.

"Would you care to hear what I think?" Auckland asked her.

"I suppose—"

"What's your name?"

"D.B."

"Your full name."

"D.B. Sadder."

"All right, D.B. I think you're bored. You've been sitting in your castle, combing out your silver locks and pining away for the hero to come and save you. I remember how you looked when you first entered Pendragon's. Scared looking, as if you were afraid somebody was going to punch your pretty face. You looked unattached inside, meaningless to yourself, then you heard the music and you looked like you'd gotten the Big Message. Am I right?"

"Perhaps."

"So now you want to meet Harry Dazier, presumably to aid him in his career. But you want to meet him as a friend, not as a wild-eyed fan. I'm supposed to be your camouflage. Right?"

D.B. didn't know if she was that obvious or if Auckland was that clever. But she had to admit that he was correct. She nodded, feeling vaguely guilty. "Something like that," she admitted.

He studied her a moment, then asked quite suddenly, "Are you related to Malcolm Sadder?"

"Yes, but how did—"

He waved his hand. "Everyone's heard of old Malcolm Sadder," he explained. "I'll be honest with you, D.B. Sadder. I'll take you to meet Harry Dazier as a friend, but it's going to cost you twenty-five bucks. I'm being very honest. I'm an opportunist, and you, to be frank, you're a sucker. And besides, I know you can damn well afford it."

She nodded, hating him.

"You want to meet your Saviour," Auckland said, "and I'll take him to you. Are we friends?"

She held her hand out of sight and childishly crossed her fingers. "Yes, we're friends," she said.

"Fine. Now, Harry Dazier lives in Darker's Bay. That's a weird little town south of Mendocino. Do you know Mendocino? That's where Kazan shot *East of Eden*. Tomorrow night Dazier's throwing a bash and a recital. Since I don't have a car, you'll have to drive me." He smiled. "Naturally, *you* have a car."

"Yes."

He rose and handed her the dinner check. "Meet me tomorrow afternoon at Pendragon's. Meanwhile, take care of my dinner. And incidentally, don't forget to bring the money tomorrow."

He left. D.B. remained at the table, glumly staring at the thick puddles of fat on Auckland's plate. Everything was going wrong. First there was Gordon blackmailing her, and now a grimy little opportunist was taking advantage of her. With a shudder, she remembered Auckland calling her a sucker. Perhaps he was right! She angrily stabbed her cigarette into a tin ashtray and rose from the table, wondering if all this was worth it.

5

Harry Dazier had gone to the Darker's Bay General Store for the supplies of food and liquor and the party began as soon as it grew dark. The first to arrive at the house were Richard Freeze and Daniel and Helga Marris, then Herman and Vivian, and later, Zeke. Birsha, as usual, was the first to become drunk. Sophie wandered off into the forest and every now and then Harry had to go out and call her to see if she was all right.

Sandro, like some disagreeable chaperone, planted himself in the corner near the piano and refused to speak with any of the others.

"Is there anything the matter, Sandro?"

"No. I feel fine."

Harry handed him a small glass of rose wine. "Here. You can have a couple of glasses tonight."

Sandro nodded and took the drink. "All right. Thank you, Harry."

Sandro was about fifty, a huge man with frozen craggy features, hard black eyes, thin cruel mouth, and white Prussian haircut. A bright pink scar ran from his forehead to his cheek, an ugly line, pulling down one corner of his eye.

"Are you sure you feel all right?" Harry asked him.

"Yes. You don't have to worry about me."

"Are you going to argue with Birsha again tonight?"

Sandro frowned, puckering his lips on the rim of his glass. "No," he answered. "I've got no arguments with Birsha. It's Sophie. I just don't like her, that's all."

"She's not hurting anyone," Harry said.

"Yes she is," Sandro said. "She's hurting Birsha. She's draining him. *All* women hurt men, Harry. You know that."

Harry nodded. "Sure, Sandro."

"We've got to help Birsha, Harry. I'm supposed to look after you boys, but it's hard for me if you don't cooperate. We've got to get Birsha away from that—that woman. She's—bad, Harry. She's not good for him…."

"All right, Sandro. I'll talk with him."

Harry left and went out onto the porch. After calling for Sophie and receiving no answer he returned to the house. Sandro's words had left no real impression on him. He had heard them too often. It wasn't Sophie that Sandro objected to—it was all women.

Birsha was in the kitchen with Daniel Marris, making Bloody Marys. Outside, the fog that had held for the past three days was beginning to thin. In the front room there was a great deal of noise, laughing, drinking, pounding on the table. It was going to be a good party. When Harry entered the kitchen Birsha handed him a fresh drink.

"Here you go, buddy."

"What's it made with?"

"Vodka and V-8 juice."

"No hot sauce?"

Daniel shook hands with Harry, "That was some drunken brawl the other night," he said.

Harry looked surprised. "Were you there?"

"We came right after you passed out."

"Did you happen to find out why my clothes were out in the front yard?"

"No. I didn't even know that they were there."

Harry turned to Birsha. "How did my clothes get out in the front yard?"

"I don't know. There was a raccoon on the porch and I seem to remember that you were chasing it."

The light bulb in the kitchen had been covered with a shade fashioned from a grocery bag, and it was difficult to see clearly; everything glowed a dull orange. Daniel picked up a drink for his wife and left the room. A minute later Harry heard the first sounds from Daniel's guitar. Birsha made another round of drinks.

Birsha was a smaller version of his brother, with long black hair and a thin mustache. He always managed to look like a turn-of-the-century sharpie; bright weskits, striped shirts, stovepipe trousers, long sideburns, and on special occasions he sported a pair of fawn-colored spats. Harry had been supporting his younger brother for the past thirteen years.

"I've been wanting to talk with you, Harry."

"Go ahead."

Birsha made a small gesture, fooling with the ice in his drink.

"What's on your mind?" Harry asked.

"Well—I think I'm going to marry Sophie," Birsha answered.

"Why?"

"I don't know exactly."

"Are you in love with her?"

"I don't think so. She's a good kid. I like her. And besides, she asked me."

"Is it something you really want to do?"

"I think so."

Harry held up his drink in a toast. "Then all I can say is,

congratulations."

"Thanks," Birsha grinned, then frowned. "Listen, Harry, I hate to ask you again, but I was wondering if we had any spare cash."

Harry shook his head. "I doubt it, kid. I'm not finished with *Kadesh* yet, and even then, I don't know how long it'll be before I get the balance on it from Amduscias. It's feast and famine around here, just like always."

"What about Sandro? Do you think he's got a couple bucks he could lend me?"

"He might."

"I'll ask him tonight if he gets into a good enough mood."

"What do you need the money for?"

"I want to take Sophie into the city, goof around a bit, maybe make it sort of like a honeymoon, or something like that."

Harry made another drink, being careful to go easy on the vodka. He had to play tonight and he wanted to stay in shape for it. He doubled the V-8 juice and added ice cubes. He had already had three strong drinks and he judged that enough for right now. He leaned against the stove and listened to Daniel's guitar from the front room.

"Do you think Sandro would do it?" Birsha asked again.

"Sure, if you asked him for it. But have you thought about what he would do if he found out what you wanted it for?"

Birsha frowned. "Naturally."

"Don't sound so bitter, kid. It's not Sandro's fault."

"I know," Birsha sighed. "But if he knew I was going to marry Sophie then he'd flip out of his goddam noodle and we'd have to put him into the hospital again—"

"That's probably what would happen, Birsha. So if I was you I'd keep it kind of quiet about wanting to marry Sophie. At least for a while."

"Okay, Harry. And listen, when the time comes and he has to know about it, then I'll let you handle him. You can do a better job than I can."

Harry nodded. When Birsha left and he was alone he deliberately picked up the bottle and added a double shot to his glass.

Like always, he was thinking. It had always been Harry's responsibility to keep Sandro on an even keel. It had been Harry who had signed Sandro's commitment papers thirteen years ago. And it had been Harry who had secured the release and had sworn to see that Sandro was properly cared for.

When Harry and Birsha had been children it had been Sandro who had cared for them. Their father, Gerard Dazier, had died in 1936 when Harry was twelve. At that time Sandro had been a famous animal trainer and the two orphaned brothers had gone to live with him, traveling with various circuses throughout the United States and Europe. Sandro had a strong sense of love and brotherly loyalty and had sworn to see that his half-brothers had opportunities to attend the best colleges. Harry, whose job with the circus had been to play the steam calliope, chose a school of music in Illinois, while Birsha remained with Sandro and the circus.

Then Sandro had gone out of his mind, shooting his favorite tigress and running berserk into the packed circus bleachers with his whip, and Harry had to take in his younger brother while Sandro stayed in the mental institution. During Harry's childhood Sandro had been his hero, a powerfully handsome man, a famous animal trainer, a star of two continents. But now he was nothing, an insane man reduced to renting a merry-go-round to the traveling carnivals and county fairs that performed nearby. He did this in order to stay in the circus atmosphere of his great past. It was a slim living but Harry knew that it was the best Sandro could do.

Helga Marris and Zeke came into the kitchen, Helga glowing, Zeke completely drunk. Harry made them Bloody Marys, then returned with them to the front room. The party was obviously in full swing. Daniel and Birsha were playing their guitars. Zeke went to the corner near Sandro's chair and passed out. Herman and Vivian were talking to Richard Freeze. The rest were at the oaken table, singing, drinking burgundy, rose wine, and vodka from waxed paper cups.

"Where've you been, Harry?"

"In the kitchen, brooding."

"Come out of it, buddy. Let's get drunk. Let's live it up."

"I'm for that," Harry said quietly. "I'm always for getting good and drunk."

Auckland sat hunched in the passenger seat of the little German car, drinking occasionally from one of the bottles of expensive Scotch that D.B. had brought. He had said very little and by the time they reached the old coast highway he was well on his way to becoming drunk. The sun passed under the dark horizon of the sea and great streamers of fog hung over the twisting road. D.B. shivered miserably. She hadn't thought to bring a jacket and the salty wind cut easily through her gray sweater and black skintight trousers. Night came and she turned on the headlights. The heater purred against her legs. Auckland finally passed out, doubled in the seat, his dirty sandals scraping on the white leather upholstery. D.B. was disgusted with him.

When they came to Darker's Bay D.B. stopped at an old hotel near a sagging pier to ask the way to Dazier's house. The desk clerk gave her the directions, then added: "You tell old Harry that Lennie—that's me—don't mind giving folks directions to his place. See, you ain't the first tonight to ask me ... I guess he's having hisself another party, unh?"

"Yes, I think he is."

"Well, don't forget to tell him I don't mind, y'hear?"

Back at the car she didn't bother waking Auckland to tell him they had arrived. She followed the winding shell road that curved around the small bay until she came to the marked turn-off. The farther she drove up the wooded slope, the more the fog thinned out. A half-moon was beginning to show through the dark branches overhead. She came to a parking area and came to a stop near a white Jeep and a battered Oldsmobile. She picked up the untouched bottle of Scotch and stepped from the car.

There was no need to wake Auckland. She had paid him his twenty-five dollars and had given him the bottle of Scotch. He had been well paid and she had him as evidence of her invitation, even if he was passed out drunk. She figured that his presence was sufficient proof that she was no stranger.

She entered the gate and picked her way along a worn path that led to the house. Party sounds could be heard now, laughter, guitar music, talking. She hoped that she hadn't missed the recital. Pausing at the foot of the sagging house she looked up at the mint-colored door, the long covered porch, the weird shape of the old house.

When she heard the sound—something like the quick shuffle of a foot—she peered to her left and saw a girl on the porch, watching her and standing in the breath of light from the narrow window by the door. D.B.'s hand froze on the porch railing. Her heart gave a sudden twitch.

She could hardly believe what she saw. The girl was green. Her skin was completely green and her lips were silvery white—

6

The girl moved away from the breath of light and stood at the head of the steps. She was asparagus green, delicate lips and eyebrows white with silver makeup, uncombed hair like wild sprays of corn silk. Her dress was a simple pullover affair, as green as her skin. She had appeared from the dark a blithe Ariel, a wonderland child green as jade. Her voice was soft, like spring grass being crushed under naked feet.

"Gee, honey, don't be scared."

D.B. was still unable to move. Could she be dreaming this? Was this girl some Halloween joke? If a green girl in the dark was any indication then what kind of person could Harry Dazier be?

"Gee whiz, honey, do you think I've got some kind of weird disease? Don't worry, there's nothing wrong with me. I'm just green this month, that's all."

D.B. nodded. Her initial surprise was gone now. "I see," she said absently. "It's a nice—color."

"Thank you. I dyed it," the girl explained. "It's a special kind of dye, sort of like that vegetable stuff, I guess. It comes right off when you wash it. I suppose if it rained I'd become all streaky. You know, last month I was a blue, a fantastic Mediterranean blue. Next I think I'll try tangerine. I've never been tangerine before, have you?"

D.B. suppressed a giggle. "No, I never have," she said.

"Hey, my name is Sophie. Who're you?"

"I'm D.B."

Sophie giggled softly, like a moth in a jade jar. "I think you're beautiful, D.B. You know, without my coloring I'm not very good-looking. In fact, I think I'm really kind of homely. Gee, I just love white hair. Like spun marsh-mallows." She smiled, white teeth against the silver and green. "Don't mind me. I'm a little drunk, or high, or maybe a little both." She wriggled her green fingers. "Bye bye." Then she disappeared into the dark under the long porch.

Now was the time for D.B. to turn and leave, to forget the whole crazy impulse and return to San Francisco to have a sane and boring life with Malcolm and Aunt Eva. After all, the Cheshire Cat might turn up any minute. And then what would she do?

The mint-colored door swung open and a tall red-bearded man stepped out, his face darkly weathered almost the color of a walnut. D.B. wondered if he had also dyed himself. Perhaps everyone in the house would be a different color, like a basket of little Easter eggs. Perhaps Harry Dazier would be polka-dotted. She wouldn't be too surprised if he was. Anything could happen now.

Redbeard asked, "Is she here? Is Sophie out here? I thought I heard her talking."

D.B. answered, quite calmly, "She just went around the corner."

"Oh. Did she scare you?"

"Yes. For a minute there I didn't know what to think."

"It's a goddam wonder you even saw her. She usually blends right in with the scenery. By the way, who're you?"

"I'm D.B. Sadder."

"And?"

"Auckland brought me—"

"Where's he now?"

"In the car. He passed out. He was drinking pretty heavily on the way up."

"Come on in. My name's Herman."

She entered the house and Herman closed the door after her. They were in a small hallway. The party sounds were louder now. Another man entered the hallway. He was carrying a guitar and seemed to be dressed in costume, something like a Victorian gambler.

"Is this a costume party?" D.B. asked.

"No," Herman said. "This is just Birsha."

Birsha bent toward D.B. and kissed her softly on the cheek. "Who's this?" he asked.

Herman explained. Birsha was obviously drunk and when Herman finished he bent again and kissed D.B.'s forehead, then he held her arm and led her through the front room to the kitchen. No one paid any attention to them. D.B. caught a quick glimpse of the room; highbacked chairs around a long oaken table, bottles and cups. Birsha, the Victorian gambler, pointed out the array of bottles along the dirty sink. "Make yourself a drink, D.B. I don't know if there's any V-8 juice left or not."

She handed him the Scotch.

"Ah, excellent. I haven't had Scotch for months." He made two drinks and handed her the stronger one. "Well, lovely white-haired, well-stacked girl, what brings you to the Dazier house?"

"Is—Mr. Dazier here?"

"That's me. I'm Mr. Dazier."

She stared at him unbelievingly. "Harry—Dazier?"

"No. I'm Birsha. Harry's my brother."

She felt relieved. Birsha wasn't her type at all. There was something about the man, lavishly dressed, underfed, lazy, definitely on the make. She was grateful that he wasn't Harry Dazier.

"Where is Harry?" she asked.

"Around. I don't know. He went off about an hour ago."

"I see—"

Birsha stroked her back, winked, then left the kitchen. Alone, D.B. took the opportunity to look about the house. A fire was burning in the stone hearth. A big, mean-looking man was sitting in a corner chair, glaring at her, his eye pulled down by a crooked scar. There were several old tapestries along the walls. The parquet floor had been recently waxed and her low shoes squeaked softly, like little leather mice, as she moved about the room. A guitar thrummed from the crowded table. She almost stumbled over a man asleep on the floor. She moved back to the mean-looking man in the corner.

"Excuse me, have I missed the recital?"

"Who are you?" the man asked coldly.

"I'm just a friend. I—"

"No," he said curtly, "you haven't missed the recital. Now get away from my corner and leave me alone."

She moved hurriedly away and bumped into Birsha Dazier. He grinned and threw his arms around her narrow waist. "Hey, just a minute. What did Sandro do? Give you a scare?"

"Yes. He seems—awfully mean—"

"He's not," Birsha answered thickly. "He's my other brother. None of us Dazier boys, are mean. Believe me, honey, it's just that Sandro thinks you're a tiger."

"A—a what?"

"A tiger, honey. You know, one of those things that Chenault had painted on his airplanes. Tigers, honey. All women are tigers to poor old Sandro."

Herman came and drew her to the table and introduced her to the crowd, but she couldn't remember any names. D.B.'s first Scotch was beginning to affect her. She hadn't eaten all day and the alcohol on the empty stomach was working quickly. Sophie came and sat down beside her.

"I'm sorry I scared you," she said. "Herman said that I scared you."

"No, that's all right. I've never met a green woman before. It was my pleasure."

"And I've never met anyone named D.B. before. I think plain initials are mysterious and awfully romantic. Don't you? My initials are S.S. But that sounds too much like something from the war, doesn't it? I hate war."

Birsha stood behind Sophie's chair, leaned forward and touched her cheek. "Isn't this something? A green woman. My little green woman. Did she tell you that last month she was blue? You should've seen that. She looked like Sophie, The Queen of the Lizard People."

Sophie beamed happily. "I love science-fiction stories. Did you see that movie, *The Thing?*"

Birsha kissed her cheek. He said, "If I kissed you with my tongue, honey, I'd leave a little white spot on you and the end of my tongue would be green."

"Like life-savers," Sophie said. "I just love lime-flavored life-savers."

Daniel Marris was singing in Spanish, not looking at anyone in particular, sitting straight in the highbacked chair, a gray-haired man with narrowed deepset eyes and grave expression. His wife, Helga, was younger, very attractive, with a rather detached expression that was probably due to the Bloody Marys.

Twenty minutes later D.B. left the table for another drink and she was surprised to find that already her footsteps seemed heavy and irregular. She still hadn't recuperated from the strange collection of people and her introduction to Dazier's house. It wasn't at all as she had imagined it.

Sandro stopped her at the kitchen doorway. "Are you a friend of Harry's?" he asked.

"No. I've never met him."

"Who invited you?"

Daniel Marris came to her side, holding his empty glass. "I invited her," he said. "She's a good friend of mine."

Sandro gave a snort, then returned to his chair in the corner. Daniel and D.B. went into the kitchen. She poured out two drinks of Scotch.

"Thank you," she said.

"That's okay. Sandro's that way, that's all. He's not all there upstairs."

"It is true that he's Harry's brother?"

"Yes. But only a half-brother."

Another twenty minutes passed and still the host hadn't shown. The front door had opened once but it had been only Auckland, looking cramped and chilled from sleeping in the car. He had fixed himself a drink and had settled at the far end of the table, casting knowing looks at D.B., and smiling like an ugly alley cat.

Whatever tension D.B. may have felt in the beginning was now gone. She was feeling mellow, having reached the perfect stage of drinking, and a warm, glowing sensation buzzed behind her eyes, numbing her sense of touch, amplifying her sense of hearing.

7

An hour before D.B. had arrived Harry realized that he was becoming too drunk to perform. He excused himself from the party, explaining that he needed a breath of fresh air, and stepped out onto the porch. He wandered to the far side of the house and sank into the wicker chair, holding his head in his hands. He had to sober up. He knew that if he remained in the house he would continue drinking.

He breathed deeply for a few seconds, then went down into the yard and knelt by a pine tree. The grass was still damp from the fog. He pulled up a handful and pressed it into his face, crushing the sweet blades against his nostrils.

Then, quite suddenly, he remembered how his clothes had come to be in the front yard. He had gone out on the porch to capture the raccoon, thinking that he could possibly tame him, and he had chased the animal into the trees. Then he had kicked off his shoes to demonstrate to himself that he was giving the raccoon an equal chance. One thing led to another and he had stripped naked. Then he had wandered around the trees, calling to the raccoon, calling the animal the Kissing Bandit and crooning loving little raccoon songs.

He stood up now, smiling, and moved off into the forest. He crossed the road near the parking area and sat on a stump, lighting a mentholated cigarette. Thinking of Sophie and Birsha he recalled how, many years ago, he had met and had fallen in love with Jessie Wilbern.

She had been a music student and he had met her in Chicago while attending a lecture on Sibelius. She had been a virgin, a lovely dark-haired violinist, sensitive, quiet. They had lived together for five and a half months, both young and very much in love. Then Harry had had to leave for North Carolina to pick up Birsha and see after Sandro's care in the hospital. And when he had returned to their apartment he learned that Jessie had left him for a jazz musician from Oregon. She had decided that Harry had no talent, no sensitivity, that he was just a half-crazy steam calliope player with brutal schemes for music and demanding ideas about love.

There had been other women since Jessie but he had never allowed himself to become serious about any them. Jessie Wilbern had been love and youth, and all that had left with her. If he was going to be serious with another then there would have to be something more substantial than love. He had decided, quite simply, to put a more realistic price on himself.

He chain-smoked two more cigarettes, feeling more sober now, but didn't return to the house. A vague, pensive yearning had crept into his mood.

After graduating he had left Illinois to study with the composer Arnold Oberhurst, taking Birsha with him. A year later he had his first break: a commission from the Theatre of Ballet to write *The Owl and the Pussycat*. The music had enjoyed a critical success but had never been recorded or included into the repertoire of the company. Harry had earned a following and a reputation but that was all. Then, seven months later, he wrote *The Legend of Peter Klaus* for Arnold Oberhurst's brother-in-law, the conductor Kenneth Amduscias. And, finally, the *Two Saints: Vitus, Walpurgis*, and the third for Amduscias: *Kadesh*, yet to be completed.

But now he could feel his juices failing him, his talent succumbing to the pressures of finances and responsibilities. In cartomancy the tarot has two cards relating to the fatality of human life: The Lovers, and The

Wheel of Fortune. And these cards were making themselves well known to Harry. He was broke, and he was feeling the long greenish ache of loneliness.

The stars were bright overhead and there was just enough light to cast a bluish pattern of shadows along the mulchy ground. When he left the stump and started back for the gate he saw the headlights creeping through the trees. The lights were far below, moving up the road toward his house, and a half minute later he saw the car swing into sight, a low-slung German make. Very expensive. It came to a stop near Daniel's Jeep and Zeke's Oldsmobile, just a few yards from where Harry stood. He said nothing, made no movement to give himself away. He had no idea who it could be. He knew no one with a car like that and he was curious.

A girl, holding what appeared to be a whiskey bottle, stepped from the car and looked at another person who was in the car. The other person was obviously asleep and the girl didn't wake him. She walked toward the gate and passed a few feet from where Harry stood. He caught his breath. Besides driving a rich car the girl was strikingly beautiful. He waited, standing behind the trunk of a pine, and watched as she approached the house. Then he saw her talking to Sophie. Then Herman came to the door and the girl entered the house.

Harry stepped from behind the tree. He hadn't recognized her, was sure that he had never seen her before. Perhaps Daniel and Helga had invited her, or the drunk, Zeke. Or she could be a friend of Richard Freeze's, or even Herman. He was pretty sure that Birsha didn't know her.

He waited a few minutes then approached her car. The other passenger was still asleep, snoring into his armpit. Harry lit a match and read the name on the registration card attached to the steering column. Debra Balmont Sadder. The name meant nothing. He reached over and shook the sleeping man awake.

"Unh—wha—what?"

"Wake up," Harry said.

When the man jerked up and saw Harry he looked nervously to his left and right. He was drunk. Harry recognized the man. Auckland, one of the North Beach creeps who played a lousy piano.

"Hello, Harry. I don't suppose you remember me—"

"I remember you, Auckland. What're you doing here?"

"I came to hear the recital," Auckland explained weakly. "Look, I hope you don't mind my barging in. It's just that I happened to overhear Birsha talking about it in a bar two weeks ago—"

"No, I don't mind."

Auckland fumbled along the floor of the car. "I had a bottle of Scotch here a minute ago—ah, here it is. Would you like a drink, Harry?"

"Just a short one."

Auckland held up the bottle. The liquor was expensive, an excellent label, warm and smoky on Harry's tongue.

"I guess I passed out on the ride up," Auckland said. He stepped from the car, shaking his head, stroking the thin point of his beard and blinking owlishly at Harry. "I came up here with a chick—the one that owns this car—did you happen to see her?"

"Yes. I saw her when she walked up to the house. How do you happen to be with her? She doesn't look degenerate enough to be your type, Auckland."

"Don't act that way, Harry."

"I'll act any way I please," Harry said quietly. "Now why don't you go in to the party and enjoy yourself with your sick girl friend. Tell Birsha I'll be up in a little while."

Auckland made no move to leave. "I brought this girl for *you*, Harry. She's not *my* chick. You must have misunderstood—"

"I didn't know that you were a pimp besides being a lousy piano, Auckland."

"Hey, don't get me wrong, Harry. It's not like that at all. You've got to hear me out. The story might amuse you—"

Harry studied him a moment, curious now about Auckland's air of heavy intrigue. "Okay, Auckland, tell me the story...."

Auckland told him of his first encounter with D.B. Sadder in Pendragon's Bar the night of the television showing, then of the second meeting in Hajek's restaurant, and finally, the trip to Darker's Bay. As Harry listened, drinking occasionally from Auckland's bottle, he realized the interest quickening in him. The girl, if Auckland's story was on the level, might just be what Harry was looking for. When Auckland finally finished, Harry stared thoughtfully at the house beyond the gate, not saying anything.

"What do you think, Harry? Does it interest you?"

"What? Yeah, sure. If it's on the level."

"I swear it, Harry."

"Quit calling me Harry. Don't be so familiar." He lit a cigarette and ran his hand thoughtfully along the curved windshield of the expensive German car. "She's Malcolm Sadder's daughter, you say? His only daughter?"

"That's right."

"And she paid you twenty-five dollars just to meet me? Just like that?"

Auckland nodded. "Sure. Listen, Mr. Dazier, she's got millions. And if she hasn't got it right there in her hand, then she's worth it. You've heard of Malcolm Sadder. The guy makes Scrooge McDuck look penniless. And this chick is the only daughter. Rich? What's twenty-five lousy bucks to her? And she thinks that a certain composer is the greatest. Get it?"

"I get it, Auckland," Harry said. He took another swig from the bottle, thinking of the possibilities of the girl and her interest in him sight unseen. Then, "All right, Auckland. Go up to the party—tell Birsha I invited you if he asks. But don't say anything to anyone about this. Got me?"

Auckland grinned wolfishly. "Sure, Mr. Dazier. I got you. But—one more thing."

"And that is?"

"Well—I was simply wondering what a good settlement would be if all goes well. Now, don't get me wrong, please. Let's just say—between you and me—that if all goes well I should get say—ten per cent for turning you on to her?"

"Five per cent," Harry said.

"Ten. After all, if she comes through, it was through my introduction."

Harry nodded. "All right, ten. But only if I con her. If I don't, then you get nothing. Understand?" .

"Sure, Mr. Dazier. I understand."

Harry returned to his stump in the forest and watched until Auckland went into the house, then he lit another cigarette and breathed heavily, taking in air to help his thoughts.

A beautiful rich girl had come to Darker's Bay to meet him. He should feel flattered, but he didn't. Auckland and his schemes were none of his affair, but still, he didn't reject the idea entirely. After all, she *was* a lovely girl, a wealthy girl, and if Auckland was right, a willing girl—

He returned to the house a few minutes later. The party noise was almost deafening now. Birsha handed him a glass of wine but he didn't drink it. He sat at the table, listened to Daniel's guitar, stole quick glances at the girl. He remarked to himself that she was more lovely than he had managed to see outside in the dark. Her eyes were large, pale green, her lips not too full. She wore very little makeup. There was an electric, animal air about her, definitely attracting. She was watching him now, seeming surprised at seeing him. She continued to study him, practically undressing him. Harry began to feel uneasy and it became difficult for him to look directly at her.

A few minutes later the girl left the table and walked to the kitchen and Harry watched the movement of her body under the skintight trousers. The palms of his hands felt damp. He decided, almost defensively, that it was time for a party intermission, time for him to play the piano.

8

During the recital D.B. sat quietly hunched in her chair, listening with closed eyes. Crystal and lavender and black leather sounds; with gongs and snowballs and pussycats and monsters; witches, sorcerers, devils and saints. While Harry Dazier played the opening of *Kadesh* he spoke the narrator's role, his voice black, sepulchral. She had envisioned the entire complex of sounds and colors, still a little drunk, hunched in her chair.

When it was over it was confusing to D.B. Not the music; but the attitude of the group. She had expected them to be enthusiastic, wanting to talk about the works with Harry, but they simply nodded, said a few words, and returned to the party. It all seemed a bit irreverent to D.B. Harry Dazier seemed at his ease, as if this was the way he preferred it. He poured himself a drink, talking with Birsha, not looking at D.B.

The man called Zeke had slept through the entire performance and now he snorted, turned over on his side, and began to snore very softly. D.B. left the room and went into the kitchen, closed the door after her. She made herself a light Bloody Mary and leaned against the sink, remembering the way Harry had looked when he had first joined the party. He was the most beautiful person she had ever seen.

A few minutes later Harry came into the kitchen.

"What's your name?" he asked.

She swallowed from her drink. "D.B."

"What does that stand for?"

"Debra Balmont. My last name is Sadder." She looked at him, wondering why he looked so amused.

"That's a nice name," he said.

"You look amused, Mr. Dazier—"

"You can call me Harry. And I am amused. I rarely meet my fans. You are a fan of mine, aren't you?"

"Yes—yes, I am."

"Then you amuse me."

"How did you know that I was a fan of yours, Harry?"

"By the way you looked when I played. You seemed more charged than the others."

"Aren't they fans of yours?"

"The others aren't the type of fans I mean. Take Daniel and Helga for instance; I feel sure they think I'm a phony. Herman and Vivian love anything that smacks of art. Richard Freeze enjoys anyone who can do something. Birsha and Sandro are my fans because they're my brothers. Sophie doesn't understand a word that I say. And Zeke, he doesn't even listen when I play. Zeke would like to be a Dark Messenger, but he's too impatient and usually too drunk to learn to ride a motorcycle. But you—" he held out his glass, "—you're an honest-to-God fan. A very rare thing."

"You don't have a very high opinion of yourself."

"Don't I? Perhaps I gave that impression deliberately—simply to bring attention to myself."

She shook her head. "I don't understand you—"

"Then I'm sorry. How old are you?"

"I'm twenty-three. I'll be twenty-four Christmas."

"Do you live in San Francisco?"

"Yes."

"With your parents?"

"No. My mother's dead."

"What does that have to do with it?"

"Nothing. I mean—I live alone. I have an apartment."

"Are you married?"

"No—I've just been divorced."

He seemed to think that over and she lit a cigarette to hide her nervousness. She suspected—which was absurd—that he knew why she had come to Darker's Bay. He acted so damned knowing, making her seem naked, a little foolish, forcing her to play a part. She knew that he was attracted to her, as well as she was to him, but there seemed to be something else.

"Who brought you here?" he asked.

"Auckland."

"Who's Auckland?"

"He said that he was a friend of yours."

"Really? Is he here?"

"Yes."

He sipped from his drink, cocking his head to one side. "Is he the piano player from Pendragon's? The dirty looking guy? Yes? Then I do know him. I just didn't know his name. Are you a friend of his?"

"No," she said. "I—I paid him to invite me here."

"Really?" He smiled and shook his head. "How much did you pay him?"

"Twenty-five dollars."

"You didn't have to do that, D.B. It was a waste of your money."

"Well, I didn't really mind—" She tried to smile, to make a joke of it.

Why had she told him that? She wasn't that drunk.

"Are you going to drive back to San Francisco tonight?"

"Yes."

He nodded. "Well—I was wondering—if you could give me a lift. Auckland can ride back with Herman and Vivian."

"Yes, I'd like that."

"Good. When you're ready to leave just let me know."

An hour later she found herself again in the kitchen, this time with Sophie and Helga Marris. Since her talk with Harry she had been drinking steadily, knowing that she wasn't going to have to drive on the way back. Harry was sober. D.B. had switched to wine, the vodka and Scotch having run out.

"Harry likes you," Sophie said.

"How do you know?"

"I can tell. Are you married, D.B.?"

"No. I'm divorced. I was married to a man—with a crewcut and—very pink cheeks."

"That shows how nice you are," Sophie said vaguely. "But don't mind me, because I always say what first comes into my head. I think I'm high. I don't know what it is but I go to sleep high and wake up high."

"You're full of Sophie," Helga said.

"That's it," Sophie said.

D.B. asked, "Have you known Harry long?"

"Two months," Sophie answered. "You know, you should never *never* marry a man with short hair. Do you remember the story about Samson?"

"Yes—"

"See? I never marry men with short hair. My first husband looked like a walking palm tree and he was one of the most beautiful men I've ever known. But he divorced me when I married my second husband. Isn't that awful? I think a woman, especially a green and blue and tangerine woman, should be allowed to have at least five husbands."

"Are you married now?"

"Gee, I don't think so." She frowned. "No, not right now. But do you know? I'm trying to get Birsha to marry me. He's got long hair. And besides, I think he likes me. He called me Queen of the Lizard People." She frowned again, knitting her green brow. "Maybe I should make myself blue again," she said.

"I like the green," Helga said.

"So do I, but Birsha says that without my clothes on I look like a little green Martian wearing green grapefruit. He says that blue grapefruit is all right, but that green grapefruit is a little too weird for him."

Helga poured another round of vin rosé and Sophie continued giving her strange advice to D.B., saying that D.B. should marry a painter because painters are definitely harder to get along with than farmers or airplane pilots. And besides, airplane pilots wear Cesar Romero mustaches and undershorts with flowers on them—

"I wish that Harry hadn't asked Sandro here," Helga said. "I hate people like Sandro."

"Gee," Sophie said, "I feel the same way, too. Sandro wears his hair short. It's just like I told you."

Helga turned to D.B. "Do you know what that guy does for a living?"

"No."

"He runs a merry-go-round for the kiddies. He's got a dismantled merry-go-round in his warehouse and he puts it up when there's a charity bazaar or a carnival nearby. I tell you, I wouldn't put my kid on that lunatic's merry-go-round if it was the last goddam merry-go-round on earth."

"He used to be with a circus," Sophie said.

"What did he do?" D.B. asked.

Helga poured more wine. "He used to train lions. You know, a goddam lion tamer with a goddam whip and jodhpurs. Tigers and panthers—things like that. A real nut on tigers."

D.B. felt a shudder go through her, as if the floor of the house had shaken. They continued talking, and when the conversation turned to a place called The Singing Frogs, D.B. excused herself. She wanted a breath of air, wanted to be alone with her thoughts, so she left the kitchen and walked twice around the veranda, slowly, enjoying the cool night air.

The second time around she was startled to see a figure standing near the railing. She hesitated, telling herself that there was no reason to be frightened, then continued past the railing. The figure had been Sandro, watching her from the darkness.

The party was over by four in the morning. Daniel and Helga had left an hour earlier. Herman and Vivian helped carry Zeke to his Oldsmobile. Richard Freeze left in a black Jaguar sedan, taking Auckland with him. D.B. stayed behind and helped Sophie clean the front room. When she finished she went out onto the porch and sat in a wicker chair to wait for Harry, who was carrying Birsha to one of the upstairs bedrooms.

Sandro came out, playing a flashlight along the porch near the steps. Sensing that he was looking for her, D.B. sat quietly, trying not to bring attention to herself. But when she moved the lacquered wicker sighed under her weight and Sandro turned, swinging the beam of light into her face. She squinted, fighting back the impulse to call for Harry.

"So, Harry's going to go back with you," Sandro said.

She tried looking away from the blinding light but he moved closer, keeping the beam in her eyes.

"It's not going to be any good for him," Sandro said.

"Please—take the light away—"

"Harry's my brother, my little brother; did you know that?"

"Yes, of course I knew."

"I don't want anything to happen."

"How—how do you mean that?"

"You know exactly how I mean it."

"I'm hardly going to hurt him, if that's what you mean. I'm simply giving him a lift into town—"

"I'm giving you a warning," Sandro said tightly.

All she saw beyond the bright circle of light was the vague outline of Sandro's huge body. She could hear his voice but it seemed detached from the body, as if his words were coming from the flashlight.

He started moving away from her, still playing the light on her, and she heard his footsteps moving out into the yard, his voice far away and crooning: "Tiger, tiger, burning bright—In the forest of the night—"

Then the light went out and she was alone.

Harry came out a few minutes later. She pressed her hand into his, and she knew that she had no intention of letting him go anywhere else but her apartment when they reached San Francisco. She wanted to have him with her, in her house, in her bed, and she wasn't going to let him slip away. She had no idea if he wanted her but she was convinced that she could impress herself on him. She had no idea why she felt so bold. Perhaps Sandro's warning had, in a way, excited her to a quick decision. Whatever, she wanted him and she didn't want to hold herself back for a more formal time.

She followed Harry to the gate, then to the car, and she handed him the keys without a word. Before he got behind the wheel D.B. heard Harry's name being called from the stand of pines on the opposite side of the road. It was Sandro, calling for his brother. Harry excused himself and crossed the road, his tall figure losing itself in the pines.

She tried to hear what they were saying but only stray bits of their conversation came across the road. She couldn't tell, but they seemed to be arguing. Furthermore, she sensed that it concerned herself.

"No, Sandro—let's not talk about it right now…. Harry, please listen—ignoring what?—I'll do the deciding if—burning bright—Yes, call at the warehouse if—No, I'm going to be—"

When Harry returned to the car she noticed his troubled expression so she thoughtfully said nothing to him—right away. He slid behind the wheel and without a word drove hurriedly down the country road to the village. When they reached the coast highway she reached over and touched his arm, as if to remind him of her presence. He smiled briefly.

"Is there anything the matter, Harry?"

"No."

"Would you rather not go into town with me?"

"No, of course not."

A dog barked when they passed a farm house. There was no traffic and the heater hummed against D.B.'s legs. The headlights reflected from the red discs on the highway markers.

"Sandro doesn't like me, does he, Harry?"

"No."

"Why not?"

"He thinks we're going to become lovers."

"And are we?"

There was a pause. She was aware that her question definitely had been an invitation. Harry Dazier turned to her, studying her for a brief second, then he nodded.

She wanted him to kiss her, as if needing that to seal the bargain, but he made no move toward her. D.B. realized that she had been right earlier: Harry had known why she had come to Darker's Bay, the same as Auckland had known why she had wanted to meet him. But she no longer felt ashamed. Perhaps she was a little too far over the edge of drunkenness to feel badly over her boldness. Instead, she felt completely at her ease, as if propositioning complete strangers was the natural thing for her to be doing.

She asked, "Did you know that I came to meet you because I wanted us to become lovers?"

"No, but it occurred to me later. It just seemed to be the way it was meant to be."

Harry drove slowly, enjoying the feel of the expensive car. His meeting with D.B. had gone much better than he had imagined. So far it seemed as if he could do no wrong as far as she was concerned. She was willing to swallow any line that he fed her, no matter how obvious it was. And, because of this, he was feeling a little guilty. But that, he told himself, was perfectly natural. He didn't feel *too* guilty, however, because he had, in a way, told her the truth. He *did* want to be her lover. And why not? After all, Harry was human, and D.B. was a beautiful, desirable woman.

True, her being very wealthy was an added incentive, but right at the moment it wasn't everything. He was aware of her warmth next to him, could feel her large breast pressing softly into his elbow whenever he moved his arm.

A white sign indicated the cutoff to Bolinas Beach and he slowed, taking the turn. To the right a field stretched to a windbreak line of eucalyptus. A white horse stood in the deep grass, watching as the car drove by. The road turned again. A few houses came into view. It was beginning to grow light, a gray false dawn.

When they entered town he stopped at an all-night café and D.B. waited in the car while he ordered beer and sandwiches. He had no definite plans, but he knew that the beach would be empty at this time of the morning, that D.B. was more than willing, and that it would be a perfect opportunity.

As he watched her through the steamy windows he felt the excitement rise in him. The fry-cook was watching over his shoulder, with beefy freckled arms, gold-toothed smile, and envious eyes. Harry smiled and nodded. He paid for the food and drinks and returned to the car. He noticed the expression on D.B.'s face whenever she looked at him. It was obvious that the girl was fascinated by him and it made him feel a bit uneasy, a bit unworthy. He had never thought of himself as a particularly fascinating person, but if D.B. wanted to think so then it was all right with him. In fact, it definitely helped his cause.

He slid behind the wheel and she bent across the seat, her eyes not moving away from his. Harry felt wonderfully amused by all this attention, this drama, and he returned her gaze, knowing that the fry-cook was watching them.

So why not give the fry-cook something to watch? Harry kissed her. No bells, no violent colors, no absurd singing strings. But then, he hadn't expected any. Her mouth was warm and moist, her body pressing into his with an eagerness that he hadn't known for many years.

"Hello," he said.

"Hi."

"Would you like to pick some shells?"

"What kind of shells?"

"Sea shells. There's a beach at the end of the street."

Her look was an open invitation. "Yes, I would," she said.

He drove to the edge of the village and parked near a broken concrete wall. The sky was pale gray, the beach deserted, the bay resembling a sheet of wet steel, dull and cold. There were no waves, only a tiny lapping and curling at the gritty shoreline. It was strange—because Harry hadn't expected it—but there was a sudden feeling of intimacy between

D.B. and himself. He knew that his reasons weren't the purest, that her reasons in turn were childish and somewhat starry-eyed, but there was no embarrassment between them, as if, in spite of their separate designs, there was a bond between them, as if each was secretly aware of the other's motives.

D.B. sat at the base of the old wall while Harry went through the motions of hunting for shells. He found a few good ones, washed them in the gray icy water, and put them in his pocket. Then he lit a cigarette and stood watching D.B. at the wall.

D.B. Debussy. Snow white hair and sea shells. Two Saints—Harry and D.B. What was it that Sandro had said to him earlier? Oh yes. William Blake. Tiger, tiger, burning bright—In the forest of the night. Harry smiled, dragging deeply on the Alpine cigarette. He wanted a drink of beer and he returned to the wall.

He no longer wanted to eat but he ate a sandwich anyway. He drank two beers and rested his back against the wall, his bourbon-colored eyes watching the dark stretch of water.

"Is this right, Harry?" D.B. asked softly.

Good God, but this girl must have gone to a lot of movies when she was a kid. Perhaps she still went to the movies. It would just be his luck if she did. He hated the movies.

He nodded solemnly to her question. "Yes, this is right," he answered.

She started asking him questions about his work, his past, his future. Then she talked of herself, telling him a lot of weird nonsense about her father, then some garbled story about some character who had visions of Christ in Ireland. And as she talked he knew that he should be listening intently, but he wasn't. He was fascinated with her looks, her body, the way she moved. But what she said seemed to be so much disconnected nonsense. She told him briefly of her feelings, but they meant nothing to him. However, when she paused and looked questioningly at him, he nodded gravely and said: "I understand."

She seemed relieved by that. "I knew that you would," she said quietly. "When I first heard your music I knew that you'd understand."

He didn't know whether to laugh aloud or groan. He did neither. He drew her close to him and kissed her lightly on the cheek.

What did he really represent to this girl? He had no idea. He saw in her a way to help himself, a way to crawl out from under the oppressive weight of his financial troubles long enough for him to finish *Kadesh*, and if things went right for him, long enough for him to start on something new, something bigger.

Malcolm Sadder, he knew, was on the art commission, was very influential with the opera league. Perhaps, if he played his cards right, he could work out some sort of a commission from Malcolm Sadder. It wasn't too unusual for a man of Sadder's wealth to help a composer. It wouldn't be an unusual experience for Harry, but it would certainly be the richest one.

The girl was kissing him again and he felt the excitement again. Her desire infected him and his schemes vanished from his mind. He returned her kiss, moved his hands along her back. He pulled the edge of her sweater free and slipped his hand on her bare flesh. Her bra had become unhooked and he found himself wondering when that had happened. She pressed into him, turning slightly. Her lips parted and she made a tiny gasping noise. He held her down against the soft sand, cupping her breast in his hand, feeling the nipple tighten against his palm. Her lips brushed his cheek and then his ear. Her arms went around his neck and her neck pressed against his mouth. It was warm now and D.B. moved against him, under him, dimming his surroundings—

The sky was pearled with tiny cobwebs of clouds as the dawn grew lighter. A string of cormorants moved over the water in rosary formation. Later, D.B.'s head rested against Harry's chest, her soft hair brushing his chin. Her voice was barely a whisper.

"How long has your heart been beating, Harry?"

"Thirty-seven years."

"That seems like such a terribly long time for something to keep operating, to keep pounding."

He stared up at the sky, completely relaxed, still enjoying her—which was unusual for him. He stroked her back. "Can you hear my stomach growling?"

"Yes."

"That's because I've got a choochoo inside me and it growls like that whenever it goes uphill."

"Choochoo," D.B. whispered. She kissed his chest. "It's all gone. I feel wonderful, lightheaded—"

"That's because you're full of flowers."

She pinched him, then kissed him. "I don't think I'll ever be your fan any more, Harry. I wouldn't want to embarrass you and I wouldn't want to amuse you the way that I did."

"What will you be then?"

"Can I be your lover? I mean—not just for a day, but for a long time?"

"Yes."

"Then I'm your lover. I want you to come with me to my apartment. To stay. I mean, you don't have to stay if you don't want to. I mean—I'd like you to stay with me for as long as you'd like."

"All right."

"Have you ever been married?"

"No."

"In love?"

"Certainly."

"Do you like me?"

"Yes. I wouldn't want to stay with you if I didn't."

"I don't think I've ever been in love. Can I be in love with you, Harry?"

"If you want."

He kissed her softly, feeling almost sad for her, but not quite. She was a grown woman and she knew what she wanted. She had gone to a guy like Auckland and had foolishly paid him twenty-five dollars to meet Harry. And now she had met him, had made love to him, and had committed herself to him. He liked her, appreciated her childish adoration, and was beginning to feel curious about her. But as far as her not knowing that he was attracted to her wealth as well as herself—that was a sad thing.

He decided that she would never find out about that part of it. There was no reason for her to ever know.

D.B. rested against him, half drowsing, listening to his regular breathing, the beat of his heart, and watched the sky turn from dawn to day. A few children came out onto the beach to throw stones at the water but she didn't move. She felt complete, blinded to everything but her satisfaction, asking herself if her feelings were true, if she could, in such a short time, fall so desperately in love with a man.

Yes, she could. Because she had already convinced herself that she had. Harry Dazier was everything that she had ever wanted. The satisfaction that she felt testified to that, and she believed that it could never change.

Book II — Dazier

1

D.B. had bought Harry a new piano and they had converted the parrot's room to a comfortable music studio, and for two weeks after the night of the Darker's Bay party, she was content to spend most of her time there, being close to him, listening to his work as it progressed. Harry was near to finishing *Kadesh* now and D.B. was trying to make herself useful to him without directly interfering. He didn't seem to mind; in fact, he seemed to enjoy her help. She had typed his correspondence to his conductor and patron, Kenneth Amduscias, and to his ex-teacher, Arnold Oberhurst.

It was difficult for her to explain, for during the first week of their affair Harry had seemed tense and uncomfortable, oftentimes moody, but then he had relaxed, coming from out of his quiet self-darkness and giving himself to her, as if a weight had been suddenly removed from his spirit. His rebirth had been so tender, so rewarding, that she hadn't questioned him about what had been troubling him.

The only shadow that now remained to threaten her new life was her father. She still hadn't told him of her divorce from her ex-husband, and she was still paying Gordon his weekly blackmail check. She was still afraid of what Malcolm would do. Aside from that single wrong note she was happier now than she had ever believed possible.

Her life had become better organized. Her drinking was no longer a problem; she confined herself to a few vodka martinis in the evenings. Harry, of course, drank from noon until it was time for bed, but it didn't bother her. She was deeply in love with him. He had given her identity, had given her completeness. He had become her life.

She sipped from her coffee now and contentedly watched as Harry made a drink from his siphon and bottle. She realized, probably for the hundredth time, that he was a terribly handsome figure, in spite of his present state of careless dress. She had bought him new clothes despite his protests that he didn't want her to pay his way. Even his protests had pleased her. He didn't seem to be interested in her money; in fact, he had been genuinely embarrassed when she had told him of her relationship with Malcolm.

"Have you decided?" Harry asked.

"Decided? I really don't know, Harry. I wish I could see it as objectively as you do—but I can't."

She had told him of her life with Gordon, of his blackmailing her. And he was right—she *should* tell her father the whole story—but still she was afraid.

"Of what?" Harry wanted to know.

"He could force me back to stay with him and Aunt Eva. And, Harry, I don't want that. I don't think I could stand it. Not now. Not ever."

"You're certainly not going to let that sonofabitch Gordon get away with milking you, are you? No. You've got to tell your old man. That's all there is to it. If your old man blows his cap and tries to get you back to his place, then why don't you and I go back to Darker's Bay and forget him."

"I couldn't do that to you, Harry. Honest. You're already supporting Birsha and Sophie, and what little money I have in the bank wouldn't last the four of us a year. And I wouldn't want you to throw Birsha out just because of me. No—if Malcolm tries to force me back, then we'll have to think of some other way."

"Look, D.B., I'm not thinking of the money. I'm thinking only about you and me—about us. We can make out all right. We own the piano and we can move it up to Darker's Bay and I'll finish the *Kadesh*. Amduscias will advance me about five hundred if I asked him."

"I don't know," D.B. said doubtfully. "Perhaps Malcolm won't try to force me back. Maybe he'll just blow off steam and give me a tongue lashing."

"Then you'll tell him? And let the cards fall where they may?"

She nodded. "Yes—I suppose that's the best—" She went to Harry and rested her cheek against his chest. She knew that it was absurd but she was afraid that Malcolm could, somehow, get to her through Harry. She was afraid that he could harm Harry's career, but she couldn't see how. The fear was simply there, coiled like a hot red snake in the pit of her stomach.

She wished that the matter could be ignored, that they could go on exactly as they had been for the past two weeks. But she knew that they couldn't. There would always be the problem of Gordon's blackmail and the shadow of Malcolm Sadder. Harry was right. Malcolm was going to have to be told and Gordon was going to have to be pried away from her pocketbook.

Harry kissed her lightly, brushing his mouth on her forehead. "It's got to come out, baby, one way or the other."

She left the room and moved through the routine of removing her robe and stepping under the shower like a sleepwalker. When she finished she toweled and dressed in a dark business suit, very severe and tweedy, knowing that it would appeal to Malcolm's tastes. She returned to the music studio and stood in the doorway.

Dazier was absorbed in his work, sitting with shoes and shirt off, hair falling in his eyes, a forgotten cigarette between his lips. The one thing that she hadn't been able to talk him into was having his hair cut, and looking at him now she was reminded of what Sophie had once told her about men with long hair. She went to Harry and kissed his bare neck, running her hands along his ribs, the flat of his stomach. He looked up at her.

"You look nice, D.B. Did you know that?"

"Yes, but I like to hear it."

"You look nice," he repeated.

"Do you like *me*?"

"Very much."

She stroked his stomach, brushing her lips on his neck.

"Not now," he said quietly.

"No?"

"No. You've got a duty to perform."

"Do you think I'm trying to escape from my duty by wanting to go to bed with you?"

"Yes."

"Isn't it a good idea?"

"You'll be back in no time at all," he said.

"Will you still feel the same?"

"I will if you put your hands on my stomach again."

"Then I'll run in and tell my father and I'll run right out again."

He reached behind him and held her leg, turning in his stool, pressing his shoulders against her thighs. She leaned forward, against him. His hands moved along her legs, then her waist.

"Have you ever made love to a woman in tweed before?" she asked.

"No, but I once slept on top of a bunch of gunny sacks. Do you think it'd be the same?"

She pulled herself away reluctantly. "I don't think so." She smiled. "You go back to *Kadesh* and I'll go see my father—my executioner."

"I don't think it'll be that bad."

"Perhaps. Wish me luck."

She left the room, then the apartment, leaving a faint trail of her perfume behind her. Down at the street level the doorman swung open the door and saluted. She continued past him, not exchanging her usual small talk, knowing that he was watching her and wondering why Mr. Fitzroy didn't come home any more.

When D.B. had left, Harry got up and stood by the piano, deliberately catching the trace of her perfume. He grimaced, then made a tall drink and moved out to the balcony. The view never failed to impress him. It was a mild spring afternoon, bright and clear, and there were many sailboats out on the bay. He leaned on one of the gargoyles and softly cursed himself.

What had happened to him?

At first he had been interested in D.B. only because of the money, but after that first morning with her on the beach at Bolinas he had grown curious about her. Perhaps that had been the beginning; he didn't know for sure. He had still been interested in the money, in the influence that he knew her father had.

Then what had changed that?

He hadn't the slightest idea. But subtly, almost unnoticed, his curiosity had grown, and as she told him more about herself he found himself listening and becoming uncomfortably responsible toward her. His conscience began to bother him. He told himself that he was a grade-A sonofabitch, no better than her ex-husband Gordon, or Auckland.

Several times he had found himself on the verge of packing up and walking out on her, returning to Darker's Bay where he belonged and quitting the whole rotten scheme. But he hadn't. He had stayed and had recognized the changes in himself. He found himself thinking—seriously thinking—of her more and more. She started to get under his skin and he felt guilty because he enjoyed having her there. He enjoyed her presence, liked to look up from his piano and find her near him, reading, typing, or simply watching him. He liked to hear her move about the apartment, humming to herself, making noises to the parrot. He liked to touch her, arouse her to such wild desire that she made love to him before they could reach the bed.

He realized that he was in love with her. At first he didn't want to admit it, but he knew that it was true. She had bought him the piano, but there had been no triumph in that. Instead, he had felt like a cheap con-man. And it had been worse when she had insisted on buying him the clothes. He had honestly protested, but she had made the purchases anyway.

Had it gone too far?

He felt like throwing himself at her, placing himself in her innocence, telling her the whole story. But he was afraid. He remembered how hateful her recollections of Gordon were. What would she think of Harry if she knew that he had originally seduced her for her money? The idea was staggering.

There was only one other person who knew of Harry's original motives. Auckland. Harry shuddered in the warm sun and quickly swallowed from his drink. Auckland.

He swore to himself that she would never learn about his original designs. He didn't want her to be hurt. It wouldn't be right—especially now that he no longer wanted her money, but wanted her for herself. He had been quite serious when he had suggested they return to Darker's Bay and make it on their own.

The whole thing was so damned complex, and yet so very simple. Harry was in love with her. It was a more solid, more mature love than his youthful affair with Jessie Wilbern. With D.B. there was no selfishness, no jealousy—he cursed himself again, wishing that there were some way to make up for his past machinations, wishing hopelessly that there were some way he could stop Auckland when the time came.

And the time for Auckland would come. He knew that. Auckland was a dangerous little schemer—especially where there was big money to be had. Harry had no delusions about Auckland's having dropped his ideas for a possible commission from Harry's so-called 'score' with D.B.

Harry sighed, staring out to the bay, thinking of D.B. again, wanting her to return, wanting to have a cold beer with her, wanting to take a warm shower with her. And, if not that, he simply wanted to sit and talk with her, be with her, listen to her move about the apartment humming softly to herself.

2

Aunt Eva's pearl-gray Bentley was parked in the graveled driveway directly behind Malcolm's De Soto. D.B. parked at the end of the curving driveway and walked across the lawn to the stone walkway which led to the front. When she unlocked the door she heard her father's voice from the main room at the end of the hallway. She took a deep breath, wished herself luck, thought of Harry back in the apartment, and crossed the hallway to the room.

"Well well," Malcolm said thinly, "this is a pleasant surprise."

D.B. nodded at the both of them. "Hello, Malcolm. Aunt Eva."

Aunt Eva smiled coldly. "My dear, you're looking marvelous. And how is that dear husband of yours?"

"I—he's fine—I suppose."

"Well, D.B.," Malcolm said, "we haven't been seeing very much of you."

"I've been—busy, Malcolm."

"I see."

Malcolm Sadder was a thin little man, carefully balding, with pinched white lips and rimless tinted glasses. He wore his usual dark suit, high topped shoes, high Hoover collar and wide necktie. He had a twitch in his left eye and when he became angry he squirmed his thin lips and winked his eye. He had never struck his daughter, but she knew that his voice could cut into her like a wire whip. His face was twitching now and D.B.'s heart sank.

Aunt Eva, Malcolm's younger sister, was tall and narrow, about forty, with absolutely no breasts or hips. Her face was a long white mask with a hooked nose and slightly protruding teeth. She invariably piled as many bracelets as she could on her thin wrists and she jangled when she gestured—and she gestured constantly.

Malcolm cleared his throat, moved to his desk.

The house always smelled the same to D.B. Dark and musty. She wished that she was back in her own apartment, in the comfortable music studio with Harry.

"I'm glad you came by," Malcolm began. "I've been wanting to have a chat with you—about certain things."

"Oh?"

He opened a notebook on his desk with a disgusted flip of his wrist. "Yes, D.B.—a little chat. I've been looking over your bills. You say you've been too busy to come by and see us? I'll say you have. You've been too busy drinking over one hundred dollars' worth of imported Scotch whisky! And here! Look at this little item! A totem pole and a parrot cage. I ask you, why should a *parrot* cage cost well over two hundred dollars?"

She didn't answer.

Malcolm sighed. "Those—gargoyles that you purchased a while back were certainly bad enough. But a *totem* pole. Is a totem pole a necessary item in a married couple's home these days?"

"I'll return the pole if you want," D.B. said.

"Forget it. I've paid for it already. But I'm going to take half of its cost from your next allowance check."

She nodded and looked at the carpet. Why couldn't she come right out and tell them? Was she that gutless? Isn't that why she came?

Aunt Eva sat on the sofa, jingling like a troika. D.B. felt like a child again. Once, in the third grade, she had been forced to sit in the school principal's office and listen to the tick of the clock.

"I've divorced Gordon, Malcolm."

No one moved for a full minute, then Aunt Eva groaned and looked to the ceiling and Malcolm slowly passed his hand over his bald crown.

"*Divorced* Gordon?"

"Yes."

"Absurd! Why, I see Gordon every day and he—divorced Gordon?

Absurd!"

When she had been allowed to leave the principal's office she had returned to the class for the singing lesson, and the other children had been in the middle of *Frère Jacques*, but D.B. hadn't felt a part of it.

Aunt Eva looked dramatic. "Surely, you're joking—"

"Eva, stay out of this."

"Now, Malcolm, after all I'm the child's—"

Aunt Eva was the child's what? What was Aunt Eva? D.B. wondered if she were pale; she felt pale. What would they say if they knew about her affair with Harry Dazier? Good God. The idea was horrible.

"When and where did this so-called divorce take place?" Malcolm asked.

"In Las Vegas about a month ago. Gordon didn't contest. As a matter of fact—he was rather nice about it—in the beginning. It wasn't until later that he became nasty—and started to demand money."

"Demand *what?*"

D.B. nodded. "Money. I'm paying him a hundred and twenty-five a week."

"What for?"

"It's blackmail. To keep it from you. I was frightened of what you'd do if you found out about the divorce. I couldn't help it, Malcolm. I didn't want to disappoint you. But I couldn't stay married to Gordon. I couldn't stand him."

Malcolm was twitching.

D.B. sighed. "I knew you wouldn't understand."

"Gordon, a blackmailer? Good God, D.B. What else have you been up to?"

Aunt Eva looked haughty. "All *I* can say is that it's a wonder the papers haven't gotten wind of this sordid affair."

"Papers?" Malcolm echoed. "Do you mean the *news*papers?"

"What else?"

Malcolm groaned. He turned to D.B. "I'm glad that you've told me about this, young lady. Gordon won't be blackmailing you any longer. He'll be damned lucky if I don't throw him in jail."

D.B. nodded. She couldn't feel sorry for Gordon.

Malcolm talked for a few minutes, then, almost to himself, he said: "I had hopes—foolish ones I now realize—of my daughter's settling down and behaving like a normal human being. I had hopes of—of grandchildren."

So it was of himself that Malcolm had been thinking. D.B. should have known that she would never receive sympathy from her father or Aunt Eva.

Aunt Eva cooed, "What more can you expect, Malcolm. After all, D.B. is her mother's daughter—"

"Keep quiet, Eva!" Malcolm snapped. "Don't say another word on that subject!"

There it was again: D.B.'s mother. What was there about it that D.B. shouldn't know? Had Marjorie told the truth, or had she, as D.B. had suspected, lied to her about their mother's death.

D.B. rose, wanting to leave before the inevitable lecture. She said, by way of an exit line: "I'm sorry about all this, Malcolm. Honestly."

"You're sorry! What good does being sorry do? Closing the door after the sins have escaped, don't you think? Isn't this familiar to you by this time? Don't you remember what you and I went through eight months ago? You'd said that you were sorry then. And what good did it do? I can tell you—it did no good. No good at all."

D.B. said, "I'd hoped that you'd understand, Malcolm. I divorced Gordon because I hated him. I couldn't stand to be with him. His blackmailing seems to prove what kind of man he really is. But you seem to overlook that. You're not interested in knowing *why* I divorced him, but only that I *did* divorce him."

"Perhaps you're being unfair, D.B. Understanding cuts both ways. I understand why you divorced him. I think you did the correct thing. Undoubtedly. If that's the sort Gordon is—then I wouldn't want him as a son-in-law, and I certainly wouldn't want him to be the father of my grandchild. I suppose you're wondering why I'm being harsh? I'll tell you. It's because you kept this business quiet for a month, not telling me that you were being blackmailed by him. That's what I object to. You ran off in Dublin with a sculptor who saw visions. Now you pay blackmail to a person like Gordon. Don't you see what I'm driving at? You're irresponsible. You're a fool, a babe in the woods. You're almost twenty-four years old and you're still a child. You're open prey for any scheming clown that happens to strike your fancy. I admit that it was my mistake in asking you to fancy Gordon, but at least I investigated the young man before I made the suggestion. But what about yourself? Did you ask *who* the sculptor was? Did you ask yourself if it was *right* to have a hush-hush divorce from Gordon, then put yourself into a position to be blackmailed? No, D.B. You're unfair to me. Not I to you. You're the fool, not myself. And, as I say, God knows what you'll be bringing to me next week, next month, next year. God knows what impulsive item you'll buy, or what lunatic you'll take up with next, what stray cat you'll feed."

She stared at him, hearing his cold words, thinking of Harry Dazier. What would Malcolm do if he learned of Harry? Would he investigate

Harry and conclude that he was simply a gold-digger? Let him! True, Harry was poor, but she knew, this time, that she had made the right choice. But would Malcolm, with all of his suspicions, believe that? No, of course not.

Malcolm continued, his voice cutting into her. "Let me remind you of something, D.B. I'm a rich man. I may not dress the role, and I may not live the role, but as you damn well know, I'm worth well over fifteen million dollars. Real estate, investments—you know the story. I know what the newspaper columnists call me. I know my money.

"But I'm afraid that you don't quite realize the value of money. What would happen if I died tomorrow, or next week? *You*, not Marjorie, not Aunt Eva, but *you* would inherit every bit of my holdings and my investments. I hate to think of what would take place if that happened."

He continued to preach, twitching and pulling his mouth, showing figures, telling her that she was a complete fool, that she had better snap out of it. When he brought up the subject of moving back into the St. Francis Woods home D.B. practically cried out.

"Let me stay in my apartment, Malcolm. Please."

"Why should I?"

They argued about it, D.B. defending the apartment and giving her reasons: her happiness, her wish to be alone for a while.

Malcolm relented. "All right. You can stay there. But if you make one more mistake I'm canceling your lease."

When they had finished, finally, D.B. left and drove slowly back toward town. She chain-smoked three cigarettes, stopped at a cocktail lounge atop Twin Peaks, and ordered a vodka martini. What could she do now? She had already made that one mistake—according to Malcolm—she had fallen in love with Harry Dazier. What was the sense of it all? She wormed her way out from under one problem and fell right into another.

"Another martini, please."

A hell of a situation. Should she tell Harry? No, she decided not to. She didn't want him to share her problem. She wanted him to feel everything was fine; she didn't want anything to interfere with his work.

"Here's your drink, lady."

"What? Oh, thank you."

Malcolm had been right about certain things. She knew that. But not about everything. How could he understand that she loved Harry, that she had fallen in love with him only two days after she had rid herself of Gordon? How could anyone understand that?

3

Three days after her visit with Malcolm she sat in the main room of her apartment, her feet propped on a white leather ottoman, drinking her second vodka martini of the day. The drink was cold and dry, sharp and clear, and outside the window the day was slowly becoming magic rose as the sinking sun reflected from the far clouds. The bridge seemed on fire, the towers and struts burning gold. She hadn't told Harry about her visit with her father; she had simply said that it had gone well and they had left it there.

Arnold Ames, a composer that Harry had met in Pendragon's the night before, had come to the apartment three hours earlier that afternoon. The two of them, Harry and Arnold, were still in the studio, drinking Scotch and banging noisily on the piano. D.B. could hear their voices, Harry making occasional comment, Arnold describing passages of his opera. D.B. knew little of the opera, even though she had heard a recording of it. It was called, oddly enough *The Needle* and was concerned with the Government's continuing crackdown on narcotics. It was all quite vague to D.B., but Harry was enjoying the whole thing immensely.

Then she heard *Kadesh* from the studio. Harry had, just the day before, completed the score and that morning had telephoned Kenneth Amduscias in New Orleans to tell him the good news as well as to ask for a five-hundred-dollar advance. Right now they were celebrating. They had telephoned Birsha and had made a date to meet him later that night. And, when Ames had arrived, they had started drinking.

Ames was talking now, his voice rumbling, talking about his brother, who had sung the title role in the opera.

D.B. had, for some childish reason, once pictured composers as playing their music in grand parlors before people of wealth and influence. Where had she got that idea? From the motion pictures? Probably, because she had always pictured Cornel Wilde as the composer—

Harry and Ames came into the room. Harry was stripped to the waist because it was a warm evening, and Arnold had removed his jacket. D.B. noticed that he wore old-fashioned suspenders.

"Did you hear Arnie's stuff?"

"Yes."

Ames turned to Harry. "Are you going to work on anything new?"

"Yes. Have you ever thought about *Alice in Wonderland?*"

"And?"

"Think of it as a three-part opera, with ballet. Wild dancing and singing on a chess board, at the seashore, at the tea party. Besides, half of the songs are already written. Have you ever heard the recording that Cyril Ritchard made of them?"

Ames nodded, sipped his drink.

"Do you have any other recordings?" Harry asked.

"*Nox Microcosmica.* I'll bring it over here one of these days."

"Do you remember any songs of Alice?"

Harry was drunk, D.B. becoming drunk more slowly. Ames started to sing a few lines from Alice and Harry laughed and poured more drinks. D.B. tried to picture Alice as an opera, but nothing came to her; however, she could see that Harry was fired up over the idea.

An hour later, Ames shook hands all around, promised to call Harry at a later time, and left. D.B. saw him to the door, then returned to the room. She felt like skipping, celebrating *Kadesh* in some wild way.

"I feel grand!" Harry said.

"So do I."

"Let's go meet Birsha and Sophie and do something."

"All right."

They staggered out to the balcony and looked out at the lights on the bay. The Alcatraz tower light was flashing, reflecting on the water.

"I can hear the trucks on the Embarcadero," Harry said. "Look at all the lights over on the Marin side. It reminds me of Lisbon."

"I didn't know that you were ever in Lisbon, Harry."

"I haven't. It just seemed to be the appropriate thing to say."

She giggled and impulsively kissed his cheek. "I think you're crazy, Harry. Wonderfully crazy. Crazy at the piano. Crazy in bed. Crazy Harry, D.B.'s lover."

He finished his drink and took her glass from her. "I want to see my crazy little brother Birsha, and my equally crazy big brother Sandro."

She had always resented Harry's thinking of Sandro as his full brother. Sandro was an evil, frightening man, and she didn't like to associate the two together. She said, a bit stiffly, "Sandro's not your real brother, Harry. He's only your half-brother."

Harry grinned. "Perhaps. But don't try to convince Sandro of that. Our father, dear old Gerard, is the same father. And when he was shot and killed in—"

"Shot?"

"Haven't I ever told you about Gerard? A character. A real-life character straight out of an Eric Ambler novel. He was a smuggler and a gun runner. His first wife, who was Sandro's mother, was a German poetess. And his second wife, mine and Birsha's mother, was an Arab whore."

"But you said that your father was shot."

"That's right. By the French police, in Marseilles on November fifth, 1936—that's Guy Fawkes Day. That's when Birsha and I went to live with Sandro."

"And your mother was really a—a prostitute?"

"Well, why not? Whores have babies, too. And from what I know about Arab prostitutes, it was a wonder my old man didn't die of something other than a bullet."

An hour later they were ready to go out. D.B. had finished two cups of black coffee while Harry cleaned up the studio and found a clean shirt and sweater. When they left the apartment and rode down to the street level D.B. paused at the mail grill and automatically glanced into her box. There was a letter there.

"Anything important?" Harry asked.

"I don't think so. You pick up the car and I'll meet you in front."

She opened the grill and pulled out the envelope. It was addressed to her in plain block letters. She tore it open and when she read, the fear shuddered through her, shocking her into a complete sobriety.

> *D.B.*
>
> *I've just lost my job, thanks to your telling your father. I don't suppose I have to remind you that it's going to be near impossible for me to find an equal position in this city, indeed, in this state. Naturally, this is something that I shall never forget. I'll make you pay for it.—Gordon.*

She stepped onto the sidewalk, fearfully crumpling the note in her fist, as if she could squeeze the words from the paper and leave them forgotten in the lamplit gutter. She hoped that her expression was normal. Harry pulled up and she stepped into the car. As he drove down toward Chinatown she tore the note and envelope into small bits, then held her hand out and let the wind suck the paper from her palm. They flew behind them, like dry snow whipping.

"You seem pretty angry about that note," Harry remarked.

"Do I? It was just some advertising. I hate to get junk in the mail. Don't you?"

Harry was feeling good. *Kadesh* was finished, done with, and it had been by far the best that he had ever done. He felt proud of himself, proud of the night, ready to tear loose and celebrate. The car shot forward, braked neatly, weaved in and out of the traffic like a white eel.

He flicked on the radio, found only Elvis and Duane and Fats, so he flicked it off. The stars were bright overhead, the streets crowded with the Saturday night mob, bathed with the hot lights of the neon.

Pendragon's was far too crowded, the mob overflowing onto the narrow sidewalk. Harry steered D.B. further up the street to a small bar aptly named The Dump. Inside there were booths along one wall and a long bar with the usual high leatherette stools. A jukebox silently whirled colored bubbles in plastic tubes. The suspended light globes were red and yellow and green. Harry led D.B. to a rear booth and ordered a pitcher of dark beer. He couldn't see Birsha anywhere.

"Are you troubled, D.B.?"

"Me? Of course not. Do I look troubled?"

"I don't know. You don't seem as jumpy as you were a few minutes ago. Did the black coffee take the edge off?"

She nodded. "Yes, I suppose that's it."

"Did you know that everyone in The Dump looked at you when you came in?"

"Why?"

"Because of your body."

She smiled then and drank from her beer mug.

What Harry had said was very true. D.B. had put on a pair of skintight trousers that fitted her like a coat of luminous paint. She also wore a dark green sweater and green shoes. He sat back, sipping his beer, contentedly watching her and enjoying his smoky drunk. D.B. was some woman. He remembered that morning on the beach at Bolinas he had thought of Debussy. Right now she was Edgard Varese's *Hyperprism*. Winds and percussion. And Harry? He felt like taking D.B. outside, finding a dark and vacant doorway, and making love to her.

When Sophie and Birsha entered the bar every head turned to the doorway. Birsha was drunk, Sophie moving quietly at his side. A few of the bar patrons started clapping.

"My God," D.B. said, "look at Sophie now!"

Sophie was a brilliant orange. She had also dyed her hair a flaming red and wore red lipstick and eye shadow. Her dress looked like a circus awning, with wide stripes of electric orange and red.

Birsha ordered Pernod at the bar and Sophie stayed to pick up the drinks. The crowd was excited by the fantastic, gaping at her as if she were a celebrity, looking from her orange legs to her red hair, asking themselves aloud if she was really orange all over, and what the hell and blue damn was this all about, anyway—Sophie ignored them and came to the table. Birsha held out a chair for her, then pulled a chair for himself near Harry.

"Do you like the orange?" Birsha asked Harry.

"Sure."

Sophie said, "Birsha says I'm hotter now that I'm orange. I wonder if that's true. Do you think my personality changes with each different color?"

"I don't know," D.B. answered.

"Harry, have you ever drunk terpin-hydrate and codeine with beer?" Sophie asked.

"No. Does it taste good?"

"I think so. I'm not too sure. Gee, Harry, I miss your piano playing at the house. I think D.B.'s lucky." she turned to D.B. and placed an orange hand on her green sweater. "Honey, you're a lucky girl, even though your hair's still snowball colored. I think you ought to change it. It'll make you feel like a new person. Look at my hair. Isn't it bright?"

"I think you look great," D.B. said.

"I feel great," Sophie said gayly. "I feel like I'm stuffed with fireflies. Harry, are you in love with D.B.? I think that's fine. I still can't get Birsha to marry me."

Harry turned to his brother. "Did you talk to Sandro about that loan yet?"

Birsha nodded. "He told me to go to hell."

"That doesn't sound like him."

"He's angry."

"Oh? About what?"

Birsha swirled his Pernod and avoided Harry's gaze.

"About what?" Harry repeated.

"You."

Harry glanced across the table, saw that D.B. was busily engaged with Sophie, discussing color and men. He moved his chair a few inches closer to Birsha's. "Why's Sandro angry with me?"

Birsha's voice was low, thick with Pernod. "You know why, buddy. He think's we've *both* betrayed him because we've gone alone into the tiger pit!" The last words were spoken bitterly. "Hell, Harry, you know how he is. Listen, if the guy wasn't my brother I'd think he was a loonie-fag, or some goddam thing, I don't know, Harry. He won't talk to me. I asked him for fifty bucks—just fifty, mind you—and he screams at me and says that he has to protect me."

"I know, Birsha. Keep your voice down."

"Okay, Harry, okay." Birsha moved in his chair. "Harry, I think he's heading for another crack-up. I'm scared of him. Me! I'm his brother. I love him, but even I'm getting scared of him. He called me at Darker's Bay the other day, said he wanted to come up, but I told him that I was going hunting and wouldn't be home. Do you know why?"

"Sophie?"

"That's right. What would happen if I got a little drunk and wasn't on my guard and that big loonie decided that Sophie was a tiger, or some goddam thing. What then? He'd probably pick up a chair and make her sit on top of a beach ball, or some damn thing. Honest. We've got to do something."

Harry nodded. Sandro hadn't been too well, that was true, but Harry doubted if he would become violent. After all, he had gone violent only that one time, and that was thirteen years ago. And the doctor in North Carolina had said that the possibility of a complete relapse was very slim. So? Sandro had been behaving himself for ten years.

"Harry, why don't you call that doctor—what's his name?"

"Bennet?"

"That's the one. Why don't you call him and tell him what's going on?"

Harry sighed. "What is going on, Birsha? I mean, what's going on that hasn't been going on for ten years? He's always thought of us as his charges, his responsibilities; what's so off about him *still* thinking so? You know that he lives in the past. And Bennet said that most likely he'd continue living in the past."

"I know. But have you seen his warehouse? Have you been up in that creepy room of his? Talk about living in the past. Jesus Christ! Every time I go up there I think I've stepped onto a set for a silent movie. I'm telling you, Harry, we've got to do something."

Harry fell silent, trying to think. He was pretty drunk still. He remembered all that Dr. Bennet had told him, that the best thing to do with Sandro was to humor him. And, if Sandro became violent, Harry was supposed to treat him as naturally as possible. But the chances of his becoming violent were pretty damn thin. A thousand-to-one shot.

"I'll see Sandro," Harry finally said. "But if he's still the same as he's always been then I'll let him alone. If not, then I'll give Bennet a ring. Okay?"

Birsha nodded.

Harry ordered another pitcher of beer and another round of Pernod. D.B. was smiling again, he noticed. She had had two Pernods and a beer and she was obviously feeling gay again. Harry shook off his gloom and clapped Birsha on the back. He wanted the party to continue, to have fun. After all, he was supposed to be celebrating, wasn't he?

"What were you two so wrapped up in?" D.B. asked.

Harry grinned. "Birsha told me that the porch of my house needs fixing. And I told him that I was in love with you."

Sophie got the giggles and nearly choked on a piece of ice. D. B.

clapped her back. Sophie blinked. "We're all four of us in love with one another. It just struck me as being hilarious. Gee, I hope I don't cry because then my cheeks would streak."

D. B.'s foot touched Harry's and he turned toward her. Her eyes held him while her foot, which was bare now, searched along the calf of his leg, then his thigh. Harry grinned at her and she grinned back. Her foot rested on him, the toes curling against him. He had to turn in his seat to put a stop to it. Any more of that and he would have to find that dark and vacant doorway.

When he moved in his chair he spotted Auckland.

Why couldn't a love affair ever be a simple thing?

Auckland was at the far end of the bar, standing near the open doorway, trying to catch Harry's attention. Harry turned away quickly, pretending that he hadn't seen the man.

"Let's have another beer," Sophie said. "I love Pernod, but I love beer, too."

When Harry turned to call the bartender over to their booth he saw that Auckland had gone. He sighed his relief, wiped his eyes, and wondered what Auckland had wanted of him. He knew, of course, but nevertheless he wondered.

A half hour later Birsha and Sophie suggested that they all move to another bar. The party was moving into high gear. Birsha, Harry thankfully noticed, wasn't becoming unmanageable. In fact, they were all holding their liquor quite well.

They rose from the booth and moved out into the street. A pair of policemen strolled by, glanced suspiciously at Harry, appreciatively at D. B. in her skintight trousers and sweater; then when they saw Sophie they stopped. One of them exclaimed: "Now I've seen everything!" The police moved on and when Harry reached the far corner he saw Auckland again.

He was standing near a yellow pickup truck parked at the curb. With him was a tall man wearing an expensive black silk suit and white vest. Harry continued on, holding D. B.'s arm. Then he felt her stiffen under his fingers, saw her eyes grow wide and her lips tremble.

"What's the matter?"

"It's Gordon," she whispered tightly.

4

Auckland moved from behind the truck with his usual crab-like shuffle. He peered at Harry with his gummy eyes, smiling his yellowed stumpy teeth through his scraggly beard. He paused first before D. B. "Hello, Miss Sadder. Do you remember me?"

"Yes—of course, I—"

"Will you excuse me, Miss Sadder? I'd like to have a word with Mr. Dazier." Still smiling, he turned to Harry. "Hello. I haven't seen you since the night of the party. I was thinking that perhaps we should have a talk—"

"I don't want to talk," Harry said. He was rapidly becoming more sober. His legs felt like they were filled with hot cellophane and his heart was hammering in his chest. He wasn't afraid of Auckland—not the man himself, but of his words, of what he could say to D. B.

Harry looked toward the truck and noticed Gordon Fitzroy. He should have recognized him from D. B.'s description; tall, boyish face, blond crewcut hair, pale blue eyes, college tan and white teeth. Harry would have laughed under different circumstances.

"I think we should talk," Auckland repeated. His voice was a little sharper this time. "I think you and I should step over to that truck and talk with the man over there. I'd like you to meet him."

"Who is he?" Harry found himself asking.

Auckland feigned surprise. "Why, that's Gordon M. Fitzroy the Second. I think you and he have something in common. Don't you?"

Harry wasn't a small man; he was well over six foot tall and weighed just under a hundred eighty pounds, and if D. B. wasn't there, at his side, he would have mashed Auckland down into the concrete. As it was, he did nothing, said nothing. He was trying to think of a way out—but nothing was coming to him.

"What's up?" Birsha asked.

"Nothing," Harry said. "Why don't you walk down to Pendragon's. You and Sophie both. I'll meet you later."

Birsha seemed to think that over for a moment, then as he looked from his brother to the thin little figure of Auckland, he nodded and said that he supposed it would be all right; he reached for Sophie and playfully pulled her down the street.

"You go with them, too," Harry said to D. B.

"No," Auckland said. "She stays."

Harry realized that Auckland was nobody's fool. Without D. B.'s presence his fangs would be removed and Harry would slap his yellow teeth down his stringy throat.

"I'll stay," D. B. said.

Harry nodded dumbly, asking himself why he didn't punch Auckland, anyway? Because of Fitzroy? Was that it? He realized that Auckland must have told Fitzroy that Harry was conning D. B. and that Fitzroy had told Auckland that he had just been cut off from his blackmailing scheme. So? So they were both on the make, hoping to milk D. B. through Harry.

Gordon stepped forward, moving not too gracefully, and Harry noticed that he was a little drunk. Gordon was smiling—or sneering—showing his white teeth and glancing first at D. B., then at Harry.

Harry was thinking of his hands. It wouldn't be good to hurt them. But he knew that the first one who opened his mouth and started to say something, he would have to shut him up the quickest and best way possible. He braced himself, spreading his legs a few feet apart, left leg closest to Auckland. No one seemed to notice his stance.

D. B., who was still obviously drunk, was looking confused now, probably wondering what Harry had to do with Auckland and her ex-husband.

"I'm Gordon Fitzroy. I suppose D. B.'s told you about me?"

"I suppose."

"And you're Harry Dazier."

"That's right."

"Don't say anything more, Mr. Fitzroy," Auckland warned.

"You keep out of this," Gordon said. He was obviously too enraged at seeing Harry with his ex-wife to remind himself of their money scheme. "You stay out of this Auckland," he said. "I want to have a few words with this guy. He thinks he's such a hot bastard because he's sleeping in my bed. He thinks that my wife is going to be fooled by his line of crap forever! Well, he's got another thought coming. Isn't that so, Mister Dazier?"

"Maybe."

"I've heard some interesting things about you, Mister Dazier. Auckland here has been filling me in—"

"Shut up, Mr. Fitzroy," Auckland shouted. "You'll give the whole—"

"*You* shut up!" Gordon snapped. "I want to tell my wife about her new big love. I want to tell her that—"

Harry swung, throwing his back into the punch, and his heavy fist smashed hard into Gordon's face, cutting off the words, breaking the lip under his knuckles, cracking a tooth. Gordon staggered back and Auckland jumped out of the way. Gordon slumped against the truck fender, shaking his head, momentarily cross-eyed. He spit out the cracked tooth and it clicked on the pavement. Blood was smeared along his split lip and the bright drops were falling on his vest.

D. B. had turned with the throwing of the punch and had thrown her hands to her face, hiding, moving to a doorway a few yards from the truck.

When men fought in the streets why do you always hear the coins jingling in their pockets?

Gordon lunged and swung wild and Harry jammed his right up into his stomach. He heard the gush of forced air oof near his ear. Gordon curled over and Harry stepped back, and thinking of his hand, he swung with his foot and jacknifed Gordon to the pavement. Breathing hard, he reached for the blond crewcut, pulled the head back, and smashed his knee into the face. Gordon fell forward without a word and spread out on the sidewalk.

Harry turned and caught Auckland's arm just as the little man tried to scurry past. Harry threw him against the fender and pushed his face close to the bearded chin. His voice came in short quick gasps.

"Now, listen to me, Auckland. If you try to shake me down I'm going to break your neck. Do you understand?"

"I wasn't going—to shake you down, Harry. Honest. This guy—this Fitzroy creep—comes to me and—tells me he'd like to meet you—"

"You make my stomach crawl, Auckland. You think that I'm playing the girl for a sucker and that you deserve a commission. When you came across Fitzroy you decided to team up with him to see how much you could get from me. Well, you've seen what you can get. And I'll crack your neck if you try it again. You understand?"

"Sure—Harry."

Harry pushed him disgustedly away. "You can roll Fitzroy if you want, Auckland. He's harmless now. And that's more your speed." He turned and went to the doorway where D. B. had gone. He found her with her face in her hands, her back in the corner near the mailboxes. He drew her gently toward him and held her close, stroking her back.

"Is it over?" she whispered.

"Yes."

"Why? Why? What was it for?"

"Fitzroy just wanted to needle me, that's all."

"I thought—I was through with him."

"You are, honey. He won't needle me any more."

They left the doorway and started down the street to Pendragon's where Birsha and Sophie were. Harry felt his muscles relax, the tension wash away, and the quivering reaction begin to set in. He needed a drink. He needed one bad. Strangely enough, he hadn't had a fight in over fifteen years, and he had found it a terrific release for him. He had almost enjoyed it. But he didn't know exactly what he thought he had proved by it. He knew that the scare he had thrown into Auckland wouldn't last, that Auckland would come again for his commission. And, he knew as well, that Gordon wasn't going to forget the whole affair now that he had been beaten by Harry.

Actually, he reflected, he was in the same position as before.

"Harry, can we—I mean—can we forget about what just happened? Can we still have a party with Sophie and your brother? Or would it bother you?"

"No, it wouldn't bother me. I can use a drink. In fact, I think if we have about six more we'll forget about it as if it never happened."

She tried to smile. "Harry, I thought—I mean, I keep thinking that what just happened was my fault ..."

"No, it wasn't your fault."

"But—don't you see? Gordon hates me because I had him fired and because—"

"Let's not talk about it, honey. We're supposed to be forgetting about the whole thing."

He cupped her face in his hands and kissed her lips and then her eyelids; the eyes were moist, tasting of salt. He was thinking, no, it couldn't have been D. B.'s fault. It had been his own fault. If he had told her in the beginning that he had been after her money and then had fallen in love with her he could have laughed at Auckland and Fitzroy tonight. But not now. It had gone too far. He was convinced that she would never believe him now. Not with Auckland on his tail. Not now. His confession would look too much like a well-timed turnabout.

Harry had been right: after five or six drinks D. B. had practically forgotten about the fight on the street—but not quite. She remembered it again at ten o'clock while they were still in Pendragon's Bar, listening to the jazz group and drinking Pernod. She turned to Harry and saw that he was drunk again, completely at his ease, and she wondered if he had forgotten about the incident or if he was still brooding about it. Harry had said that the fight hadn't been her fault—but she knew that that wasn't true. It *had* been her fault. It had been because Gordon had warned her. She knew now that he must have meant to get even with her by needling Harry into a fight. But Harry had beaten him. She smiled to herself. She hadn't liked the fight but she had to admit that it had excited her in some purely animal way. Harry had hit Gordon so beautifully, so perfectly.

Then she forgot about the fight and gave herself to the party, to the riotously drunken night with orange Sophie and Victorian gambler Birsha. Harry kissed her, moved his hand along her thigh, sang songs to her. She became happier as the clock hand moved toward midnight. And when Harry suggested they all go on a trip she was delighted. She couldn't think of a better, a more fitting idea. She was gloriously drunk.

"Do you remember the Donner Party?" Harry asked thickly.

She shook her head. "No, I've only been to a few parties."

"No, it wasn't that kind of a party, honey. The Donner Party was a group that was a'goin' West, a pioneer type-thing, and they got stuck up in the Rockies in the middle of winter. Snow falling all over the place. See—they were starving and they ended up eating each other— cannibalism. They were hungry."

"What's the point?" Birsha asked.

"Well, I was thinking that if we went up there—to Donner's Pass— maybe we could find us some bones, or something. Think of it. We could sell them to museums. We could write a rock'n'roll song about it, maybe make a fortune. Just the sort of thing for Johnny Mathis to sing—"

Birsha nodded like a marionette on a loose string. Sophie said she thought it was a grand idea. D. B. immediately agreed and Harry rose from the table, standing unsteadily.

"Let's go."

"In my car?" D. B. asked.

"What else?"

"But it only fits two."

"Sophie can sit on your lap and Birsha can sit on the trunk deck. There's plenty of space behind the seats for his legs."

They left the bar and while Harry went to pick up the car, D. B., Birsha, and Sophie went to the all-night surplus store on Columbus Avenue and bought two Army blankets and a vacuum bottle for the trip. Harry drove up just as they came from the store. The car radio was playing music-till-dawn, Bach pouring out, the motor racing.

Before leaving the district Harry stopped at an Italian grocery and bought two fifths of Pernod and a bottle of mineral water. D. B. sat with Sophie on her lap, barely able to hold her eyes open. She wished that Harry would hurry up and drive so that the night wind would revive her. She was having a fine time, a wild time, but if only she wasn't so sleepy—a deep licorice, dark beer sleep. What was Harry doing? She saw him pouring the two bottles into the huge Thermos, then adding the water. How wonderful.

"Let's have a drink," Sophie said.

There was a spigot and D. B. had to hold the jug up over her nose to get a drink. The car roared, Bach harpsichords jingled from the dash, and lights flashed by, passing D. B.'s dulled vision. The wind rushed against her face, whipped her champagne hair, lulled her into a gentle sleep. Her final thoughts were amusing, thinking of their finding Donner bones at the bottom of the Pernod jug.

5

When D. B. awoke she had no idea of the time, and when she looked out of the car she discovered that she also had no idea of where she was. The roof of her mouth tasted sweet and she had a slight headache. She tried to recall what had happened, but, for the very first time in her life, she realized that there had been blackout periods. The realization didn't frighten her; in fact, she felt rather amazed about the whole phenomenon. She merely smiled at the idea that she remembered so little. It seemed quite comical, like reading a book with pages removed here and there.

She remembered the fight, then drinking, then a few small towns flashing by in the night, and a stop at a café for frying chickens. She remembered that the bright neon sign over the café canopy had been a huge chicken, winking and pointing to the roof of the building.

She sat up in the car. There was a rich sweet odor of pine trees in the air. Overhead the sky was smeared with a million stars, like sugar sprinkled on dark blue velvet. She knew that they were somewhere in the Mountains. Crickets chirped steadily under the forest and she could hear the gentle rushing of a creek.

Then she saw the small red glow of the fire to her right, heard Harry's muffled voice, smelled the frying chicken. She left the car and cautiously followed the path down the mulchy slope to the small clearing in the pines.

Sophie, Birsha, and Harry were sitting cross-legged around the fire, looking like scheming demons, sipping from the Thermos spigot and staring at the flames. Twigs snapped and sparks floated slowly into the sky.

"Howdy, D. B.," Harry said. "I was just going to call you. The chicken's almost done."

"Where are we?"

Sophie giggled. "We don't know."

"You mean, we're lost?"

"Ah reckon," Harry said.

She settled beside him, kissed his cheek. "Are we in a Western mood,

Harry?"

"Yep. Ah'm Wyatt Dazier. How y'all doin', D. B. gal?"

"Fine. I passed out, didn't I?"

Harry nodded, forked a piece of chicken from the tin sheet over the fire and handed it to her. She sat and nibbled, then ate hungrily. Harry passed her the jug and she took a small drink.

"How long did I sleep?"

"About five hours, I guess," Harry said.

"Whooopeee!" Birsha shouted. "Ah'm dronk, Sophie woman. Ah dronk and ah'm rarin' t'go. I don't know where, but I'm willing. I wonder where the hell we are, anyway."

Harry shrugged. "I don't know. We got off the main road a while back. We drove for about six hours, so we must be in Nevada somewhere. Maybe we're near Tahoe. Hell, maybe we're in Golden Gate Park."

Birsha laughed. D. B. ate another piece of chicken and drank more Pernod. She was thinking how wonderful it would be if they could stay there for months, perhaps even longer. Away from Malcolm, from people like Gordon and Auckland, from Aunt Eva. How fine it would be to simply eat chicken and drink Pernod and make love under an Army blanket under the stars. No liquor bills, no appointments with the hairdresser to touch up the champagne strands, no credit cards, department stores, cocktail lounges, people. Just herself and Harry.

Sophie finished the last of her chicken and tossed the bone into the fire. "It's going to be dawn pretty soon," she whispered. "And do you know, I just love this hour. It's so secret. Harry, didn't you once tell me that the dawn was a boundary for something?"

Harry settled back against D.B.'s lap, smoking and staring sleepily at the fire. "Yes, I said it was a boundary. Between the domains of good spirits and bad spirits. But I was only kidding."

The fire burned low, the tin sheet curled to one side, and there remained a small bowl of glowing red coals. The four of them became silent and D.B. had to strain her vision in order to see the vague reddish outlines of their figures; Sophie, orange and red; Birsha sleepily bent wizard-postured to the fire, bright weskit and striped shirt; Harry, sleepily gazing at the slowly burning coals. It was a time—as Sophie had remarked—of secrets, a boundary line, a confession.

D.B.'s voice was a bare whisper and she was sure that if the others hadn't been attuned to the mood of the forest clearing they never would have heard her. She asked Harry, "Why do you write music?"

"Because I don't want to die."

"Are you afraid of death?"

"That's not what I said. I said that I wrote music because I didn't want to die. I don't have to fear death simply because I disagree with it."

Sophie leaned forward. "What month were you born in, D.B.?"

"December. On the 24th, the day before Christmas."

"Then you're a Capricorn. And Harry's a Libra. I know that Harry's symbols are supposed to be a tuba and a banjo. He told me so. But what's D.B.? If I had my book I could tell you."

Harry smiled. "She's an Edgard Varèse. A *Hyperprism*"

"Harry, you ought to tell fortunes, or something like that. Honest. What's Sandro?"

"He's a Leo," Harry replied.

Birsha snorted. "Wouldn't you know it."

"Do you believe in horoscopes?" D.B. asked Sophie.

"Not really. But I think it's fascinating. I mean, when I look at the stars I like to think of them as being sort of personal. I mean, responsible. I don't like to think of them as just being targets for rockets, and silly things like that. I'd rather believe in magic than science."

The Thermos was becoming empty. When D.B. lifted the jug and shook it there was a shallow swishing sound. Birsha broke the spell of the clearing, throwing more twigs on the fire. The flames caught at the fresh wood, popped, spewed sparks, and the light threw their shadows against the bowl of tree trunks. A few minutes later they heard the sound of an approaching truck, moving up the grade, then gearing down. D.B. sat up, but no one else moved; no one seemed to be concerned. After she heard the squeal of the brakes and the slam of the truck door she heard the footsteps moving toward the clearing down the path.

The figure that entered the clearing was short and round, almost bear-shaped, and wore freshly pressed suntans. Small glasses were perched on his little pink nose and he moved toward the fire with short, apologetic steps.

"Hello—"

Harry looked up. "Hello. Who're you?"

"Uh—I saw your car parked up on the road, saw the fire—"

"We're having some chicken," Birsha explained.

"I see." He smiled sheepishly and looked at the faces around the fire. When he saw Sophie he stared—and the glasses threatened to slide from his nose. "Say," he said open-mouthed, "Are you really orange colored? I mean no offense, but—"

"Of course I'm orange. I dyed myself. Are you a ranger?"

"Yes—well, sort of. You see, I work at the fire watch up on the mountain and I was just on my way to—I don't suppose you folks know about open fires up here—"

"I know," Harry said. "But we were hungry and we figured it'd be all right if we built the fire properly and kept a good close watch on it. I was in the Boy Scouts once. They taught me all about those things."

"Yes, well—that's fine," the fire-watcher said. "But you'd better put it out now—"

"We were just talking about demons," Sophie said. "For a minute I thought you might be a demon. But I can just tell by looking at you that you aren't."

The fire-watcher smiled. "Thank you. I—"

"Are you Smoky the Bear?"

"No, Miss. I sort of work for Smoky the Bear."

Birsha looked impressed. "Well! In that case I suppose we'd better put the fire out."

The fire-watcher nodded, apologized for having had to ask them, said he hated to disturb their party; then he retreated from the clearing and returned up the path.

They put out the fire, scooping dirt over it and putting the guard stones over it, then picked up the blankets and marched back up the slope in single file. Harry stopped by the fire-watcher's truck. "Incidentally, where does this road lead to, anyway?"

The fire-watcher pointed down the road, making vague gestures. "If you go straight you'll find a blacktop—not dirt, like this—and if you follow that it'll take you onto the highway direct for Reno."

As the truck pulled away, Harry crawled behind the wheel and the others squeezed in beside him and behind him. Sophie turned to Birsha. "Let's go to Reno and get married."

Birsha lifted the jug for the last drink and clapped Sophie on the back. "All right, let's you and me get married. I think that's a great idea."

The car bounced down the road. D.B. settled Sophie on her lap and, as the dust swirled over the windshield, she wished that it was Harry and herself who were going to Reno to be married.

"We'll gamble," Sophie said. "Reno's full of gambling and marrying."

"We'll win a million bucks and we'll buy a yacht. We'll sail away for a year and a day. We'll go to the land where the bong-tree grows."

"And there in the wood," D.B. added over the rush of the wind, "we'll find a piggywig with a ring on the end of his nose."

Birsha whooped. "And we'll be married the next day by the turkey who lives on the hill."

Eight hours later, while the bright afternoon sun flooded the street outside, D.B. stood at the crap table and watched, almost hypnotized, as the stick flashed over the green, over the white lettering and numbers, passing chips and jingling silver dollars, sweeping, clicking, flicking across the table like a snake's tongue. The dice were passed and a red-faced cowboy with yellow sunglasses shook and rolled. More passing of the stick.

Before coming to the club the four of them had stopped at a small motel on the outskirts of the city and had slept for six and a half hours. Then they had gone into town to watch the action and gamble a few dollars. Harry gave D.B. a ten, explaining that they had very little money left.

While the others planted themselves in the club bar to drink cold beer and gin fizzes D.B. moved into the fascinating rooms of the casino. She played several one-arm bandits in the gleaming nickel and chromium machine room, and when she had won eight dollars she moved on to the greater mystery of the roulette wheel. When, an hour later, she tired of the uninteresting fluctuation of win and loss, she moved to the crap tables.

Now D.B. was ninety dollars to the good; and this, since she had never before gambled, she considered something fantastic. She had always thought that winning at games depended a great deal on familiar knowledge. When she had stayed in Vegas while waiting for her divorce she hadn't gone to the clubs, but had remained on the dude ranch, watching TV, brooding, swimming, and reading novels. But now, what with the lights and the spinning silver coins, she realized that she had missed an entirely different world. She was even a bit frightened of it all.

The cowboy pulled out while he was fat and the stick slid the dice to D.B.

"Would you like to shoot, Miss?"

"Well—do I have to?"

"No, Miss. You can pass."

"Well—I've never done it before."

"Just shake them and throw them against the back here. That's all there is to it."

Hesitantly, she picked up the dice and threw them where he had pointed. The stickman called her point eight. With an encouraging nod from the man, D.B. clumsily threw again. The dice returned and again she threw. She was feeling a little foolish now—Another eight.

"Did I win?"

"Yes, Miss. The dice are still yours."

It was amazing. So simple. Her point came eight again, and again she repeated it after several tries. She played again, watching the coins move, the wooden discs slipping into her "come line" domain. She hadn't any idea how much money she had won. A few people stopped by the table to watch. The other players were following her play.

"The dice still have the young lady."

"Four point."

"Four's your point."

"Go to it, lady."

She hesitated, then threw again. Eight. Again. Five. She knew that she had to get a four. She tried to count how many times she had won after the ninety dollars had been left on the come line. Three times. That was more than seven hundred dollars. The other players were crowding, a few dollars tossed to the "don't come." The stickman tapped the green.

She rolled them in her hands and threw them to the back.

"Four, the lady's a winner, the dice belong to the lady."

Almost fifteen hundred dollars!

"Do you want to let that ride, Miss?"

"Could I—could I quit if I want?"

"That's up to you, Miss."

The man on her left whispered don't quit while you're hot, but she felt flushed and terribly frightened, so she apologized for having been any trouble, quickly scooped up the discs and dollars and squares, and carried the pile in her purse to the cashier's window near the Wild West display and cocktail lounge. The cashier smiled and without any sign of being impressed flicked out a sheaf of fifty-dollar bills. It came to almost fifteen hundred.

Even though she realized that she had eight thousand in her private checking account, that she was worth almost fifteen million, she felt as pleased as a child with her winnings. Her hands shook as she crammed the money into her purse. With her back to the wall she nervously lit a cigarette and stood apart from the casino, terribly excited, feeling supreme, proud of her luck. The roller coaster roar of the casino gushed on. Noise, clatter and whir of the gleaming one-arms, shouts and groans from the crowded tables, blinking and buzzing of jackpots, dice rattling, the twenty-four-hour roar of Reno. She told herself that she had better move out of the casino before she was tempted to return. Terrified again, and feeling like a successful thief, she returned to the cocktail lounge.

In a corner booth with cowhide seats, Harry, Birsha, and Sophie sat glumly before a black table littered with empty fizz mixers. D.B. could see by their expressions that they had come to the last of their money, that they felt the party was over.

"What's the matter? You all look half dead."

"Sad news, honey," Harry said. "We're broke. We've got just enough for Birsha's wedding, a cheap bottle of vodka, and gas for the car."

D.B. beamed. "I'll write a check."

Harry's face tightened. "No you don't. I won't have none of that."

"Have we enough for one more round of beer?" Birsha asked.

Harry nodded. "I think so." He smiled. "Hey, let's cheer up. We've had a ball. We'll get Birsha and Sophie hitched and we'll celebrate with a fifth of vodka. We can go throw stones in the Truckee River."

D.B. couldn't hold it off any longer. With a dramatic flourish she opened her purse, drew out the thick sheaf of bills, and spread them on the table. Then she sat back proudly and watched as the three of them gaped at her winnings.

Harry's face broke into a wide grin. "Now *where* in God's good name did you find *that* funny looking stuff?"

She explained how she had played the one-arm, the roulette, then the crap tables. When she finished, Birsha leaned across the table and kissed her joyously on the mouth. Sophie bounced up and down and started to sing Jingle Bells, which made no sense to D.B. Harry called the bartender and ordered another round of fizzes.

Flushed with luck, excited with the casino action outside the bar, laughing and talking wildly, they started to become drunk again; not a senseless drunk like the night before, but a slow, careful drunk, keeping careful watch on their moods.

Harry ordered sandwiches, which the bartender made in a chromium machine with infra-red lamps, and D.B. ate hungrily, drinking gin fizzes with the food, and feeling a condition of forever gayety steal over her. She looked at Harry, studying his profile, watching his gestures, and she wanted to make love to him. Her trousers felt tight on her thighs, her bra felt confining. Without a single thought for her surroundings she could have easily seduced him under the booth table.

"What're you grinning at?" Harry asked.

"You." She leaned, whispered in his ear: "I was thinking how nice it would be to seduce you under the table. Right here in front of everyone. I mean, near everyone. But hidden."

"You're a funny girl."

"We're all funny."

"I'll let you in on a secret. I was thinking of approximately the same thing."

"Are you drunk?"

"No," Harry whispered. "Just feeling very good. Are you drunk?"

"I feel fine. I feel like I've always wanted to feel. Does that sound strange?"

"No."

They had two more rounds, drinking very slowly, talking about marriage. Again, D.B. felt the twinge inside her. She wished that she

could ask Harry. But she was afraid that he might not want to be tied
down in that way. He had told her that he had been in love once before,
but had never married. She assumed that he hadn't wanted to be
committed, and she was afraid to approach him with an offer of
marriage and put him in an embarrassing position.

It hadn't seemed as if they had been in the club very long but when
they stepped out into the street D.B. saw that it was evening already.
The sky was a deep dark blue. The main drag was a bright neon forest.

"Look," Birsha said, "they must be making a goddam movie down
there."

Half a block down the street, in front of a large club, there were several
sound trucks, property trucks, and rented limousines. Tourists clustered
near the doorway, watching the technicians prepare the walkway for the
scene. Huge drum lights, rises, cables, reflectors, booms, sound and
camera equipment choked the street. Several police guards held back
the press of tourists.

"I've never seen so much neon," Sophie remarked.

"The sun never sets on the Reno empire."

"I'll bet people think you're a character player in the movie, Sophie."

"Let's get some more beer."

The police detoured them from the set and they moved on to a
package store where D.B. bought a bottle of tequila and a six-pack of
beer. Then they strolled through the town, enjoying the tree-lined
streets, the soft warm mountain air. They stopped at a small park at the
bank of the Truckee River.

Harry spread the blankets out under a tree and settled down. Birsha
and Sophie talked in whispers for a few minutes, then picked up some
beer and excused themselves, Sophie explaining that she had to talk to
Birsha.

"I wonder what that's all about?" Harry said.

"Maybe they think we want to be alone."

Harry frowned. "I don't think so. Sophie seemed to have something on
her mind. Birsha looked a little worried when she talked to him just
now."

D.B.'s blanket still held the odors of chicken and wood-smoke. She
huddled next to Harry, and as they shared a can of beer together, their
eyes met and held. Harry kissed her, then whispered against her cheek.
She couldn't tell what he was saying, but it didn't matter. Returning his
kiss she felt the flat of his hand on her stomach under the sweater.
Settling back, Harry drew the second blanket over them and cupped his
hand on her breast. She felt her breath come shorter, the nipple harden
to his touch, and she moved closer, arching herself to him.

There.

Gripping his shoulders she moved under him, kissed his neck and tasted the sweet salt of his skin on her lips, smelled the musky forest odor of the blanket, felt the warmth of him against her now naked stomach and thighs. The river whispered to their right, curling in long wet strands under the bridge. She no longer knew where she was; the world was under the blanket, under the darkly spreading tree.

What a crazy thing to do.

What an absolutely crazy way to live.

Moist grass pressed against her cheek and she slowly opened her eyes and gazed up at the branches, feeling the earth moving under her. She relaxed, became drowsy. Full of flowers. The taste of Harry's skin on her lips.

6

Harry stood and watched D.B. sleep. He opened a can of beer, tipped the tequila, swallowed beer, and sighed. He moved to the water's edge and sat on a gray rock, lit an Alpine, watched as the dark water flowed past his feet. He waited for Birsha and Sophie to return. He felt more sober now, having drunk himself far beyond the foggy gayety of the past two days. His thoughts were cold and clear.

He cursed himself for a juvenile dingaling. Why didn't he tell D.B. that he had known about her long before he had met her? He knew that she was in love with him. Certainly she would understand. Then what was it? Why did he dwell on his problems? Was it a camouflage for a greater fear?

He realized that he wanted to marry her. Was he afraid to ask her? Was it because she had money?

Harry was honest with himself about music—yes. But about his social self—no. Whenever he tried to open a door he always found another, then another, and still yet another. It seemed as if he could never find an answer. Just more goddam doors. One right after another. Each one a little darker than the one before it. So, he gave up trying to search inside himself for the answers. He fell to lying to himself, accepting the first room beyond a door which satisfied his present mood, answered the question the way he wanted it to be answered.

With his music he was pretty much the same way. He allowed his instincts to take over, his demons do the work for him. The end result was always what he wanted, so he never questioned the method. It was easier. Just shout it out with all the musical training, all the mad hours, all the sounds and colors, and what came out was a solid picture of the man. What difference did it make if the man hadn't the slightest idea who or what he was?

He was in love with D.B. Sadder. Was he, hidden somewhere behind one of those unopened doors, still after her money? He *had* to put the question to himself now. It would be wrong to ignore it. Marriage was a big step. D.B. was a very wealthy woman and anyone who wanted her for his wife *had* to ask himself if he was still after the money.

So?

He didn't think so.

"Why not?" he asked himself aloud.

Because he honestly intended to live from his music. He didn't want one penny of the Sadder millions.

That was true.

And what about the other thoughts? About the shouting and spewing and waiting to see what happened with his work? Did all men know *what* they were doing, and *how* they were doing it? If they did, wouldn't the end result be studied, cold, clinical? If they didn't, and acted as Harry acted, a trained-in-art about-to-explode emotional bomb, was the result still true? It must be true. It was up to the cold ones to write the articles and tell Harry Dazier *what* he had said and *how* he had said it. That wasn't Harry's role. His role was simply to burn, writhe, explode, speak his unknown soul in the recognizable tongue of art.

Explode.

God, he was a bundle of nerves. He tipped the tequila bottle, silently thanking Mexico for such a wonderful drink, such a wonderful damper to the fire. Without the liquor Harry felt that he wouldn't be able to slow down, that he would burst in one glorious Adrian Leverkuhn explosion. He felt that he would be a madman, a hotrod without brakes going down the Matterhorn, an airplane without wings zooming earthward. But the liquor acted as the brakes. The liquor gave him time to pause and amuse himself with life.

D.B.

She was another brake. He knew, that in spite of his problem over Auckland, he was going to ask her to marry him. He was going to tell her the whole story.

He rose from the stone and returned to the tree, stood and watched D.B. while she slept.

He had been a lonely man, and now, for the past three weeks, he hadn't been lonely. He knew that loneliness was something that could never be cured by company, or by a bottle and a good-looking girl. Loneliness existed in the soul of the man, under the skin, and that's where D.B. had finally reached him.

Birsha and Sophie returned, arguing softly, looking sadly at Harry when they drew up to the tree.

"We're not going to get married," Birsha sighed.

Harry stared unbelievingly at his brother. "Why not?"

"I can't," Sophie said.

He turned to her. "Why not?"

"Because she's never gotten a divorce from her fourth husband," Birsha explained sadly. "In fact, she never even divorced her first one. Sophie's been a bigamist for the last three times."

"Is that true?" Harry said.

Sophie sniffed and looked miserable. "Yes. But don't you see, Harry? I *want* to marry Birsha. I want to *really* marry him. And how can I get married if I've got all my past marriages all balled up like that? I don't want to marry Birsha just to go to bed with him with a piece of paper saying that it's all right. I can go to bed with him any old time. I want to marry him with all my past marriages cleaned up. See, Harry, it'll make me feel—feel so clean."

Harry nodded.

Birsha put his arm around Sophie. "It's okay, little orange Martian. You get it all straightened out and we'll get that piece of paper that says you're clean with your past."

She leaned forward. "Kiss me, honey. But don't French me because you'll make my lip run."

Harry went to D.B. and woke her up, shaking the blanket gently. "Hey, wake up, D.B."

She drew herself up and looked at him, the love still warm in her jade eyes, her mouth still slightly swollen. He kissed her softly. "How do you feel?" he asked.

"Fine. Wonderful. Still full of flowers. How do you feel?"

"Sophie and Birsha aren't going to get married," he said.

D.B. blinked, looked at Sophie and Birsha who were walking arm and arm on the path near the bridge. "Why not? Did they have a fight?"

"It's a long story. They're crazy about each other. I'll explain the whole thing to you later." He knelt beside her, thinking that it was now or never. He said, "D.B., I want to ask you something—Do you want to keep on living on your old man's dough?"

"I—I don't know—Why?"

"I want you to marry me. Will you?"

She didn't hesitate. "Yes."

"But, I don't want anything from your old man. Nothing. Ever. Is that understood?"

"Yes."

"Good. Now I have something else to tell you. Maybe it'll change your mind. But that'll be up to you—Did you know that the reason Auckland and Fitzroy approached me the other night was to shake me down?"

Her eyes grew wide. "Shake you down? Why should—"

"Because—I'll tell you, honey. That first night—the night you came to Darker's Bay—Auckland and I had a little talk out in the parking area. That was *before* I met you. He told me everything about you. Your name. Your money. Your starry-eyed thoughts about me. The dilettantism. The whole bit—"

"And?"

"Don't you see? The reason I made it with you was because I was after your money. Worse than Auckland. I wanted the money, the influence that your old man might want to swing with the opera league and the concert routes. I didn't give a good goddam about *you*. You were just a good-looking kid with a very susceptible hero-worship hang-up on me. And I naturally took advantage of it."

Her voice seemed far away. "Naturally," she said.

"I'm sorry."

"Harry." She put her fingers to his lips. Her lips were trembling. "Poor Harry—No, don't say anything. Please. I love you. And I *do* want to marry you. I knew that something had been bothering you during that first week. Don't ask me how I knew. I don't know. Perhaps it was woman's intuition. It doesn't matter what it was. But I knew. Then, when it was over I saw that it was going to be all right. Honest. I saw that, Harry. I wondered what it had been, but you were so sweet, so—real after that, that I forgot about it."

She pressed her fingertips on his lips. "Poor Harry," she whispered. "If you were after the money, then it's just as I said: it's natural. Malcolm pointed that out to me just the other day. He said that I was prey to the first stray cat that came by. And, you see, he was right. But not about you. How could he understand about you. I love you, Harry. You're not a sculptor, a Gordon Fitzroy, or a stray cat. You're my lover, baby, my honest-to-God lover. You made me become my own dreams. You made me real." She slowly pushed the blanket from her knees. "Let's go get married, Harry."

He couldn't describe the relief, the gratitude, the quiet happiness that he felt. He helped her to her feet and kissed her, then without a word they left the park and joined Birsha and Sophie on the bridge.

The first marriage chapel they came to was a small white stucco cottage with a Disney-like charm about it; pink neon outlined the roof and a sign that gave the preacher's name, and there was a small garden with cleverly trimmed hedges that looked like something from *Alice in Wonderland.* A hidden loud speaker softly poured out Mendelssohn.

The preacher turned out to be a little man with a Roy Rogers cowboy shirt and flowery Mexican boots. He gaped at Sophie, then at Birsha's Victorian costume, then at D.B. and Harry. His little brown eyes moved mice-like behind his pince-nez glasses. He clapped his hands and a flat footed sad-eyed girl with pimples shuffled out into the chapel.

"Who—which couple wishes to be married?"

Harry pointed at D.B. "Us."

"Ah, how wonderful. If you'll come this way—a few papers to be filled—I—may I ask you a question?"

"Yes."

The mice-like eyes darted to Sophie and Birsha. "Are you people from Hollywood? I mean, are you here in Reno with the movie company?"

"Sure," Birsha said.

The preacher grinned broadly and turned to the sad-eyed girl. "This is my daughter Kim. She adores the movies—"

Birsha bowed. "Hello, Kim. We're very pleased to meet you."

The preacher moved hurriedly about, fixing seals, signing papers, pointing to Harry and D.B. where they should fill in the information necessary, cooing words about the grave responsibility of matrimony. It all sounded pretty well rehearsed. Then the preacher returned to Sophie.

"Yes, now that I think of it," he said excitedly, "I'm sure I've seen you in the movies." He nodded to Birsha.

"I usually play Westerns," Birsha said modestly. "Did you ever see *Gunfight at Darker's Bay?*"

"Why, yes, I believe I have," the preacher said, obviously impressed. He puffed out his chest and rocked on his heels. "May I ask who—I mean, I'm not very good at names—"

Birsha smiled politely. "Certainly. I understand. I'm Rock Fabian. And this—" he nodded to Sophie, "—this is Brian Donlevy."

"Oh! Ha ha, you're joking—"

"I'm Tuesday Wednesday," Sophie said.

Kim, the preacher's daughter, pulled out the register and asked for their autographs. Birsha complied with a graceful flourish and a serf-important sigh. Sophie paused, asked Birsha how to spell Wednesday, then signed with a large scrawl. The preacher and his daughter were delighted. Kim left the chapel and returned with a small Kodak flash camera. The bulb popped and caught Birsha posing in an assumed Hollywood stance. They shook hands all around.

"And now," the preacher announced, "to the happy couple."

The Mendelssohn recording began again and the preacher started the ceremony. There was the smell of orange blossoms in the air, probably out of a spray can from the supermarket.

Then, while Harry's mind became a blank and he watched the white string of spittle shift rapidly in the little preacher's mouth, he realized that he was getting married. He reached for D.B.'s hand, nervously squeezing it, wondering what in God's name was going to happen now.

Afterward, they went out into the preacher's garden, drank tequila, and told the preacher wild stories about Birsha's experiences as a Hollywood star. The preacher ended by becoming drunk and chasing away two couples who also wished to be married, and Kim made flat-footed, sad-eyed passes at Birsha and Harry.

7

Harry awoke in a white and blue bedroom and when he turned his eyes up toward the ceiling he saw only a gently swaying silk overhead. He tried to sit up but his muscles were stiff and his hands shook. After a few minutes he crawled from the bed and staggered into the shower. The lukewarm spray stung into his face, washing the itch away, forcing his eyes open. For a second there he hadn't known where he was. He was home—in D.B.'s apartment—and he had come awake in an empty bed.

He shaved carefully, combed his hair, surveyed the damage of the three-day drinking bout. He decided that he hadn't changed too much. He hunted up his clothes and went into the kitchen. He found the note that D.B. had left him propped up against the plugged-in coffee maker and the bottle of tequila. He poured coffee, laced it with tequila, and sat down to read the note.

It simply said that she had decided to go to see her father at his office building and get it off her chest.

Good, he said to himself. The night before, when they had returned from Reno, he had decided that it was time for D.B. to have a talk with him. He had told her that he wasn't going to live on the Sadder money another day, that she was going to have to tell her father and take the consequences. And, no matter what Malcolm said, they had decided to return to his house in Darker's Bay and live on his music. When they had returned, dropping Sophie and Birsha in Darker's Bay, Harry had picked up his mail and had found the short note and five-hundred-dollar check from Amduscias.

So, D.B. had agreed, that they would remain in the apartment on Nob

Hill for the rest of the month—until Malcolm could make arrangements to find new occupants.

There was also the matter of almost eight thousand in D.B.'s account. Perhaps it had been foolish but Harry had suggested she return that as well. D.B. had agreed.

He felt good. All the small ends were being cleared up and he was in the mood to start work on his old piano at Darker's Bay. He finished his coffee, made a sandwich, opened a beer, and went into the front room. He picked up the phone and called a moving company. D.B. wanted her couch, the parrot cage, the totem pole, the bar, and the plants and gargoyles, as well as her clothes. He asked the moving company how much it would cost to have a large van and labor move the items to Darker's Bay. They assured him of a standard price and he thanked them. Then he called Dr. Bennet.

"This is Harry Dazier. Do you remember me?—Yes, that's right, Sandro's younger brother—Yes, I hate to disturb you but Birsha, that's the youngest, wanted me to call you—That's right, about Sandro—Well, no, he hasn't. He's been just about the same. No violence, no real threats. Just about the usual thing—Well, Birsha wants to get married—and I got married myself two days ago—Thank you—But about Sandro, do you think—I see." He lit a cigarette and drank his beer, listening to the bored, reassuring voice of Dr. Bennet. "Yes, well, Doctor, I was wondering if I could call on you in case anything comes up that— Yes, that'll be fine—Yes, he's still working with the merry-go-round— I'll keep an eye on him—Fine."

He hung up and stared moodily at the carpet for several long minutes. Then he rose from the couch and cleaned his breakfast things. There was plenty of work to be done. He had to start packing items that they wouldn't be using for the rest of their stay in the apartment. There was his music, some of D.B.'s clothes, and several crates of books. He went into the studio, deciding to begin there.

8

Waiting quietly in the red leather chair in the outer room of her father's office D.B. felt surprisingly calm over having to tell Malcolm that she had remarried and that she was going to cut herself off from the family money.

She felt, without actually saying it, like a new person. She tried to recall the person she had been in Dublin, in San Francisco before that, in the apartment last month with Gordon, but it was like trying to remember a bad bit-player in a film she might have seen many years before. The character was misty, unreal, small.

Almost without realizing it, D.B. was changing from a rebellious, starry-eyed girl to a mature, self-assured woman. The change wasn't complete, but it was there, reflected in her eyes, in her speech, in the way she gestured and carried herself. She couldn't define it, but she felt free. Not the hysterical freedom that she had experienced in Dublin, but a true freedom, solidly founded, confident.

She started to remove her dark gloves, then changed her mind; she didn't want the small wedding band that Harry had bought in a Reno pawnshop to be seen. She wasn't ashamed of it; she simply felt that it wasn't the proper time.

"How much longer, Selma?"

The secretary looked up from her John O'Hara novel and smiled politely. "Not too much longer, Miss Sadder. Your father's on the phone right at the moment—he knows that you're waiting." She looked at her intercom. "Shall I remind him for you?"

"No, thank you."

She saw, almost without registering the fact, that it had started to rain outside. She was thankful to herself for having put the car in the St. Mary's Garage. She lit a cigarette and picked up a copy of *Time*. She smiled, thinking that it was typical of Malcolm to have *Time* magazine in his office.

When Malcolm came to the door he raised his hand to catch her attention, then disappeared back in his office. D.B. rose, crossed the room, and closed the door softly after her. She still very calm.

"This is my usual lunch hour, so I have a little time for a chat," Malcolm said briskly. He sat behind his walnut desk and watched her, the overhead light making occasional yellow pools of his rimless glasses. "Have you been to a steam room, D.B.?"

She sat in the chair facing the desk. "No, I haven't; why do you ask?"

He shrugged. "You're looking—rather well."

She looked at him without expression. "I was just wondering if that was your first compliment to me, Malcolm."

He smiled thinly. "I believe you're aware of your physical assets without my telling you."

"Perhaps." She lit a cigarette and crossed her legs, and as she did she became aware of the soft hiss of pylon on her thighs and she immediately thought of Harry. She smiled to herself.

"You're looking amused, D.B."

"I have some news for you, Malcolm," she said.

"Oh? Have you bought another totem pole?"

She put her cigarette in the crystal tray that he pushed toward her. "I've remarried," she said quietly.

His left eye twitched and the color of his cheeks paled.

The only sounds were the traffic moving along Montgomery Street far below, the rain splattering on the stone window sill.

"What the deuce do you mean you've remarried?" Malcolm asked.

"Yes. I married—"

"No." He closed his eyes. "No, I don't want to hear about it," he said wearily.

There had been none of his usual anger, and this surprised D.B. She was a bit awed by it.

Malcolm left his desk and moved slowly to a walnut cabinet against one wall. When he inserted a tiny key and swung open the doors she saw that it was a compact office bar. She sat, staring, not knowing what to think.

"Do you prefer Scotch?" Malcolm's weary voice asked.

"What?"

"Scotch? Or would you prefer bourbon." He sighed, gestured as though it didn't matter. He drew out a bottle of Dewar's and a siphon. Carrying that, and two glasses, he returned to the desk and silently built two strong drinks. He handed one of them to D.B.

D.B. was still amazed with his resigned air, his secret liquor cabinet. It seemed that, after all the many years, she hadn't known Malcolm as well as she had thought. She didn't know what to make of the whole idea; she sat with the glass in her hand and tried to puzzle her father's ways.

Malcolm finally turned to her. "I'm sorry that you've done this, D.B. I don't know why. It's obviously something that you believed you had to do. At least, I hope that it was." He glanced at her while he paused to drink from his glass. "Why are you staring at me, D.B.?"

"I—I'm a little shocked, that's all. I never knew you to take a drink. I mean—that, coupled with the fact that you aren't—aren't ranting at me. I—" Her voice trailed weakly.

Malcolm shrugged. "I'm hardly above taking a drink, D.B. In fact, I usually have several here in my office for the lunch hour. Of course, I don't go down to any of the saloons along Montgomery. My employees drink there. It's not proper for a man of my position to be seen in an ivy-league cocktail lounge with a businessman's martini clenched in my fist."

"I see—"

"About my being angry with you. Why should I? I've 'ranted'—as you say—for the past twenty-three years and it's gained me nothing. So, why should I rant now—" He sat on the edge of his desk. "What I started to say was that I hope you haven't remarried simply to prove something to yourself—and perhaps to me—I see that you're still surprised. Do I sound so strange?"

True, even his voice seemed different. She swallowed Scotch and soda and nodded, feeling a curious bond growing between herself and her father. And she asked herself: why hadn't this happened years ago? Why now?

"You see, D.B., doing something to prove something to yourself—or to me—is nothing new with you. You've always done what you knew in your heart I could never approve of. Witness Dublin; witness your school days; witness your allowing yourself to be blackmailed by that Fitzroy scamp—I don't know quite how to put what I feel into words— father and daughter relationships are hardly my line. Business—yes. What I'm saying is that you've been trying, in your own way, to draw attention to yourself—no, please allow me to finish. You see, Marjorie was the favored child. That's true. Why should I deny it. I loved Marjorie because—because she was very much like me."

He poured another shot into his glass. "And do you know who you're like, D.B.? You're very much like your mother. You look amazingly like her, even now with your hair dyed that strange Hollywood shade, your up-to-date clothes. Your mother is a very beautiful woman, D.B. You were named after her. Debra Balmont—What's the matter? You're looking at me strangely. Did I say something wrong?"

D.B. had paled and had set her glass down, her hands trembling.

"Is there something the matter, D.B.?"

"No, nothing, Malcolm. It was probably a mistake. You said that my mother *is* a beautiful woman. You didn't say that she *was*—"

The lights in the office windows across the street seemed brighter, and somehow more melancholy. The sky was darker, the rain falling quicker, heavier, twisting in wet gray streaks on the window pane.

"Is my mother still alive, Malcolm?"

"No. She died eight years ago."

"I was—sixteen years old?"

"Yes."

"When did she leave?"

"When you were three years old." Then he added, "I'm sorry."

"Why should you be sorry?"

"Because I kept it from you."

"Did Marjorie know about this?"

"Yes, she did."

"Why didn't you tell me, Malcolm?"

"I thought that it would be best—perhaps I was wrong."

D.B. had, by now, forgotten her reasons for having come to see her father. She said, "My mother left you, didn't she?"

He nodded, then slowly unlocked his desk drawer and drew out a package of Parliament cigarettes. As he lit one, D.B. realized that it was the first time she had ever seen him smoke.

"Will you tell me about my mother?"

"I'm afraid it isn't a very pleasant story."

A mood of confession settled in the air and D.B. refilled her glass from the Scotch bottle.

Malcom sat back in his chair. "I came home one evening after work and Marjorie was next door, playing with the Anderson child—someone you wouldn't remember—at any rate, that evening I came home and found you—in the kitchen, alone, and you'd managed somehow to climb a chair and get into the bread and peanut butter—" He smiled, his expression looking back over the years. "Debra—your mother—had left no note. Not a word. I called an agency to have a nurse sent out to look after your sister and yourself. I set out looking for my wife. And I'm afraid I wasn't very successful. After two or three days I swallowed my pride and called in a firm of private investigators, then, when they failed, the police—"

"But you found her?"

"Yes. She wrote to me, asking for money."

"Where was she then?"

"Quebec."

"Had she run away with a man?"

He nodded. "Yes, a man who published a horse-racing journal in Canada."

"She died in Canada?"

"No. She ran away from the horse-racing chap and took up with a retired French policeman, who she happened to meet while he was vacationing in Quebec. They moved to Paris a year later."

D.B. nodded gloomily, staring at her cigarette burning in the crystal tray. "What was she like?"

"Young. Very young. From a good family. George Balmont had been one of my best friends—"

"How did she die, Malcolm?"

His eye twitched and he narrowed his lips over his teeth, then he sighed. "I—that's something that not even Marjorie knew—it's something that—You see, D. B., there was something about Debra that had always puzzled me. Something wild, rebellious, doing things—simply to punish me—"

"How did she die?"

"She was murdered—Strangled and beaten with a—a sledge hammer. Her lover, the retired policeman, had been the guilty party—They'd quarreled during a drinking bout—I'm sorry, D.B."

She shuddered, not doubting the truth of his story. It was obvious that the telling had upset him, had raked over the ashes of the past to reveal a spark still smoldering. She said the first thing that came into her mind: "Do you love me, Malcolm?"

"Yes."

She remembered now why she had come to see him. She hadn't expected the story that she had been told. She wanted to push it out of her mind—but it was difficult; she kept seeing a woman, resembling herself, strangled and mashed with a hammer.

"Do—do you want me to be happy?" she asked.

"Yes."

"Do you disapprove of me?"

"I—I don't know. If I do, I suppose it's because you resemble your mother so very much. And because you've always had that same wild streak that had caused her death."

D.B. felt like crying, breaking the tightness in her throat and laying her head in her hands. Her father's life had become very real in the past half hour. She realized that he had a past, and this upset her. She had never thought of him as a human being before.

They were silent and again the rain sounded on the hill and the traffic purred on the street far below. D.B. clutched at her bag, remembered what she had inside it: a cashier's check for seven thousand six hundred forty-two dollars. It was the exact amount of her now-closed account.

"Wouldn't you like to know now who I married?"

"I suppose it's necessary."

"His name is Harry Dazier."

"A Frenchman?"

"No, just the name."

"Are you in love with him?"

"Yes. Very much."

"And when were you married?"

"Two days ago. In Reno."

Malcolm sighed. "What kind of work does he do?"

"He's a composer."

"Indeed? Not a jazz composer, I hope?"

"No. He's quite serious."

"Does he happen to earn a living with his work?"

"Yes."

"Oh? I've never heard of him."

"I'd be surprised if you had," she answered politely.

"Does he love you?"

"Of course." She opened her purse, drew out the cashier's check, the apartment lease, the title papers to the car. She placed them on his desk and he hesitated before picking them up. When he finished looking at them he raised his brow and pursed his lips.

"What is this?" he asked softly.

"Everything."

"Why are you giving it to me?"

"Harry wants it that way."

"Really? Doesn't he like money?"

"Yes. He doesn't want your money, though. He told me to tell you that he doesn't want anything from you."

Malcolm nodded, dropped the papers on his blotter. "All I can say is that if the man is sincere I admire him. But if this is a grand-stand gesture to put me off my guard then I pity him."

"It's not a gesture, Malcolm. He first seduced me knowing that I was wealthy, wanting the money and wanting your influence with the opera league."

"He told you that?"

"Yes."

"Before or after you were married?"

"Before."

"I see." Malcolm smiled and poured another drink for himself, then added a shot to D.B.'s glass. "He sounds like a fine young man. If he's real. I can find out, you know."

"I don't doubt that you could," D.B. answered.

He nodded. "Does he drink? Is he one of those wild, drunken artists one reads about?"

She hesitated. "Yes, he drinks."

"Very much?"

Why did she feel the urge to lie? Was it because she felt that Malcolm was about to accept Harry, that a few white lies wouldn't hurt? At any rate, she answered that he wasn't a very heavy drinker, that he was in fact practically a teetotaler. Then, with that lie so easily told, she lapsed into her old scheming self. She told her father that Harry was everything other than what he was. Malcolm was quite pleased by the time they finished their talk. He had drunk quite a bit and she knew that he was in an expansive mood. And she wasn't too surprised when he made a suggestion.

"Perhaps I *could*, after all, help the young man with the opera league."

"He wouldn't like that. He'd be angry with me because he'd say that it was the Sadder influence. It was a nice thought, Malcolm. Very nice. It's just that I don't think it would work."

"Is he ashamed of the Sadder name?"

"No. It's not that. Harry's a proud man, I suppose. He just wouldn't want help because he happened to marry the only daughter of a rich man. He's not that kind."

"I appreciate that, D.B. I like that kind of spirit in a young man. However, if I could—arrange, shall we say, a consideration with the opera league—and I'm sure I can—it wouldn't come about simply because he happened to be my son-in-law. The committee, Mr. Richard Lippmann—one of my board members—would hardly settle for Harry Dazier if he didn't honestly come up to the standards set by the committee. No, the final deciding factor would be the young man's talent—*not* his connections. I didn't make that suggestion a moment ago in a moment of Scotch whimsy, you know. I was quite serious. Lippmann is a capable director, well versed in the field of music, and the final word would naturally be his."

D.B. saw the logic in what Malcolm said. She felt herself giving in, raising only feeble arguments with herself. "I—I don't know. If Harry ever found out—"

"Credit me with discretion, D.B. I'm certain I can keep my name out of it. I'm serious about wanting to help this young man. I'll be honest with you. It's not only Harry Dazier, it's you that I'm thinking of. I hardly want my daughter to live the life of a struggling artist. I understand—as you've explained—that your young man earns enough from his work, but I rather doubt he wouldn't appreciate a commission from the opera league. And there would be no reason for him to know that his being my son-in-law had brought him to the committee's attention. And believe me, D.B., that's *all* I could do—bring his name to Richard Lippmann's attention."

D.B. was weakening, excited by the idea, but she still had her doubts. "I still think that he would suspect something. I hate to refuse such an opportunity for him—for us, but he'd become suspicious if he received an offer like that only a few days after marrying me—and a few days after I talked with you."

"I can remedy that," Malcolm said. "Believe me. I've been in the business world for many, many years, my dear, and I can doctor an offer to fit any situation I so desire."

She nodded, completely surrendering herself to the scheme. Half drunk now, she began to feel somewhat proud of herself.

It was true, Harry wouldn't have to know. And, after all, it wasn't as if she were buying him the commission. It wasn't that at all. Malcolm would bring Harry to the committee's attention and it would be Harry's talent which would win or lose him the offer. That wasn't *buying* him the job. The Sadder influence would be the catalyst and that was all.

Already she imagined Harry's surprise, and she flushed with pleasure. She had drunk too much, but she felt sure that she was thinking logically. What was wrong with helping the man you love? Nothing. Absolutely nothing wrong with it.

Malcolm walked her to the door, still talking, telling long-ago anecdotes of D.B.'s childhood, of Marjorie's. When they left each other they were each aware of the bond between them. They shook hands shyly, then D.B. walked to the elevator. She stopped at the first bar on Montgomery Street.

"A Scotch and soda, please."

Outside, the rain fell in dark gray streams; umbrellas scurried by, and the skies darkened, reflecting D.B.'s turning moods.

"You said soda, Miss?"

"Yes, please."

Oh God. Why did she have to tell Malcolm those ridiculous stories about Harry's sobriety? Why had she gone overboard? She hoped that she hadn't failed Harry with her foolishness. She loved him. God, how she loved him. But it was only natural that she wanted to see him succeed.

But still, despite her arguments, she suspected that she had, once again, crawled from one problem to another.

"Another Scotch and soda?"

"Yes—make it double, please—"

Would she ever be able to bring her two lives together? What would Harry do when he found out about the committee offer? Where would it all end?

9

Three days later, Harry sat sprawled in the studio in the black Gothic chair, drinking beer and listening to rock'n'roll on the radio, tapping time with his bare foot. D.B. had gone to the hairdresser's, and Harry knew from past experience that she would be gone for another four hours at least. He chuckled aloud. While the cat's away, the mice will play. Rock'n'roll mice. He turned up the volume and wallowed in the primitive shouting and banging. He almost didn't hear the phone when it rang, but during a comparative lull in a record which sounded like tribal

music from Tanganyika, the insistent ringing came through to him. He
turned off the radio and picked up the phone.

"Hello—Who?—Okay, what do you want?—What!" He listened, turned
pale, asked several questions, nodded. He didn't know what to think,
what to say. "I—*when* did you consider this, Mr. Lippmann?—Two
months ago? Are you sure of that—What? No, of course I'm not being—
Yes, certainly—Belphegor? Yes, I can find it—I will—Thank you."

He dropped the phone in the cradle and stood in stunned silence. He
pulled on his shoes, lit a cigarette, his thoughts racing suspiciously
around in his head.

"She couldn't have," he said aloud. "She *couldn't* have!"

The parrot winked. "I'm in hell!"

"Shut up!"

He opened his packed suitcase, pulled out his new drip-dry suit, soft
Brooks shirt, dark necktie, and dressed in the hallway. Out in the
street, the doorman saluted him and said that it was a fine afternoon,
Mr. Dazier. Harry glared at him. "Call me a cab, goddamnit."

The doorman looked startled and hurried down to the near corner and
blew his whistle for one of the cabs in the Hotel Fairmont waiting line
a block and a half down the street. A minute later a yellow slid to a stop
under the apartment's green canopy and Harry quickly piled into the
rear seat.

The driver dropped the flag. "In a rush, unh?"

"You know where the Belphegor Club is?"

"Sure do, buddy. It's for members only—"

"Just shut up and take me there."

He slumped in the leather seat, chewed his thumb, listened to the
metallic click of the meter. There was nothing to be gained by snapping
at strangers. He felt a twinge over his cursing the doorman and the
driver. But what the hell—Harry was badly shaken inside. He hated to
doubt D.B. but the coincidence seemed too great. He married Malcolm
Sadder's daughter and less than a week later he received an offer from
Richard Lippmann, director of the San Francisco Opera League.

Coincidence?

Perhaps.

"Hey, buddy. Here's the Belphegor."

Harry tipped him a dollar. "I'm sorry I snapped at you back there. I
just received some bad news, that's all."

"Sure, I know how it is, buddy."

The Belphegor Club was housed in the lower level of a faded brick
building that was completely covered with Kenilworth ivy. A small,
graying colored man wearing a red velvet jacket stopped him just as he

pushed through the oak and brass doors. Harry gave the name of his host and the colored man led the way down a thickly carpeted hallway to a small dark-paneled tap room. Richard Lippmann was sitting in a corner booth. Harry drew up to the table and politely announced himself.

"Ah, Mr. Dazier. How nice of you to be so prompt. May I suggest a drink before we eat?"

Richard Lippmann was a large Nordic-looking man with a wild shock of yellowish gray hair, thin blue eyes, flat face, and a grave, responsible expression. His voice, surprisingly, was a soft undertaking purr; his handshake was moist and warm.

Harry ordered a Scotch on the rocks, feeling uncomfortable in the deep redwood paneling and red velvet trim of the tap room; his doubts seemed almost foolish now in the official presence of his host.

"Well! I believe you know why I asked you to meet me, Mr. Dazier."

"Yes, you mentioned—" His voice trailed off.

Lippmann nodded briskly. "We've given this matter considerable thought, Mr. Dazier—Believe me, there were several eliminations before we decided on you. Maestro Amduscias, I might add, influenced us considerably."

"Amduscias?"

"Yes. We contacted him, as well as Arnold Oberhurst and the Theatre of Ballet. We understood that you've been committed to two works for Maestro Amduscias and the Philharmonic—We had to know if you would be free and open to our offer."

"I see. I suppose the Maestro informed you that I'd completed both commissions."

"Yes. He seemed quite enthusiastic—"

That was a twist Harry hadn't expected. "I—may I ask you a few questions, Mr. Lippmann?"

"Do call me Richard. The Mister business always seems so unnecessarily formal. May I call you Harry?"

"Please do. About my questions—"

Lippmann signaled for two more drinks. "The questions, of course, Harry. Ask anything you wish."

"First, where did you get my San Francisco phone number?"

Lippmann seemed surprised with that. "Why, I phoned your residence in Darker's Bay and a man who identified himself as your brother—a certain Burt, or Burda—and he was kind enough to give me the number where you could be reached—Ah, did I do wrong?"

"No," Harry assured him.

Harry sipped his drink, the exhilaration of what was happening finally dawning on him. It seemed that the offer was on the level so far. He had certainly been a fool for having doubted D.B. He should have known better.

"And you say that you've been considering this offer for almost two months?"

"Yes, that's correct. You see, we haven't had a new work for more than three years. Frankly, it was I who made the suggestion to the committee that we consider a fresh approach to next year's season. You understand naturally that symphonic and operatic presentations rarely make money on a municipal level. We're always trying to plan new ways to spark public interest, to pep up the program, so to speak. And, considering yourself, you're a—if you'll pardon my saying—you're rather a controversial voice on today's musical scene."

"Thank you."

Lippmann smiled warmly. "I'm glad to find you're not easily offended." He sipped from his martini, winking his thin blue eyes. "I've been familiar with your works since the New York premiere of *The Owl and the Pussycat*. Yes, I was there. And I found it very good."

Harry said, "Why don't you say what you really thought of it."

Lippmann studied him a moment, then chuckled. "You're right. I found it interesting rather than very good. The choreography was marvelous, the settings superb, and your score the strangest I've ever heard. It's never been recorded, has it?"

"No."

"I thought not. The *Peter Klaus* has, though?"

"Yes."

"Well, you're still a young man, and you've a bright future ahead of you. Please don't take what I say too seriously. I'm a real-estate man, not a music critic. I'm director of the league simply because my wife once sang in a small Texas company and had a terrible crush on Jan Peerce."

Harry smiled, the Scotch warming him, lulling him. He was convinced that the entire conversation was legitimate, that his suspicions had been groundless, and he relaxed before his host did. When the luncheon came to an end, Lippmann put the question to him. Was Harry interested in the offer?

"Yes."

"Excellent, Harry. I'm very pleased."

When Harry finally left the club and stepped out onto the street he found himself too pleased with himself to want to return to the apartment and wait for D.B. Walking down the steep hill he felt like going to the hairdresser's, invading the sanctum of robot machines and cold cream and barber bibs, and telling D.B. the news. He felt like celebrating, like having some people up to the apartment for a party. After all, they would be moving from the apartment in another week, so why shouldn't they take advantage of it? For once they would be able to make noise in the place!

While Harry was sitting in the bar, an idea came to him and he started to jot notes and symbols on a stack of dice cards and cocktail coasters. He ordered tequila, drank it straight, and worked at the bar for the remainder of the afternoon. When he finished with the outline he penciled in a title, half humorously—*St. Cado, the Cat, the Devil, and the Bridge at Cahors*.

"What's so funny, mac?" the bartender asked pleasantry.

"Have you ever heard of St. Cado?"

"That's a new one on me," the bartender said.

"Good. It always makes more sense if no one's ever heard of him. Give me another tequila, please—and some more dice cards."

10

Two nights later, the celebration party was in full swing. D.B. had to send Zeke out to buy a case of vodka and soda because, even though Harry had invited only fifteen people, the word had spread and now there were more than forty people crowded into the Nob Hill apartment. The carpet had been rolled and placed on end in the far corner and the floor was littered with paper cups, melting ice cubes, bits of paper, and mashed cigarette butts. D.B. had to press herself flat against the wall in order to pass through the short hall to the kitchen. The air was stained with layers of tobacco smoke. Everywhere there seemed to be a face, a smile, a drink, or an elbow.

She filled the oak bucket with ice and pushed her way back to the bar. She was weaving and was well on her way to becoming drunk. When Harry had told her the glad news of Lippmann's offer, and when she listened to his humorously told tale of how he knew that it had been offered on his own merit, she had felt an intense surge of relief. It had been difficult for her to hide her feelings, so she had buried herself in his arms and kissed him, congratulated him, told him how proud she was of him. She had felt like a cheat for only a brief moment, then because of Dazier's genuine pleasure over the news, she forced all else from her mind.

"How're we doing with the liquor?"

"We're all right now," Zeke answered.

"You were at the Darker's Bay party, weren't you?"

"That's right."

"Are you a friend of Harry's?"

"In a way. I'm a friend of a friend."

"Zeke—is that your name?"

"It's one of them," Zeke said.

"Harry said that you wanted to be a Dark Messenger. Is that right?"

"Only when I have a dark message to deliver. Otherwise I'm one of the good guys."

Two men pushed near the bar, arguing, gesturing wildly. One was tall and dark with black olive eyes, Vandyke beard, and a white turban. The other, who was shouting and waving, wore a deerstalker cap and a London raincoat.

D.B. made herself a small drink at the bar and moved through the crowd. She talked, without listening to herself, with Arnold Ames, Sandro, Helga Marris, Birsha and Sophie, and finally reached the open door of the music studio. There were three couples sitting on the floor in the dark. She stepped past them, excusing herself, and paused at the french windows. Harry was on the balcony with Daniel Marris and Richard Freeze. Freeze had arrived with Zeke, carrying a violin case like a movie gangster.

When she returned to the main room she saw Gordon Fitzroy standing near the hallway, a drink in his hand, talking to a dark-haired girl who had arrived with a TV bit player. Gordon's upper lip was bandaged and there was a purplish lump over his left eye.

She moved toward the kitchen, hoping he hadn't noticed her, but he glanced up quickly, excused himself from the dark-haired girl, and pushed his way past the turbaned man and a knot of five others. When he reached her side he tried to smile but the lip bandage seemed to get in the way. "Hello, D.B."

"What are you doing here, Gordon?" she asked.

"Don't sound so damned icy, D.B. I was invited."

"By who?"

"Auckland."

"*He* wasn't invited."

"Well," Gordon said casually, "he heard about the party and he invited himself."

She controlled herself. "You'd better leave."

"You don't seem to understand, D.B. You're in no position to order me about—"

"I think that I am. If you think you're going to shock me with your dirt concerning Harry you've got another think coming. He's told me *why* you and your nasty little friend tried to shake him down. So, you have nothing to hold over us. Now you'd better leave."

Gordon's expression hadn't changed. "Harry told you, did he? Well, I'm surprised."

She smiled through her anger, "And besides, I married him. He's my husband."

Gordon nodded. "So I heard. I suppose you've told Malcolm all about this new marriage of yours?"

"Yes."

Gordon's smile faltered. "Have you? I doubt that *very* much. If you had, you wouldn't still be in this apartment. You'd be in St. Francis Woods, living like Jane Eyre."

"You believe that? Then you're a cluck. I've told you that before, haven't I? It's true. You're a cluck. Now, if I were you I'd round up Auckland, and get out."

"I suppose if I don't leave you whistle for Tarzan. Well, if you think I'm going to let him lucky-punch me again, you're badly mistaken." Gordon's cornflower eyes glittered and his blunt jaw thrust itself out. "I've got a score to settle with that cuckolding swine! Last time I was drunk, and he was sober. Well, the tables are turned now. I hear he's pretty drunk. And I'm sober. Believe me!"

For the first time since the beginning of their talk D.B. was feeling uncertain, fearful. She didn't want a fight—not now. She reached for Gordon's coatsleeve, her concern showing in her voice. "Gordon, please, I don't want any trouble. Leave the party. Take Auckland. Malcolm knows about Harry, knows about you. Honestly, there's *nothing* here for you—"

"We'll see about that," Gordon said tightly. Shaking his arm free, he pushed his way toward the studio.

Harry and Daniel were just coming through the door and heading toward the bar when Gordon drew up beside them. Daniel continued walking past and Harry stopped.

"Harry!" D.B. shouted.

The forty people in the room seemed to sense that there was about to be trouble and a hush fell, allowing D.B. to hear a few words from Gordon and Harry.

"Out—

"You think you're a goddam—

"Just a sneaky punch—"

"Take it easy, Fitzroy—"

D.B. started to push through the crowd. She dropped her cup of vodka, elbowed her way past a couple, and when she came to the clearing by the bar she could see immediately that Harry was too drunk to fight, that he was smiling, attempting to placate Gordon.

Gordon puffed out his chest, lined Harry for a punch, and pulled back his fist, but it was stopped in mid-air. A huge hand shot out and caught Gordon's arm, then grasped his fist, twisted, and Gordon rose on his tiptoes, screaming painfully.

It was Sandro.

"Harry!" D.B. shouted.

Harry was smiling, still holding his glass and leaning against the wall for support; he didn't seem to be listening to D.B.

Gordon, still on tiptoes as Sandro squeezed his fist between his enormous hands, struggled to break free, still squealing from the pressure. Then Sandro released him. Gordon staggered back, hugging his hand to his stomach, red-faced with embarrassment and anger, glaring hatefully at Sandro.

Sandro was smiling, his thin lips drawn back and revealing no amusement at the situation. His black coalchip eyes glittered under the thick white brows, set in the scarred craggy face, and he towered over Gordon by a good five inches.

Gordon started for the door.

Sandro followed him and when they reached the doorway Auckland spoke a few words to Gordon. Sandro grabbed the little man by the neck, muttered something, and threw him into the hall, then jerked open the door and shoved them viciously out into the outer hallway.

Hating herself for it, D.B. felt grateful to Sandro and when the big man stalked past her she touched his sleeve. Staring up into his massive face, she thanked him. Sandro merely grunted disgustedly and went into the kitchen.

"He's a venomous bastard," Harry said.

"He threw them out, though," D.B. said.

"I don't mean Sandro, for God's sake. I mean Fitzroy. He's cooking in his own venom. What makes a guy like that so much a bastard? I don't know. He was mad enough to stick me in the ribs."

"Well, he's gone now."

"Yeah."

"I'm glad that Sandro stepped in, Harry. You're pretty drunk."

He grinned. "Yeah? I guess I am at that. If Sandro hadn't stepped in Daniel would've clobbered him. I'm too drunk to fight my way out of a blown-up paper bag."

The turbaned man and deerstalker were still arguing in the hall and when D.B. passed by deerstalker turned to her and asked: "I say, Mrs. Dazier, would you say this character looks like an Indian?"

"Yes, he does."

Deerstalker pointed angrily to the other's turban. "Do you see that—that exotic looking rag? Do you? Well, inside that damn thing is a transistor radio. He's secretly listening to a program of Mexican music from San Jose. He's a Mexican. Say, Pedro? Don't lean on that door! You don't know who's going to op—"

The door swung open and Helga Marris had to quickly step aside as the turbaned man fell into the room.

"I say, Pedro, I told you not to lean on that door."

Turban man cursed in Spanish.

Helga put her arm around D.B. "I never had a chance to congratulate you on marrying Harry."

D.B. thanked her and they started for the bar together. "I need a drink."

"So do I," Helga said. "Then we have something in common."

Sophie and Daniel were at the end of the bar, and Zeke was sitting on a stool near a fern, drinking vodka and scratching his chin. Daniel said, "The last time I saw Sophie she was green."

"I'm going to be purple next. Like an egg-plant. And I'm going to dye my hair white, just like D.B. That's a wonderful combination. Purple and white, don't you think?"

"Very regal," Daniel said.

"What was the fight about?" Helga asked.

Daniel shrugged. "Search me, honey."

"The other one was my ex-husband," D.B. explained.

"Oh. One of those."

"Sandro really moved fast," Sophie remarked. Then, "I hate talking about Sandro, but he keeps popping up, doesn't he? Sort of like a Kleenex."

Daniel said drily, "The next time I want to blow my nose I'll look for Sandro."

When D.B. left the bar and went to look for Harry she saw Sandro standing against the far wall near the rolled carpet, his glittering black eyes detached from the scene, as if he hadn't the vaguest idea where he was. D.B. realized, as if for the first time, that she was actually related to an insane man! A sudden shiver almost caused her to spill her drink.

Harry was still on the balcony, his arm around a gargoyle, his tie and jacket gone and his hair falling in his face.

"Hello, Harry."

He grinned, a happy, lopsided pose. "Hello. We've missed you. That is, the Gargoyle and I. Sounds like the title to a book, doesn't it? The Gargoyle and I. Pennzoil. Gargoyle. Popeye and Olive Oyl—Nov Schmoz

Kapop."

"You're having a good time."

He grabbed her, upsetting her drink. "I'm having a great time, honey. I'm glad you and I know each other. I think we're a fine couple. I'm going to finish the songs for Lippmann then you and I'll cut out for—Tahiti, someplace like that."

He kissed her and her back rustled against the fern and bamboo. He said, "I like to watch gargoyles flying in the sky. Flapping their wings and crying out with their stone lungs. You know what a gargoyle sounds like when it cries? It sounds like a mountain falling. Just like that."

He kissed her again and she pressed against him, pushing her hips up into him, her tongue touching his lips, warm and moist. "I kind of like you, too, Harry. And I'm glad you didn't fight with Gordon."

"Forget Gordon. Let's have music. I'm too drunk to play the piano and the record-player's all packed away—"

"What about Richard Freeze," D.B. said. "Does he really play the violin? Or does he carry a machine gun?"

"He plays the violin. Ask him to play you *Red River Valley.*"

"Why? Does it sound like a mountain falling?"

"No. It sounds like an old John Ford movie. If this balcony had a fire escape we could go up on the roof and—watch for Halley's Comet."

"Halley's Comet only comes by whenever Mark Twain dies."

"I know, but we could think of something to do while we waited for Mark Twain to die."

They finished their drinks and returned to the noisy, crowded main room. They joined Birsha and Richard Freeze. Zeke had passed out and Daniel was serving as bartender. Sophie started to dance, humming and clapping her orange hands. D.B. doused the overhead light, leaving only the one stand lamp, and they sat in the shadowed darkness and watched as the dancing took shape. The man with the deerstalker cap joined Sophie, then another couple. It looked as if the party was going to move to another plane.

11

Someone had dragged D.B.'s totem pole to the center of the room and fifteen minutes later they were still dancing. Herman and Vivian had collected the empty bottles and had set them in staggered rows of two along the edge of the dance area. They were striking them with teakwood swizzle sticks, changing sounds by flicking the sticks rapidly from neck to bottle to label, switching from one bottle to another. The effect was like a tumbling waterfall of bits of glass and tinfoil and ice.

Sophie twirled and stamped her feet and Harry drunkenly cast admiring glances at her legs, naked orange feet, lovely orange thighs flashing whenever the circus awning of her dress flew to her hips. Harry sighed fuzzily and covetously slipped his arm around D.B.'s waist. Sex was a wonderful thing. So was liquor. And so was D.B. and himself. He liked himself immensely and he poured himself another drink. Here's to St. Cado. Wherever he may be.

Harry realized that he had never seen Freeze as drunk as he was right now. Freeze had unpacked his violin and was now playing *Old Black Joe*, ignoring the beat of the bottle waterfall; then he played a bit of *Humoresque*, then Harry's favorite, *Red River Valley*.

The dance grew more wild, more primitive, the figures beginning to hop up and down, reminding Harry of Daffy Duck in the movie cartoons, whooping and bouncing. The floor shuddered. The bouncing became infectious and others joined in.

"I can't stand it!" D.B. said excitedly. "Look at them bounce! My God! The noise!" She squeezed Harry's arm, her green eyes shining, her cheeks colored with joy. "This is insane," she said breathlessly.

Turban man joined the others, and when he started to bounce up and down his turban fell to the floor and a red plastic transistor radio clattered to the bare wood. Harry laughed then, bewitched, caught in the mad whirl of shadows and whooping, leaping figures, and he started to bounce with the rest of them.

He saw the front door open but it meant nothing to him. He didn't stop dancing until he saw Gordon Fitzroy enter the room. He stood, breathing heavily, eyeing D.B.'s ex-husband, wondering if he was sober enough to throw a good punch. He decided that he was. He started across the room but was stopped by D.B.'s hand on his wrist. Then he saw that Fitzroy wasn't alone this time. There was a little man with him; a little bald man with smoked glasses and Hoover collar, his white face twitching, his thin lips compressed into a razor line.

D.B.'s nails dug into Harry's hand, practically drawing blood, and when Harry turned he saw that her face had become ashen, her eyes wide with horror.

"It's my father!" D.B. gasped.

Book III — Sandro

1

The telephone poles were black outlines against the dawn and long rosary rows of blackbirds slept perched on the wires. A lazing Holstein cow stood in the nearby field, velvet eyed, watching the silent gray road that wound through the rolling coastal farm lands. It was five o'clock in the morning and a car hadn't passed in four hours.

The cow's ears perked when the low-slung German sports car roared around the far turn near the cypress stand and skidded at the rise of a gentle dip. Then the car straightened, gathered more speed, and headed for the next bend, which was opposite the livestock road that led to the barns and milking sheds. The yellow headlights swerved, tires squealed again, then the car spun on the soft road shoulder and crashed into the whitewashed fence near the livestock road.

The cow bolted. The blackbirds exploded from the wires and filled the dawn air with the rush of their wings. Then it was silent save for the still-purring car motor.

"I'll be a sonofabitch," D.B. mumbled thickly to no one.

The headlights were still on and the motor was still running, so she decided that there hadn't been any real damage. She put the car in reverse and pulled away from the fence. There was no wobble, no scraping, so she knew that she hadn't had a flat. The only damage, save her left fender, was to the farmer's fence.

"The farmer can go to hell," she said.

The car moved forward again and as she drove she pulled the flying strands of champagne hair from her mouth and eyes. Now, where was she before she had been so rudely interrupted by the farmer's goddam fence? Oh yes—Birsha. She was sure that Birsha had been lying to her. He must have known where Harry had gone to. Perhaps she would have done better if she had offered him—what? Money? That was ridiculous. She had only sixteen dollars left in her purse and was driving a car that no longer belonged to her.

She had gone to Darker's Bay to look for Harry. She had tried every other place she had been able to think of during the past five days. She had phoned Birsha, but she hadn't believed that Harry wasn't there. After all, he had to be somewhere. And when she found him she would ask him to forgive her.

She fumbled at her feet, found the bottle of bourbon, pulled the cap and tilted it. As she drank she was vaguely aware of blinding headlights rushing directly toward her. Then an ear-splitting horn. She jerked disdainfully at the wheel and the monstrous truck roared past her, missing the car by a bare two inches.

"Goddam road hog," she said.

It was almost seven o'clock by the time she reached San Francisco. She parked the battered car in the brick court and staggered upstairs to her half-empty apartment. She didn't want to face the bare floor, still littered from the party, the packed crates and suitcases. Fully clothed, she threw herself on the bed and dropped the bottle of bourbon on her pillow.

Why didn't anyone tell her where Harry was? Had they all lied to her? Were they all involved in some plot against her? It was impossible for her to accept the fact that Harry might not love her now. It had been too real, too solid to dissolve, simply because she had been a fool, had deceived him with the one small lie.

She had told Birsha that she would find Harry. She would continue looking, but right now she desperately needed sleep, needed to sober up and view her search with a clear mind. She had said that she would try Daniel and Helga's, Sandro's warehouse, Richard Freeze's place in San Anselmo.

She dozed fitfully, tossing on the bed, perspiring under her thick sweater. As she dreamed she knitted her brow and shook her head as if to deny the pictures entry—

—The night of the party, wrapped in a mist, chopped sequences flitting by like a poorly spliced film.

Sandro's enormous hands crushing Gordon's fist as though it were an orange poised over a glass. Screams of pain. Daniel and Sophie at the bar and the eavesdropping Zeke. Harry on the balcony with the gargoyle. Richard Freeze and the rhythmic tinkle of the bottles. Dancing. Yes, the whooping and bouncing about the totem pole.

Malcolm's appearance was another magic-slide to the night's madness, but when his figure didn't disappear she grew cold and deaf—the party sounds vanishing, leaving a void—only Malcolm's face left in the irregular shadows. "It's my father!" she had gasped.

White with horror, Malcolm stood before her, on the edge of rage. "Which of these pigs happens to be Mr. Dazier!"

Harry drew himself up, glaring at Malcolm, at the traitorous Gordon. He said, "Just a goddam minute, you—

"Then you're Dazier?"

"That's right."

D.B. tried to lunge at Gordon, clawing with her nails, screaming "You dirty sonofabitch," but Harry grabbed her and held her back while Gordon leaped to one side, behind Malcolm the way a child sought protection from an elder. Malcolm looked disgusted, enraged, pained, vicious.

"Drunken pigs! All of you! I'm completely through! And you, Dazier, you can send your herd of swine back to their pens! The party is *definitely* over!"

"Listen, you—"

"No! You listen!" Malcolm's voice raised to a new pitch, threatening to become a squeal. His face shivered and spittle gathered at his thin lips. He pulled himself up to his full five foot five, controlling his hands at his sides. "I have *nothing* to discuss with you, Dazier! *Nothing!* And I speak for Dick Lippmann, too! Expect nothing from the league, Dazier! I wouldn't help you now if you were the last composer on the face of this earth! *Do you hear?*"

D.B. was near collapsing. Harry's face was that of a stranger. A mouth, a mask, a pair of anguished eyes. It was over! The air was ripped between them and she could feel the floor grow soft, like gelatine, drawing her into the boards to safety.

No! Please, Harry!

The floor floated toward her and mercifully struck her forehead, blinding her, erasing Harry's burning eyes, Malcolm's wrath, Gordon's proud sneer, and the wild whooping party. When she awoke she found herself on the couch. The apartment was silent, littered with party filth. She was alone. Harry had left her—

"No!" she muttered.

She drew herself up, found that she was still on her bed, twisted in the blankets, itching with perspiration. It was still morning. Her platinum wrist watch said that it was a little before eight and she realized that she had slept only an hour. She found the bottle, tilted it, drank two full shots, and fell back on the bed. Couldn't she ever sleep? Wouldn't her brain allow her rest? She stared blankly up at the blue silk overhang and wondered what Harry was doing right at this minute.

2

Harry bit into his bacon sandwich and gazed across the bright blue water of the oval pool to the practice green where a few early players were faking drives and pegging short shots at the cups. Arnold Oberhurst sat across the breakfast table from Harry, following his eyes to the green. "Have you ever golfed, Harry?"

"No."

Oberhurst poured more coffee. "You're too emotional, Harry."

Harry nodded.

"You always did drink a great deal."

"Yes," Harry replied.

Arnold Oberhurst said nothing after that and he settled back in the wrought-iron patio chair and sighed compassionately. He was a tall man, thin, sixty years old, with a narrow face that was spider-webbed with fine wrinkles. He had pale gray hair, dark brown eyes, and a prominent nose. There was something of the hawk about him, with his sharp white teeth and hungry expression.

Harry watched the men on the practice green with envious eyes. He knew that they had problems—everyone had them—but they seemed relaxed at the moment, self-contained, concerned only with a stick and a shining white ball. At any other time he would call them morons, but now he felt a peculiar yearning to be with them, dressed as they were in white shoes and pastel slacks, calmly swinging their sticks and looking sleek and fat.

Then he called himself a fool for his envy. Harry was a better man, in spite of his problems. And envy was never a solution, neither was stubbornness. And, he reflected, he was being stubborn.

When the party had ended Harry had left with Richard Freeze, Sophie, and Birsha. He stayed at Darker's Bay for two days, wandering the hills, collecting blades of grass and pine cones, working occasionally on his St. Cado. When the phone finally rang it wasn't, as he had hoped, D.B. It was his ex-teacher and friend, Arnold Oberhurst. Arnie was in Salinas, visiting his son, passing through on his way to a music festival in Honolulu. He invited Harry to visit with him at the Salinas motel near the golf links and Harry accepted. He had been at the motel for almost three days now, telling his troubles to Arnie, talking over old times, and in the evenings, playing four-handed Liszt on the two pianos in the motel's recreation room.

Arnold Oberhurst cleared his throat. "I'm leaving for San Francisco this afternoon, Harry. The *Lurline* sails tomorrow morning. I was wondering—would you like to ride back with me?"

"I suppose," Harry said indifferently.

"Are you still in love with D.B.?"

"Yes."

"Then why don't you go back to her?"

Harry shrugged.

Arnold Oberhurst smiled knowingly. "Stubborn," he said.

"All right then—stubborn."

"One thing before I leave, Harry. Have you given any thought to what I told you yesterday? The Hollywood business?"

"Yes, I've thought about it, Arnie."

"I hope you don't mind my helping you this way. Do you resent my acting like an agent with you?"

"No."

"I do this because I know that you're afraid to hustle for yourself, Harry."

Harry nodded. That was true. He knew that without Arnold's help he would never have received the Amduscias commissions, *or* the Theatre of Ballet work. And, knowing this, he asked himself, for the first time, why did he resent D.B.'s trying to do the same thing? The obvious implications, the simplicity of their meaning, was painful and confusing to Harry. He resented help from a woman. That was all. Nothing more.

"I've tried to be more than a teacher to you, Harry," Arnold was saying gently. "I've tried to be a friend. I know you think of me that way as well, and I'm grateful. I speak to you as if you were my own son. Incidentally, my own son sells electrical appliances here in Salinas. His only contact with music is through his collection of Dixieland and Frank Sinatra records. You were my best pupil, Harry. From the steam calliope to Oberhurst's star pupil. I'm very proud of you, my friend."

"Thank you," Harry said, his voice soft.

"Returning to the Hollywood business," Arnold said. "I took the liberty of telephoning Robert Betseka this morning by long distance. I told him that you were thinking it over and he was delighted. Do you think you'd be interested?"

"I don't know," Harry said doubtfully. "I hate the movies."

"They're not all bad. I worked for Warner's for four and a half years. Betseka is an artist—Listen, Harry, others have done it before. Many great men have. There wouldn't be anything about it to feel ashamed over. Believe me."

Harry shrugged. "Who ever hears movie music? Answer me that."

"You do."

"I don't write for myself."

"Many film scores are recorded."

"Sure—if you're Tiomkin."

"Harry, let me tell you about Robert Betseka. He has a passion for the film as an art. A devotee of Eisenstein. His name is up there with George Stevens, Bergman, Kubrick."

"Names mean nothing," Harry said.

"They would if you were in Hollywood. And I want you to go, Harry. After all, it's for only one film. You wouldn't have to commit yourself for life."

"I think I'd get trapped. I'm a weak person."

"I doubt it. Look, Aaron Copeland did it. Do you remember his score for *Of Mice and Men?* A beautiful piece. Virgil Thompson did a score. And so did Lennie Bernstein. He even won an Academy Award for *On the Waterfront.*" Arnold smiled. "You might win one, too. Think of that, Harry."

"What would I do with it?"

"I suppose you could crack walnuts with it," Arnold laughed. "I'm serious about this. All you have to do is call Betseka and give him your name. He said he would pay your fare down there—and back, if you change your mind."

"I'll think it over, Arnie. But *one* film—*if* I decide. If Copeland and Lennie Bernstein did it, then I guess I'd be in good company."

Harry sipped his coffee royal and found it weak. He added another dash of brandy. The bright sun reflected from the pool. It was a beautiful day. He wondered what D.B. was doing.

"I want you to be happy, Harry," Arnold said.

"I want to be happy, too."

They finished their breakfast and retired to the recreation room at the far end of the motel cabin row. Arnold suggested another round of Liszt and they pushed the pianos together. Seated back to back they played for half an hour, then, finished with Liszt, they played scales, adding comical side excursions to trip one another up. For the first time in days Harry found himself enjoying what he was doing. He felt settled. He knew that he was going to return to D.B.

"Will you play the St. Cado again, Harry?"

"Sure. Maybe I can work it into an octet. Follow me. Opening horn."

As he played he thought again to the night of the party. He had known, even then, that D.B. hadn't been malicious when she had tried to help him. But still, stubbornly, he had stalked off to brood and nurse his wounds like a child. He found himself incapable of condemning D.B. for what she had done. His love was too strong to dissolve so simply, so whimsically.

"Beautiful, Harry," Arnold said when he finished playing.

"Thanks. Can you see octet?"

"Yes, of course."

"Arnie, I'm going to call my brother Birsha. I want to find out about D.B."

"Then you're going back?"

"Yes."

"I'm very glad, Harry. Very glad."

Harry left the room and found the phone booth near the poolside bar empty. He broke three dollars into coins from a passing waiter, and entered the booth. He pumped quarters into the slot and dialed his residence number.

"Birsha?—Harry—I'm fine—No, Arnie just wanted to see me—He told me about an offer from Hollywood—No, what the hell would I be an actor for? It's about writing background music for a film—No, how the hell should I know who's starring in it—Listen, the reason I called— have you seen D.B.?—Oh?—She was drunk?—Bad?—Going to see *who* to look for me?—*Sandro!*—And you let her go? You didn't try to stop her?—I don't give a goddam *how* drunk you were!—So she's probably asleep by now! So what! When she gets an idea in her silly little mind she usually follows it through—Of course, I'm mad, goddammit!—No, absolutely not. You'll just botch it up. And besides, you wouldn't know how to handle Sandro—I'm coming right back—And listen, I'm going to break your goddam neck if anything happens to her—No, it *wouldn't* be Sandro's fault! It'd be *yours!* Sandro can't help himself—No, I'll be right in—Goodbye!"

When he hung up he discovered that his hands were moist, his legs shaking. The booth was stuffy and he could hardly breathe. He shoved the door open and hurried back to the recreation room where Arnold was still at the piano, playing boogie-woogie.

Harry's thoughts hammered madly in his brain. He could catch the return train in twenty minutes, maybe less. He could be at the Third Street station by late afternoon. Then, if he caught a taxi, he could be at Sandro's in a matter of minutes.

"Something wrong, Harry? You look pale." Arnold stood up quickly, concern wrinkling his hawk-face. "Bad news? Is something the matter?"

"There's plenty the matter, Arnie. Can you drive me to the station? I've got to get back right away."

3

When D.B. awoke she saw that it was late. She had finally slept and, for the first time in days, she felt refreshed. Her thoughts were clear, in spite of her hangover. She noticed the bottle of bourbon at her side, made a wry face, and pushed it out of sight. She didn't want a drink now. She went into the bathroom and drank a three-capful Bromo-Seltzer. After a leisurely shower and a fresh change of clothes she felt much better. She slipped into a moss colored cardigan sweater and stepped into low Capezio shoes, then in the kitchen, she made a pot of black coffee.

She carried the phone to the breakfast nook and dialed Daniel and Helga's number. Then, "This is D.B.—Have you seen—you haven't—If you hear from him—Thank you—I know you will, Helga—Thanks. Goodbye." She dialed Richard Freeze's San Anselmo number. "Richard Freeze?—He's not home?—He drove to where?—Arizona?—Thank you."

What next?

"Information?—Do you have a listing for Sandro, S-a-n-d-r-o Dazier, D-a-z-i-e-r—Yes, in San Francisco—No, I'm not sure—You haven't?— Thank you."

She glanced at her wrist watch. Almost seven o'clock. The sun was setting and the outline of the skyline was bathed in soft apricot gold. Gulls moved in the sky, Old St. Mary's chimes echoing in the twilight. She drank two cups of black coffee and ate a sandwich. Her stomach rumbled for a minute but after the food was down she felt better. She brushed her hair, wondering if she could find Sandro's warehouse simply by going to the district and asking around. Surely, such a huge and ugly man must have attracted some attention during the past few years.

As she gathered her purse and car keys she remembered that Harry had warned her against going to Sandro's by herself. She felt a twinge, then shrugged it off as coffee nerves. After all, she didn't have to go *inside* Sandro's house. She could simply talk to him at the door.

The car rocked gently back and forth and the deck throbbed rhythmically over the ties. The empty Scotch and soda glittered on the thick white linen, the Pullman-marked condiment tray and dishes reflected the bright club car light. Harry sat smoking, impatiently watching the small houses flash by, watching the landscape blur into a green and brown smear, touched with soft gold from the setting sun. He turned his eyes back to the club car, to the photo-muraled walls, the thick carpets. A porter stopped by his table, smiling politely. Harry ordered another drink, a double, and reluctantly turned back to the window. When the porter brought his drink he asked for the time.

"It's almost seven o'clock. Five to, to be exact."

"Thank you. How much longer?"

"Not too much now, sir."

Harry lit another cigarette, noticed that he still had one burning in the Pullman tray, stumped one of them out. He tried to tell himself that Birsha may have been mistaken, that D.B. hadn't said that she would see Sandro to ask where Harry had gone. She knew that she should never go there. In spite of Dr. Bennet's reassurance, Harry was worried, recalling what Birsha had said to him the night before they had gone to Reno. *"What if that big loonie decided that Sophie was a tiger, or some damn thing. What then? He'd probably pick up a chair and make her sit on top of a beach ball—"* And what else had Harry's younger brother said that evening in the bar? Harry had been pretty drunk then, but the conversation was slowly returning. *"Talk about living in the past! Every time I go up there I think I've stepped onto a set for a silent movie ..."*

Harry lit another cigarette, ordered another drink from the porter. Why didn't the train go faster? The sun had sunk behind the hills now and the first stars were showing. The soft music from the train intercom poured into the club car. The last rays of the sun retreated. The houses, as they whished by the wide window, showed yellow lights.

D.B. parked her car at the edge of the produce district and walked two blocks south. There was a breath of rotting vegetables clinging to the warm air. The sun was setting now, the great rays stretched across the sky. A few of the big produce warehouses were open, naked lights burning. Limp rags of lettuce and fallen produce littered the gutters. Great stacks of fruit blocked the sidewalks and she had to move along the gutters. Trucks, like sleeping dinosaurs, crouched in the narrow streets.

She stopped at a shed and peered into the gloom. A small, dark man noticed her and came to the loading ramp. His eyes flicked along her face, her breasts, and he smiled appreciatively.

"Do you happen to know of a man named Sandro Dazier?"

"He in the produce business?"

"No. He lives around here. Or at least he's supposed to."

"Well, I don't know the name, but—" he jumped from the ramp and stood beside her. "—maybe if you describe him to me I'd remember him. Does he hang around here?"

"I don't know." She was beginning to feel resentful. Why do men always stare at women's breasts? "He's a big man, very big, with white hair and—and a scar."

"A scar?"

The dark little man pointed to a café that was between two warehouses. "Why don't you ask over there? Most of the people that live around here—and there ain't too many—eat there."

"Thank you."

The café was small and narrow, shaped like a railroad car, with nickel coffee urns and plastic pie towers that were gray with rust. She ordered coffee from the colored man behind the counter.

"Do you know a man called Sandro? Sandro Dazier?"

"Gee, ma'am, not by name I don't. Does he work around here?"

"No. He lives nearby."

"I'm sorry. I just don't know him. Have you asked around?"

"Yes. I was told that anyone who lived in the district would eat here."

"Yeah, I guess that's true, ma'am."

"The man I'm looking for is very big, with a white crewcut and—"

"Oh, the big guy? Does he have a kind of scar?"

"Yes," she said excitedly. "That's the one!" She felt as if she had actually learned where Harry was. Harry *had* to be there! She could sense it. "Where does he live? Can you tell me?"

"Well—"

She fumbled in her purse and took a five-dollar bill from her sixteen-dollar roll. She slid it across the counter, looking at the man with an expression of expectancy.

"You don't have to go do that, ma'am."

"Take it. Can you tell me?"

He took the bill, folded it four ways and tucked it into his watch pocket. "Well," he said slowly, "the guy I'm thinking of has a truck. It's a merry-go-round truck. Sometimes he drives by and I see him. And I seen that truck parked three or four blocks from here. You just walk straight down—toward the docks—and keep looking in the little side alleys until you see the truck. That's probably where he lives."

She thanked him, left the café, and headed down the street toward the Embarcadero. A ship's whistle sounded, a truck rumbled by, and she noticed that it was night. Her watch said eight o'clock. She peered up the narrow alleys, seeing nothing. Then, when she came to one three blocks from her starting point, she saw the truck. It was parked up on the cracked sidewalk and the side of the van was lettered in bright gold. Sandro's Magic Merry-Go-Round—Rides 25¢.

A small red-lettered mailbox beside a double garage door and wooden entrance door announced, DAZIER, S. There was a rusted bell-push and she thumbed it nervously, imagining Harry inside, beyond the doors, waiting for her. However, she wouldn't enter if Sandro answered the door. She would just ask to see her husband. Nothing more. She was sure that Harry would hear her voice and would tell Sandro that it was all right.

The alleyway was dark. There was no street lamp. And when the door opened a crack she could see no figure there. She stepped back, suddenly frightened, and she looked nervously about her. The crack didn't widen, there was no questioning voice from the darkness. She could feel the eyes beyond the door, watching her.

"Is that you, Sandro? I—I want to see Harry—Is he here?" She gathered courage, assured herself that there was nothing to fear, and stepped a few inches closer. "Is that you, Sandro? Sandro? Why don't you answer me—"

The door swung open and a huge hand shot out. She tried to run, but the hand caught her wrist and jerked her through the door. Then the door slammed and she was in darkness.

4

When D.B. turned and faced in the direction of the door she saw nothing; her vision wasn't adjusted to the sudden darkness, and strange brass-colored visions ghosted in the dark. She heard the doorlatch whisper in its metal groove, then the snick of a padlock. Her heart hammered wildly in her breast and her purse fell from her trembling hands. Her voice quavered from her lips, "Is—is that you, Sandro? Are you there?"

His answer purred. "Yes, I'm right here."

"You gave me quite a fright," she stammered.

"Why did you come *here?*"

"I—to find Harry—naturally. Couldn't we have a light? It's awfully dark."

A small click from the wall brought a weak yellowish glow from a single bulb deep in the warehouse. She saw Sandro by the door, dressed in cream-colored jodhpurs and gleaming black riding boots. He was naked at the waist and there was a faint odor of perspiration about him.

"Is Harry here?" D.B. asked.

"Harry? No, he's not here. Why should he be?"

"Well—" she smiled politely, "then I guess I'd better be running along. I only dropped by for a minute."

"Go upstairs," Sandro said.

"I'd like to, but I can't right now. I—"

"Go upstairs," he repeated.

He gave her a small shove and she followed his advice, telling herself that he simply wanted to chat with her, that it would be all right if she humored him for a few minutes. But even as she reflected, she knew that she wasn't convincing herself. She was frightened, and as she walked, prodded from behind by Sandro, she stared with open-mouth wonderment at her surroundings, momentarily forgetting her fear.

She was following a narrow, curving path through a fantastic jungle of dismantled merry-go-round equipment.

There seemed to be horses everywhere, captured in wild, forever positions—plunging, standing, cantering; carved from wood and brightly lacquered in a carnival of colors—red, yellow, white, orange, green, black. Some with flowing manes of gold, gilt hoofs, glittering glass eyes. D.B.'s eyes were wide with awe. There were tigers, crawling, poised to leap, with bright ruby tongues, white wax teeth, and glittering diamond eyes. She saw elephants and zebras and giraffes and sparkling white swan chairs. Here and there she saw her reflection in huge mirrored panels with Victorian fringes of gilt and blossoms and crawling tendrils. Then came masses of circus awning, twisted brass poles, heaps of oily black machinery, rococo decorations, and a polka-dotted ticket booth with a nickel-plated window grill and a tinseled sign that read, *Rides 25¢*.

"What's this?" she asked.

Sandro stopped before a turntable. "This is a record machine," he said softly. "I play my steam-calliope records, my carousel music, while the merry-go-round goes around—and around—" He looked down to D.B. "Harry plays the steam calliope," he whispered.

"Yes, Sandro, I know.... This is all *very* interesting, but I really *must* be going. I'm sorry—"

"I'm not," Sandro interrupted. "You're lying to me."

"No. Honestly. I—"

"Go upstairs or I'll hit you."

He had threatened her so casually that she felt herself grow cold. She nodded dumbly, resignedly, and started for the staircase which led to a loft room near the top of the warehouse where another light glowed. Sandro touched a switch and the warehouse proper was in darkness again.

Was she going to be raped? Her thoughts were stumbling frantically about in her mind. She felt helpless, terribly alone, and when she entered the living quarters she moved automatically to the center of the room.

Sandro stood behind her, staring at the floor, his hands hanging limply at his sides, as if he were unaware of her presence. He didn't speak, made no movement toward her. However, D.B. noticed, he was standing near the short narrow hall, completely blocking the way to the staircase.

She gazed at her surroundings. The first odor was of fur. Stretched full length on the floor at the foot of the huge carved bed was an enormous tiger skin, beautifully black and orange, pure white at the edges where the belly had been. The mouth of the cat was open and she saw the false pink tongue, the bone white teeth, the glistening plastic eyes.

The room, aside from the musty odor of fur, smelled deeply of the past: camphor, saddle soap, and sour yellowing paper. The walls were covered with hundreds of photographs, billboards, circus posters. One poster showed Sandro as a young man, proudly smiling, holding a whip and surrounded by colored sketches of snarling beasts mounted on red platforms and leaping through hoops.

She saw photographs of Theda Bara, Rudolph Valentino, Pola Negri, Von Stroheim. There were posters in French, in German, in Italian. Posters of high-wire acts, animal acts, ringmasters, and clowns.

In spite of herself, D.B. felt a great wave of pity sweep through her. She could easily imagine Sandro's life of self-confinement. She noticed that there were no ashtrays in the room, neither books, nor radio, nor television set. There was only one lamp, a huge ball of colored glass beads that cast a dark pattern of colors on the walls.

"It's a very nice room," she said.

Sandro lifted his head and looked at her, his stolid face pale in the dim light, his massive chest faintly gleaming with perspiration, his black eyes dull. He nodded.

"You don't have any books—"

"No," he whispered, "of course not."

"I see—"

The air of lifelessness seemed to leave him and he stepped forward. He pointed to the wall, his eyes glittering now. "Look at this picture," he commanded. "Here! This one. Do you know who that is?"

"No, I can't say that I—"

"Hagenbeck! The greatest animal trainer of them all. Look at this one. It's me. That was taken in Paris in 1928. And here. Look! Berlin. 1933." He drew himself up, towering over her. "I traveled with only the great circuses of the day. Look at my posters!"

Was this why he had insisted she come upstairs? Because he wanted to explain himself? She looked at the posters, nodded, made what she felt was proper comment.

"They're very beautiful, Sandro."

"You sound frightened," he said suspiciously.

"Why should I be?"

"Aren't you?"

"No, of course not."

"Why do you say, 'of course'?"

"Because there's no reason for me to be afraid of you, Sandro. After all, I *am* your sister—"

His eyes narrowed. "I have no sister," he said.

"But, I thought—"

"*Hush!*" He held up a hand and cocked his head. "Did you hear something?"

"No, I didn't hear anything."

His scar was vivid on his face. He twitched, then looked at D.B. and smiled grotesquely. For a brief moment she had the impression that he had no idea who she was.

"Is there anything the matter?" she asked.

"Yes. You. What are you doing here?"

"I told you. I came to find—"

His hand swung up quickly and hit the side of her head. She gasped and staggered back, her footing catching in the tiger's mouth. She fell back on the bed. She sat on the edge, staring unbelievingly at him. She started to protest.

"*Hush!* Hush, tiger, hush!"

She calmed herself, watching him as he moved back a few feet from the tiger skin.

"They put me in a small white room," Sandro whispered. "There was a light, but it was too high, and it was in the ceiling, out of my reach. And it burned all the time. The light never went out. Never went out."

"I understand," D.B. said. "Honestly, Sandro, I—I understand."

He didn't seem to hear her. He continued in his soft voice. "The door had a small hole in it, but it was too far away for me to reach it. At times the hole would open and people talked to me. Once every week they put vaseline against my temples, my chest, my legs, and they set me on top of the table in the white room—Then the light, always burning in the ceiling."

"Please," D.B. whispered, "let me go now. *Please*, Sandro."

He reached for something black that was coiled and hanging on a wall peg. She saw, with a sinking sensation in the pit of her being, that it was a trainer's whip.

"Look there on the wall," he said. "By the lamp!"

It was a photograph of two small boys standing next to a calliope, both wearing collarless shirts and baggy knickers. It was Harry and Birsha. Beside that picture was another of Sandro and Harry; Sandro proud and terribly handsome, holding a whip; Harry youthful and gangling, wearing a straw hat and holding a monkey on his shoulder. She saw more photographs, yellowish and cracking at the edges. Fatty Arbuckle. Charlie Chaplin. Alla Nazimova. Clara Kimball Young. Emil Jannings. Marie Dressler. And another of the man Sandro had identified as Hagenbeck.

"Look at me!" Sandro said sharply.

She stared, recognizing Sandro's pose as being the same as the one on the large circus billboard. Then he raised his whip and it cracked in the sour paper air. His eyes looked feverish. The whip popped again.

Hoping that he was too absorbed with his whip to notice, she left the edge of the bed and started slowly for the door. Sandro continued to swing the whip, snapping his wrists. She passed him and made for the door. Then, like the bite of a gigantic insect, the whip flicked around her ankles and wound tightly on her flesh. She was jerked to the floor. Sandro picked her up and roughly freed her. Her skirt ripped at the seam when she arose from the floor. She stepped aside, pressing her back against a billboard of Clyde Beatty.

Sandro smiled and reached for her throat. She twisted past him but his outstretched fingers caught at the neck of her sweater and the material tightened against her breasts. Then the buttons popped free and clicked to the floor.

Trying to hold her sweater closed, she started frantically for the staircase again. Sandro stepped quickly before her and swung his fist into her stomach. She felt the hot rush of air expel from her lungs and she stumbled back toward the carved bed. His hand grabbed for her again and she felt the back strap of her brassiere break in two. Then his fist crashed against her head a second time, and she fell across the bed, unconscious.

5

"Would you care for another Scotch and soda, sir?"

"What? Yes, thank you."

Harry handed the porter his empty glass. One more would be all right. He figured that by the time he finished his drink they would be pulling in to the Third Street station. When the porter returned, he settled his bar bill and tipped him a dollar and a half. He sat drumming his fingers on the thick linen, glancing from his glass to the window. He was surprised when he saw his reflection; his forehead was wet with perspiration and he had to mop his brow with his handkerchief. Then, cupping his hands on the window, he was able to peer out and recognize the landmarks as they swept by. They were damn near there. He finished his drink with three swallows, picked up his small overnight bag, and impatiently strode down the aisle to the free space between cars. A sudden rush of air and train noise greeted him. He stared down at his feet, watching as the overlapping walkway swayed between the coupled cars. Finally, a few long minutes later, the bar porter came out to the coupled landing and nodded. "We're pulling in now," the porter announced. "I'll let you out the first thing, sir."

Harry handed him another dollar and picked up his bag. "Thank you," he said.

When D.B. came to she raised her head and saw that Sandro was again cracking his whip, working himself into a frenzy, shouting commands to imaginary cats, holding up imaginary hoops and watching proudly as the great beasts leaped through them.

She had no weapons. Nothing. She looked about her, seeking a suitable weapon to strike him with, but she saw nothing. Only faded pictures and—the lamp. She gazed at the huge ball of beaded glass burning on the night table near her hand.

"In my room!" Sandro shouted. "In my room with the light! Ha ha ha! The light never went out!"

Lunging desperately, she swung at the lamp, and the beads exploded and showered like glass confetti. The bulb and heavy base teetered, fell, and shattered, and in the sudden darkness she raced for the staircase. Knowing that the front door was padlocked she clattered down the stairs and ran for the protective forest of merry-go-round equipment.

Sandro was directly behind her, his screaming voice echoing in the cavernous warehouse.

D.B. plunged into the maze, worming herself into the bowels of figures and brass poles and machinery. She worked her way silently past the elephant; then she waited, controlling her loud breathing, while her eyes accustomed themselves to the darkness. Slowly the figures around her took shape. True, she couldn't see well, but she consoled herself with the fact that she could see well enough not to stumble over anything.

"You think you can escape?" Sandro's voice boomed, losing itself in the rafters far above. "You can't! I'm going to find you and whip you! I've trained many like you before! Lions—tigers—yes, even panthers. My reputation bears me out!"

She crouched behind a ghostly swan chair. Behind her, looking over her shoulder, was a leering golden horse with eyes of blue glass. Above her, a giraffe craned its long spotted neck, watching Sandro. Fifteen D.B.'s reflected in fifteen mirrored panels.

"*Lay-deeez* and *gentle-men!*" Sandro announced, roaring like a ringmaster. "With great pride we in-trow-duuuce—*Sandro!* This famed per-former of two con-ti-nents, will perform with—"

At that moment a yellow horse slowly raised a tinseled hoof and struck the fat gray back of an elephant. Sandro stopped in mid-fantasy and whirled toward the sound. D.B. held her breath, crept quickly and silently away from the swan chair, and, after threading past a zebra and a black horse, she hid behind a snarling tiger.

"Do you think you can yell for help?" Sandro called out. "Do you think you can be heard over the music?"

D.B. frowned. What music? There was no music. She peered in the gloom and discovered that she was nearing the front door. Her heart pounded, her legs felt weak, her mouth was dry. If only she could reach the door! If she pounded and screamed a passerby might possibly hear her and send for help—

Sandro's voice boomed, "Carousel! Calliope! Music!"

Then she heard the hoarse electrical whisper of an open loudspeaker, the sharp rasp of Sandro's finger on the needle, amplified a thousand times. Then the music crashed out, shattering the darkness with— merry-go-round music! Steam calliope music of gay Sunday afternoons and cotton candy and brass rings and merry children.

Sandro's whip cracked in the air.

He charged into the maze of animals, whipping, shouting curses. D.B. had to run. It would be senseless now to remain where she was. Her only chance was at the door. She removed her shoes and started away from the tiger statue. A figure suddenly leaped before her! A zebra. Another figure! A white horse with crimson mane and glass studded reins. Then another figure loomed before her.

It was Sandro.

She panicked and turned to run for the rear of the warehouse, but the whip struck her shoulder and she stumbled, hardly aware of the burning on her flesh. The sweater ripped again. She fell across a jeweled horse and screamed. Sandro whipped again—and again, striking blindly at the wooden animals, the twisted brass poles. Desperately, D.B. lunged at him and staggered into a swan, then she swung wild and caught a giraffe in her arms. The whip seemed to lash from nowhere, popping against her back. She felt the warm moistness of her blood trickle on her shoulder blades.

Sandro swung the whip again, but it didn't come down. It had caught and coiled tightly around the light fixture directly overhead. Sandro cursed and tugged at the whip. D.B. rushed into him and bit into his arm, into the straining bicep. She sunk her teeth until she tasted the hot gush of his blood on her tongue. Sandro screamed and swung his fist. She fell to the concrete floor, exhausted, beaten, burning in several places from the whip, unable to fight back. Her wounds weren't great, she knew, but fatigue and fright overcame her and she welcomed the closing blackness when it came and swallowed her.

Harry had heard the haunting sounds of the steam calliope before his taxi had slid to a stop in front of Sandro's warehouse door. He threw a five-dollar bill to the driver, told him to move on, and when the cab made the turn onto the one-way street at the corner, he hurried to the door and shouted his half-brother's name, pounding and kicking on the door. He thought he heard a scream, and that was enough. He kicked frantically at the door, aiming waist high near the jamb. A second later he was rewarded with the harsh splinter of wood against his heel. The calliope record seemed to come to an automatic end. It was silent. He continued kicking. A second later the door gave way and he quickly stepped inside and threw on the light switch.

"Sandro!"

Sandro released his grip on the suspended whip and slowly blinked his eyes. He turned, breathing heavily, his great body streaked with sweat, and faced his brother. When recognition finally passed across Sandro's face he broke into a shy smile, and for a brief moment, Harry was reminded of a child who had been caught playing at a game that had been forbidden him by the adults.

Forcing himself to remain calm, to keep himself from taking the whip from the light fixture and lashing it across Sandro's smiling face, he entered the warehouse. He *had* to act as if this were an everyday occurrence, as if he couldn't care less what had gone on just a few short minutes ago.

Meanwhile, Sandro seemed to be genuinely ashamed of himself and when he looked down to D.B. Harry had the impression that the big man was just now recognizing what he had done.

Fighting his anger and revulsion, Harry leaned against a fallen giraffe and slowly lit a cigarette. His first concern was for his wife. He looked at her as she lay on the floor and he saw that she hadn't been hurt as badly as he had feared. From his many years of circus experience, he noted that, although her back had been cut in several places, Sandro hadn't been able to lay a truly direct whip on her.

Harry surveyed the chaos that surrounded them. From the positions of the animals he concluded that D.B. must have eluded Sandro's whip by ducking in between the figures.

He almost broke into an appreciative chuckle when he saw the bloody teeth marks in Sandro's bicep. So, D.B. had fought back. Good. He felt his own anger subsiding.

Sandro's voice was vague, very soft. "You came to see me—"

"Sure," Harry said. "I like to drop in on you now and then and see how you're getting along."

D.B. stirred, moved slowly. Then, a few seconds later, she stood on shaking legs and moved to a swan chair. She sat and tried to repair her torn sweater, cover her bared breasts. And, as Harry had suspected, she was able to move her limbs without wincing from pain. She finally looked up, obviously wondering at the light, at the absence of the whip, and when she saw Harry she started to rise from the chair. Harry shook his head and signaled her back. She did as she was bid, sat and looked at him, her eyes filling with tears.

Harry winked at her. She returned the wink.

"How are you, D.B.?"

"I'm—I've been—" She didn't complete her sentence, but her glance toward Sandro was sufficient.

"I've been whipping your wife," Sandro explained softly.

Harry nodded, again acting very pleasant about the affair. "So I see, Sandro. So I see. And did you have a good time?"

"Yes."

"I'll bet you're tired after all that, aren't you."

"Yes, I am."

"Can I have the whip now, Sandro?"

"What? The whip? Yes, it's all right—"

Harry grasped the handle and freed the whip from the light cord. He coiled it as he would a garden hose, then looped it over the giraffe's raised foot.

D.B. was silent, watching them both.

"I'll bet you're *real* tired," Harry said again to Sandro.

Sandro touched his scar with his fingertips, then his forehead. "Yes, I'm very tired, Harry. I'm really very—tired now. I think I'd better—lie down."

"Would you like to see Dr. Bennet, Sandro?"

"Who? Dr. Bennet? Why, yes, I suppose so—"

"All right," Harry soothed. "You go to your room and lie down on the tiger skin and in about two hours I'll come back with Dr. Bennet. Then you'll be all right. You'll feel a lot better."

"Yes," Sandro said. "Harry? Did Gerard die?"

Harry's throat tightened and he felt the sour bite of the tears against his eyelids. "Yes, Sandro. Gerard died. I was wondering—I was wondering if you could take care of Birsha and—and myself until we grow up. Could you do that?"

"Yes," Sandro said. "I will. I'll look after you."

"Thank you. Now you lie down on the tiger and I'll come and see you in a little while."

Sandro nodded and retreated from the clearing. Harry watched as the big man tiredly climbed the rickety stairs leading to the loft, then disappeared.

Harry went to D.B. Taking her hands into his, he said, "Sandro's completely gone now, honey."

She touched his cheek, his eyelids, felt the moisture of his tears. "I'm—sorry, Harry," she whispered gently. "I'm terribly sorry—"

"Don't be. First, I want to say that I'm glad you're only hurt a little bit. Second, I want to say that I'm sorry I ran out on you. I'm back. That's all that counts. I'm back."

She nodded, still holding his hands. "I—I want to get out of here. Please, Harry—Let's leave—"

He gave her his jacket to wear and she winced when she pulled it over her shoulders, then she smiled and nodded that she was all right. Out in the street she told him where she had left the car and they headed in that direction.

A trucker stood before the café, chewing a toothpick and pulling on his gloves. A Chinese groceryman quietly argued with a produce seller over the price of lettuce. And in the gutters, webs of cornsilk and crushed vegetables lay rotting. A fat gray cat crawled from under a car, looked suspiciously at Harry and D.B., then darted across the street to another car.

THE END

For more from the Beat era, try...

Malcolm Braly

Shake Him Till He Rattles / It's Cold Out There

"*Shake Him* is the best novel I've ever read about the intersection of the Beats and criminals in the San Francisco heyday of Neal Cassidy, Jack Kerouac, etc. It is grim, bleak, and one of the best novels GM ever published." — Ed Gorman

"There is much in *It's Cold Out There* that reminds me of Nathanael West at his best..." — H. Bruce Franklin

Felony Tank

"*Felony Tank* is written from the heart on a gravel road of conviction and authenticity. It's a stellar first effort (nominated for an Edgar) and one that cements Braly's position in the 'prison drama' niche of novels." — *Paperback Warrior*

False Starts: A Memoir of San Quentin and Other Prisons

"A reflective, painfully honest account of prison life." — Brian Greene, *CriminalElement.com*

STARK HOUSE — In trade paperback from: **Stark House Press**

1315 H Street, Eureka, CA 95501
griffinskye3@sbcglobal.net / www.StarkHousePress.com

Available from your local bookstore, or order direct with a check or via our website.

Made in the USA
Columbia, SC
11 August 2022